The Full Moon Bride

Also by Shobhan Bantwal

THE UNEXPECTED SON

THE SARI SHOP WIDOW

THE FORBIDDEN DAUGHTER

THE DOWRY BRIDE

Published by Kensington Publishing Corp.

The Full Moon Bride

SHOBHAN BANTWAL

KENSINGTON BOOKS
www.kensingtonbooks.com

KENSINGTON BOOKS are published by

Kensington Publishing Corp.
119 West 40th Street
New York, NY 10018

Copyright © 2011 by Shobhan Bantwal

All Kensington titles, imprints, and distributed lines are available at special quantity discounts for bulk purchases for sales promotion, premiums, fund-raising, educational, or institutional use.

Special book excerpts or customized printings can also be created to fit specific needs. For details, write or phone the office of the Kensington Special Sales Manager: Kensington Publishing Corp., 119 West 40th Street, New York, NY 10018. Attn. Special Sales Department. Phone: 1-800-221-2647.

Kensington and the K logo Reg. U.S. Pat. & TM Off.

ISBN-13: 978-0-7582-5884-7
ISBN-10: 0-7582-5884-4

First Kensington Trade Paperback Printing: August 2011
10 9 8 7 6 5 4 3 2 1

Printed in the United States of America

Acknowledgments

As always, I offer my initial prayer of thanks to Lord Ganesh, the remover of obstacles.

My heartfelt appreciation goes to my warm and supportive editor, Audrey LaFehr, who has placed her faith in me again and again. Special thanks to Martin Biro and Vida Engstrand, consummate professionals who make my writing career a pleasure.

The friendly and dedicated editorial, production, public relations, and marketing folks at Kensington Publishing richly deserve my gratitude and praise for yet another job done well. I look forward to working with you on my future projects.

To my agent, Stephanie Lehmann, I thank you for your invaluable help and guidance at every step. I would not be here without you.

The Writers' Exchange at Barnes & Noble in Princeton, New Jersey, and the Writers' Group at the Plainsboro Public Library deserve my thanks for their insightful comments and suggestions. I offer a grateful hug to my many other friends, who are my cheerleading group.

To my super-supportive family: I am deeply grateful to have you all in my life and for putting up with my idiosyncrasies— and for loving me in spite of them.

Chapter 1

Like most second-generation Indian-Americans, I'd dismissed arranged marriage as a ridiculous and antiquated custom. Tying oneself to a man one hardly knew, and pledging lifelong love and fidelity on top of that?

"For a modern woman it's nothing short of insanity," I'd mocked many a time.

But after reaching adulthood and realizing that everybody in my big South Indian Telugu family was married in that fashion and looked utterly content, except for my uncle Srinath, whose wife was suspected of being a hermaphrodite, the concept didn't seem so absurd. I figured I'd even give arranged marriage a try. That is, if I could find a man to marry me—and it was a huge *if*.

So far, I'd acquired an Ivy League education and moderate success as a big-city attorney, but I'd come up empty in the marriage department, perhaps because I'd distanced myself from the madness of the dating scene.

If it weren't for the fact that I really and truly wanted to get married, I wouldn't have ventured into the old-fashioned Indian form of torment called bride viewing. Fortunately it wasn't as bad as it was in India, where girls were often put on display and expected to tolerate their potential in-laws' scrutiny like cows at a cattle auction.

Here in the U.S. it was just a matter of boy meeting girl and family meeting family in an informal setting. There was generally no undue pressure exerted on either party to marry. But convention required them to be polite and respectful of each other. However, the system was biased in our male-worshipping culture. The respect shown by the girl and her parents to the boy and his family often bordered on sycophantic.

At the moment, standing before the oval mirror in my elegant bedroom with its honey oak and pastel furnishings, I gave myself a once-over. In spite of the clever use of cosmetics, the face staring back at me seemed rather plain—ordinary nose, full mouth, curious eyes fringed by dark lashes, tweezed eyebrows. Nothing beyond plain Miss Soorya Giri.

Being the potential bride in yet another bride viewing was hardly pleasant. The mild fluttering in my tummy was gradually escalating into an anxiety attack at the thought of meeting one more eligible man.

With a damp palm pressed against my belly, I waited for my bachelor and his family to arrive. I stood in my bride-viewing finery—the whole nine yards—or in this case, six. The sari happened to be six diaphanous yards of silk—soft, glossy, South Indian silk.

My suitor and his family were coming all the way from Kansas City, Kansas, making the occasion all the more unnerving. Looking outside the picture window, I contemplated if I should make a quick and silent escape into the backyard.

The weather was perfect for lounging around our kidney-shaped swimming pool, shimmering like a sheet of turquoise glass in the balmy afternoon sun. Mom's lovingly tended zinnias, marigolds, and impatiens were fat and bursting with vigorous colors. The copse of pine trees in the distance looked cool and darkly forbidding, but no more forbidding than what perhaps awaited me in the coming hour.

Fleeing was tempting, but I couldn't summon the courage to do it. In fact, I'd never had the stomach for it. Good Hindu girls didn't indulge in blatant disregard for convention. Conformity and duty to family above all else were deeply embedded in our DNA. All the Americanization in the world could not eliminate what was intrinsic to the Hindu psyche.

Although Indian-American kids are often branded as "co-

conuts"—brown on the outside and white on the inside—girls and boys like me can talk, eat, party, work, and think like Americans during the adolescent years, but once we're no longer teenagers, our Indian-ness starts breaking through the brittle plastic façade.

I had discovered I was a dark Telugu-American some ten years ago, no matter how much imported-from-India Fair & Fabulous bleaching cream I rubbed over my skin.

Besides, our community was small and close-knit, and rumors of my wayward behavior would spread fast, humiliating my parents, my grandmother, who happened to live with us, and me in the process.

I could picture Dad frowning down at me with his enormous arms folded across his equally enormous chest. "Soorya Giri, I am appalled at your behavior. Did you have to ruin the family name in such a reckless manner? If you weren't interested in meeting the young man, you should have told us in the first place. We could have saved those folks and ourselves a lot of grief."

Mom would put on that wounded basset hound look, with her head tilted to one side and her big eyes blinking. "Baby, did we do something wrong? Is that why you are behaving in this strange manner?"

My paternal grandmother, Pamma to me (short for Papa's Amma), was too deaf to know what was happening around her most of the time, but even she would have a seizure at my shocking behavior. "If I do this kind of nonsense things when I was a small girl, my father squeeze my throat and throw me in river," would be her reaction. Then she'd remind me that in my next life I'd have to pay very dearly for bringing such shame upon the family. "God always watching, baby. You do bad-bad things in this life, you get bad-bad things in next life."

Taking into consideration family honor and dignity combined with bad-bad karma in my next incarnation, running away was definitely not an option at this time.

The doorbell chimed downstairs, sending a mild ripple through my system. Oh God, they were here.

"Soorya, they have arrived," Mom announced from below, confirming my thoughts.

I listened while my parents welcomed the visitors and ushered them into the living room. After a minute I quietly tiptoed down the stairs and slipped into the kitchen. I would wait there until the time was right for my planned and practiced entrance. There was an established procedure.

The pistachio-colored kitchen curtains looked fresh and crisp from a recent wash. The appliances gleamed and I could literally lick the smooth, waxed hardwood floor if I had a mind to. A garland of fresh, turmeric-yellow marigolds was strung around the picture of Lord Balaji in its silver frame. The mildly pungent odor of ammonia cleaner combined with sandalwood incense and spices lingered in the air.

Everything looked warm and welcoming in the sunlight filtering in through the towering sunburst windows, down to the multicolored roses arranged in the Waterford crystal vase on the sill. Mom, the perfectionist, didn't leave anything to chance.

Voices in the living room were clearly audible and the thick Telugu accent unmistakable—each *R* rolled around with relish and the dialogue flowing in the present continuous tense. "We are coming for the first time to New Jersey. Do you always have so much traffic congestion here or what?" asked a male voice. *Always* sounded like *aahl-vays*.

A few other voices, including my parents' and grandmother's, came to mingle with the man's. Pamma spoke mostly Telugu, although she knew a fair amount of English. The old lady conversed with me in English, read the *New York Times* each morning, and rarely failed to watch the evening news on TV.

My father's accent was a shade less pronounced as he proceeded to respond to the honored guests' comments. "Newark Airport and the main highways are naturally congested, but our vicinity is quiet—no apartment buildings and condos."

Dad loved to throw that in—the fact that we lived in an exclusive area of New Jersey. Bergen County bordered New York and was more like an upscale suburb of New York City. God forbid we should have apartments within a ten-mile radius.

Catching my image in the smooth surface of the stainless steel refrigerator, I couldn't help but adjust the *pallu* of my sari, the loose end that goes over the left shoulder and cascades down the back. The green sari with red border embellished by gold thread or *jari* had me looking like a Christmas tree decorated with tinsel, but Pamma and Mom had convinced me that green and red were auspicious colors.

My lips still looked glossy. My shoulder-length, iron-straightened hair looked salon-perfect.

But the gold thread abraded and itched where it touched my neck. I scratched at the three ugly welts that were getting larger and redder by the second. Good thing they weren't all that visible on my dark skin; there was no reason to panic yet.

The wet stains on the underarms of my red blouse were a different matter. My industrial-strength antiperspirant wasn't performing so well today.

Mom came prancing in from the living room, a hundred-watt grin lighting her face. She approved of the family from Kansas. "They seem like nice people, Soorya. And so cultured," she informed me, then went to the oven to inspect whatever was in there.

The aroma of fried food came at me with a whoosh as she pulled on her pistachio green oven mitts, deftly removed a loaded pan of goodies from the oven, and placed it on the beige speckled granite counter. Whatever lay on that pan continued to sizzle for a few seconds.

I offered no response to Mom's statement. I preferred to reserve my comments until after I met the folks from Kansas. Instead I discreetly scratched my hives and inhaled the curly wisps of aromatic steam traveling toward me.

"Don't scratch, Soorya. You know it leaves scabs." Mom threw me a stern look, or at least as stern as she knew how. My dear mother didn't know what stern meant. "You remembered to take your antihistamine?"

"Yes, Mom. Don't worry, I'm fine." Honestly, I wasn't all that fine.

After countless times, I should have become a pro at this. But no such luck—I was still reduced to a nervous glob of dark, pudgy female at the thought of being on parade before people whose names I didn't know. Oh boy, I really didn't know. "Mom, what did you say their name was?"

"I told you the other day, dear, Vadepalli."

Vadepalli—a nice, old-fashioned Telugu name, pronounced *Va-they-palley.* My mother had a knack for discovering them—families that had similar backgrounds to ours in terms of language, religion, and culture.

"The Vadepallis are good people with healthy genes according to your auntie Prema. And you know Prema is very smart in these matters." Mom opened the refrigerator and retrieved a crystal bowl covered with plastic wrap.

"Yeah, I know. She's arranged the marriages of no less than thirty-two people." I was kept abreast of Prema's impressive record on a regular basis.

"It's thirty-three now; she arranged one more last month. Every one of them with healthy genes," Mom boasted.

"No kidding!" My aunt's idea of healthy genes included most anyone who wasn't dying of advanced tuberculosis or AIDS. On the other hand, Alzheimer's, heart disease, hypertension, Parkinson's, and even lunacy were considered minor ailments and were to be overlooked, especially when the lack of marriageable young men was bordering on dire, as in my case.

"First you get married; afterward you discuss all those unpleasant genetic things," my aunt had said to me once, after having lectured me on the advantages of marriage.

I couldn't imagine how such grave genetic health inquiries could be put off until after marriage, when it was way too late. But I wasn't in any position to argue with my aunt, who was like a runaway steamroller when it came to arranging a match. Thirty-three was an impressive number, though.

I watched Mom carefully lift the hot snacks off the metal pan and arrange them on a sterling silver platter—a variety of spicy fried delicacies that smelled divine and had acquired a perfect golden tint—crisp lentil *vadas,* onion *pakodas,* and vegetable *samosas.*

The crystal bowl filled with bright green mint-coriander chutney sat in the center of the arrangement. I knew how it would taste: tangy and fiery hot—pungent enough to strip the top layer off one's tongue. Beautiful and oh so enticing! My mouth watered.

A carved silver bowl held luscious-looking *gulab jamuns*—the round, dark brown orbs of fried pancake flour that resembled chocolate Munchkins floating in rich syrup. I eyed them with longing. They were a definite no-no on my latest diet: the Red, White, and Green Vegetarian Diet—anything that didn't fall within those colors was not even to be looked at.

I lived on salads, red and green fruit, select cooked vegetables and sprouts, skim milk, Diet Sprite or diet cherry soda, and plain nonfat yogurt.

And damn if brown, yellow, black, and everything in between didn't look and smell divine.

"Mom, is my sari still all right?" I cocked an eyebrow at my mother, hoping to force my attention away from the food. Mom had patiently wrapped the sari around me in the traditional style with lots of safety pins to keep the complicated folds and tucks in place. Once or twice she'd had to yell at me to stand still and not wriggle.

I didn't know how to wear a sari any more than I knew how to steer a fighter plane. The fabric was like an endless bolt of interconnected bedsheets. But no South Indian girl worth her blood would find herself at a bride viewing in anything less than a Kanjivaram silk sari.

At Pamma's insistence, I wore the traditional diamond earrings and necklace, too. Several twenty-two-karat gold bangles jangled along my wrists. The red dot on my forehead was nice and big to suit my face.

Her own purple sari with a saffron border slightly askew from her exertions, my nearsighted mother blinked and studied me critically for a moment. "It looks fine, dear. But try not to fidget with it too much." Then she offered me a warm, reassuring smile. "You look nice, baby, really pretty."

"Yeah, right, and Mars is inhabited by little bald men, Mom."

My wry comment earned me a tight frown from Mom.

Laughter floated in from the living room. Dad was doing his part in keeping the Vadepallis sufficiently entertained while Mom took care of the food. He could be quite a lively host, especially when it came to impressing important people—like potential in-laws.

Gregarious and witty, Dad was often the soul of the party, especially after consuming a couple of stiff martinis garnished with his favorite pearl onions. But there was no liquor on this afternoon's menu. What if the Kansas folks were teetotalers? Worse yet, what if they frowned on alcohol? One had to be politically and culturally correct in such delicate matters.

Mom placed the platter and bowl on an oblong wooden tray alongside the rose-pattern Lenox plates and pale pink cotton napkins. Then she filled the silver coffeepot with South Indian coffee—strong and thick, with loads of frothy whole milk and sugar. "Be an angel and get the matching cups and saucers, dear," she said to me.

I gathered up the necessary items and stacked them on the tray set aside for the coffee service, then took a deep breath. Another minute and I'd make my grand entrance.

At least the previous bride seekers had come from within the tristate area—near enough to make a hasty exit and drive home when I didn't measure up to their standards.

Soon I'd be gawked at and inspected from all angles by the Vadepallis. Despite having lived over three decades in the U.S., some folks still subscribed to this manner of matchmaking. Traditions often died a very slow death in conservative Hindu households.

But to give credit where it's due, if I didn't want this method of meeting a future spouse, my family had offered me the option of dating—within reason, of course, meaning it had better be an Indian boy, or at least Asian. And also, no premarital sex, and positively no shacking up together before marriage.

Mom's eyes twinkled with barely contained excitement behind her plastic-framed glasses. As a wealthy woman Mom should have been wearing stylish designer eyeglasses and elegant clothes, but her humble Indian background still lingered inside her. Her wardrobe was mostly furnished by discount department stores: slacks in different colors topped with coordinated short-sleeved tops in the summer and pullover sweaters in the winter.

Somehow the gold, diamonds, and silk saris that were considered solid investments didn't quite go hand in hand with the $19.99 shoes and the $49.99 watch that were viewed purely as consumer goods, not worth throwing good money at.

"Never pay too much for anything that loses value the minute it comes out of the store, and don't buy unless there is a half-price or better sale," Mom preached, and habitually scanned the newspaper ads for special end-of-the-season clearance events at the local department stores. A seventy-five percent reduction sale could make Mom giddy with delight.

That philosophy didn't extend to my dad, of course, since he was a prominent doctor and had to look the part. He always wore designer labels, drove an expensive car, and had his offices lavishly furnished. They were all investments. Mom's life, on the other hand, was an eclectic mix of cheap and pricey, elegant and tacky, drab and colorful.

"So, what do you think of the boy, huh?" my mother asked in a conspiratorial whisper as she placed the lid on the coffee-pot.

"I haven't even seen the boy yet." I'd been trying to postpone the inevitable as long as I could.

"You mean you have not taken a secret peek yet?" Mom looked shocked. She always assumed I was as wildly excited about these occasions as she was.

"Of course not. I don't spy on people."

"It is not spying, dear; it is simple curiosity. Every girl does that, you know. When your dad came to see me, I hid behind the wooden screen in my parents' home and took a good look at him. He looked so nice. He was a lot thinner then, too." She giggled. "Your Pamma caught me at it, but she didn't seem to mind."

"Good for you, Mom." I couldn't help smiling.

"Just wait till you see this Kansas boy, and tell me if he's not handsome." Mom looked like an eager little girl waiting for my reaction to her first kindergarten project. Except in place of pigtails, she sported a short, bouncy bob that was dyed a shade too dark.

Mom's bathroom cabinet held a jumbo pack of Clairol hair color. All her toiletries came in discounted multipacks.

"Handsome, too? Looks like you and Dad have outdone yourselves this time," I said. This was the first time I'd heard any suitor described as handsome. But then, in Mom's opinion, practically every fourth man she came across was nice-looking or distinguished-looking, so I had serious doubts about this Kansas guy.

Mom's face settled into a troubled frown. "I hope you are not going to be difficult about this, Soorya. You will behave like a good girl, right?"

"Yes, Mom, I promise." Sometimes she seemed to forget I had outgrown the toddler stage a long time ago.

Mom's tone softened. "I know this is tough, but the Vadepallis have come a long way to meet you, dear." Good thing Mom was a forgiving sort and had overlooked the first few bride viewings when I'd deliberately worn faded jeans and sweatshirts or short skirts and tank tops that revealed my rolls and bulges to the point of driving away any potential young man and his family.

Those were the days when I didn't want to marry and get saddled with a husband and a couple of kids.

However, along with maturity had come the slow realization that I did want all those sentimental and wholesome things. My thirtieth birthday some months ago was a sobering experience. Many of my girlfriends were married, and a couple of them had babies already. Even my best friend, Amy Steinberg, a rebel who'd denigrated marriage for many years, was now engaged.

All of a sudden, I wanted a husband, too—a guy who'd bring me flowers, help me chop vegetables for the salad, shovel the snow, warm my bed, and hold my hand when I went into the delivery room to bring his babies into this world. Besides a fabulous career, I wanted marriage. I wanted a family.

Why couldn't I have it all?

But it meant seeking out the right man first, or at least letting my parents find him for me. And that's why I stood there dressed in a sari, wearing diamonds and makeup, and trying not to let it get to me. Nonetheless, my bland reply to Mom was, "Kansas isn't the end of the world. I'm sure they can hop on the next plane and go home."

I had subjected myself to this torment since I was twenty-three. Not that I counted the bride viewings anymore. The occasions were too numerous to keep a tally, too humiliating to acknowledge, too frustrating to ponder.

It wasn't Mom and Dad's fault, though—this was the only method they knew. If I were to find someone on my own, they'd accept him wholeheartedly. In fact, they hoped I'd find someone and get married as fast as I could. They dropped enough hints on the subject. Since I hadn't obliged, they were trying their level best to get me to the proverbial altar—or in my case the *mandap,* the ceremonial Hindu marriage canopy.

Each time a potential groom came to meet me, the outcome was the same: rejection—for one reason or another. I was either too tall or too heavy or too dark-skinned, or a combination. After the barrage of negative responses, I'd become even more apprehensive about going out and finding a man on my own.

I often wished I could summon enough nerve to go to bars and parties, get myself a boyfriend and put an end to this husband hunting. Amy had managed to find her perfect Jewish man in David Levine through the Internet. But I couldn't. I had learned my lesson as a teenager when no boys in school had noticed me.

My fear of dating was pathetic for a grown woman whose spirit was intrepid in every other sense, but I just couldn't get over my inhibition. It had left me more or less out in the cold, to use a trite cliché.

Despite wanting to know what a kiss felt like, I'd never had a taste of it. Imagine that—I'd never kissed a man in my entire life. I had often wondered what it would feel like to have a man's lips touch mine, his tongue dueling with my own, his arms holding me in a passionate embrace.

But I was too damned afraid of rejection to go out and find all those sexual experiences I dreamed about. I was afraid to fail. At least when my parents tried to find a man for me, any failures were as much theirs as they were mine.

Initially, I believe what enticed the would-be grooms and their families to come bride-seeking to our house was the BIG DOWRY sign around my neck—my father's flourishing medical practice. He owned three clinics around New York City, where he performed his own brand of magic: cosmetic surgery.

My father's clients included a long list of celebrities—movie stars, models, singers, business moguls, and sports heroes. A certain real estate tycoon had his puckered lips enhanced and his face lifted so he could bag his fifth trophy wife. A basketball legend had an unsightly birthmark removed from his armpit. A middle-aged gay singing sensation had his penis reshaped.

Then there was the blond movie star whose breasts were enlarged so many times that she nearly fell on her face a couple of times, after which Dad was asked to refashion them to a more manageable size.

I had a feeling Dad had perhaps played God more times than he could remember—he had probably adjusted, reshaped, rearranged, and remolded more body parts than anyone on the East Coast. Dad's list of famous patients and their fascinating stories could fill a book.

Too bad Dad's charmed scalpel could do little for his only child. Unfortunately, I had inherited his looks, and he had inherited his from his father. But to his credit, he had tried very hard to use every ounce of his medical and cosmetic skills on me in conjunction with other specialists who'd given my looks a boost.

In the end, after a few layers of fat had been surgically removed from my hips and belly, my nose cleverly restructured, teeth aligned with orthodontics, hair removed permanently from my upper lip and arms, and some elaborate beauty treatments, I had made the happy transition from unappealing to slightly better than plain.

"Look, baby, Dad made you so beautiful!" Mom had clapped her hands with girlish delight and held the mirror before me when the last of the procedures was over. I was twenty years old then. "Now all we have to do is find a good husband for you."

Pamma had nearly lost her dentures from grinding them too much and shedding tears of joy at the sight of her granddaughter's improved appearance.

I had merely walked away from the mirror with a long, tired sigh. From that day on I'd be known as Pramod and Vijaya Giri's homely daughter. But *homely* was significantly better than *ugly,* I'd consoled myself.

My latest birthday resolution had been to do whatever it took to look attractive.

"Soorya." Mom's voice pealed like a bell to shake me out of my depressing thoughts. "Stop daydreaming now. It's about time you came out and met them."

"Can't you and Dad entertain them and send them on their way?" I pleaded with her.

"I realize you're nervous, but the boy seems very friendly, dear. I'm sure you'll like him. He's different from the other boys you have met." She wiggled her eyebrows and grinned. "And don't forget handsome."

"They're all very friendly until they meet me, Mom," I murmured. Even our eye-popping mansion, complete with fountain, swimming pool, hot tub, and Dad's steel-gray Porsche sitting in the garage, didn't appear to matter once they laid eyes on me. Then they all seemed to panic and run like hunted rabbits.

The irony was, even the ugliest suitors wanted a pretty bride. It was all part of the male-worshipping Indian culture. The potential groom could be short, overweight, bald, or even disabled, but the prospective bride had to be perfect in every way. Centuries of technological and cultural changes hadn't managed to bring about a shift in the double standards.

"But his horoscope and yours match beautifully, Soorya. Besides, by a happy coincidence, today is *purnima,* full moon," Mom chirped. "It is an auspicious moon. Maybe this time it will click." She thrust the coffee tray into my hands while she put the finishing touches to the other one loaded with snacks and sweets.

Mom always found something auspicious about every day. She was the eternal optimist, cheerful as the lark that heralds the dawn with a burst of song. But her temperament had its advantages. Thanks to her boundless faith in me, I had excelled in school, college, and then law school, and eventually become an employee of a prestigious Manhattan law firm at a young age.

Of course, one of the reasons I got hired at the firm was Matthew McNamara, or Mac, the firm's senior partner and one of Dad's most grateful clients. Despite knowing the job was granted as a favor to Dad, I knew I deserved it. I wasn't just a good lawyer, I was an outstanding one, and an asset to Mac and his august team of legal professionals.

Mom finally picked up her tray. "Okay, baby, let's go," she announced.

Pulling in a deep breath, I followed Mom's slim figure down the hallway toward the living room. Even after three decades of knowing and loving Mom, I still felt this slight pang of envy whenever I noted her trim hips and slender arms.

Although not exactly pretty by most standards, my mother was nonetheless petite and generous and charming in her own South Indian way. Her sweet, munificent personality drew people to her like bees to her prize roses.

Why couldn't I have inherited Mom's skinny genes, or at least her sparkling nature? Why did Dad's DNA have to be so dominant? I asked myself that every time I looked in the full-length bathroom mirrors that captured my image from every imaginable angle.

After yo-yoing on Slim-Fast, Weight Watchers, Jenny Craig, and LA Weight Loss, I was still a large woman. The anorexic, hollow-cheeked look still continued to be all the rage in this decade. My current diet had knocked off several pounds, but the red, white, and green fixation was beginning to turn my nerves into live, exposed high-voltage wires.

The potent scent of coffee on the tray rose to meet my nostrils, reminding me to walk upright and smile. It was a bit of a challenge balancing a tray of hot coffee and china cups and trying not to trip over the bulky sari that swished and swirled around my ankles.

Okay, Soorya, this too shall pass, I told myself and proceeded to check out the man who was waiting to meet me.

Chapter 2

Entering the living room, I took quick note of the people seated on our pink and white floral-patterned furniture. Mr. and Mrs. Vadepalli seemed normal enough—typically dressed in their own conservative discount-store apparel.

Mr. Vadepalli was a lanky man in a pale blue shirt and gray pants that went out of fashion some five years ago. His salt-and-pepper hair was slicked back with some kind of oil or pomade. His skin was the color of glossy ebony, with a few deep lines etched on its surface. Sitting on the couch next to my dad, Mr. Vadepalli looked almost gaunt.

Mrs. Vadepalli, seated beside Pamma on the other couch, was a small woman with buckteeth. She wore glasses and ruby-red lipstick that emphasized the teeth. She was lighter-skinned than her husband. Her long hair was braided but looked as black as Mom's. If nothing else, the two women could discuss hair color and exchange tips on buying it at wholesale prices.

At a second glance, I realized these people were rather thin. They were likely to dislike me on sight. Slim individuals invariably had this disdain for fat people.

Looking at Mrs. Vadepalli's periwinkle blue pantsuit and black sandals, I wondered about the dress code. If the old lady was wearing American-style clothes, why had Mom and Pamma insisted on my wearing Indian attire and heavy jewelry?

But old folks aside, it was the son, if that young man sitting in the recliner by the fireplace was indeed their son, who nearly caused me to drop my coffee tray.

Oh my God!

My mouth went dry. The cups rattled ominously in my trembling hands. Coffee dribbled out of the pot and into the tray.

Dad sprang to his feet. "Let me take that, sweetheart," he said and relieved me of the tray. As a rule Dad never lifted a finger to help with anything remotely connected to housekeeping. He must have been desperate to make a good impression on the Vadepallis to actually touch a coffee tray, dressed in his favorite white Ralph Lauren shirt and black slacks, no less.

He didn't want the guests to think I was a klutz.

Meanwhile, oblivious to my disoriented state and my near mishap, my mother introduced me to the visitors. "This is our daughter Soorya, the lawyer," she announced, her voice brimming with maternal pride. I was never just Soorya or Soorya Giri to my mother. I was Soorya the lawyer. To Mom it was a matter of prestige, but to me it was somewhat akin to being introduced as Xena the Warrior Princess.

Regaining my equilibrium to some degree, I joined my palms in the traditional *namaste* to greet the Vadepallis. Mr. Vadepalli returned my gesture. "How do you do, Soorya." With his bushy eyebrows and dark eyes, he looked rather serious and unapproachable.

His wife adjusted her glasses and studied me for a long moment, her eyes traveling up and down my body a few times, making me feel like a rare exhibit at the natural history museum.

So how did I measure up? I wondered. T. rex or woolly mammoth? And did I really care what they thought of me? These people would eat our delicious food and drink our imported coffee and be gone within the hour.

By next week they'd be history, and Mom would put a check mark next to their name in her little blue book of matrimonial prospects. Then she'd move on to the next name on her list.

Once again Pamma would pray to the Lord to bless me soon with a nice-nice husband.

Despite my reservations, my eyes scooted right back to the guy in the recliner—the potential groom. There was something about him that drew my eyes to him. He was a human magnet.

The young man, or rather the Greek god with silky-looking black hair that curled at the neck, unfolded his long legs and rose to shake my hand. "Hello, Soorya. I'm Roger."

Roger? What was a guy with brown skin and a South Indian Hindu surname doing with a name like Roger?

I accepted his hand with a practiced smile. "Nice to meet you." His hand felt long and bony and warm, and his handshake firm. His voice was deep—just raspy enough to make it interesting—like the cool, gritty texture of crushed ice in a tangy margarita.

And . . . oh joy, he was taller than I. This was the first suitor I'd had to look up to, in spite of my one-inch heels. He was well over six feet.

As I lifted my eyes to his, I realized his were big and cinnamon colored and fringed by incredibly long lashes—like Bambi's. But unlike Bambi's endearingly innocent ones, Roger's eyes had a sexy, come-hither look. Bedroom eyes. What an attractive but deadly combination—bedroom eyes and bedroom voice.

Oh my God. I breathed a long, wistful mental sigh.

This time Mom was right. Handsome.

Roger waited to sit down until Mom and I were properly seated. He had sweet manners, too—something I rarely came across in spoiled Indian men. From the corner of my eye I noticed he had a slim, tight body and a slightly crooked but captivating smile. His teeth were white and even, not at all like his mama's buckteeth. Orthodontics or just pure luck in inheriting genes from the right ancestors? He wore khaki trousers, cream shirt, and brown loafers. Preppy and appealing.

So what was this Roger doing here, looking at me? Right about now he was probably checking out all the exit routes, dreaming up a dozen excuses for hightailing it out of here. But this guy appeared to be clever and sneaky. Instead of looking bored or fidgety like the others I'd met, he looked relaxed and genial. His legs were stretched out in front of him and crossed at the ankles over the oriental rug and his hands were loosely locked over his middle.

He looked more at home in my living room than I did.

I caught him eyeing the food with interest. Perhaps he was hungry after his long flight from Kansas. Airlines were notorious for not providing meals on board these days. If Roger was a true Indian at heart, he was likely to take full advantage of a free meal. And my mother's cooking was outstanding. The size of Dad's, Pamma's, and my waistlines could attest to that.

After another covert glance at Roger and then at my wrist-watch, I figured this guy would be leaving soon. Didn't they all? I could then change into comfortable clothes and get some research done on the Internet for one of my cases while I scratched at my hives and found some relief. After that I could curl up with a good romance novel and fantasize about having wild sex with a tall man with . . . cinnamon eyes.

Where the heck had that X-rated thought come from? I privately scolded myself for fantasizing about a stranger named Roger. I'd just met the man, for heaven's sake. I had to blame such uncharacteristic cogitation on my diet. The hunger pangs were making me light-headed.

Meanwhile Mom poured coffee and Dad passed around the snacks on dainty plates with a solicitous smile on his face. Since I wasn't supposed to speak unless spoken to, I sat with my back rigid and my eyes trained on the coffee table, as though I'd never seen it before. The itch on my neck was making me squirm. I could feel the wet spots under my arms getting larger. Twenty more minutes of this and the sweat was likely to start running down my arms.

When would this visit end?

"What kind of law do you practice, Soorya?" Mrs. Vadepalli's voice seemed to reach me through a mental fog.

I respectfully turned to face her. "Environmental law." I made sure to look at her without letting my eyes make direct contact with hers. One did not look an elder in the eye. It was a mark of disrespect. I had it down to a science now, this business of looking at people without really looking at them.

Mrs. Vadepalli's arched eyebrows climbed up. "Oh, so you are like that movie heroine, Erwin Broncowitch?"

Movie heroine? Hardly. Julia Roberts was gorgeous. Mrs. Vadepalli's pronunciation of the protagonist's name was atrocious, but I smiled and nodded. "Something like that."

I was tempted to point out that Erin Brockovich was not a lawyer, but a high school grad and single mother who just happened to work in a law office. However, condescension was another no-no during bride viewing.

"So you fight to preserve the environment?" chimed in Mr. Vadepalli, the pockets of his cheeks filled with food.

"Yes and no. My job is to make sure my clients don't break environmental laws in the course of doing business. But I also see that they're not penalized irrationally by the lawmakers. My colleagues and I work for preserving the environment but not at the cost of hindering progress."

"I see." Mr. Vadepalli nodded, then frowned a little. "But is there money in that kind of law?" The old man was obviously making some hasty mental calculations about my earning potential.

Before I could come up with a suitable reply, Dad interceded smoothly on my behalf. "Soorya works at McNamara, Simmons, Poindexter. Their primary clients are major oil companies, land developers, and manufacturers. Soorya earns well." Dad, with his vast experience in dealing with upper-crust patients and golf partners, was a seasoned and diplomatic conversationalist. I threw him a look of warm appreciation.

"Very good." Mr. Vadepalli finally swallowed the wad in his mouth and took a sip of coffee. "And a law degree from Columbia, too," he added with relish. "Very creditable." More dollars and cents probably somersaulted across his brain.

Pamma obliged by adding her own remarks. "Very clever she is, our Soorya. All the time top of class she was."

"Just like Erwin Broncowitch." Mrs. Vadepalli appeared pleased with her analogy.

Looking sufficiently impressed with my credentials, Mr. Vade-palli seemed to relax. But the lady continued to study my clothes and jewelry, probably assessing their worth.

Meanwhile Roger got up and took a generous second helping of everything on the table, much to Mom and Pamma's delight. The man seemed to have a healthy appetite and yet managed to maintain that flat belly. How did he do it?

I wondered what Roger did for a living. My parents and Pamma weren't asking him about it, and it wasn't my place to bring up such a touchy subject. As usual, I had failed to pay attention to my mother's glowing account of the man I was scheduled to meet today. I regretted it as I indulged in some mental drooling over Roger's biceps and bedroom eyes.

All of a sudden, Mister Bedroom Eyes spoke, startling me. "Soorya, do you like going to the movies?"

"S-sure," I said, blinking a little.

"What's your favorite kind?"

"I rather like . . . mysteries." In reality, I adored horror movies—the spookier the better. I had a collection of DVDs that could make the bravest man's hair stand on end. But I didn't want to shock these people's delicate sensibilities by mentioning my passion for terror and gore on the screen. Even Mom would find that hard to forgive.

Bedroom Eyes beamed at me. "Excellent. There's a good one that just opened this week. Would you like to go see it with me?" He put his plate down and turned the brilliant smile on my parents. "Uncle, Auntie, you don't mind, do you?"

My stomach lurched. Was this some sort of prank? Nobody had insulted me to this degree. Overweight yes. Unattractive yes. Dark-skinned yes. But no man had made me the butt end of a cruel joke. "I beg your pardon?" My voice was cold enough to freeze a lake.

"A movie. Didn't you say you liked mysteries?" Roger Vade-palli's face looked perfectly serious, and his tone sounded rational.

"I'm not sure. I have a lot of work to catch up on this evening."

"Can't you take a Saturday evening off?" Roger's eyebrows, which were arched like his mother's, cocked up, and his big eyes twinkled with wry amusement. He had seen right through my flimsy excuse. And he wanted me to know it.

"Well, I suppose I could." This was getting more awkward by the minute. All my communication skills had abandoned me for the moment. So much for being a member of the Toastmasters Club for two years.

Sending a "help me" look to Mom across the room only got me a gentle, encouraging smile. Pamma, despite her money-back-guarantee hearing aid, looked like she hadn't heard Roger's words or mine. Oblivious to the tension in the room, she was still chewing on her *vadas,* her false teeth clicking like knitting needles.

Dad's face split up in a satisfied grin. "Go on, you two young-sters." He made shooing gestures at us with his big hands. "We will entertain ourselves here."

I glanced at Roger's parents. Having consumed a fair amount of food, Mr. Vadepalli burped and didn't care to excuse himself. But I seemed to be the only one disturbed by such lack of manners. Everyone else was smiling and carrying on as if they didn't have a care in the world.

Burping after a satisfying meal was all part of Indian social life, something I'd never accepted. In fact, Pamma always assured me burping was a way of complimenting the host on a superb meal. The Japanese believed in it, too, as Mom often reminded me.

The Vadepallis seemed quite nonchalant about their son asking a strange woman out on a date, like they'd been through this scenario before. Exactly how many girls had Roger interviewed so far? And how many had he taken to the cinema? Was he in the habit of groping and fondling in the dark? Was that why he'd suggested a movie? If so, he could spell trouble.

I didn't want a strange man laying his hands on me. Although on second thought, those long, manly fingers touching me didn't seem like such a bad notion. It could even be . . . well . . . fun.

With some reluctance I agreed to the movie idea. What did I have to lose? Once outside the house, Bedroom Eyes was likely to show his true colors. He'd probably say he was merely going through the motions to please his parents and then tell me to my face that he wasn't interested in me. Or, like my last suitor had done, that gutless weasel, lie to me by claiming he was gay.

At best I'd get a free movie out of this highly contrived date with Roger—perhaps even a slice of pizza afterward. The Vadepallis appeared to be middle-class. After all, wasn't the size of my inheritance the main reason all these so-called eligible men came to meet me?

Bedroom Eyes couldn't be any different from the rest of them.

I trudged upstairs to my room, took off all the jewelry, the sari and its accompanying garments, and tossed them on the bed. It felt like heaven to be able to shed all those layers and stand in my underwear for a minute. I rubbed some cortisone cream over my welts.

Then after changing into comfortable slacks and my signature baggy shirt that managed to conceal my generous hips, I repaired my makeup. Grabbing my purse, I went back downstairs.

Pamma, dressed in her widow's best for the occasion, white silk sari with a thin green border, threw Roger and me a suspicious look. Even if our respective parents seemed to be in favor of us going out together, Pamma was likely to frown on such nonsense. "Where are you going, Soorya?" she asked.

"I'm going to a movie, Pamma," I replied, trying not to be too loud, and hoping I wouldn't have to repeat myself. Pamma's hearing problem could be a real pain sometimes, especially when there was company around. Yelling at the top of my lungs was embarrassing. Looking at the others, I realized they were occupied with chatter and ignoring us. Anyway, satisfied with my explanation, Pamma waved us away.

Roger and his parents were drinking more coffee. Disturbingly, Mom was dropping hints that the Vadepallis should cancel their hotel reservations and stay with us overnight. I winced inwardly at the thought of more torture. Bedroom Eyes under the same roof as me? Perhaps sleeping in our guest room in his birthday suit? Oh dear.

This wasn't supposed to happen. I'd assumed the Vadepallis would be polite and slip out of here with a few mumbled apologies and promises of calling back within a day or two. Then the call would come—a rejection with some cockamamie excuse tacked on, like "personalities don't match" or "diverse interests" or "not ready for marriage just yet." The most original pretext was the one where the guy's father had said I was overqualified for their son—their doctor son with an MD-PhD, no less.

And now this. Things seemed to be spinning out of control.

With a resigned glance at the two sets of parents laughing and reminiscing about their respective hometowns in Andhra Pradesh, the Telugu state in India, I motioned to Roger that I was ready to leave. The elders were getting along beautifully, digging into each other's ancestry and common acquaintances.

If one came from the state of Andhra, it was inevitable that one would bump into either a relative or a relative of a relative by marriage. Between in-laws, out-laws, and everyone in between, there was generally a common thread somewhere—if only one was tenacious enough to delve deep enough to find it. Even Pamma was chuckling heartily about something. Her hearing aid seemed to be working rather well this afternoon.

I heard Mom's high-pitched giggle. "Oh, looks like we know many of the same people back home. Who knows, we may even have some common relations, right?"

Mr. Vadepalli's guffaw followed. "It's possible. By any chance do you know the Gullapalli family from Hyderabad?"

Pamma cackled with delight. "Gullapalli? Oh yes, I am knowing quite well." She switched to Telugu after that.

An uneasy sigh escaped me. I wasn't sure if all this camaraderie meant good news or bad.

Chapter 3

The second shock of the day came after we stepped into the foyer, when Bedroom Eyes coolly decreed that we should forget the movies and simply go for a leisurely walk. "Let's get to know each other a bit, shall we?" he suggested.

I gave him a deliberately bored look. Somewhere within the next ten minutes I'd be hearing his lame excuses. How original would his lies be? He didn't appear to be gay. He spoke like an educated man. I assumed all his male parts worked adequately, so impotence didn't seem a likely reason. He didn't look like a hermaphrodite like Uncle Srinath's wife, either. And he carried himself well.

And, oh my, when he smiled, he made my pulse take a dizzying leap.

"If that's what you want," I said, putting some starch into my voice, surprised but pleased to note that my nervousness didn't show. I seemed well in control of the situation. "There's a park about a quarter of a mile from here. We won't need to take the car."

Roger nodded. "Excellent. I like walking."

He'd said *excellent* twice in the last twenty minutes. He was either very pleased with the way things were going, or he had a limited vocabulary.

We crossed the street and walked for a while in silence, my high-heeled sandals making a clip-clop sound on the sidewalk. It was a grand day for a stroll—temperatures in the eighties, a light breeze and the sweet, heady scent of late summer roses in the air. The neighborhood's lush green lawns and professionally landscaped shrubberies and flower beds looked as perfect as something carved and polished and carefully painted by hand.

Nearby someone's automatic sprinkler system came on and droplets of water started to dance in the sunlight, making tiny rainbows as they whirled around and around, releasing the pleasant odor of damp earth. An elderly couple walked their two identical Pekingese dogs, the happy canines wearing jeweled collars. The old lady carried a discreet little pooper-scooper and a plastic bag.

Half a block down, the aroma of someone's backyard barbecue met us, making me think of hot dogs and burgers smothered with ketchup and mustard and onions. It always came down to food. Was I the only one, or were all dieters similarly obsessed with food?

I could feel Roger's eyes on me and as a result I nearly tripped over the concrete sidewalk a couple of times. Gallantly he reached out and steadied me by grabbing my elbow. I felt like a graceless baby elephant. Generally I walked with a purposeful stride and plenty of confidence. I rarely stumbled. But then I never got to walk alongside a gorgeous sample of the male of the species either.

To make matters worse, Mr. Shah, an Indian businessman who lived in the neighborhood, was just stepping out of his convertible BMW. It was a great day to ride with the top down, but his comb-over had a windblown look, with a few long, scanty locks spilling onto one shoulder, revealing the entire top of his gleaming head. Comb-overs weren't meant to go with wind and speed. I knew he would give us an enthusiastic greeting.

Sure enough, he lifted an arm and waved at me from across the street. "Hellooo, Sooryaaa, hellooo!"

I waved back. "Hello, Uncle Shah." I had to raise my voice to be heard over the splashing sound of more water sprinklers.

"Long time no see." Shah took off his sunglasses. "Been out of town or what?"

"I've been busy," I yelled, embarrassment making my face

and neck feel hot. This walk with Roger was turning out to be quite an experience.

"Daddy and Mummy doing okay?" Mr. Shah asked.

"They're fine, thank you."

A couple of women taking a power walk were staring at us for disturbing the peace in this tranquil neighborhood. Loud conversations on street corners were not considered polite in refined communities.

Besides, dark-skinned folks were still eyed with some wariness in primarily Caucasian neighborhoods—especially after the 9/11 disaster. It was best not to invite unnecessary attention to ourselves. I began to walk faster to get away from Shah.

However, I noticed Shah keenly eyeing Roger. Oh great! Now Shah would spread it around that Soorya Giri had a boyfriend. Short of placing a bulletin in the India Association's newsletter, he'd do everything in his power to broadcast the news.

Next thing there'd be phone calls asking my mother whether I was engaged—at last. Every Indian family in the neighborhood knew about my parents' frantic efforts to get me hitched. Many of them kept my mother informed about some eligible Indian guy or other.

Even our non-Indian friends and neighbors were getting involved in the matter. Old Mrs. Singleton had suggested a motel owner with one eye. I had nothing against that, except he was only five feet two inches tall and weighed about one hundred pounds.

Dad's golf buddy, Simon Stokes, had found an Indian student at a community college for me, a guy who pumped gas for a living. That wasn't what bothered me. It was his illegal alien status that irked me.

The last one, suggested by none other than Mr. Shah, really took the cake—he was a fifty-three-year-old Indian widower with three kids. Apparently he owned a lucrative chain of fast food restaurants and the poor man was lonely.

Mr. Shah had helpfully added, "Soorya will be a good companion for him and in other respects also—she is young and healthy and he is missing some necessary things in life." The implication was that a younger woman would likely give the middle-aged man's starved libido a badly needed workout.

All those friendly suggestions were meant well, but remaining single was beginning to look more and more attractive.

Mom's little blue book was brimming with names, addresses, and phone numbers. "Getting the Giri girl married" had become a mission for our relatives, friends, acquaintances, and neighbors.

After we'd made it past Shah's elaborate Tudor-style home, Roger broke his silence to make a polite comment. "Nice neighborhood you have here. Some beautiful houses." I guessed he didn't know what else to say. Besides, the homes in the area were rather nice. And why not? They were mostly custom-built, and maintained by professional landscapers, housekeepers, cooks, and maids.

"Yes, it is rather lovely," I said. Not being used to much exercise other than walking the block and a half from the subway station to my office, my legs were beginning to get tired as we continued to saunter. I breathed a sigh of relief when the park came into view.

The place looked a bit crowded because of the ideal weather. But maybe that was a good thing. Surrounded by lots of people meant less opportunity for private and intimate conversation. I wasn't sure what to say to the enigmatic Roger, although his nearness was disturbingly pleasant. His cologne was cool and citrusy, like a shady orange grove on a blistering summer afternoon.

Oh no, I was doing it again—drooling over a man who was probably laughing at me right now. But a quick peek assured me his face was serious and attentive.

When we found an ice-cream vendor at the park's entrance, I turned to Roger. "How about some ice cream?" Although Roger had eaten plenty at my home, I hadn't eaten any of Mom's food, and my stomach felt hollow.

"Sounds good." Roger was already reading the menu displayed on the side of the ice-cream cart with narrowed eyes. "Chocolate-pistachio. Single scoop," he said, after carefully pe-

rusing the list with the kind of concentration we attorneys reserved for studying complex legal documents.

"One single chocolate-pistachio cone and one sugar-free
cherry ice, please," I said to the ice-cream seller. I would have
loved to sink my teeth into some chocolate-pistachio myself, but
the cherry ice was the only thing with a bright red color, no fat,
and no carbs.

When I opened my purse to pay for our purchase, Roger didn't
even make a token effort to pick up the tab. Cheap! I doubted
whether he even carried a wallet. For all his earlier chivalry, the
guy seemed stingy. And thank goodness I'd remembered to
bring my purse, or it could have proved embarrassing.

Happily licking his ice cream as we strolled toward the small
lake with ducks floating on its surface, Roger was quiet for a
while, then shot me a quizzical smile. "Why the glum look? Am
I that repulsive?"

Boy, did he have some nerve! Coming to a complete stop, I
turned to him, right there in the middle of the park, surrounded
by walkers and joggers and dog exercisers. "Look, there's no
need to add insult to injury, okay. I know why you suggested we
go for a quiet walk. You're going to tell me in private, very po-
litely, that I'm too fat and unattractive, aren't you? So cut out
the BS and cut to the chase."

A few passersby stared at us, but I didn't care.

"What are you talking about?" Roger's puzzled frown
looked genuine enough, making me wonder if his question was
indeed innocent or if he was just a gifted actor.

Marching over to an empty bench located under a Norway
maple, I sat down with all the feminine daintiness I could
muster. The result was a rather clumsy plop, with the cherry ice
landing in my lap. Thank goodness I was wearing dark brown
slacks. I hastily cleaned up the icy red mess with my napkins
and tossed the ball into the nearby trash receptacle.

"I'm not impressed by the innocent act, Roger," I snapped,
suppressed annoyance making my voice quiver.

Joining me on the bench, Roger methodically finished the last
of his ice cream and tossed his napkins in the trash, then

combed his fingers through his long hair. A sheepish look came over his face. "Actually . . . my name's not Roger."

"What!" My scowl must have been ferocious, because his head jerked back a bit.

"I apologize. My real name is Rajesh."

"Rajesh? Then why did you tell me your name was Roger?" My notorious temper was beginning to do a tap dance in my head.

"That is something I use for professional reasons."

"Why?"

A long sigh escaped Roger's full lips. "I'm not exactly your average Indian male."

As if I hadn't noticed? My cursed brain was still singing *cute-sexy, cute-sexy*. "What does that have to do with lying about your name?"

"Quite a lot."

"I don't appreciate being lied to." I slid away from him to the end of the bench to show him just how much I disliked liars.

"But you're a lawyer, for Pete's sake."

I was incredulous. "I resent that—the pot calling the kettle black." Drawing a deep breath, I counted to five. "I realize lawyers aren't viewed as icons of society, but I happen to be a respectable lawyer with scruples. I do *not* lie."

"I'm sorry. I didn't mean to imply you were a liar. I meant you should be used to other people lying to you."

"Even so, I don't tolerate people who pull a fast one on me." Roger was getting on my last nerve. "So what's with this Roger alias?" I demanded.

He winced, showing me he wasn't used to dealing with girls with fiery tempers. "Friends and teachers started calling me Roger because it was easy and familiar when I was in elementary school, and it stuck. It was a more acceptable name while I was growing up in a mostly white neighborhood and attending an all-white school in a conservative state like Kansas. Americans react better to Roger than Rajesh."

"My family is very Indian in their ways, thank you very much. I'm sure they'd have handled Rajesh perfectly well, much better than Roger, in fact," I ground out, still fuming. "And Roger Vadepalli sounds a bit silly, by the way."

Roger shook his head. "I have to tell you something else. It's not just the name that's outside the norm. I generally sport long hair and a beard. I wear wrinkled T-shirts and jeans. I told you I'm not your typical Indian guy with an engineering degree, a nine-to-five job, a 401K plan, and a fat year-end bonus for being a good boy. My dad lectured me and forced me to clean up specifically for this occasion."

"I see." Inwardly I didn't see at all. So he'd showered and shaved and cut off his locks for his meeting with me. Big deal. It wasn't enough to diminish my anger.

Besides, his hair was still too long. And so darn silky-looking. I tried not to let my eyes linger over it.

"Being a young, modern attorney and all, I thought you might like Roger better than Rajesh, too."

"And your parents don't mind this sort of deception?"

He shrugged. "They don't appreciate it, but I convinced them it was only for a few hours. Eventually I was going to tell you and your family the truth. And I just did, didn't I?" he added with a disarming smile.

Despite my attempts to hold on to my sense of outrage, Roger's quirky logic was beginning to get the better of me. It appealed to my odd sense of humor. He was a rare masterpiece, this man with the long legs, soft hair, the Adonis face, and a ridiculous name like Roger Vadepalli. After a long, heavy silence, my lips began to twitch with amusement. "Beard and decrepit togs, eh? No kidding?"

"No kidding. Here, take a look at this." Roger dug into his pocket and pulled out a dog-eared photograph of himself.

A hoot of laughter, loud and unladylike, erupted from my throat. The snapshot looked like a mug shot and the young man in it looked like a hobo, nearly as wild and crazy as the Unabomber. For one brief, uneasy second I wondered if this individual sitting next to me was as twisted as the lunatic who'd terrorized the academic and scientific communities for so many years.

The outward charm, the lies, and the assumed name. Were they all part of a sick mind? Was it a mistake coming here alone with him? An unconscious shiver shot through me. I slanted a wary look at Roger. "So what's the catch? Are you so desperate to get my dowry or does someone in your family badly need my father's cosmetic makeover for free?"

"Neither," said Roger, or rather Rajesh, on a chuckle. "My dad owns an engineering consulting company and is rolling in dollars. He employs about sixty people and lives in a huge house. And nobody in the Vadepalli family is quite that anxious for your father's scalpel."

I couldn't keep my curiosity locked up any longer. "And what do *you* do for a living, Roger? Work for your father?"

"No. I don't like engineering. I'm a writer and producer."

Well, that more or less explained the scruffy look. He was the untamed, artistic type. I took a slow, deep breath. My nerves settled a bit. At least he wasn't a demented genius who built bombs in his basement. "Producer, as in movies?" I asked.

"As in plays. I have a degree in theater arts."

"You mean like Broadway?" Well, now that I'd established he wasn't a mad scientist, Roger was suddenly beginning to take on fascinating proportions in my view. A young man from a conservative Telugu family working as a drama producer? This surely had to be a first.

"Not right now, but I'm hoping to get to Broadway someday soon."

"So where do I fit into this? I'm guessing you don't need an Indian woman lawyer to play a role in one of your plays?"

Roger stared at the ducks gliding over the lake in quiet contemplation for a long minute, his cinnamon eyes narrowed. I wasn't sure if he was trying to compose a suitable reply to my question or a painless way to let me down, or perhaps both.

The sun was low over the horizon—a giant fireball shimmering over the lake and the ducks, casting golden fingers through the rhododendron bushes and the giant weeping willows skirting the water. Bees buzzed around us. It was nearing dinnertime and many of the walkers were heading for the exit gate, leaving Roger and me sitting more or less by ourselves.

And still Roger continued to stare into the distance in silence. My patience was wearing out. I'd give him thirty more seconds.

Finally I rose from the bench. "So, which is it going to be, Roger? Am I dark and unattractive? Or way too qualified? Or you're gay perhaps? Impotent?"

What he said next wasn't all that unexpected, but the stark honesty of it left my legs feeling a bit weak. So I sat down again. Despite all the lies he'd told me so far, the man seemed brutally honest in this one answer.

"None of those," he replied quietly. "What I need is a rich wife."

Chapter 4

I stared at Roger, my eyes wide. Had I heard correctly? Had he actually come out and admitted what most men wouldn't? Or couldn't?

"Look, I'll be honest," Roger explained earnestly.

"You mean you'll tell me the truth for a change." I was still bristling from the chain of lies and the shock of one harsh truth.

Roger had the grace to blush. "I need to move to New York to pursue my work. I have no money of my own and Dad refuses to help me out unless I do something stodgy and uninspiring like consulting."

"Why?"

"He has no faith in anything that's remotely related to show business."

"How about friends or siblings?"

"None of my friends are rich. I have only one older sister, Renuka, and she's married to a regular scrooge. Renu's husband is comfortable but even more conservative than my dad."

"I suppose that's where I come in?"

"Well, I was hoping that if you agreed to marry me, maybe I could ask your father, or perhaps even you, to invest in my production."

"And you don't feel any discomfort in that, Roger?"

"It'll only be a loan that I intend to repay—every last penny of it with interest...." His voice trailed off on a disheartened note. "Never mind. It's all so far-fetched and hopeless."

Despite my efforts to resist his eccentric charm, I felt myself getting reeled in like the fish that bites the shiny lure. "No, your career doesn't sound all that hopeless. Tell me more about your work."

"You're sure you want to hear the boring details?"

"I'm sure." I watched Roger Vadepalli's eyes light up as he told me about his play, *Mumbai to Manhattan,* the story of a young, idealistic diamond merchant named Satish Sharma.

Satish migrates from Mumbai (originally called Bombay), India, to New York to start a jewelry business. Walking home late one night, he witnesses the murder of a young woman and calls 911. That single fateful incident lands the naïve Satish in a tangled web of drug deals and killings, eventually making him a target for the killer. Meanwhile Satish is befriended by his neighbor, a mysterious and slightly crazy clairvoyant who calls herself a voodoo priestess. Despite his doubts about her mental stability and her motives, she helps him overcome his troubles and achieve his dream of starting a successful diamond business in Manhattan.

Realizing Roger's tale was filled with dark secrets and gruesome murders—exactly my kind of macabre drama—I smiled. "Sounds wonderful."

Bedroom Eyes looked stunned. "It does? So, you think this might work? Marriage, the drama company?"

"Whoa, wait a minute. Who said anything about marriage?"

"But you and I? Our meeting today—" His frown looked perplexed.

"Don't take me for granted, Roger Vadepalli." Some nerve the man had, presuming I'd be so grateful for his largesse that I'd fall at his feet and accept him as my lord and master. I wasn't that desperate for a man.

"Pardon me." He didn't look all that contrite.

"Marriage is very premature at the moment. We've just met." I raised a hand to stop him when I saw his lips move. "I realize this was a bride viewing, but that doesn't mean I subscribe to the meet-once-then-marry philosophy. I want to date the man I'll eventually settle with. So forget instant marriage."

Roger held up both hands, palms facing out. "All right, okay. I understand."

"Good. Besides, for all I know, you could be a serial killer." The teasing note slipped through the seriousness I was trying hard to preserve.

"Sorry, I got a bit carried away." His mouth curved in the most attractive way, and his eyes twinkled, turning the cinnamon to liquid copper.

"But you don't think I'm too chunky and plain?" I asked, hearing disbelief in my own voice. No matter how outlandish his plans were, the man didn't have to marry a girl he didn't like and consequently ruin his personal life, just to fulfill his career dreams.

He shook his head. "Not at all. My last girlfriend was also a big girl."

I couldn't help the shocked gasp. "You don't say!" His honesty about my size stung a bit, but I had asked for candor, hadn't I? "So how many girlfriends have you had?"

"A few."

A few could mean anywhere from two to ten. It was best not to delve into that. "So what happened to your last girlfriend, the big one? Did she dump you?"

"No, I ended our relationship. She took it hard, but I couldn't do that to my folks, you know, marrying a non-Indian girl. Being an Indian dude has its obligations."

"Yeah, I know how that feels," I said, recalling my obligations to my family. "But don't your parents expect you to marry a pretty girl?"

A wicked grin spread across Roger's striking face. "They'll be happy to get an Indian daughter-in-law, period. Every girl I've met so far has rejected me."

"Why?" He was one of the most attractive Indian men I'd seen.

"They all wanted a nice, clean-cut doctor or engineer or some other respectable professional with a healthy income. I obviously didn't fit the mold."

I could see some Indian girls wrinkling up their noses at an unkempt and unemployed writer-producer with no real prospects. "How many girls?"

"Exactly a dozen. I suppose you'll be the thirteenth," he said with a resigned sigh. "Thirteen is never a good number. I told Dad this wholesome new image wouldn't work any better than my destitute look, but he wouldn't listen."

Just like Roger had done earlier, I watched the ducks floating over the sun-kissed water. For some reason the bees were buzzing more loudly now—maybe they'd found a piece of candy or something lying around, or it could be Roger's cologne.

I wasn't sure what to say to Roger. Sure, he was cute and likeable. He was probably quite bright, too. But did I want to marry a jobless guy? I was a well-paid lawyer working for a classy firm in Manhattan. I had standards to maintain.

But I was undecided. Why did he have to be so darn attractive? If he were ugly as a warthog, it would have been simple. "Like my mother said, it's a full moon tonight, with potential," I finally said and rose from the bench. "Come on, let's go see a movie and discuss a few possibilities, Roger."

We headed back to our house so we could pick up my car and go to the movies. The walk back was much less stressful than the earlier stroll. At least now Bedroom Eyes and I were talking. I was no longer afraid of him. He even had both hands thrust in his pockets in that relaxed way men seem to have.

Mr. Shah was nowhere in sight, thank goodness. Everybody else we ran into was a stranger to me. Absently I scratched my neck.

"Contact dermatitis," pronounced Roger.

"Excuse me?"

"Your hives. I noticed them earlier. The gold border on your sari might have irritated your skin. It's called contact dermatitis."

"I know what it's called, but how do *you* know that?" Roger's knowledge of things was fascinating, but I hadn't realized he'd noticed all that much about me. What else had caught those dreamy eyes? The wet patches under my arms? The tiny mole on my upper lip? The funny shape of my right middle toe?

"I was a pre-med student a long time ago," he replied.

"So how did you end up in theater arts?"

"The theater's more appealing than slicing up cadavers."

"I know what you mean," I said with a shudder. Cadavers had never appealed to me, either. Our house came into view and we crossed the street.

"We could take our rental car," Roger offered, referring to the white Chevy Malibu parked on the street in front of our house.

The offer was unexpected, but I considered it for a second. The idea of making him pay for something, even if it was only half a gallon of gas, sounded great. But I was afraid the Vadepallis were probably debating the idea of staying at our house, and having no car would give them the perfect reason to accept Mom's invitation. I was against that notion.

Having the Vadepallis in our home overnight was unsettling. I had no idea how things would go with Roger, and I didn't want to establish any sort of relationship with these strangers. Besides, I'd discovered they were rich. They could afford a hotel room. "No, let's take my car," I said. "I know the roads and it's faster that way."

When we reached the house, I found the elders cozily settled in the family room, watching television. The volume was extremely loud for Pamma's benefit. Oh dear, in the hour or so since Bedroom Eyes and I had left for the park, things had obviously progressed from the formal living room to the more informal family room.

Mrs. Vadepalli looked comfortable with one foot tucked under her other knee on the couch. Her husband sat next to her with his head thrown back against the backrest, his long, skinny legs stretched out in front of him. They looked like they'd been in our house forever. Mom and Dad sat side by side on the love seat, looking equally relaxed. Pamma was fast asleep in the recliner.

Instead of considering all this conviviality a good thing, I had the most uncomfortable feeling in my gut.

Because of the way the furniture was placed, they all had their backs to me, all except Pamma. Perhaps because of the

TV's deafening volume, they appeared not to have heard us coming in.

I stood on the threshold in silence to see what they were watching with such rapt attention. When I realized what it was, the blood surged into my face. I could feel Roger's presence directly behind me. He had come to a standstill, too.

There I was on the screen, a larger-than-life three-year-old, plump and brown as a roasted turkey, frolicking in the bathtub in all my naked glory. Two rubber ducks floated in the suds while I splashed water over my mother and everything else in the bathroom.

I'd forgotten that old video was still around. It was actually an old home movie that had been converted to a video after VCRs became the rage. Soon it would turn into a DVD.

I must have made a sound, because four sets of eyes abruptly turned to look at me. If it were possible to die of embarrassment I'd have been a heap of ashes. "What are you guys doing?" I managed to squeak out and glare at my parents.

Typically oblivious to my discomfort, Mom grinned. "We're sharing some of our precious memories with Sharda and Venki, dear."

Sharda and Venki? When had my parents gone from calling these people Mr. and Mrs. Vadepalli to using their first names? And Venki was a shortened version, sort of a nickname for the old-fashioned Venkatesh.

This visit was turning more absurd by the minute. Mom and Dad were starting to treat Bedroom Eyes's parents like old friends. Knowing Mom was a hopeless case of sentimental mush, I pinned Dad with a blistering look. "Of all things to show people, you had to pick *that* video, Dad?"

Dad shrugged. "Hey, family life is pretty much the same everywhere, princess. I'm sure Sharda and Venki have similar videos of their children."

Venki, or rather Mr. Vadepalli, removed his glasses and wiped them with a handkerchief. "Not exactly like this, but very similar."

His wife nodded in enthusiastic agreement. "Venki always

carried his movie camera everywhere when Renuka and Rajesh were little."

The conversation had woken Pamma, who looked at me and smiled serenely. "Oh, you are back already?"

"Yeah, we went for a short walk before going to the movie."

I heard an amused chuckle behind me, so I turned around to face Roger with narrowed eyes. "That's enough out of you," I hissed, keeping my voice to a whisper meant only for his ears.

Roger shrugged in a helpless gesture. "What did I do?"

"Come with me." I proceeded to the living room, Roger close on my heels. He was still snickering and I subjected him to the full measure of my indignation. "Stop that." When he raised an amused brow, I pointed a finger at him. "Just stop it."

"Okay, but you were a cute kid."

"Round and big-nosed with wild hair is not cute. And don't patronize me, Roger Vadepalli."

Throwing his hands up in mock surrender, Roger sank onto the couch. "My name is Rajesh, remember?"

"To me you're Roger. It's your own fault for lying about your name in the first place. Now you're stuck with it." His jaw tightened and I rejoiced instantly. A little revenge felt good. He was getting too cocky.

"All right, calm down. There are plenty of videos of my sister and me running around in our underwear, too. So don't get yours in a knot." He had the nerve to grin. "Your underwear, that is—"

"Pervert." My embarrassment and anger started to simmer down despite his ribbing. It was probably his infectious grin that did it. I had to admit Bedroom Eyes had a way about him that made me forget why I was angry in the first place. I'd even started kidding with him—me, the levelheaded attorney.

He was right, though. So what if I was a chubby toddler? I was still big, so body fat was nothing new. In fact, now my nose and chin and eyebrows were rather nice compared to that picture on the screen. I wondered if the Vadepallis had noticed the difference in my features and whether they'd thought to ask my parents about it. If they had any social graces at all, they wouldn't.

Had Roger noticed? I slanted a glance at him. "Did you notice my face in the video?"

"Sure."

"So do you see the difference now?"

He chuckled again. "You want to know if I noticed whether your daddy used his scalpel on you? The answer is yes."

"And you have no problem with that?"

"Nope. I had a honker for a nose when I was little. I was at least sixteen before the face fit the nose."

I frowned at him. "But you have a perfect Adonis nose."

Roger ran his artistic fingers through his tresses and batted his eyelashes at me. "*Moi,* Adonis?"

I had to laugh. No wonder he was in show business. He would be perfect for the stage or the screen. I pulled out my car keys. "What kind of movie would you like to see? The theater's going to be crowded on a Saturday evening, so we may not get tickets for exactly what we want."

He shrugged. "I'm open to anything. You choose."

"Tell your parents we're going to the movies. I'll get the car out of the garage. Meet me out front."

"Yes, ma'am." He rose from the couch and wandered off in the direction of the family room.

I couldn't help but admire his body—long legs and firm, masculine muscle in all the right places. Oddball though he was, there was something dangerously attractive about Roger that left me with a funny feeling I couldn't analyze. This was like no other bride viewing I'd ever had.

But eventually the outcome would be the same. In the end, they were all cut from the same *samosa* pastry cutter.

So, exactly when was Bedroom Eyes going to turn tail and run?

Chapter 5

Roger adjusted the passenger seat to accommodate his long legs, then looked about the interior of my car. "Nice wheels. But I thought you'd be driving something fancier."

"Like what?"

"Like a luxury sedan or a sports model. You're a successful lawyer, so I assumed you'd like the good stuff—status symbols."

"You assumed wrong." Roger's comment wasn't anything I hadn't heard before. Lots of people assumed that about me. "My dad's the one who likes status symbols, not me, and certainly not my mother or grandmother."

"Sorry, I didn't mean to imply you're a snob or anything."

"That's okay. Others ask me that, too." I happened to like my very boxy and very practical three-year-old black Volvo. It lent me a sense of sturdiness to go along with my square attorney image. It probably came from my need to get away from the pampered princess impression.

As I'd predicted, the movie theater was mobbed. With sixteen theaters crammed into one building, the parking lot was packed, too. I found a spot for my car in the farthest row and we were forced to walk some distance to the building. It seemed like a day for long walks. Hopefully those fat cells were melting off my hips.

We stood in a long line outside the ticket booth and Roger picked up a casual conversation with the elderly grandma type standing behind him in the line. By the time we reached the ticket window he'd managed to find out the lady's name, how many children and grandchildren she had, that she suffered from emphysema, and that she was afraid of dying.

"Poor Mildred," he whispered in my ear. "In spite of having five grown and married children, she lives alone. She says she's afraid she'll die in her sleep some day and they won't even know until her body is decomposed."

I shot Roger a dubious look. "She told you *all* that?" He made it sound like Mildred was an old and dear friend.

"It's preposterous that a woman her age and in her condition should be living alone and that her kids don't care."

"You're absolutely right," I said before realizing it was our turn at the ticket counter.

I managed to get tickets for an Indian movie produced in the U.S. Most of the dialogue was in English, but the Hindi portions had subtitles. It turned out to be quite entertaining, with a zany mix of Hollywood and Bollywood—song, dance, love and romance without a hint of sex—not even a real mouth-to-mouth kiss.

Bedroom Eyes surprised me when he got us giant-size sodas just before the show started, and paid for them on his own, too. So he did have money on him, unlike what I'd thought earlier. He hadn't offered to pay for the tickets. Clever, underhanded— and entirely sneaky.

The big disappointment, however, or should I say the surprise, was Bedroom Eyes's behavior in the darkness of the theater. He was the perfect gentleman. Not once did he make an effort to touch me or whisper anything lewd in my ear.

Was this the same guy who'd claimed to have had a number of girlfriends? His eyes seemed glued to the screen. Once or twice I stole a peek at him, but he appeared enthralled by what was happening in the movie.

I'd never know how those slim, bony fingers would feel against my skin. But then, if he'd tried anything funny, I'd probably have smacked him and told him to keep his groping hands to himself. So his lack of interest was good for his reputation but bad for my already bruised ego. Oh well, I'd have to get over it.

Once when I sniffled during a touching scene, Roger turned to me with an understanding look, then went right back to watching the movie. I'd hoped he'd pat my hand and offer sympathy, or at least a handkerchief like they did in romance novels.

When the show ended, he turned to me with a pleased smile. "Pretty entertaining, wasn't it? The writer's a whiz at making up these Indo-American fusion stories. She seems to have the right touch," he enthused.

We made our way through the darkened corridor and then out into the bright lobby. Knowing I was a bit red-eyed from the film's emotional finale, I kept my head down. Despite my pragmatic and cynical personality, I was a sucker for a good love story and a happy ending. The hero in the movie was attractive and long-haired like Roger, making my mind spin a few fantasies around him.

And it didn't help matters one bit when Mildred, Roger's recently acquired friend, tapped me on the shoulder. "Your young man is so nice, dear, just like the hero in the movie."

I thanked Mildred and kept moving despite noticing Roger's grin at the remark. My eyes remained on the ground so Roger wouldn't see me as a sniveling, sentimental blob of a woman. My tough image was something I worked hard at maintaining, so I kept a tight rein on my tear ducts.

Lord knows why I cared about Roger's opinion of me. He was just another man who'd be gone from my life in the next hour or less.

It had turned dark outside except for the light coming from the lampposts, and the full moon was clearly visible in the velvety black sky—a perfect *purnima* moon. As we walked across the parking lot crammed with automobiles, I noticed the stars were delightfully bright on this crisp, clear, late-summer night. Hundreds of moths circled the lamps.

We got into the car and headed back home. I figured if the senior Vadepallis had gone to their hotel during our absence, like I'd hoped, then I could turn around and drop Roger off, too.

Roger once again settled back in my car and went on and on about the movie. He also told me about his role model, M. Night Shyamalan, the writer and director of the movies *The Sixth Sense* and *The Village*. "Such a talented guy. Boy, would I like to be the next Shyamalan!" he said, his expression wistful. "At least the Broadway version of him."

"So you think you can rise to those heights in the theater industry?"

"You don't think I have what it takes to make it to the top?" He sounded offended, but the sly smile belied it.

"It takes not just talent but mountains of hard work to get there." Looking at his relaxed posture, I got the feeling he wasn't quite the workaholic. How old was he? At least my age, to be considered eligible for me by my parents and his. The Indian norm was to pick a boy slightly older than the girl. At thirty-something he was still without a job or any kind of personal savings.

"I happen to have plenty of talent and capacity for work," Roger announced with supreme male confidence. "I won an award for my play in my master's program. I sold the rights to an off-Broadway producer."

Sufficiently impressed, I raised my brows. "What school did you go to?"

"Yale School of Drama," he said quietly.

Wow! An award from Yale wasn't anything to sneeze at. He was smarter and more diligent than I'd assumed.

"Surprised?" he asked, as if reading my thoughts. "You're not the only one with an Ivy League degree, Soorya. And my undergrad is from Johns Hopkins, by the way."

Holy cow! This was getting more and more interesting. The man had to be a whiz to get into the Johns Hopkins pre-med program and then into Yale for his master's. He was a madcap genius after all. "Then why are you struggling to make a living now, Roger?"

"I told you why," he said, rolling his eyes. "My dad washed his hands of me when I decided to go into theater arts instead of med school. He grudgingly paid for school, but he won't fund my play."

"You've never worked for a salary? No savings whatsoever?"

Roger exhaled slowly, thoughtfully. "I've saved a little from working the last few years at a community theater in Kansas City, but it's just about enough to cover my grocery bills in a place like New York."

"So how much money do you need to produce *Bombay to Manhattan*?" I regretted the question the moment it left my mouth. I didn't want Bedroom Eyes to think I was interested in financing his project. I had absolutely no intention of getting involved with him on any level.

"Mumbai to Manhattan," he corrected me before mentioning the dollar amount. "Around half a million dollars, and that's a very conservative estimate."

"Ouch, that much?"

"Have you ever thought about the cast's salaries, the costumes, the sets, the musicians, the rent, the overhead, the sky-high insurance? It's immense. What I quoted is the bare minimum."

He was right. I'd never thought about most of those things whenever I'd sat in a theater and enjoyed a performance. The trust fund Dad had set up for me had that amount and much more in it, but it was still a huge sum of money Roger was talking about. And why was I thinking about my own savings? His father was a multimillionaire, probably much wealthier than my family, and Roger was quite capable of convincing his old man to cough up the money to fund his venture. His very risky venture.

The rest of the drive home was filled with Roger telling me more about his play. His voice had a deep, soothing quality, so I listened without interrupting. I realized, to my surprise, that he had done considerable research, even to the extent of talking to set designers, sound technicians, stage actors, and a variety of people connected to the professional theater business.

He'd made several trips to New York City in the past year.

But still, was the play merely Roger's unreachable dream or a tangible goal?

I wasn't surprised when I found the white Malibu sitting in the same spot outside our driveway. The Vadepallis were still hanging around. I hit the automatic door opener and drove directly into the garage. Roger and I entered the house through the door that led into the laundry room. We walked past the washer and dryer and Mom's super-organized shelves with the detergents, stain removers, and fabric softeners.

As we approached the kitchen, voices and the aroma of South Indian food drifted toward us. The clink of ice cubes in glasses mingled with the Telugu music playing in the background. The elders were still at it—cozying up to each other.

Roger glanced at me. "Isn't it nice that our parents get along so well?"

"Hmm." Nice for Roger perhaps, but not for me. I didn't want his parents and mine to become friends. I didn't want to keep discovering Roger's finer qualities, either, only to be informed later that he, although an unemployed guy, had rejected me and gone back to Kansas.

Dad's back was to us when we entered the kitchen. He stood at the island, holding a martini glass with two pearl onions floating in its frosty depths. A tall crystal glass filled with a golden liquid that looked like scotch and soda graced Mr. Vadepalli's hand. Ah, so the Vadepallis were drinkers. Dad could enjoy his martini without feeling guilty.

About as tall as Dad, but thin and narrow-shouldered, Mr. Vadepalli stood on the other side of the island. The men appeared to be discussing the stock market. "I'm not sure the market will go back to the nineties high for a long time, Pramod," Mr. Vadepalli announced, looking unhappy. "I've lost faith in the market."

"Tell me about it," Dad groaned. "Even my blue chips took a nosedive. I'll never recover the losses. I'm not putting my money into those risky sectors again."

Two rich men discussing their portfolios, I observed with

some amusement. The women were at the stove, each stirring a simmering pot and talking about something I couldn't hear—most likely food and jewelry.

This was a typical Indian social scene: the men conversing about politics and investments over a drink, while the women cooked and chatted about the price of Basmati rice and the latest fad in saris and gold necklaces.

Pamma, who generally ate early and went to bed before nine o'clock, was at the kitchen table, eating yogurt, rice, and lime pickle. Although a large woman by Indian standards, she looked wizened and tired at eighty-four. Her white-haired bun looked even whiter in the light from the chandelier. She had already changed into a plain white cotton sari, more or less ready for bed.

I glanced around one more time. The tableau looked heartwarmingly sweet and domestic.

Roger beamed at the picture. "Something smells great. It's making me hungry."

"Didn't you eat and drink already?" I whispered.

He patted his stomach. "I'm a growing boy."

Mr. Vadepalli was the first to notice us. "Look, here they come." He smiled at us in that indulgent fashion parents reserve for their children.

Dad turned around. "Just in time for dinner. So, what movie did you guys see?" His pristine white shirt had a grease spot right where it stretched across his belly. He'd been eating a few too many *samosas*.

Was it my imagination, or did Dad look particularly smug as he asked the question? Roger and I both replied at precisely the same moment. I wished we hadn't, because it looked like we'd rehearsed it—a sure sign of guilt.

I wished there had been something to be guilty about, a little hanky-panky at least. It would have given me a chance to experience what Roger's skin felt like. Maybe it would have helped me make up my mind about Roger.

"Was it a good film?" Mom asked as she moved to grab dinner plates from the cabinet.

"It was very interesting—a Bollywoodized version of a Hollywood movie," Roger announced with such zest and launched into such a positive description that the elders immediately started to discuss the possibility of going to see the movie the next day.

I groaned inwardly. That meant the Vadepallis would stay at our house that night.

At Dad's offer of a drink, Roger opted for a beer and I decided on a diet cherry soda. I went to the dining room to set the dinner table while Mrs. Vadepalli helped Mom bring the dishes of steaming food to the table.

Everything smelled delicious, but I knew I could eat only the tomato *pappu,* a spicy split pea and tomato curry served over plain rice, and the spinach salad.

Just before we sat down to eat, Pamma announced she was going to bed. Mr. and Mrs. Vadepalli promptly bent down to touch her feet in the old-fashioned Hindu way of bidding goodbye to an elder. Obviously thrilled at their show of respect, Pamma patted their heads, heaped blessings upon them, and then hugged the petite Mrs. Vadepalli, who barely reached Pamma's chin.

It was a pleasant surprise to see Roger follow his parents' example. Pamma's eyes lit up. I could tell she hadn't expected this young man with his American ways to touch her rough and wrinkled feet. "You are such a good boy," she said. And her teeth clicked more than ever.

Roger was clearly unleashing his boyish charms on my unsuspecting grandmother. Pamma twinkled at him and asked how he liked his trip to New Jersey so far, and he replied in nearly perfect Telugu, albeit with an accent, that he was having a wonderful time.

Looking more impressed than ever, Pamma turned to Roger's mother. "Very nice boy you have, Sharda. He is speaking very good Telugu." Naturally Sharda looked pleased.

Roger glanced at me with a gleam in his eyes. I had to give the boy credit for speaking Telugu, which I didn't. He'd made Pamma a happy old woman.

Of course, I'd have to endure the lecture from my parents and grandmother tomorrow about how awful I was for not making an effort to speak my mother tongue. I remembered having spoken the language fluently in my childhood, but somewhere between grades one and three, I'd switched entirely to English.

Sometimes I regretted it, like right that minute, when my parents and grandmother were looking at Roger like he'd just established peace in the Middle East and won an Olympic gold medal—all on the same day.

Once again, the Vadepallis made a hearty meal out of Mom's cooking, making me wonder how this family could pack away so much food and manage to remain so thin. How unfair was that?

While I nibbled on dainty bites of tomato, rice, and spinach, I watched Mrs. Vadepalli, whose weight was likely no more than a hundred and ten pounds, devour second helpings of every dish.

The men ate everything in sight. My dad seemed ecstatic at having guests who ate as heartily as he did.

The conversation turned to Roger.

"Your father tells me you turned down medical school offers to take up theater arts, Rajesh. Why is that?" Dad asked with such a somber face that I almost felt sorry for Roger.

Defending his choice of occupation to me was different from doing it before an elder, especially a dedicated doctor who thought the sun rose and set over the medical profession and its esteemed practitioners, especially those who could fix oddly shaped chins and noses.

But Roger did a superb job of explaining to my father why he'd chosen show business over medicine. At the end of a long conversation, Roger seemed to have convinced both my parents that writing, producing, and directing plays was a perfectly reasonable way to make a living.

Mom's soft eyes gazed in rapt attention while Roger made his impassioned speech and Dad nodded like he usually did when something made complete sense to him.

Roger was articulate and very convincing. If being a playwright wasn't in his stars, I concluded he could always go into a sales career. The man could sell stripes to a herd of zebras and crude oil to a bunch of Arabs. Being a huge Broadway fan, Dad asked him questions about some of the more popular shows and they discussed them at length.

The only person who still had a look of disdain on his face was Mr. Vadepalli. "Useless, I say. What is the use of entertaining people for a living? There are so many useful and productive occupations in the world, and my son decides to go into entertainment. And calls himself Roger."

"Entertainment is a legitimate business, Dad," Roger explained with infinite patience.

"What is legitimate about men putting on lipstick and wearing dresses and dancing on stage? Besides, there is no stability in that. What is the guarantee that one will succeed? Look at all those Broadway and Hollywood flops. Only one in a hundred movies or plays will make it to the top. Doing something consistent and earning a decent living is the only way to survive."

"But, Dad, my heart is not in any of the things that *you* like doing."

The veins in Mr. Vadepalli's neck seemed to expand. The look on his face was beginning to scare me. I hoped he wasn't about to have a coronary attack or something. "Damn your liking, boy! Who says *liking* has anything to do with earning a paycheck?"

"Dad, there's nothing wrong with liking one's—"

"When you *like* something, it is a hobby, not a career. When I came to this country with eight dollars in my pocket, if I became a playwright, do you think we would be where we are today? We would be living in a ghetto somewhere, not knowing where our next meal would come from." With that said, Mr. Vadepalli pushed away from the table and rose to his feet, essentially calling an end to a hitherto enjoyable meal.

An uncomfortable silence fell over the dining room.

It was a good thing most everyone had finished eating. All at once we all scrambled to our feet and pushed our chairs in. Mom and Mrs. Vadepalli picked up the pans and carried them to the kitchen. I applied myself to gathering up the plates and flatware.

A glance at Roger got me an apologetic shrug. I gave him a sympathetic look in silent support and went back to the task at hand.

For the first time that day, I felt genuinely sorry for Roger. I had no idea what it was like to be yelled at and lectured about my choice of occupation. My father had been supportive of me all through my school and college years, even though I'd chosen to go against his dream of his only child following in his footsteps. He'd encouraged me to apply to medical schools but never forced me.

Roger's mother obviously didn't have anything to say about his theater career, but then Mr. Vadepalli's contempt and rage seemed more than enough for both of them.

Poor, poor Roger, I said to myself and went into the kitchen.

Meanwhile, Dad, our resident diplomat, saved the evening by deftly leading the fuming Mr. Vadepalli back to the family room. "Venki, have you seen that new Telugu movie yet? We have a DVD right here, so let's watch it together, shall we?"

After helping Mom and Mrs. Vadepalli load the dishwasher and tidy the kitchen, I quietly slipped out the back door to the deck and sat in a chair by the picnic table. After witnessing the heated outburst in there, I needed some quiet time. Other than some well-deserved reprimands during my rebellious years, I'd never been lambasted like Roger had been by his father, and certainly not before an audience.

But then, I'd chosen a lucrative profession with a lot of prestige attached to it, while Roger had picked something few Indian-Americans wanted to touch. I was beginning to see why Roger couldn't count on his rich father to finance anything he'd dream up.

What about his mother? I wondered. She'd been silent and kept her eyes on her plate all through her husband's diatribe. What were her feelings about her son's career? At least my mom, despite her old-fashioned deference to Dad, had some opinions of her own, unique and separate from his. And she had no qualms about voicing them, either.

Dad was an accommodating husband and always offered Mom the privilege of speaking her mind. I was given lots of independence to say exactly what I wanted, too. Foul language was frowned upon, but I never really got chastised for using it occasionally. Pamma could be an opinionated woman at times, but Dad and Mom always let her air her views, too.

The mosquitoes were all around me, but I managed to keep them at bay with the can of bug repellent spray left on the table. Mom's roses smelled lovely in the moonlight. The pool's surface resembled a mirror, except when an occasional bug landed on it and caused tiny ripples.

I looked at the shadowy woods in the background. Strange how earlier that day I'd almost been tempted to hide amidst the trees rather than meet the Vadepallis. If I'd followed through on that impulse, I'd never have met the odd, intriguing character called Roger Vadepalli.

Some small night creature scrambled through the weeds growing underneath the deck. Laughing voices somewhere nearby reached me along with the splash of water—a pool party—a happy sound that eliminated some of the bad taste left in my mouth from Mr. Vadepalli's tirade.

I secretly hoped Roger would seek me out and join me outside. But too many embarrassing things had been said at the dinner table for comfort between us. He was probably too mortified to talk to any of us anymore. I wasn't sure what he was doing at the moment—watching the Telugu movie with the elders or sitting all by his lonesome somewhere and licking his wounded ego.

So what were his thoughts about us? I wondered. While returning from the movie theater he hadn't really said anything of substance. He hadn't mentioned meeting again or made any suggestions about staying in touch.

After having spent half a day with me, he'd probably reached a decision. I was likely not his type. Besides, I'd shown him only the ornery and sardonic side of myself while he'd been polite and affable.

I stayed outside for as long as I could without insulting our guests. As a host I couldn't neglect my visitors, even if they were sure to reject me with a careless phone call in the near future. Besides, it was beginning to get a bit chilly to stay outside for too long.

When I went back inside, it was a relief to hear the Vadepallis laughing about something. The idea of watching a movie had obviously been scrapped. Things appeared to be on an even keel once again, and I breathed more freely.

I found Roger in the living room, reading the latest issue of *Time* magazine. He looked up when I walked in and smiled that crooked smile that made him both an angel and devil rolled into one sexy package.

I smiled back but didn't sit down. From what the elders were saying, it sounded like they were getting ready to leave soon, like the evening was definitely coming to an end.

Whatever had transpired while I sat on the deck was probably for the best. The elders emerged from the family room into the foyer. Roger and I joined them. The Vadepallis were going back to their hotel.

Good-byes were exchanged all around. Mom and Mrs. Vadepalli hugged briefly, but the rest of us shook hands. Nice and efficient. No strings attached.

Roger held my hand with unexpected warmth. "Thanks for everything, Soorya. I enjoyed my visit."

Liar! He'd probably disliked every minute of it. Nonetheless I mumbled something appropriate.

Mom and Dad went outside to their car to give them a proper send-off while I stood uncertainly on the porch. I heard Mom expressing regret that they had turned down her invitation to spend the night at our house. Then the car's engine cranked up and they drove away, with Roger at the wheel.

I turned around and went back inside. Yet another bride viewing was now behind me. This one was unusual, wacky actually. I should have felt relief that it was finally over. Instead I felt an odd sense of restlessness. Roger was the only man who'd left an impression on my mind.

Noticing the light on in Pamma's room on the first floor, I walked in, wondering if something was wrong. She should have been asleep long before this.

"Pamma?" The bedspread was turned down but her bed was empty. Her bathroom door was closed. Had she fallen or passed out in there? I panicked. But in the next instant she came out and my breath eased. "Are you all right?" I yelled, not sure if she was wearing her hearing aid.

She motioned to me to pipe down, meaning her hearing aid was working. "Just using the bathroom, baby." Carefully lowering herself to the bed, she took off her glasses and placed them on the nightstand. Then she patted the spot beside her, inviting me to sit down. "Everything good?" she asked me, her tired eyes trying to focus on me. She used to be nearly as tall as I in her younger days, so her eyes were level with mine.

I nodded. "Everything's good." I hoped she wouldn't bring up the Vadepallis. Frankly, I didn't know how I felt about them. But of course she had to talk about them after the enjoyable day she'd had with them.

"Very good family, no, Vadepalli?" Pamma patted my cheek, eased her legs over the bed, and stretched out. "You know what is another good thing?"

"What?"

"Venki's aunt's sister-in-law is from my village in Andhra."

"That's nice, Pamma," I said. Finding some distant link to her village back in her homeland had to be a thrill for Pamma. Ever since she'd come to live with us some sixteen years ago, after my grandfather's death, she'd looked like a lost soul. Despite all the attention and luxuries Mom and Dad gave her, she missed India. But my father was her only son, and although she had two daughters in India and one in Arizona, and all of them well-off, it wasn't customary to live with a daughter.

The son was always the one who provided for elderly parents. So poor dear Pamma was stuck here in a foreign land, where the weather was too cold, the food too bland, the culture alien, and the streets depressingly empty. But she rarely complained.

I pulled the cover sheet and blanket up to her chest. "Good night, Pamma." I didn't think she heard me. She was already pulling out her hearing aid and setting it on the nightstand, next to the glasses and the ceramic bowl that held her dentures floating in some kind of frothy cleaning solution. Turning out the bedside light, I left her room and went upstairs.

As I got ready for bed that night, I tried to imagine a Broadway sign in lights: MUMBAI TO MANHATTAN—WRITTEN, PRODUCED, AND DIRECTED BY ROGER VADEPALLI.

Chapter 6

The next morning, I sat at my computer for hours and worked on my briefs. I'd never worked so long and so hard on a Sunday morning, but after the strange Saturday I'd had, I needed work to keep my mind occupied.

At noon, I padded downstairs to eat lunch with Pamma and my parents. Mom and Dad were in a pensive mood. I had the feeling they were digesting the Vadepallis' visit, just like I was.

Pamma appeared cheerful nonetheless. She couldn't stop talking about Venki's aunt's sister-in-law. Her voice and the clicking of her teeth were the only distinct sounds at the kitchen table. This was perhaps the most exciting thing in Pamma's life in over a decade and the most emotionally exhausting, too. After lunch she went back to her room for a long nap.

Since the afternoon was pleasantly hot, I changed into a bathing suit and indulged in a leisurely swim. Dad joined me in the pool for a while and we competed with each other, doing laps. It was a game we'd played since I was a little girl, splashing each other and going crazy.

Dad always lost the race, whether by design or lack of skill I'd never know, but it was always fun to tease him about it.

Exhausted, we flopped onto the poolside chairs under the shade of the dogwood trees and Mom treated us to cold sodas. Dad, as usual, claimed he was starving, so she brought him cheese and crackers, cautioning him not to overeat. Naturally Dad polished off the last crumb and went looking for more.

At about four o'clock, Amy called on my cell phone, wanting to know all about the latest bride viewing. "So, how did it go?" she asked.

"Okay, I guess," I answered in my usual indifferent fashion. By now Amy knew that these things had become routine in our household. "Although—"

"What?" I could hear the alertness creeping into her voice.

"This one's different."

Amy chuckled. "So he asked for a Bud Light instead of Indian tea?"

"I'm serious. He's charming but he's . . ." Now that I had to describe him, I wasn't quite sure what to call him. "I'd say crafty."

"How?"

"He lied to me about his name—told me it's Roger when it's really Rajesh. And he's very handsome in an offbeat sort of way."

"No shit!" Amy sounded delighted. "An Indian man called Roger? And he's handsome?" All these years, when I'd shown her pictures of the guys who'd come to meet me, she'd been entirely disappointed. They were nerdy guys with impressive degrees from well-known universities, lucrative jobs or businesses, little or no sense of humor, and solid, Telugu backgrounds. Adjectives like *handsome, good-looking,* or even *personable* hadn't factored in at any time.

"Yeah, go figure that. Mom found a cute one this time. He's even taller than I am. And talk about great eyes and a terrific physique."

"Get out! You're saying he's sexy?"

"Mmm-hmm," I sighed. "Again, in a different sort of way. He kind of looks like the long-haired guys on the cover of a romance novel."

"Wow, those cover guys can be hot. That's great!"

"It's not great. He lied to me, Ames. Lied about something as basic as his name."

"But you did say he's cute."

"So?"

"That's a big improvement over the others. So tell me what happened."

"The usual—nothing. He came, he saw, he left."

"Oh." The single syllable was enough. I could hear the disappointment and almost see Amy's almond-shaped eyes lose their luster for a moment.

We chatted a little about David. Apparently he was invited to dinner with Amy and her mother that evening. She told me her mom was making David's favorite dishes. "She's in her Wonder Woman mother-in-law mode, so I'm trying to stay out of her way," said Amy. "I'm doing my nails instead."

"Good for you." I was happy for Amy, but a slight twinge of envy cast a shadow over my thoughts. If I ever managed to get engaged, I could only imagine how wild Mom would go over making my fiancé's favorite foods. She'd import ingredients if necessary. "I'd better return to finishing up my briefs. Enjoy the evening with David," I said, and hung up the phone.

During dinner, Mom threw me a concerned look as I toyed with my salad. "Baby, shouldn't you eat something more substantial for a change? Aren't you tired of red and green salads?"

I shook my head. "I ate some vanilla yogurt earlier. I've had my day's quota of protein."

"Then at least drink some warm milk before you go to bed."

Pamma joined Mom in admonishing me. "It is not good for children to starve."

"I haven't been a child for the last fifteen years or more, Pamma," I reminded her.

She either ignored me or didn't hear me. "You eat good, you feel good—otherwise, you get sick. Now eat!"

I nodded absently. Mom and Pamma worried about my nutrition. Their old-fashioned Indian wisdom included spicy food in humongous quantities. A full belly was considered healthy for the body, mind, and soul. They were both against my dieting, period, whereas Dad, more attuned to how the outside world treated overweight people, spurred me on.

What did a perpetually slim woman like Mom know about the trials and tribulations of fat people, especially in a beauty-

and youth-oriented society like America? And Pamma, though still a big woman, was at the end of her life. As far as Dad's eating habits were concerned, he ate like a sumo wrestler.

Dad was successful in his career and his personal life. He had nothing more to prove. He could eat all he wanted and get as big as he pleased. His scalpel spoke a charming language all its own. People flocked to him no matter what he looked like. As far back as my memories went, Dad looked like a dark-skinned version of Santa Claus, round-cheeked, big-bellied, and instantly ready for a hearty laugh and a plate of food.

At one point during the quiet dinner, the topic of Roger Vadepalli came up, when Mom reflected, "Such a handsome and smart boy. I can't imagine why Rajesh didn't become a doctor."

Dad agreed. "Especially after he supposedly did well in premed." After a long, thoughtful moment, he added, "But you have to give the young man some credit for standing up to Venki and going into the profession he wants."

Mom made a clucking sound. "That poor boy. It was not right for Venki to insult his son in front of us."

I entirely agreed with Mom, but kept my mouth shut. I wasn't in a mood to discuss the Vadepallis. I was wondering why the expected rejection call hadn't come yet. Their son might be a hippie with empty pockets, but that didn't mean they were going to settle for me, especially since it was I who had made it clear that marriage wasn't in our immediate future. That meant Roger, who was hungry for instant funding for his project, would be looking elsewhere for a rich bride.

Suddenly my appetite was gone. With my salad only half-finished, I took my plate to the sink and dumped the rest in the garbage disposal, then took myself off to my room to work some more and pack my briefcase for the next day.

Monday morning's commute was the usual frantic rush through the parking lot and into the train station. Once seated on the train, I generally liked to get my mind organized and focused on the day's impending activities, but I had a hard time doing it this morning.

Instead I dully observed the people around me—all the Manhattan folks going to their offices or stores or wherever they worked—the Chanel and Gucci suits and dresses mixed in with the Macy's and Walmart togs.

Inside a commuter train, everyone seemed to blend into this middle-of-the-road blandness—everybody going out to make a living, be it in a fancy high-rise or a humble grocery store.

There was something about New York City that homogenized people—America's true melting pot. I noticed a couple of people glancing at their watches anxiously. Were Mondays usually rough for the rest of them, too?

Later, the staff meeting at our Lexington Avenue office was stiff and boring as usual, with all the junior attorneys delivering a progress report on their respective cases. Mac was conspicuously absent. I'd noticed that lately he'd started to miss the routine weekly staff meetings. I wondered if at the age of sixty-six he was beginning to phase into retirement, or if his notorious extramarital life over the weekends kept him away on Mondays.

Al Simmons and Larry Poindexter, the two other senior partners, did show up and stayed through the customary meeting, asking tough questions and doling out advice and directives.

My mind refused to focus on the issues, and my eyes wandered to the windows often. When I'd finished my brief presentation and the meeting ended a little after 10:30 A.M., it was with relief that I picked up my folders and headed back to my small private office.

Being the most junior associate, I had the tiniest office, with only one window which overlooked another skyscraper across the street. My room's size and view indicated my lowly status as the new kid in the firm.

But I still had it better than the men and women who worked as paralegals, law clerks, and secretaries in our organization.

Happily, the afternoon turned out to be brighter than the morning. I had a meeting scheduled with an attorney who worked for the New Jersey Department of Environmental Protection, or NJDEP. He was assigned to work with the Pinelands Commission and the Natural Resources Defense Council.

The DEP, the Council, and the Commission were making my most prominent client's life difficult at the moment.

My client, Solstice Properties, was a major real estate development corporation that had acquired a prime piece of land bordering New Jersey's picturesque Pinelands. The company was being hassled for endangering various species of snakes that called the protected area home. And that was only the tip of the iceberg, because other government and nonprofit environmental organizations stood in the long line of complainants.

I'd always wondered why my client couldn't build those fancy homes someplace else. Why go through so much grief and expense just to develop land that everyone thought was so damned precious?

Personally, I couldn't care less about snakes. My fondness for horror did not extend to reptiles and arachnids. Slithering and crawling critters gave me the creeps. Ever since I'd seen a cobra slide into my maternal grandparents' home in rural South India when I'd visited them as a child, and subsequently had nightmares in the following years, I'd developed a serious fear of them.

To this day, recalling the incident made me break out in goose bumps.

It was ironic that I'd been assigned to this case—the one person in the office that was terrified of snakes. I considered it baptism by reptile—in a sense therapeutic, since psychoanalysts advocate conquering one's fears by meeting them head-on. As part of taking on the case, I had to view videos of the snakes that were on the Pinelands Commission's endangered list.

At precisely 2:30 P.M., Sandy, our group's secretary, announced the visitor I was expecting. "Send Mr. Draper in," I instructed her. "And please see if he'd like a cup of coffee or tea, will you, Sandy?"

I had mixed feelings about this meeting with Louis Draper. I looked forward to meeting him in person and at the same time felt a bit anxious. I had talked to him over the phone and e-mailed him several times, and he seemed like a reasonable man. And very intelligent, different from the government bureaucrats I'd met in the recent past—men and women who'd graduated from law schools I'd never even heard of in some cases.

Draper and I had developed a rapport over the long-distance lines during the past few weeks. He had a sense of humor and we'd laughed about various things. We knew each other well by now, except we'd never met face-to-face. In a certain fashion, we had become friendly adversaries.

But we were still on opposite sides of a sticky legal battle. Today's meeting wasn't going to be easy.

I knew Draper would come armed with data, including tests run by the Commission on the wide varieties of fauna, and how and why they were threatened by the housing developments that were slowly cropping up around the neighborhood.

My client was one of the largest housing developers in the Northeast. It was a lucrative business, with customers willing to pay insane prices for homes adjoining scenic wilderness. Why anybody would want to live side by side with frogs, snakes, and swamp creatures was beyond my comprehension. However, my job was not to question the wisdom of backwoods living, but to protect my client's interests. And to bring in the revenue Mac and his partners expected.

My first surprise came when Draper was ushered in by Sandy. He was African-American!

For some inexplicable reason I'd expected a white man some-where in his late forties. But this man was easily ten years younger. Over the past few months, I'd visualized him as a man of fair skin, medium build, blond hair, and blue or perhaps hazel eyes.

Well, so much for mental images. Draper was very tall, very wide-shouldered—about as large as my dad, but minus the flab. He appeared to be all hard muscle, like a football player. And he was black.

I felt ashamed of my racist stereotyping. Why had I expected him to have a certain accent, or a certain attitude, for that matter? Wondering if he'd perhaps typecast me in a similar fashion and drawn up a mental picture of me wearing a sari and a red dot on my forehead, I stepped forward and shook his hand. "Mr. Draper, nice to finally meet you in person."

I put on my most charming smile. Of course, all my charm couldn't compete with the delightful sweetness Sandy happened to be expending on him at that moment. Sandy Minski was a slim, petite redhead with lovely blue eyes, and she had the friendliest personality this side of the Hudson.

Sandy asked Draper if he wanted coffee and he graciously accepted. Poor man, just like every other male who came in contact with our Sandy, he seemed dazzled.

I could have hated Sandy for her stunning looks, but it was impossible. She was warm and caring and didn't have a malicious bone in her body. "Thanks, Sandy. I'd love a Diet Sprite myself," I said when she arched a questioning eyebrow at me.

Draper took a seat across from my desk. I noticed he was dressed well: neat navy suit, well-pressed gray shirt and silk tie. His attire was not much when compared to the Brooks Brothers outfits my male colleagues favored, but for a public-sector employee, Draper looked well groomed. And he was a pleasant-looking man. Better than pleasant.

Again, I mentally reprimanded myself for typecasting bureaucrats.

He threw an appreciative glance around my office, taking in the watercolor landscapes on the wall, the Bokhara rug, and my eclectic assortment of *tchotchkes* from around the world. "Nice office. Very classy," he purred. "So this is how and where the other half works."

I sat down in my swivel chair and grinned. I liked Louis Draper. I had begun to like him as a deep, masculine voice on the phone, but I liked him even more in person. He had an easy way about him that I hadn't expected from a stuffy bureaucrat. "You mean to tell me you don't have a plush office that overlooks the enchanting Pine Barrens?" I asked him.

A chuckle escaped him. "Don't I wish! I have a small square area in a dusty old building with no view whatsoever—not even a skinny little pine tree. I have no windows, either." His eyes wandered to my window and the jade plant flourishing on the sill. "Why do you think I offered to come here instead of having you drive down to my office?"

"Because you were being gallant by saving a lady a long haul across the Garden State?"

"That, too," he added with a laugh.

"Why, thank you, Mr. Draper," I said, amazed that I was batting my eyelashes and putting on the pleased female act. I never did that, not even with my parade of eligible suitors.

His lips twitched with amusement. "Mr. Draper makes me feel like an old geezer. Why don't you just call me Lou?"

I nodded. "Lou it is. And I hope you'll call me Soorya."

"Pretty name. I meant to ask you about that. Does it mean something?"

"Soorya means sun—as in Sun God."

"I like the way some cultures have names that mean something." He studied me for a moment. "It suits you."

"Thanks." The remark seemed sincere. It warmed my insides instantly.

"You mind if I take my jacket off?" he asked.

I shook my head and watched while he placed his jacket on the back of his chair. Then he pulled out various folders and manila envelopes from his briefcase and methodically placed them on a guest chair. I had my own paperwork stacked up in front of me. We were both preparing for a friendly battle.

Sandy walked in with a tray. As always, she was the perfect hostess, smiling and radiant while she made sure Lou got his coffee just the way he liked it and my Sprite was poured in an elegant glass filled with ice.

For the next hour and a half, Lou and I went over his vast storehouse of scientific studies accumulated by the DEP and the Pinelands Commission. He had photographs, CDs, books, papers, and even sworn testimonials by environmental scientists.

In that short span of time, I learned more about the mating habits of the Eastern Timber Rattlesnake than I'd ever learned about human mating. Mrs. Westerly's eighth-grade sex-education class had taught me nothing compared to Lou's lecture on reptiles making out in the wilderness. With all that sexual activity and the resulting baby snakes I wondered why the rattlesnake was an endangered species.

I was impressed by Lou's presentation. But in the end I turned to him with a shake of my head. "Excellent work, but you still haven't told me how building a few dozen homes on the periphery of the Pinelands is going to kill off the snakes, Lou."

He clucked in mock exasperation. "Soorya, don't you know that building homes means putting in roads, sewer pipes, gas lines, electricity, and water? Do you have any idea how much trash and sewage a bunch of people can generate? Toxic trash that can pollute the snakes' nests and extinguish their species?"

"We have woods in back of our development, and the wild animals there seem quite happy," I replied, knowing full well that I sounded cocky, but then Lou had seemed a bit condescending in his remarks, so I felt justified in mine.

"I guess rich folks in New York don't generate any of the garbage that the heathens in New Jersey do."

"Of course not! And by the way, I live in Jersey, too."

Lou chuckled. "Is that right? Let me guess. Bergen County or Morris? Somerset?"

"Bergen." I stole a peek at my wristwatch. Nearly 4:30 P.M. It was my turn to bombard Lou with the data I'd collected. I'd done my homework, too. Besides, my client had spent enough funds on hiring scientists to do their own studies.

I tossed out statistics and morsels of information at Lou. He might have had the experience that I lacked, but I had plenty of brain and mock court practice at law school to counter his arguments. Plus I was learning daily from some of the best environmental lawyers in the business. Naturally, Lou threw in his viewpoint at every opportunity.

At one stage I actually began to enjoy the verbal sparring. This was my first really big case and my chance to argue with a strong foe. It was with a sense of euphoria that I realized I was good at this. This was excellent practice for real court time, too.

Eyes looking a little glazed from my rhetoric, Lou put up both hands. "All right, I get the picture."

I turned on my most innocent face. "You do?"

"Listen, Soorya." He sighed. "We're both intelligent people. As lawyers, we're only going to dig up more and more data to refute the opponent's argument."

"No kidding." I smiled at Lou, ridiculously gratified that he'd acknowledged my intelligence.

"There's no end to this bickering. It could go on for years. Neither your client nor we want to arrive at an impasse. I'll talk to my bosses and see if we can't work out a compromise."

When a lawyer used the word *compromise,* it meant only one thing: the defending party would be the loser. I slanted a wary look at Lou. "Exactly what do you mean by that?" I'd die before I lost my first big case.

Lou rose and walked to the window and looked outside for a few seconds. I was pretty sure it wasn't the view he was admiring. His mind was computing something.

He turned around and faced me, hands in his pockets. "Soorya, I don't make the rules. The lawmakers make the laws harsh in the hopes that would-be developers will think twice before taking on such a daunting task. Your client is one of the daring ones." He pointed an accusing finger at me. "But Solstice doesn't exactly do this as a community service. They make zillions selling those mansions."

I took a deep, defensive breath. "America is all about capitalism, Lou. Every business exists to make a profit. Nothing wrong with that."

"I agree, and I'm willing to look at the fair balance between protecting the ecosystem on the one hand and planned development on the other. But I can't talk the Commission or the DEP into letting your client go wild with building those monstrous homes with complete disregard for nature, either." Lou sounded almost angry.

"My client is not some evil predator, Lou." My own short temper was beginning to stir. "Solstice will abide by your rules. They'll hand-carry the damn snakes to another location if necessary."

Lou had his arms folded across his middle in unspoken defiance. I had a feeling my not-so-genteel speech had made him even more resistant—rebellious even. Big mistake on my part. My temper was always my biggest downfall. Well, if nothing else, I was learning a lesson in going head-to-head with an equally tenacious attorney. I lowered my voice. "Look, Lou, all we're asking for is to drop the ridiculous penalties that run into the millions of dollars."

"They're not penalties. They're the legitimate cost of development in an environmentally sensitive area."

I started to laugh. If I didn't, I'd end up throwing my prize crystal paperweight at Lou. "Legitimate cost is another name for egregious exploitation of a business to the point of beating it into the ground."

Perhaps my words had struck home or maybe it was just exhaustion, but Lou's stance relaxed a bit and he came back to his chair and sat down. "You're good with words, lady. You'll go a long way in this firm," he said with reluctant admiration. "Listen, I'll do my best to give your client a break, but I will not assist in breaking any rules."

"But you can help bend them a little?"

An unexpected spark of humor appeared in Lou's dark eyes. "Don't tell me you're asking me to do something illegal, Counselor."

"Illegal, never! Friendly arm-twisting, yes." Lou was growing on me despite our heated argument. "Hey, you're not so bad with words, either."

Lou smiled—a rather attractive smile. Gathering up his files and shoving them into his briefcase that looked more like a worn suitcase, he shrugged back into his jacket. "I guess I'll have to start that arm-twisting early tomorrow morning. Convincing a bunch of bureaucrats isn't going to be easy."

"I know. Thank you, Lou." I flashed him another brilliant smile. "I owe you one."

"Don't thank me yet. I may not get you what you want." He looked at his watch. "It's late. I might as well find a place to eat around here. I'll never make it home in time for dinner."

"You're welcome to use my phone to call your family if you'd like." I had noticed the ring on his finger, and Lou came across as a family man. Probably had a nice wife and a couple of kids. I envied him. Must be nice to be able to go home to a spouse and talk about the day, then tuck a kid or two into bed.

An image of Mrs. Draper, a pretty thirty-something woman with dark hair and coffee-toned skin, came to mind, standing beside two small children. Another one of my silly stereotypes.

But Lou shook his head. "I don't have a family."

"Oh, I'm sorry." Once again my eyes fell on his ring finger.

"I lost my wife last year."

An awkward silence fell over us. I lowered my gaze to my desk. What could one say to a man who'd recently lost his wife? The quick flash of pain on Lou's face told me exactly how much he missed the woman he'd lost. "I'm sorry. I had no idea."

"You had no way of knowing." He glanced out the window, probably gathering his thoughts once again. "Any recommendations on restaurants around here?"

Talk of dinner made me realize my stomach had been gently rumbling for some time. "If you make a left turn outside the building and walk to the end of the block, there's a nice little Italian place on the corner. I stop there often for lunch and sometimes dinner if I work late."

An idea came to me in that instant. Lou had been more than generous in traveling all the way to Manhattan and offering to work out a fair deal for my client. The least I could do was show a little gratitude. "Lou, why don't I treat you to dinner?"

Lou's eyes narrowed in suspicion. "You're not by any chance trying to bribe a government employee, are you, Counselor?" He laughed at my expression of horror. "Thanks for the offer, Soorya, but I'm not allowed to accept meals or gifts."

"Forget it, then." I was too young and new at this game of playing hotshot lawyer. How could I have been so stupid?

Perhaps recognizing both my naïveté and my embarrassment, Lou came back with a suggestion. "Why don't we go to the restaurant together, if that's okay with you? We'll go Dutch. That way it's all aboveboard."

"Okay." I was grateful to him for finding a graceful way to

handle my faux pas. He was an experienced lawyer and had probably been in situations like this before. I tidied up my paperwork and left a Post-it Note for Sandy with a few instructions for the next day.

Retrieving my purse from the desk drawer, I joined Lou and we walked out into the hallway together. I asked him to meet me by the elevator in five minutes. I needed a chance to freshen up. "The men's room is in the other direction," I told him and pointed the way before I hit the ladies' room.

As I stood before the mirror to fix my makeup and hair, I hoped dinner would prove as interesting as our meeting. It had been a most stimulating encounter. Most of my other business conferences thus far had been quite boring—nothing like the unpredictable, fun-filled meetings in all those TV shows about lawyers and law firms.

I wondered what Lou Draper's idea of a compromise was. I couldn't wait to find out.

Chapter 7

Some fifteen minutes later, Lou and I were seated at one of the small tables at Joseph's Sicilian Kitchen. The place was packed as always. Most of the tables were occupied by people like Lou and me, working people in business clothes, folks who had put in a long day at whatever they did for a living.

Snippets of conversation around us seemed to center on shop talk. At a nearby table, a bunch of lawyers were passionately discussing a tax fraud case. I felt right at home.

The restaurant smelled of Italy, the aroma of virgin olive oil and garlic mingling with the sweet scent of the vanilla candle burning in an ashtray at our table. The worn red tablecloth and dull lighting combined with Pavarotti's voice playing in the background could have come out of a scene from *The Godfather* or from a *ristorante* in Sicily.

Posters of Sinatra decked the walls alongside pictures of well-known Republican politicians from the state of New York. The restaurant owner, Joseph Travaglione, was a staunch Republican, but thankfully his prices were more Democratic and affordable for this part of Manhattan. Lou's expression as he studied the menu said the fare was definitely suitable for his wallet, too.

The waiter, a baby-faced young man named Vincent whom I'd gotten to know well, greeted me with a familiar hello. "The usual?" he asked me with a knowing smile. I nodded, which meant my standard antipasto, with no black olives or anchovies or any kind of meat.

Lou ordered lasagna and a glass of Chianti. He seemed surprised when I ordered Diet Sprite. "What, no alcohol? Is it against your religion?"

I had to go into yet another long explanation about my unusual diet.

He merely chuckled and took an appreciative sip of the wine Vincent brought to him in literally seconds. "That was prompt service!" Lou seemed impressed with Vincent.

Minutes later, Lou dug into his tossed salad with the enthusiasm of a five-year-old attacking a triple-decker ice cream sundae. I started on my antipasto with little eagerness. But I was starving and needed nourishment.

Needless to say, all those wonderfully fragrant sauces and gooey cheeses being served at the neighboring tables were driving me nuts. I tried hard not to look.

Dinner turned out to be a remarkable meal—even more interesting than I'd hoped. But instead of more business, our conversation involved personal topics. Lou didn't believe in spoiling a perfectly good dinner with shop talk.

He was an easy man to talk to, so I asked him questions about his job, his life, his town. I was genuinely interested in the life of a bureaucrat. And Lou told me his whole history while I listened to his low-pitched voice with rapt attention.

I'd never expected that a black man, raised by foster parents in a poor neighborhood in Philadelphia, would turn out to be so intriguing. Compared to his life, mine had been a cocoon of indulged luxury composed of private schools, ballet lessons, catered birthday parties, trips to the theater, exotic vacations, and finally Ivy League universities followed by a plum job.

I'd never really paid attention to anything beyond my safe little world.

Lou's life reflected the opposite end of the spectrum. He had attended a variety of urban public schools, dropped out at one time, experimented with drugs, almost joined a gang, then eventually returned and finished high school.

He had managed to get a degree from Temple University on a football scholarship. My guess about football was accurate. After that he'd studied law on a part-time basis at the same school while working in a mayor's office.

I looked at him wide-eyed. "My God! It's amazing what you've done with your life, and against all those odds. You must be so proud of what you've achieved, Lou."

I sincerely hoped he didn't consider my remarks condescending. I couldn't even begin to imagine the horrors he'd lived through: going to bed hungry most days; sleeping on a cold floor with no blankets; shoot-outs and stabbings on a regular basis near his home; drug pushers hanging out on street corners; teenage girls getting pregnant at thirteen.

How had Lou dug himself out of that dark, depressing pit? How had he motivated himself? How had he become such a polished professional?

"I'm satisfied with the way my life turned out," he said, twirling the stem of his glass as he stared into its depths. "There were times when I never thought I'd get anywhere, do anything more than scavenge for food for the rest of my life."

"What changed?"

"Reverend Bronson, pastor of the local church. He nearly beat me into attending school." Lou's face broke into a nostalgic smile. "He said I was smart and God had put me here for a purpose, and if I didn't heed my calling, I'd rot in hell. I resented the old man then, because he lectured and bullied me into studying."

"But it paid off?"

Lou nodded. "Today I think of Reverend Bronson as my personal savior and guardian angel."

How touching. Despite the surge of emotions that threatened to flood my eyes with tears, I matched Lou's smile with one of my own. "I hope you remember to tell him that often."

"He's been dead a long time. I wish I'd told him thanks. But I was a cocky punk then. Anyway, now I remember him in my daily prayers."

Lou's lasagna arrived, an enormous plate stacked high, redolent with the aromas of ricotta and basil. And he stabbed it with his fork with renewed zest, as if talking about Reverend Bronson had given him a fresh perspective on the meal.

I tried not to stare at the lasagna. I was dying to plunge my own fork into the endless layers of curly noodles and sauce and stuff my face till my belly groaned. Only the thought of shocking Lou's sense of gentility kept me from making a pig of myself.

"That's nice, Lou," I said instead. "I'm sure the reverend hears your prayers."

Mom and Dad had never exposed me to anything that remotely smelled of unpleasantness. At that moment, I wasn't sure if I should be grateful for their overprotectiveness or irritated that they'd never let me learn about the darker side of life.

Even now, finding me a good husband was their main goal. Although they were doing that in my best interests, the pressure it might exert on me was something they'd probably never considered. The husband-hunting game was unpleasant for me, even painful at times.

Of course, I couldn't lay the entire blame on my parents for my keeping myself aloof from the repulsive side of life. As a grown woman, I had every opportunity now to explore and educate myself about the world outside my immediate circle.

I'd had everything in life that Lou hadn't. It had taken me this long to realize the deeper meaning of it—because only now was I sitting across the table from a man who had drawn a vivid picture of it, a man who was a product of that scary other world.

Polishing off his sauce with a piece of bread, Lou sat back in his chair and patted his stomach, pulling me out of my thoughts. "That was delicious! Thanks for recommending this place." He looked about him and nodded in satisfaction.

"They sure make a mean Italian meal."

Vincent returned to pick up our empty dishes and Lou ordered coffee while I shook my head at Vincent's raised eyebrow. I'd already overstepped my quota of food for the day by eating every last bit of my antipasto.

"Hey, that's enough about my pathetic life. Now tell me about yours," said Lou while we waited for his coffee to arrive.

"Mine's rather boring, Lou. I'm an only child of doting parents. What can I say?"

"I'd like to hear all about how the rich and spoiled folks live," said Lou with a good-natured grin. Since Lou didn't seem the type who'd be envious of my privileged lifestyle, I told him everything about my childhood. He frowned. "Tell me if it's none of my business, but as a young Indian woman, isn't there a husband or fiancé in the picture?"

Reluctantly I told him about my parents' obsession with arranging a marriage for me. However, I didn't mention the number of failed bride viewings. I couldn't.

"Amazing!" Lou seemed fascinated by arranged marriage. "I've read about the custom and wondered about it. It actually works?"

"That's the way my parents and aunts and uncles and even some cousins got married, and they're all happy."

"But you're in America. You don't mind this arranged marriage thing?"

I thought about it for a second. "Not really. I'm not the type to date, so why not go the traditional way?" I didn't want to tell him I was too afraid to date. First of all, I had never been asked out by any man. Secondly, I feared that if on the off chance I got lucky, the guy would be asking me only out of pity or because no other girl was available. Why else would a guy approach someone like me?

And at some point, dates would likely involve sex. Deep down I was terrified of sleeping with someone who would find my body unattractive and get turned off entirely. How crushing would that be? It was best to stay away from that kind of experimentation.

"You've never dated anyone, period?" Lou's dense brows shot up.

"No. My girlfriends and I have been going out with a bunch of boys since we were teenagers, but it's a friends group. Nothing even remotely romantic there."

"Mostly wealthy Indian girls and boys, I presume?"

"That's presumptuous of you, Lou," I said.

"Sorry, I didn't mean to be. I'm just curious."

"Well, we're not highly wealthy. We're upper middle class, and not all of us are Indian."

"Still, must be nice, having most everything," Lou reflected, but with no trace of jealousy or grudge.

"Even the richest folks don't have *everything*. I hate to bring up the old adage, but money really can't buy happiness."

Then Vincent brought Lou's coffee to the table and we stopped talking for a few seconds while Lou added cream and sugar to his cup and stirred thoughtfully.

"How long were you married, Lou?" I said, wanting to switch subjects and break the long, awkward silence. Lou's life was much more inspiring than mine and I was curious about his late wife.

He stared at his cup for several seconds. "Nine years and three months."

"Long time." I got the feeling this wasn't something he talked about much.

Lou sipped his coffee and sighed. He looked tired. "Lynne was the best thing that ever happened to me." His deep-set eyes seemed to stare at nothing in particular on the table. "She gave me what I'd never had growing up: stability, unconditional love, and pride in being black."

I wanted to lay a hand on his to offer comfort, but I didn't. Despite having come to know him somewhat well, I'd met him face-to-face only hours ago. My heart constricted nonetheless. "You mean . . ." What did he mean by pride in being black?

"Lynne was a white woman, part Polish, part Italian," he added, guessing my thoughts.

"Any children?" I wondered if I was prying too much and if he'd be offended, but I had an inquisitive mind that refused to quit.

"Sadly, no. At first we put off starting a family because both of us were trying to get our careers in order. Lynne was a high school counselor and I was just starting out as a law clerk. But Lynne was diagnosed with breast cancer three years after we were married, so children were out of the question by then."

Dear God, his wife had suffered for six years? "Long illness," I said, finding nothing else to say.

"Initially, after the mastectomy and radiation, the doctors said she was in remission, and Lynne was doing fine. But a year or so later the damn thing came back with a vengeance. After that it was pure hell."

He closed his eyes for a moment, as if to shut out the painful memories. "In a way it was a good thing we had no kids. I'd never be able to care for the kids and Lynne at the same time, in spite of switching to a nine-to-five job."

"Is that when you went to work for the DEP?"

He nodded. "I worked long hours for the law firm I was with and I couldn't do that and take care of Lynne, so I applied for various government jobs, and ended up at the DEP."

"No regrets?"

He set his empty cup aside. "Not many. Government jobs have easier hours and they let me take several weeks of family leave when Lynne needed me."

"Hmm." I really had nothing to add. It was heartbreaking all the way around.

Lou offered me a half smile. "But I sometimes wish we'd had a kid. A child would have been something pleasant to go home to every night."

This time the tears gathered in my eyes, in spite of my iron self-control. Lou must have noticed my expression, but was too much of a gentleman to comment on it.

We settled our respective bills. When Lou turned to head out, I quietly left an extra tip on the table for Vincent, my favorite cherub-faced Italian waiter who made sure my antipasto arrived just the way I liked it.

There was still light outside but the pedestrian traffic had thinned out. Manhattan took on a different flavor as soon as the office crowds went home. The atmosphere was more casual, with shoppers wearing jeans and sneakers, mommies pushing baby carriages, seniors strolling, and dog owners exercising their pooches.

We stood on the sidewalk for a couple of minutes. "Give me

a few days, Soorya," Lou said. "Like I said earlier, I have to work on a number of individuals to get them to see my point of view."

"Whatever you can do will be appreciated, Lou."

With a warm handshake Lou walked off in the direction of the train station. I watched his large back recede and blend in with the crowd.

In a single evening Lou had altered my image of a black urban male.

Chapter 8

When I reached home, I found Mom and Dad sitting companionably at the kitchen table, sorting the day's mail.

Dad, dressed in comfortable shorts, T-shirt, and flip-flops, was tearing open the clear plastic cover from a medical journal. He glanced up when I walked in. "Hey, princess. How was your day?"

"Very busy," I said, looking up at the cuckoo clock on the wall and noting it was late. Pamma had probably gone to bed.

On the table, Mom had neatly separated the bills from the junk mail so she could put them in her pocket folder marked "Unpaid." Twice a month she sat at the desk in the upstairs study and wrote checks to settle those invoices. She didn't believe in online accounting, but Mom's old-fashioned record keeping was still thoroughly organized.

I sometimes wondered what sort of working woman Mom would have made, had she ventured out to find a job. She'd probably make an excellent office manager.

She rose to give me a maternal squeeze around my waist. It was her way of saying she missed me at dinner. Mom had many such nonverbal ways of communicating her sentiments. I squeezed her shoulder in turn.

She felt so tiny. The top of her head barely touched my shoulder. For every pound of weight Dad appeared to gain, it seemed like Mom lost one. Instinctively I placed my cheek on top of her head. She was already in her long cotton nightgown. Around nine o'clock each night, Mom slipped into her old-fashioned nightclothes and slathered generic-brand moisturizer over her face.

It rarely failed to bring a fond smile to my face, and the memories of childhood.

When I was little, Dad used to kiss me good night and then Mom used to slip under the covers next to me in my bed and read to me until I fell asleep. The scent of Dad's aftershave and the Downy fabric softener on Mom's nightgown combined with the herbal odor of her moisturizer would always remain with me.

Sometimes I wished I'd stayed about eight years old. Being a little girl was so much simpler. Back then, I couldn't wait to grow up and do all those mature grown-up things like drinking, driving, going to late-night parties, and holding down a job.

Well, now that I was there and had done all those things, none of it felt half as exciting as it had seemed when I was itching to get my hands on it.

"I hope you ate something decent, baby," Mom said, interrupting my thoughts.

"I had a hearty Italian antipasto, Mom. Very decent." Her expression clearly spelled *not decent enough*. So I quickly added, "Maybe I'll have an apple before I go to bed."

"You went out with friends?" Dad tried to be casual about it, stretching his big legs out in front of him and crossing them at the ankles. But I knew where his mind was. He was always hoping I'd go out with an eligible Indian guy.

Wedding bells had never been far from his mind or Mom's since the day I'd reached puberty.

It seemed Indian parents lived for only one thing in life—getting their kids married. Pamma had come to live with us and made marriage even more of a priority in my life. In her old-fashioned mind, a woman of thirty years had no business being without a husband and kids.

I grinned at Dad. "Don't look so hopeful. I had dinner with a widowed attorney who works for the NJDEP." I laughed when Dad's face fell. "It was business, Dad."

It was now two days since the Vadepallis' visit and, judging from the expressions on Mom and Dad's faces, no word had come down yet. Since neither of my parents brought up the subject of Roger, I didn't mention it, either.

This was more or less standard procedure in our home. Unless there was something to tell, my parents sort of pretended the bride viewing had never occurred, and I went along with the farce.

When the rejection call or letter or e-mail arrived, they informed me with the saddest faces. Pamma quietly shed tears into her sari's *pallu*. I had to remind them it wasn't exactly the end of the world, although I felt just as deflated.

"Good night, you guys," I said on a cheery note and headed upstairs to my room.

"Don't forget your apple, Soorya," Mom reminded.

"I'll get it later." I had no intention of getting that apple. I already felt bloated.

When I sat down at my computer to scroll through my messages, one in particular caught my eye. The subject line read: *Hi from Raj V.* Who the heck was Raj V? I wondered.

It took a few seconds to register. Roger! How had he found my address? After a moment I knew it had to be Mom who'd given it to him. So what did Roger want with me now? It had to be a polite and friendly rejection. What would his excuse be? Incompatibility? His lack of finances? Too sexy for his own good?

Unable to suppress my curiosity any longer, I opened the message.

The note was friendly all right, but it wasn't a rejection. How about that? *Hi Soorya, Just wanted to thank you and your parents for your warm hospitality this past weekend. I enjoyed the movie, the company, and your mom's cooking. I'm thinking about moving to NYC . . . soon as I can find an investor to put enough faith in me and* Mumbai to Manhattan. *So long. Rajesh V.*

Nice and cordial, but impersonal all the same. He'd said nothing about us meeting sometime or even talking over the phone. On the other hand, he'd mentioned moving to New York if he could find an investor. Was this yet another oblique way of asking me to sink my money into his play? He'd said something about my marrying him and financing his project, but then I'd put a quick stop to that.

It was just my luck that when a charming, bright, young Telugu man wanted to marry me, I couldn't say yes to him—for various reasons.

To Roger, marriage was business, pure and simple. He'd marry a plain woman like me to further his career—a commonplace occurrence in India. But this wasn't India, and I wasn't the typical shy and sweet India-born-and-bred girl who'd settle for anything that primitive.

Where did Roger's kind of philosophy leave me, then? Wouldn't I, a woman considered a loser in the marriage market, be marrying a bigger loser, just so I could get a husband?

To me, marriage was a serious commitment, not merely some legally binding contract. I had more than enough legal contracts to deal with at work.

I could only imagine introducing him, all six feet plus of long hair, jeans, and killer smile, to my friends and stuck-up coworkers. *Meet my husband, Rajesh Vadepalli.* To their questions about his occupation, I'd have to say something like, *He's unemployed and has no immediate plans to find a job. He wants to produce a play that may or may not see the light of day. Until then I'm supporting him.*

When analyzed in such practical terms, marrying Roger and squandering away my nest egg on his project sounded insane. I reluctantly deleted his message and went on to the next.

End of Roger Vadepalli.

Chapter 9

Some three weeks after my meeting with Roger, I ended up in Seattle with my boss, Matthew McNamara. We were scheduled to meet with the owners of Murzak Pulp and Paper, a large pulp mill that the EPA had targeted for polluting the Puget Sound and destroying its salmon population along with other types of aquatic life that called the sound home.

Up until then, my cases were pretty much confined to a two-hundred-mile radius. As a junior attorney, during my first year, as part of my initiation and training, I had merely assisted the veteran lawyers, mostly doing research, preparing briefs, and conferring and coordinating data with other junior attorneys like myself.

In my second year, I was given my own cases, but minor ones that didn't require a lot of deep knowledge or sophistication. They were tedious but good experience nonetheless. I'd traveled to a few nearby states in the course of my work. Now I was into bigger and slightly meatier issues.

This was my first coast-to-coast business trip. I was excited to be chosen by Mac to accompany him during this initial fact-finding conference. And I was nervous. Despite his notoriously sleazy private life, he was still my professional role model.

Someday, in the not-too-distant future, I wanted to be in his shoes—senior partner in a posh law firm in midtown Manhattan.

And here I was, side by side with my idol, going to a meeting across the country.

Neither Mac nor his partners took on an important or high-profile case without personally meeting with the party interested in hiring their services. After the fact-finding meeting, if they felt strongly that there was substance to the case, they would take it on. There had to be a reasonable chance of winning, or at least reaching a resolution the client could accept and live with. And the case had to be lucrative. If not, they turned it down.

Curious as to why Mac had requested *me* to go with him, I'd puzzled over it all through the limo ride to the airport and then some. It was a last-minute request, too, with less than a day's notice.

I didn't need to worry about my personal safety with Mac. He could never have designs on me. First of all, I was neither pretty nor Mac's type—slim, blond, and lovely. Secondly, Mac was never known to fraternize with his staff—it went against his own official rules.

Something about this trip didn't quite add up, and I was dying to know what it was.

I couldn't summon the courage to ask Mac outright why a junior employee was hand-picked for this trip. As we both sat on adjacent chairs at the boarding gate, waiting for our flight to be announced, I sort of hemmed and hawed around the subject, but Mac's answers were vague and I didn't want to push him. I couldn't afford to pester and antagonize a man who hired and fired people at will.

All I knew was that the Seattle client was a pulp mill owner with pollution-related legal problems. I assumed the blood-hounds from the EPA and/or the Washington State Department of Ecology had been sniffing around for a while. Didn't they always? At least where our clients were concerned?

Besides, I figured, why not enjoy the first-class travel accommodations and go for the ride, if nothing else? I'd never been to Seattle before and never had more than a few polite words with Mac outside my job interview and our Monday staff meetings.

This was my opportunity to see Washington state's renowned

and breathtakingly beautiful Puget Sound, and get to know the enigmatic Matthew McNamara—brilliant lawyer, playboy, and one of the best known deal-makers in the country.

With a full head of gray hair, a tall, well-preserved physique honed with weekly trips to the gym, and a disarming smile that effectively hid the steel underneath, the man had a magnificent presence. He had an air of measured sophistication that many men strived for but never quite achieved.

I'd always been curious as to what kind of surgery Dad had performed on Mac. It had to have been something significant for Mac to pick me for a job when he'd had his choice of top law graduates in the country.

After we'd boarded the flight and been in the air for a few minutes, the stewardess came by to take our drink orders. Mac asked for a double scotch on the rocks and I got my usual diet soda.

Mac gulped his drink and promptly fell asleep, making me wonder if some sweet young thing had wiped him out the previous night. How did a man in his late sixties keep up with the young beauties he caroused with? He probably lived on a steady diet of Viagra or some such drug in those TV commercials featuring middle-aged men looking deliriously happy.

Unlike Mac, I couldn't fall asleep right away, so I opened the Stephen King paperback I'd purchased at the airport. Reading always helped me unwind. The book held my attention for a half hour, after which our meals arrived.

I toyed with the food on my plate. Other than the salad, there was nothing I could eat. Mac woke up and ate his steak accompanied by more scotch. With a mumbled apology to me about being such poor company, he fell asleep again.

I was glad, since I felt a little tongue-tied with him. Besides, my novel was getting more horrific by the minute. I was really getting into it.

In the end, I managed to get about three hours of sleep.

Since we'd taken an evening flight after a full day's work at the office, by the time the flight was ready to land at Sea-Tac Airport, it was something like three in the morning by our body clocks. I was exhausted, but Mac looked refreshed from his nap. A trip to the plane's restroom had his gray mane looking neat and fresh. He smelled good, too. The old fox probably kept a bottle of cologne in his pocket.

While I was beginning to yawn and wilt, he was turning downright chatty, asking me if I'd ever been to that part of the West Coast before. When I shook my head, he started telling me little anecdotes about his previous trips until our plane landed and came to a stop. The old charmer was back.

It was drizzling outside, but the dampness was refreshing after spending hours in the dry atmosphere of the plane. Fortunately we didn't have to wait for our transportation. The limo arranged by Sandy was waiting for us at the airport exit and transported us to a downtown hotel that was plush and attractive. It boasted an atrium tastefully spilling over with orchids and tropical ferns.

Mac and I got our key cards at the registration desk and headed for our respective rooms—mine was on the fifth floor and his on the sixth. I stole a covert look at Mac as we rode the elevator together. He was positively humming with energy, making me wonder if there was perhaps a woman waiting for him in his room.

My room was big and comfortable. The bathroom was grand, with an oversized tub and two marble sinks. This was one of the things I liked about my employers—everything they did was first class. But the splendid bathtub would have to wait. I barely had the energy to brush my teeth and sink into bed.

Just before shutting off the light, I said a quick prayer to my small, laminated picture of Lord Ganesh, the elephant-headed god who removed obstacles and bestowed confidence. Whenever I traveled, I carried the Ganesh in my purse.

In less than fifteen minutes after I'd entered the room I was asleep. The alarm was set for 6:30 A.M. since I was supposed to meet Mac in the restaurant adjoining the lobby at 7:30 A.M.

I had the weirdest dream. Roger Vadepalli featured in it in all his quaintness—bearded face, hobo jeans, and crumpled T-shirt.

The details were a bit fuzzy, but we parted with angry words in the dream. When I woke up, it bothered me for some reason. We had argued in some ways the day he and his parents had visited us, but we hadn't had a fight as such. So why did a silly spat with a virtual stranger, especially one that occurred in a dream, bother me?

Well, Roger had no business invading my dreams.

Chapter 10

I was up well before the alarm went off. My mind and body were on East Coast time, wide-awake and raring to go. What was I going to do at 5:20 in the morning? Maybe I could go for a brisk walk. But it was still raining outside. So what else was new in the Pacific Northwest? How did people live with such dreary weather day in and day out?

On an impulse I looked up the hotel's directory of services and found out their gym was open twenty-four hours a day. Dragging on exercise shorts, sneakers, and a T-shirt, all of which I'd fortunately thought to pack at the last minute, I took the elevator downstairs to the well-equipped but nearly empty gym and walked on a treadmill for forty-five minutes.

The only other folks using the gym at that ungodly hour were two middle-aged men. One of them grunted as he lifted weights. The attendant on duty at the front desk was a young man with a crew cut, reading what looked like a heavy textbook. College student working part-time, I concluded. When did the poor guy get to sleep?

As I walked away from the treadmill and toward the door, wiping away the dripping perspiration with a towel, the young man smiled at me. "Fly in from the East Coast?"

I nodded. "How'd you guess?"

"Who else comes here at this hour? See those two guys?" he said, indicating the man on the bench press and the other one using some contraption that looked like a medieval torture in-strument. "They got here before you did. I bet they're from the east, too."

I chuckled. "I'm sure you get to know all the guests' habits after a while."

"Yep. You here for the big conference?"

"What conference?"

"The software guys' conference."

"I'm here on legal business. I'm an attorney."

Obviously impressed, the guy arched a brow. "East Coast law firms must pay really well if they're putting you up in *this* place."

"They do okay." I glanced at his textbook. "Exams coming up?"

He grimaced. "Yeah, physiology."

"Are you a pre-med student?" Roger came to mind again.

"Physical therapy major. But if a young attorney can stay in this hotel, maybe I should think about switching to law," he said with a grin.

I shook my head. "It's not at all like the stuff you see on TV. It's pretty boring."

"So you're saying I better stick to PT?"

"Definitely," I replied, grabbing the door handle. "Good luck on the exam."

"Thanks. You have a good day now," he said as I pushed the door open and stepped outside.

Upstairs in my room, I lowered myself into the giant bathtub in a sea of steaming, lilac-scented bubbles and read more Stephen King. It felt wonderful to wash away the exercise-induced sweat and exhaustion. I hadn't felt this relaxed in years. And I hadn't been to a gym in a while, not since my membership at the Bergen County gym had lapsed. Maybe it was time I bought a treadmill of my own.

I put on a caramel-colored suit made of lightweight wool and paired it with a cream silk blouse with pearly buttons. Pearl studs in my ears and soft brown shoes with sensible two-inch heels completed the ensemble. Hopefully I was neither over-dressed nor underdressed for my meeting with a bunch of exec-utives.

After my hair and makeup were done, the clock read 7:23 A.M., so I quickly picked up my purse and briefcase and ran for the elevator. Nervousness made my palms a little damp. Going to a power meeting with Mac by my side was both scary and exciting.

I was going to learn how to deal with an important client, how to extract information and make a profound decision. The next time I met with Lou Draper, I'd give him a tougher time than ever, I decided with a mental grin.

In the lobby, right outside the hotel's main restaurant, I waited for Mac for over thirty minutes, pacing the floor, my temper escalating with each passing minute. I hadn't had enough sleep, and I was hungry. Was he still frolicking with some woman while I'd given up an extra fifteen minutes in the tub just to be punctual? Was he at least up and about?

Just then he came sauntering through the lobby, with his usual air of male confidence and a formal greeting. "Good morning, Soorya. Let's get some breakfast, shall we?" No apologies or explanations for his tardiness. But then, men like Mac probably didn't see the need to apologize to junior employ-ees who were of no consequence.

As we were shown to a table by a waiter, I noticed Mac's eyes looked a little red around the rims. But he seemed to be in high spirits, dressed in a gray power suit and white shirt that looked bandbox perfect.

While Mac ate a hearty breakfast of eggs, toast, bacon, and coffee brimming with cream, I drank a glass of skim milk and toyed with wedges of watermelon and honeydew. Mac looked lean and fit despite the fat- and cholesterol-laden food on his plate, while here I was, starving myself and drooling over the aroma of buttered toast.

How was I supposed to believe in God when He made life so unfair for so many of us?

Mac had the concierge call a cab for us and we headed downtown for our meeting. Although the Murzak pulp mill was located in some suburb, the administrative offices were in the heart of the city. The building was a typical chrome-and-glass urban high-rise.

On the ninth floor of the building, we were welcomed by John Murzak, President and CEO, Kevin Gillies, Executive Vice President, and Rosemary Worth, Vice President of Operations. Murzak, a small, slim man in his sixties with wispy gray hair, was a friend of Mac's. From their conversation I gathered they'd known each other from their college days.

So that's why Mac had taken on this case himself instead of assigning it to someone else.

I patted myself on the back for wearing what I did. These people, despite the rumors about khakis and casual shirts—the dress code supposedly made popular by Microsoft and other West Coast software companies' young and casual crop of employees—were dressed in conservative suits. Both the men wore dark gray and the woman had on a burgundy pantsuit.

While we made small talk about our flight the previous night and Mac and John reminisced about their college days, a pot of coffee was brought in.

Then we plunged into the business end of it, or rather Mac did. "John, what exactly can you tell us about your operation and why the EPA is focusing on Murzak Pulp and Paper?"

John explained to us in great detail that their pulp mill, the largest around Puget Sound, was being blamed as one of the major polluters of the sound. "The government's conclusion is that the organochlorides discharged by our mill are harmful to the salmon residing in the sound and to the people who live nearby."

Mac, who'd been taking copious notes, nodded gravely. "Mm-hmm. I get the picture."

John gave an angered sigh. "They're threatening to penalize us to the tune of a million dollars a quarter if we don't do something." His face was turning a dull red from what appeared to be frustration and rising rage.

"Rather steep. And what exactly are you doing to address the issue?" Mac asked.

Just like Mac, I was scribbling notes on my legal pad. I had to look as official as I could. I noticed Rosemary Worth doing it, too, her long, pale fingers looking like the icicles hanging off our home's eaves in the winter. She was a tall, broad-shouldered woman who reminded me of the late Julia Child, the famous chef.

"We treat our wastewater and test it before it's discharged into the surrounding surface water, removing most of the toxic chemicals. Whatever is discharged has no effect whatsoever on the sound, but trying to get that through the EPA's thick skull is another matter. That's where you come in, Mac."

"Uh-huh." Mac was writing something at a furious speed.

"Windham is good," said John, speaking about his local attorney, "and he works well with the Washington State Department of Ecology and the EPA's local office, but he's never crossed swords with the feds, Mac. That's why I requested you to step in."

I realized why Windham wasn't included in this meeting. His shortcomings were being discussed—he was a corporate attorney but had no experience in environmental law.

"Any major problems with DOE so far?" Mac finished his coffee and pushed his cup aside.

John shrugged. Despite the chilly, air-conditioned atmosphere of the room, the sheen of perspiration on his face was apparent. "Windham's managed to keep DOE off our backs. But now the EPA is all stirred up. They're poking into our labs, running their own tests. They've turned their so-called findings over to their DC office. Our production is down to a mere twenty-five percent of its capacity."

"What kind of damage are we talking about?"

"Damage? More like devastation!" John Murzak's face had gone from dull to beet red and his face was dripping with perspiration. He pulled out a handkerchief from his pocket and mopped it.

I was afraid the man was going to have a stroke. Rosemary threw a worried glance at him, too. Kevin's frown intensified. I felt sympathy for John Murzak. His mill was clearly a family business, probably had been in the family for generations, and if he lost it, it would be the end of him.

Mac held up a hand. "Take it easy, John. That's what we're here for. Damage control is our business." His voice was quiet but stern, the voice of a friend-cum-counselor. It immediately served to calm the ruffled Murzak, who dabbed his face once again. "What's the feds' attorney's name again?"

"Vasudev Rao."

My head snapped up. Bingo! In that instant I knew why I'd been picked to accompany Mac. The mystery that had been bugging me for the past day and a half was solved. John's pronunciation made it sound odd, but Vasudev Rao, pronounced *Vah-sue-dev Rahv,* was an Indian man. And from his name, it was quite likely he was a Telugu like myself.

Rao was the precise reason I was here.

Mac was going to use his neat little trick of throwing Vasudev Rao and me together and see whether we could work something out—as one Indian attorney to another. If things came out according to his plan, and from the look on Mac's face he expected they would, I'd simply use my feminine charms or my Indian wiles on my fellow *desi* or countryman at the EPA. And I'd have to tie things up as neatly and expeditiously as possible.

Then the firm would bill John Murzak's company for a tidy amount that would cover our trip to Seattle and then some. Murzak would be happy about getting away with only a few thousand dollars instead of millions, and Mac would have done his old college buddy a huge favor. The firm would have one more grateful client who might come in handy in the future.

I had learned that Mac held such IOUs in escrow—to be cashed if and when necessary.

He was clever all right. They didn't call him Mighty Mac for nothing. And his multilingual and multitalented staff was only one of the weapons in his war chest. I was the only Indian in the bunch, so despite my relative inexperience, I was his only choice to be pitched against Rao.

Worried about my role in this case, I wondered how old this Rao was. If he belonged to the older generation like Mac and my father, I'd be doomed. If he was a young man, there was a remote possibility that I could try to reach him on some level.

The feds were trained to be difficult. It was their job to nit-pick and prod and pester and pursue. If I failed to bring Rao and the EPA around, would that be a black mark against me? I was still desperately trying to prove myself worthy of working for the firm. I had a long way to go yet.

After a few minutes of discussing some more facts, Mac came to a decision. He would take on the case.

He immediately put me in charge, too. "Soorya, I'm going to leave this to you. Why don't you stay in Seattle today and get acquainted with John's attorney, then get in touch with the local EPA? Maybe you could confer some more with John and Kevin and Rosemary here and take it from there." He turned a brilliant smile on me that sparkled.

I nodded. Coming from the emperor, it wasn't a mild suggestion, it was an order. "Sure, Mac—no problem." I noticed Rosemary giving him the eye. She seemed dazzled by Mac. But then, he had that effect on a lot of women.

Mac got ready to take his leave. "John, can we please talk a bit in your private office?" He turned to Kevin and Rosemary. "Don't worry too much. We'll do our best to get you folks out of this." He shook hands with them warmly. "I have a meeting in DC tomorrow, so I'll be heading out after John and I confer." He briefly placed a paternal hand on my shoulder. "I'm leaving you in Ms. Giri's capable hands."

He made me sound like a bright, shining star. He had accomplished what he'd come out to do and handed over the reins to me. In sports lingo, the ball was in my court now.

I clutched the imaginary ball close to my chest and stood on the court, a little bemused but furiously trying to work out a strategy. Best-case scenario: Vasudev Rao would turn out to be a ball of putty and I could mold him to my way of thinking. Worst-case scenario: He would turn out to be a demon and I'd lose. Either way, I'd have to find a way of dealing with him.

Rosemary shot another worried glance at John, who still looked flushed. She then ushered me out of the conference room and introduced me to the company's legal counsel, Craig Windham, a gentle and quiet man in his fifties with a balding head, glasses, and a neat goatee.

Windham's records were meticulous, so getting copies of the required paperwork was not a problem. He and I went over dozens of files and folders over the next couple of hours.

When Rosemary stopped by to offer to take me out to lunch, I realized it was well past noon and I was starving. The drizzle outside continued. It had been only hours since I'd landed here and already I was homesick for the sunshine in New Jersey. Another couple of days of this weather and I'd be crying from depression.

Rosemary drove me to an upscale café that served an endless variety of salads. It was exactly my kind of place. She turned out to be a very friendly and chatty lady. Lunching with her was a pleasant experience.

Later, hoping to keep my stay in Seattle to a minimum, I worked with Windham late into the evening. Windham seemed relieved to have someone more knowledgeable about environmental matters take the load off his shoulders.

As soon as I returned to the hotel that evening, armed with loads of paperwork, I called the airline. Thankfully they were able to move me from an afternoon flight to a morning one the next day. I decided to skip dinner that evening and went straight to the gym.

Some thirty minutes of fitness torture and I found myself back in the giant bathtub. That thing held the same kind of fascination for me that a pond filled with squiggly tadpoles held for a little boy. This time, instead of Stephen King, I settled back in the luxurious bubbles with Murzak's legal documents.

Much later, just as I was about to go to bed, the phone rang, startling me. Wondering who it could be at this late hour, I gingerly picked up the phone.

It turned out to be Rosemary. Her voice told me something wasn't quite right.

"I have some bad news, Soorya," she said, confirming my hunch.

My stomach dropped. "What is it?"

"John Murzak had a heart attack earlier this evening."

"Oh no!"

"He was taken to the hospital by ambulance."

"Is he—" I didn't know how to ask. Was he dead? Dying?

"He's been stabilized," Rosemary replied, reading my thoughts. "But he's still in the ICU according to Beth, his wife."

"I'm so sorry." No wonder the man had been perspiring so much and looking ill during our meeting. "Thanks for letting me know." I wondered about how it would affect Mac and me. "In that case, do you think I should hold off on the legal work?" I asked gently.

"No. John wants you to keep working on it. He's adamant about it." She paused. "I think it's all these legal problems that brought on the heart problems to begin with."

"You may be right. I'll continue doing what I'm doing, then. And I'll inform Mac about John, too."

We spoke a little longer before ending the call on a grim note. When I tried to call Mac's cell phone, I got his voice mail, so I left a brief message explaining the situation.

I tossed and turned most of the night, worrying over John Murzak and his future. My first real big case, and it had started on an inauspicious note.

But John wasn't an old man yet, and he had plenty to live for. He'd pull through. He had to. I promised myself that I'd work extra hard to make it all right for that poor man. I'd do everything in my humble power to save his paper mill.

I fluffed my pillow and turned on my side yet again, wondering what Roger the rogue was up to. He had a way of creeping into my brain at the oddest times. I tried hard to banish him from my mind and get some sleep.

All I could do was sigh deeply and stare at the ceiling. And think some more about Roger.

Chapter 11

When my flight landed at Newark Airport the next day, it was nearly five o'clock in the evening. And it was raining. And here I'd thought I was heading home to some sunshine.

I called Sandy from the airport for my messages, then retrieved my car from the airport's parking lot and drove home in the mad rush-hour traffic, first on the New Jersey Turnpike and then the Garden State Parkway. Statistics said they were two of the highest traveled highways in the country. I could see why.

Sandy had said one of my messages was from Lou Draper. I was impressed at Lou's quick response. He wouldn't have called if he didn't have news for me. I certainly hoped it was good news. John Murzak's heart attack had left me more depressed than I'd realized, and I needed a pick-me-up.

And I certainly got one when I reached home. Mom gave me such an exuberant hug one would have thought I'd been gone for years instead of a day and a half. "Welcome home, baby. You look tired. Worked too hard?"

She had on hunter green pull-on pants with a green and white flowered top. She smelled of herbs and Downy. Any other scent and it wouldn't be Mom.

"I am a bit tired, Mom. Guess it's jet lag." I didn't want to dampen her spirits by telling her about Murzak. "I'm hungry, too." I sniffed and guessed Mom had made tomato *rasam,* a fiery hot South Indian soup—just what I needed on a rainy Wednesday night. It felt good to be home.

"Dad is on his way home," Mom informed me. "You want to eat now or wait for him? Pamma is already eating, so you can join her if you want."

I shook my head and said I'd wait for Dad. It was always nice to sit down to dinner as a family, although poor Pamma needed to eat early. She often ate alone.

Stepping into the kitchen, I realized Pamma hadn't even heard my arrival or Mom and me conversing in the laundry room. She sat in her white sari, her white hair in a braid, her blouse looking a bit loose around the sleeves. Had she lost weight? Her feet were generally clad in socks and fuzzy blue slippers, even on a warm evening. Compared with her hometown in India, any day in New Jersey was cold.

At the moment, she was chewing on her soft-cooked rice and *rasam* at a painfully slow pace and staring out the window. I wondered what went on in her mind when she gazed at the landscape like that. Whatever her thoughts were, she kept them to herself. I sensed that she missed her home in India and all her neighbors and the servants she'd had for years. Mostly I thought she missed her late husband and the children and grandchildren she'd left behind.

Perhaps sensing movement, she turned her head and broke into a delighted smile. "Baby, you came home! Business finished so soon?"

I walked up to Pamma and squeezed her shoulder. "I got done a bit earlier than I'd thought."

"Good, good. Now you eat dinner."

I loved seeing that expression on Pamma's face. Although Dad and I lived in this house, it was like she'd never expected to see either one of us here. She always looked startled and elated when Dad and I returned home each evening.

That's what was great about coming home from work. Mom and Pamma were thrilled to see me. Dad, although not quite that overtly ecstatic, was still mighty pleased to have his only child with him at the dinner table. It was my favorite time of day.

Dad and I talked mostly about the kind of day we'd had and

swap stories about the clients we'd seen—without compromising their privacy, of course. Ethics was of the essence in both our professions.

The only way I found out about Dad's celebrity patients was if and when the media somehow got wind of it, after which I'd pester him for details and ferret out a morsel here and there. After he'd inadvertently given away some tidbit, he'd shake his head in mock regret. "I never should have sent you to that fancy law school. You've become too clever for an old man like me."

I picked up my suitcase and went upstairs to my room to unpack and change into something more comfortable. As I put on jeans I realized how wonderful it was to be in my own room. Lou Draper came to mind. He was the reason I was beginning to take a more objective look at my life. I was surrounded by love, laughter, and luxury, while Lou had grown up in hunger, despair, and hopelessness.

It was time I appreciated my life more, enjoyed Pamma's presence while she was still alive and relatively alert, soaked up the warmth and joy my parents laid at my door.

I savored a hot meal with my family. After dinner, finding myself in the mood for some quiet time with Pamma, I went to her room and found she was awake. So I sat on her bed for a while.

She seemed pleased but wary of my unusual behavior. "You feeling okay, baby?" she asked me suspiciously, picking up her hearing aid from the nightstand and placing it in her ear.

"I'm fine. I missed you when I was in Seattle."

Pamma cackled. "Oh, you silly child, why are you missing your old Pamma? What you are needing is a good husband. Always nice for young ladies to have husband and children."

"That's because women your age had no jobs outside the house. Having a husband and babies was the ultimate achievement."

"When I was thirty years old, I had four children—Prema, Pushpa, Pallavi, and Pramod. I was always busy-busy. No time for thinking too much," she said and methodically soaked her dentures in the liquid sitting in the ceramic bowl.

"Nice," I agreed. In spite of its obvious lack of glamour, the simplicity of it sounded wonderful. Pamma had had a happy life until her husband had died and left her sad and lonely. She was married at fifteen, had given birth to my aunt Prema at sixteen, and then the other two girls and my dad had come along at regular intervals after that.

I also knew Dad was the darling of the family, the precious boy who'd been born after three girls. And he was bright and successful and had done the family proud. To this day Pamma and Dad's sisters talked about what a clever boy he was and what a super-clever man he'd turned out to be.

"Pamma, did you ever have a chance to meet Ajja before you married him?" I asked.

"Never! I don't see him until marriage day. But my mother told me he was a good man."

"And that was enough for you?"

"Oh yes. What more I want? Your Ajja was a very serious-type person, but he had a good job and loving nature. He took nice care of me and the children. We had a big house, the children had education, good marriage . . . everything."

"Mom says you caught her sneaking a peek at Dad when he came to see her and that you didn't mind."

Pamma laughed, the lines around her eyes and cheeks turning into deep creases. "Your mother's generation is very different." The laughter subsided into a fond smile. "I saw Viju hiding behind the screen to look at your daddy. Very pretty girl she was."

How sweet was that—and so nonjudgmental. "Did you ever think of going out and finding a job, Pamma? Have your own money and some independence?"

"No. Why I need a job? Your grandfather gave me money. I had my children, cooking all day, taking care of big house, servants, and elderly in-laws. Where was the time for a job?"

"I guess working outside the house wasn't an option in those days." I shot her a grin. "Did Ajja ever tell you he loved you?"

Pamma's face turned that funny shade of plum, making me laugh. It was such fun to embarrass her sometimes. Romantic love was an alien concept for an elderly Indian woman, but I'd always been curious about how old folks expressed themselves to their loved ones.

I could only imagine what Pamma would do if I asked her about her sex life. She'd probably shoo me out of her room and never talk to me again. But she replied with a good-humored chuckle, "Why he will say love? That is only a silly-silly word, no? Love is inside the heart," she remarked, patting her chest.

I nodded, absorbing the fact that life was so simple for both Pamma and Mom. Their parents had picked a suitable man for them and that was plenty to keep them happy. They didn't need to hear fancy words or receive flowers or birthday presents. And they had reason to be happy, too. Both my grandfather and my father were fine men, good providers who, despite their lack of sweet words, doted on their families.

I'd sometimes wondered what kind of sex my parents and grandparents indulged in. Was it fun and playful, or was it serious and intense? How often did they do it? Did they ever talk about it to each other?

Sex was never talked about in traditional Hindu households, at least not as a subject for discussion. But judging from the contented look on Mom's face and her caring attitude toward Dad, I could only presume that my parents had a healthy sex life.

If I could only find a small measure of the happiness Mom and Pamma had, I'd be content, too.

Pamma startled me when she asked, "Why you don't like Rajesh?"

Why was Roger featuring in our conversation all of a sudden? She peered at me through her glasses with a scowl. Naturally she was thrilled with Roger, because he'd charmed her out of her mind by touching her feet and speaking a couple of sentences in the mother tongue. Now she was obsessed with how nice-nice he was.

I responded with a question of my own. "Who said I don't like him?"

"You go to cinema together, you go for walk together, but he don't telephone you. And you don't talk about Rajesh."

"There's nothing to talk about, Pamma. He hasn't called and neither have his parents. I really don't know what's going on." I didn't want to share with her that he had e-mailed me, but that it was only a brief message and nothing more.

But Pamma was a shrewd woman. She smiled a toothless smile that looked both serene and wise. "Ah, but he is a nice boy. Venki and Sharda are good people also." She picked up my hand and stroked it with her rough, gnarled fingers. "Don't worry, baby. You wait and see. He will telephone you, and then everything will be good."

I didn't want to discuss Roger anymore, and it was well past Pamma's bedtime, so I got to my feet. "Whatever you say, Pamma. Now try and get some rest."

Pamma had an uncanny instinct. Maybe she was right. If there was no news from the Vadepallis, perhaps I would get a phone call or another e-mail from Roger—a more promising one. The only thing was, supposing he did, what was I going to say to him? His circumstances had still not changed. He was still a penniless writer-producer wannabe.

Nevertheless I booted up my computer, my foolish heart full of hope.

Chapter 12

There was no message from Roger. My e-mail was crammed with notes from my girlfriends about the bachelorette party we were planning for Amy.

Since Amy's parents were divorced and finances were tight for her single mother, Amy and David had decided to buy one of those small, private Jamaican resort wedding packages that included the ceremony, the champagne and cake, and the honeymoon. It meant there would be no reception or any of the hoopla associated with big weddings.

For me it was a good thing because I dreaded going to friends' weddings. I was the only one who went alone while my friends brought a significant other.

My idea about having the bachelorette party at my house was shot down unanimously. Instead they all opted for a popular strip club in Manhattan, Monk's Hunks. Oh well, so much for clean, wholesome fun. Manhattan and the Hunks it was.

There'd be lots of drinking, ogling at men in thongs, and generally going crazy. But a girl got married only once in her life—hopefully. And Amy deserved a great bachelorette bash. She'd waited long enough to decide to tie the knot and she'd have a roaring party.

We had the logistics figured out within the hour. Amy was in on the plans since this wasn't going to be a surprise. "I'm expecting a funky bachelorette party since I'm not having a big wedding, you guys," she'd told us with unabashed glee. "And you better tell me when and where, since I'm going to go out and splurge on a slutty dress for my last big hurrah before I become Mrs. Levine. And don't even *think* of inviting David's sister," she'd added as a warning. "Sara is an old fuddy-duddy—and she hates slutty dresses."

I made a mental note about not inviting David's older sister Sara. It was an awkward situation, but we had to honor Amy's wishes. Thankfully David's mother was deceased—one less person to worry about.

The rain stopped the following morning and a fog descended, but it was a relief to drive to the train station in relatively dry weather. The forecast called for a sunny day after the fog burned itself out.

At the office, I went through my messages and started returning calls in the order of importance. Lou was toward the top of my list. It was pleasant to hear him—better than pleasant, since his greeting was warm and smooth. "Hello there, busy lady."

"Hi, Lou." I tried to keep the pleased purr out of my voice.

"So the weary attorney is back from her travels?"

"Two days of rain and gloom in Seattle was really exhausting. It made me appreciate good old New Jersey all over again." Now that the small talk was over, I was dying to hear what kind of news he had for me. "So, you called yesterday with good tidings or bad?"

"Both, but mostly good."

A small smile played inside my mind. "Want to tell me about it?"

"It's a bit complicated to discuss over the phone."

"Uh-oh, it sounds ominous."

"No, I think you and your client are going to like the compromise we've worked out."

I wondered what his idea of a compromise was. "So when can you come here to discuss it?"

"You know, I was thinking," Lou said. "Why don't you come over to my office this time and I could fill you in?"

I generally disliked leaving my comfortable office, but since Lou had come all the way to the city the last time, despite the fact that it was my client who was on the defensive, it seemed only fair that I reciprocate. "Is this so-called compromise worth driving all the way down to south Jersey?" I inquired nonetheless. Lou's hedging was making me suspicious.

"Always the cautious attorney." He gave a full-throated laugh that sounded like tribal war drums. "It could be worth your while. Why don't you come in casual clothes? I could take you around the Pinelands and you can see for yourself what wilderness preservation is about."

"Sounds very attractive, Lou, but I can't get away until early next week. I have to work on the Seattle case right now." I flipped the pages on my daily planner while I listened absently to Lou go on about the virtues of the Pinelands. "How about next Tuesday?"

"Okay with me, except I hope the weather's nice enough to walk. Rain isn't exactly conducive to a hike in the Pinelands."

"We're going hiking?" Exercise of any kind was a bit of a drag for me, but hiking amongst snakes and raccoons sounded worse than three straight hours on that awesome torture machine I'd glimpsed at the hotel gym in Seattle.

"Come on, Soorya, a brave, modern woman like you shouldn't be afraid of a tiny walk amongst a few pine trees. You're an *environmental* attorney, aren't you? Shouldn't you be in tune with the environment?" Lou's voice held all kinds of amused sarcasm.

"My bravery is confined to Manhattan and its urban perils. I'll leave the reptiles to you."

"Listen, it's actually quite beautiful. We'll drive up there and walk only around the nice and safe areas, all right?"

It sounded harmless enough. "I suppose we could. . . ."

"I promise to keep the wild animals away from you. I'll even show you a couple of neat lunch places around our backwoods. Not exactly Joseph's Sicilian Kitchen, but we do eat civilized food besides roots and wild berries and rabbit stew."

"You don't say!"

"We've got a rather nice deli that makes great sandwiches and salads."

I chuckled. Lou's kind of humor was exactly what I needed after the last couple of days. And food always did it for me. I hadn't even glanced at a good sandwich in ages. I'd have to find out if they had anything with red, white, and green—and vegetarian. "All right, you twisted my arm. I'll come in jeans and sweatshirt, so we can explore the boonies."

Lou sounded pleased. "I'll e-mail you the directions to my office. I'll see you Tuesday. And don't forget to wear walking shoes," he added with a mocking laugh.

I hung up the phone feeling good. Snakes or not, I was looking forward to seeing Lou again. The man was an inspiration. And he was . . . good-looking.

My last call was to Vasudev Rao. A little nervous, I waited for him to answer his phone. He sounded stiff and formal. He probably had to be, in his position. He had an Indian-American accent like my father's, and spoke good English. That meant he'd been educated in an English school in India. I wasn't sure if that was good or bad. He could be as bright and charismatically slick as my dad or as uninspiring as some bureaucrats I'd come across.

After going back and forth on our respective calendars, we decided that I would meet with him on the following Friday afternoon.

I figured Friday would be perfect for the trip. Perhaps I could stay in DC that night and see if my friend and classmate from law school, Brenda Coleman, was free to meet me for dinner. She had just started working for a law firm in Northern Virginia, in the DC area.

When I called Brenda, she was surprised but happy to hear from me. We agreed to meet at my hotel on Friday after work. It would be a girls' night out and a chance to catch up on our lives since law school.

A little past noon, I stepped out from my office and wandered out into the street to get some lunch and a wedding card for Amy. Twenty minutes later, with my Hallmark card tucked in my bag, I headed for the nearest Indian restaurant, Tandoor

India, to pick up something to eat. I ordered a takeout veggie burger with no bread.

While I waited for my order, I stood at the window and looked out on the hustle and bustle of Lexington Avenue. I felt at home here despite the crowds and traffic jams. The morning's fog was gone and the warm sunshine bounced off the chrome and glass of the buildings across the street. Even with my dark glasses, the glare was blinding.

A one-legged man in an electric wheelchair made his way past the window and my mind automatically went to the ailing John Murzak.

As I stood rocking on my heels, waiting for my lunch to arrive, I heard someone call my name and whirled around.

My heart skipped a long, painful beat. Oh my God!

Roger stood before me, smiling that oddly crooked smile. He had on a black T-shirt with *Bombay Dreams* printed on the front. His hair looked longer and wavier. I swallowed hard. "Roger!" I managed to choke out. "What are you doing here?"

"Buying lunch, just like you." His eyes looked luminescent in the sunlight slanting in through the floor-to-ceiling window. Lots of girls would give an arm to have such gorgeous eyes.

"Yeah, but what are you doing in Manhattan?"

His smile widened. "I found an investor for my play, Soorya. I've been in Manhattan for the last two weeks, getting a crew and cast together."

"That was fast." He'd been in town for two weeks and yet he hadn't bothered to get in touch. The message was clear as Windex-cleaned glass: He hadn't *wanted* to get in touch. I didn't want to admit, even to myself, that he had indeed e-mailed me, but I had chosen not to respond.

The problem was, he had shown no special interest in me. It had been just a casual and friendly electronic message, with no hint of wanting to get together or anything remotely like that. And now, although I was happy for him in a way, my stomach sank. He'd found a nice rich girl who'd agreed to marry him and fund his career. Investor indeed.

"Remember what you said about full moons bringing good

luck sometimes? I think you were right," he said. "Things have been going rather well since that moon."

Sure, things seemed to be going well for him. But I wanted to turn around and run from there—from him. I didn't want to hear about his marriage plans or his play. The front desk guy came around carrying a brown bag, and thank goodness it turned out to be my lunch. I paid for it and turned to Roger. "So, looks like you'll be following your dream after all."

"I hope so," he said. "So, how are things with you, Soorya?"

"Fine, thanks. I just returned from a business trip to Seattle last night." I awkwardly shifted the brown bag from one hand to the other. I wasn't sure if it would be too rude to walk out of there without an explanation. "I've got to run, Roger. My lunch break ended a while ago."

"Uh . . . maybe we could get together for lunch or a drink one day?" He seemed a little unsure of himself—rather unexpected for this highly confident man.

"Maybe. Why don't you give me a call sometime?" I said a hasty good-bye and hurried down the street to my office. By the time I reached my desk, my hands were trembling and my heart was pounding madly.

Soorya, old girl, don't walk so fast the next time, I scolded myself. *When you're out of shape, jogging causes your heart to go a little crazy.*

But this girl's mind refused to accept the logic. Why did he have to be so charming and so damn cute? Now he'd gone and spoiled my day. I'd have to work twice as hard to focus on my work. The rest of the week and the weekend were pretty much ruined, too.

It was all Roger's fault.

Chapter 13

To prevent myself from thinking too much about Roger, I spent a good part of Saturday with Amy, helping her shop for clothes for her honeymoon. On Sunday I worked on my Seattle case. After debating over whether I should tell my parents about Roger's move to New York, I decided to keep it to myself.

No sense in getting them excited over nothing.

Monday was too busy to think about anything but the staff meeting where I had to present my two latest projects. The afternoon flew by with so much work that both Sandy and I had to work very late.

However, the evening ended on a positive note when I called Rosemary once again in Seattle and learned that John Murzak was on the mend. He had been released from the hospital and was recuperating at home. Just to make sure Mac was kept informed, I sent him an e-mail about John's progress.

The next morning, as the alarm radio came on with a cheerful female voice wishing listeners a pleasant morning, I dragged my sluggish feet to the window to look outside. It was a lovely, sunny day with hardly a cloud in the sky.

I was happy for one brief second before I remembered I was going down to Pemberton to meet with Lou. Although the prospect of seeing Lou was exciting, I dreaded the hike in the woods. Secretly I'd hoped for rain, something I almost never prayed for. Of course, with my luck, Mother Nature had to be uncooperative on the one day I wished for rain.

Later, when I'd showered and dressed in jeans, sweatshirt, and sturdy sneakers, I saw the puzzled look on Mom's face. She was used to seeing me in cool business suits and high heels on weekday mornings. "You have the day off?" she queried.

"No, Mom. I'm going to Pemberton to look at the Pinelands."

"The Pinelands . . . in south Jersey?"

"More like south central. One of my clients is building homes there and has some problems with the environmental people."

Mom thought about it for a second. "You want me to drive you to the train station?"

"No train today. I'm driving to Pemberton." I went to the refrigerator and poured myself a glass of skim milk.

"Shall I make you a hot breakfast?" Mom was already reaching for the pancake mix in the pantry.

"No breakfast, Mom. I expect to eat a big lunch in Pemberton. My contact said there's a great deli there."

"Okay then." She shut the pantry door. "Be careful driving on the highway, dear."

Mom said that every time I drove outside the town's limits. I looked around. "Where's Pamma this morning?"

"Little bit under the weather today. She has a cold."

"Oh, the poor thing!" Pamma rarely got sick. At this time of the morning she usually sat at the kitchen table with her second cup of coffee and either had her nose buried in the *New York Times* or she'd be chopping and slicing vegetables in an effort to help my mother. "I'll look in on her before I leave."

I finished the milk and checked my briefcase to make sure the printed e-mail directions Lou had sent me were there. If I still got lost, I had my dependable GPS in the car.

When I went into Pamma's room, I found the curtains shut tight and Pamma huddled under the blanket. The strong smell of her Indian cold remedy was everywhere. Assuming she was asleep, I tried to tiptoe out of there, but she must have sensed my presence. "Soorya, you are going to work?"

"Yes, Pamma. Mom says you have a cold. Is there anything I can do for you before I leave?"

"No, baby, you go to office. I am using *Amrutanjan* and homeopathic tablets. I will be better soon." She sounded like her nose was stuffed up.

"If you want me to pick up something from the drugstore on my way home, tell Mom to call me on my cell." I headed out, the medicinal fumes following me out the door.

How ironic. Pamma's son and daughter were noted doctors and she still used her old, time-honored cures—*Amrutanjan,* a pungent-smelling yellow balm, and homeopathic pills. But whatever she used seemed to work for her. She was in better shape than many folks her age.

The ride along the highways was pleasant, perhaps because the weather was perfect or because I'd learned that John Murzak was on the road to recovery. Ever since Murzak had suffered a heart attack, to me he had become a symbol of how easily pesky government regulations could break a decent, hard-working man and ruin an established business.

Traffic on the notorious turnpike was lighter than I'd anticipated, more than likely because I was traveling against the flow of traffic. Most folks were driving toward New York at this time of day and not away from it. I hadn't driven this route in over a year and it was fun to note the passing billboards, office buildings, and Linden's oil refineries as I sped by at seventy-five.

The trees flanking the roadway were showing the first hint of fall color. It was the end of September. Another week or two and those trees would turn to lovely shades of red and russet and gold.

When I finally took Exit 7 for Bordentown and followed Lou's directions to go southeast to Pemberton, I realized I'd made it there in about two hours. As I exited onto the county roads, the area turned more wooded and less traveled. What a difference from northern Jersey.

When I parked in front of the rectangular brick building that housed Lou's temporary office, I could see why he'd chosen to come to my office the last time. This structure looked like an old homestead converted into a government place of business.

As I stepped out of my car and retrieved my briefcase, Lou appeared at the door with an outstretched hand to offer me a welcoming handshake. In corduroy slacks and sweatshirt, he looked even bigger than he did in a suit the other day. The shirt stretched across massive shoulders and a wide chest. The sneakers were easily a size thirteen. My kind of guy.

He gave me an approving nod. "I see you came prepared for a hike. Nice to see you again, Soorya."

"Good seeing you, too." Did I sound a little too pleased?

He ushered me into the building. Low, acoustic tile ceilings, old wood-paneled walls that had lost their polish ages ago, framed posters of the surrounding wilderness, and worn blue carpeting met me as I stepped inside. The odor of stale coffee hung in the air.

We walked down a narrow hallway to Lou's office at the rear of the building. He wasn't kidding when he'd said it was a small room with no windows and no view. Industrial fluorescent tubes were the only source of light.

He had a basic desk and chair, a bookcase, a file cabinet, and one lone guest chair. Lou motioned me to sit down. "Sorry, but I warned you about my little hole in the wall. My main office is in Trenton, at the DEP building—much nicer than this, but for the last two years I've been assigned part-time to this place."

"Don't apologize, Lou. I have no problem with this." We all had to make do with what was given to us. Looking at Lou's quarters, I felt particularly grateful for my little corner office with its window.

"Would you care for some coffee?"

When I shook my head, he raised a brow. "Goes against your diet, I suppose?"

"Something like that, but you go ahead if you want." He said he'd had a big breakfast to fortify himself before the long hike ahead of us. My eyes roamed the small room and the clutter of files, books, folders, and binders. A map of the Pinelands was pinned to one wall, yellow highlighter marking zigzagging trails. There was a coffeemaker sitting atop one of the file cabinets.

My gaze reverted back to the cramped desk, mostly swallowed up by Lou's computer and printer, and came to rest on a photograph in a carved metal frame. A woman with soft eyes, wavy blond hair, and a Madonna-like smile looked out on the world through the frame.

Lynne! She was attractive. Oh God, how unfair that such a sweetly pretty woman should die so young. I looked up and met Lou's dark brooding eyes.

He nodded. "That's Lynne."

"I gathered that. She is . . . was beautiful, Lou."

"Yes." Abruptly he picked up his car keys from the desk. "If you're ready, we can leave now." It was curt—like an order.

I tore my eyes away from the woman in the photograph and looked at Lou, a little confused. The other day he'd seemed very open, talked so much about his wife, and yet now it seemed like the topic was taboo. "I thought we were going to discuss my client before going out," I said cautiously.

"We're doing the survey first," he snapped.

Clearly I hadn't been cautious enough. "Fine."

"You'll understand some things more clearly after a walk in the woods," he added, his tone softening a bit.

Without another word I followed him. Had I said or done something to tick him off? It was as if a switch had been turned off.

He turned to me as we approached the front door. "You had better use the ladies' room now. The park's restrooms aren't exactly worth recommending." He smiled faintly. It looked like Lynne had been forgotten for the moment. Thank goodness.

I took his suggestion and used the ladies' room. Then we drove away in Lou's car, a white Dodge Neon with official New Jersey government license plates, complete with a toll-free number on the bumper that vigilant taxpayers could call if they noticed the vehicle being used for purposes other than official business.

Smiling, I turned to Lou. "So, is this trip official or is someone going to call the hotline and report you for illegal use of the vehicle?"

Lou returned the smile, obviously in a good mood again. "This is as official as it gets. But you won't believe how many calls the hotline receives each week. People see a government-issued car parked outside a McDonald's and they immediately pull out their phones and lodge a complaint. They feel a public employee has no business eating."

"One of the perils of public service?"

"Only one of the *many* perils."

We veered off the main road and took a more rural route. I had no idea where we were going, but all of a sudden we were surrounded by shadowy, piney woods. They looked mysterious and uninviting. I turned to Lou. "Home of the Jersey Devil, right?"

"Maybe you could come again sometime when they have a Jersey Devil hunt," he suggested.

"If you promise it's not during the night. I like to see where I'm going so I don't step on snakes."

"Chicken! It's no fun in the light of day. The Devil is known to come out of his lair only at night." Several minutes later, Lou came to a stop in a large clearing and shut off the ignition. "All right, Counselor, get ready for some serious walking."

Reluctantly I followed him to what looked like a well-used hiking trail. The path was free of grass and scrub and tamped down to hard gray soil. It was wide enough for two people to walk side by side, so we ambled and talked. Only a handful of people seemed to be using the trail at the moment.

Lou explained that on weekdays the place was quiet. Weekends were apparently more crowded. Besides, it was the start of the fall season, and the crowds thinned out after the kids went back to school and the air turned cooler. The dense canopy of pines kept out the sun and I realized it was a bit chilly. I was glad I'd picked a thick sweatshirt for this outing.

While we strolled, Lou pointed to different shrubs and ferns, and their complex botanical names rolled easily off his tongue. It appeared he had taken his botany lessons as seriously as his legal ones.

As we went deeper into the forest, it turned darker and quieter, but it had a haunting beauty all its own, with the occasional twitter of birds and the smell of damp earth mixed with the sharp scent of pine.

Every once in a while a tiny patch of blue sky became visible, only to disappear in a second. It was lovely and peaceful, but surely a problem for allergy sufferers. Good thing I'd remembered to take my antihistamine, or I'd be sneezing endlessly by now.

Now and then, little forest critters seemed to scramble invisibly. Once, the sound was close enough to startle me and Lou smiled at what must have been a look of alarm on my face. "Only rabbits and squirrels. They don't bite."

"Good." The trail wound around and it seemed like we were going in circles. "You're sure you know where we're going?" I asked Lou.

"Positive," he assured me, easing my mind on that score. I didn't want to be lost in the wilderness—possibly my worst nightmare. The idea of getting lost in the Bronx at midnight was far less intimidating than losing my way at 10:30 A.M. in a forest filled with crawling, slithering creatures.

After we'd walked for what seemed like a mile and my breath was becoming labored, Lou must have felt sorry for me, because he suggested we sit down and take a breather. So we sat on a fallen pine log and I rested my legs. I was pitifully out of shape. It was embarrassing, considering Lou seemed barely winded.

Pulling out a roll of mints from his pocket, he offered me one. "They're white, sugar free, and vegetarian." With a chuckle I took one before we resumed walking.

A little later, he stopped me abruptly by grabbing my arm,

then pointed to something to one side. I held my breath. A herd of deer stood amongst the trees, looking like a scene from a wildlife painting. A few full-grown deer and several smaller ones grazed peacefully. One was an adorable baby with spindly legs and enormous eyes.

Roger's big, cinnamon eyes came to mind. Even here, in the middle of the backwoods, Roger wouldn't leave me in peace.

I stood staring at the picture. Although there were deer in the small thicket behind our home, we had a high wire fence that kept them out. This was the first time I'd seen wild deer this close. They were beautiful. They looked up and spied us but continued to graze nonchalantly. They were probably used to seeing humans along these trails.

"How enchanting," I whispered and continued to observe the herd.

Lou nudged me to start moving again. "You up to seeing a rattlesnake now?"

"No, please no. I—I'm allergic to reptiles."

One glance at my face and Lou gave a bark of laughter. "I was kidding. For a moment there I thought you were going to faint, Soorya."

I shot him my fiercest look. "Just because I don't like snakes, it doesn't mean I'm susceptible to feminine fits of vapors or anything of the sort."

"Big-city yuppies!" He burst into laughter once again. "What are we going to do with you?"

"Who're you calling a yuppie, Mister Philadelphia-born-and-bred?"

He chuckled some more at my retort.

When we came to a fork in the trail, he motioned to me to bear right. "Let's go look at some pretty flowers, then. They're nicer than snakes, I promise," he said in mock condescension.

We came to a stagnant pond entirely covered with lime green algae—and masses of white water lilies. Tiny tadpoles wriggled just under the pond's surface, creating small ripples in the murky, green-brown water. Flying insects hovered around the lilies and landed on the water's surface every now and then, making the slime jiggle.

It was so utterly peaceful, I couldn't imagine that people lived and worked only a few miles from here, that New Jersey's busy highways weren't all that far. Again, I stood in mute wonder for several minutes and took in the scene.

"The lilies are gorgeous, Lou," I said.

Large arms crossed over his middle, Lou rocked on his feet. "Now do you see how lovely all this is? Why nature lovers don't want people like your client to ruin it by building homes?"

I rolled my eyes. "Is that why you insisted on bringing me here? You could have talked about this and I would have understood just as well. I've gone camping once or twice in my childhood, you know. We could've easily skipped the ecology lesson."

"Skip the hike and miss seeing the look of panic on your face earlier? Nah." He grinned. "I wish I had my camera with me. The brave New York lawyer isn't afraid of muggers and murderers and mean old district attorneys, but she fears a harmless little snake."

"Just out of curiosity, where are these famous snake nests? Did we pass any so far?"

Lou shook his head. "They're deep in the interior. The hiking trails have too many humans so the snakes tend to keep as far away as possible. It's basic survival instinct—they're just as afraid of us." He checked the time on his watch. "You ready to head back to the office?"

"Oh yes!" My thighs had been complaining for a while. We'd been walking for well over an hour, but I'd actually enjoyed the outing. As we retraced our steps, I noticed the deer had disappeared.

Lou pointed out a few birds' nests in the trees and told me how to distinguish between the different kinds. He showed me a variety of wildflowers whose botanical names sounded more like exotic diseases.

At one point, Lou took my hand and tucked it in the crook of his arm. Something like an electric current shot right though me.

He must have felt the same thing, because he gave me a strange look, blinked, and dropped my hand. "Better get back to the office and I'll tell you what I've got," he said.

Just like that the camaraderie between us had vanished. Something strange had touched us both. I for one couldn't explain it. It was almost a sexual awareness. My pulse was racing and my hands were shaking. The sensation diminished by the time we returned to Lou's office.

Whatever it was, it had to have been some freak sensation caused by the dark atmosphere of the woods and my fear of it. I was certain that hunger had something to do with it, too. I told myself I'd be fine after eating a decent lunch, then followed Lou into his office.

Lou had worked out a fair enough deal for my client. Instead of twenty-two homes in the development proposed by Solstice, the DEP and the Pinelands Commission wanted it pared down to fifteen, with larger lots. Also, there was a lot of fine print in Lou's proposal. I'd have to go back to my office and read it carefully.

He had talked the authorities into reducing the atrocious development fees by nearly sixty percent. I was happy with Lou's efforts and I hoped my client would be, too.

"Thank you, Lou. That was a fine job you did of convincing your bosses. I couldn't be more pleased." I beamed at him and tucked the papers in my briefcase.

"Tell me the truth, Soorya. If I hadn't taken you out along that beautiful hiking trail, would you have accepted the compromise that easily?"

I gave it some thought. "Probably not," I admitted grudgingly. I would have argued for more leeway. "I'm glad you showed me around. Of course, I have to present this to my client and see how they feel about it. Unlike me, they're hardened businessmen and can't be swayed by a herd of deer and a pond with tadpoles and water lilies."

"It'll be months before both parties will be able to agree on some things, but this is a good start—and much more generous than any others I've worked on." He sounded like a man who'd been through similar cases many, many times.

"Yes, and thank you so much." I wasn't so sure my client would like the idea of building fifteen homes instead of twenty-two, but I would deal with that later.

"Now let's go get some lunch, Counselor. Would you like hot or cold food?"

"Let's go to your deli, shall we? I'm in a mood for a sandwich. Must be that endless hike," I said.

This time Lou drove me in his personal vehicle, a black Ford Explorer. The deli in the heart of Pemberton was small and crowded, and to my starving body it smelled like heaven. I ordered a grilled vegetable sandwich and promptly discarded most of the bread, but kept the onions, zucchini, and the red and green peppers.

While I ate my semi-sandwich and drank bottled water, Lou polished off a pile of roast beef shavings and horseradish on thick slices of rye bread, a plump kosher pickle, and a can of Dr Pepper.

It was nearly three o'clock by the time I was ready to head back home. I realized I'd had a very tiring but wonderful day. Lou had been great company. As he walked me to my car, instead of shaking hands, he both surprised me and threw me off balance by placing a light kiss on my cheek. "Let me know how it goes with your client."

"I will," I murmured. "And thanks for everything."

"My pleasure, Counselor."

As I drove out of the parking lot, I looked in my rearview mirror and noticed Lou still standing with his hands on his hips, watching the back of my car. He looked so alone standing there. His wife's photograph came to mind. He must miss her a lot.

He was a nice man—way too nice to lead a lonely life.

The next day, I got in touch with my client about my meeting with Lou. They didn't seem as pleased as I'd hoped. They were thoroughly opposed to the idea of only fifteen homes. They wanted me to negotiate for more—at least twenty.

I had a feeling Lou would work something out for me in that direction. So far he'd proved to be a more of an ally than an adversary. He'd been more than kind and helpful. He had even mentioned that he'd never gone to such lengths for other law firms.

But did other attorneys get to go on a private guided tour of the Pinelands?

Chapter 14

The next couple of days were spent in getting my homework done in preparation for my visit to DC to meet with Vasudev Rao. I was nervous, even more so than during my Seattle visit. In Seattle I had the indomitable Mac to guide me. He had been in charge.

Now I was the one responsible for the ailing John Murzak's business. Hundreds of folks' careers and futures lay in my hands. It was a humbling thought.

I'd made other trips to DC, where I'd conferred with lawyers, scientists, engineers, and administrators, but that was minor stuff, mostly groundwork I was doing for senior attorneys in our firm, work that didn't place the entire onus on me.

During the train ride, I furiously studied my notes. By now I had memorized all the statistics: pH levels, effluent water, surface water contamination, air quality, the flora and fauna surrounding Puget Sound, and sundry bits of information I considered useful.

My research on Vasudev Rao said he had an undergrad degree in pharmacology from the University of Maryland and a law degree from the same institution. It was a good combination for his kind of job, but essentially bad news for me. A bunch of facts and figures would neither fool nor impress him.

I couldn't expect everyone to be as cooperative and helpful as Lou.

Charm and beauty not being my strong points, I'd have to depend on my brains and quick wit. With any luck I'd have Rao recognizing the wisdom in saving a harmless pulp mill that provided jobs to so many. Fortunately, at this early phase, the case would go to an administrative law judge serving as a neutral and impartial party in deciding whether the case had enough substance to go into litigation.

If the judge decided the case could be dismissed, it would end there, but if he didn't, it would go to the next level. That could mean months, even years of proceedings, and in the end, our client would still suffer harsh penalties. I prayed it wouldn't go that far.

Vasudev Rao turned out to be a fortyish man with a lanky build and a cynical attitude. He reminded me of the men I'd come across in the Customs Department at India's airports—abrupt, unsmiling, uncooperative, and aloof.

Rao seemed to be steeped in India and his Indian-ness. He complained about the weather in DC, the parking situation, the people he worked with, his job, and just about everything. I wondered why he didn't live in India if the U.S. made him so unhappy.

Rao didn't have one good thing to say about America or Americans. It was ironic that he worked for the federal government, a proud symbol and the embodiment of what America stood for. He didn't even bother to shake hands, merely wishing me a good afternoon and asking me to take a seat in his austere office.

Vasudev Rao was a complete antithesis to Lou Draper. So much for Mac's and John Murzak's assumptions that I'd be the perfect individual to bond with Rao. *Desis* were generally a warm bunch when it came to dealing with one of their own. But I didn't know how to handle a guy like Rao.

An image of Roger flashed through my mind. I could have used some of his brand of natural charm and ease of manner right about now. But it was bothersome that Roger was invading my thoughts when I was in the midst of a serious legal discussion.

Considering Rao's attitude, I got directly down to business. I put all the facts on the table—very methodically.

In response Rao said, "Ms. Giri, let me tell you, American companies are sharks. The almighty dollar rules their actions. They think nothing of polluting rivers, lakes, even the deteriorating ozone layer. Profit is all they think about. Your client is no different. They should all be taught a lesson."

Secretly his tirade made me wonder if he'd been refused a position in the private sector sometime in his life, forcing him to take a government job, eventually turning him into this bitter, humorless individual. I went into a long-winded explanation, sticking to the facts.

"Your facts and figures may very well be correct," he said with grudging respect. "But this is still capitalism taken to extremes," he pronounced with visible contempt. He seemed intent on punishment.

The man was insufferable, and I was tempted to say a few unkind things myself, but I bit my tongue and took a few deep breaths. Antagonizing an already biased man would only get me in trouble. Besides, in my line of work, I was likely to bump into Rao again and again. I couldn't afford to make an enemy out of him.

Instead I focused my thoughts on Murzak and Rosemary. So I tried to put a slightly different and more human spin on my argument. "Mr. Rao, my client is one of the oldest pulp mills in the Northwest. The high penalties could drive them out of business and put several hundred people out of jobs."

Rao pushed his glasses up his nose and looked at me with about as much emotion as the antique Chinese jade dragon I had in my office. "Hundreds of companies go out of business in this country every month. The EPA cannot feel sorry for all of them, Ms. Giri."

"I realize that, sir, but my client has put in extensive control systems to avoid any kind of pollution—air, soil, or water."

"Not enough, Ms. Giri." Rao shook his head and tucked my papers inside his already bulky folder.

"Do you know that a lot of Indians work for this company, Mr. Rao?" That had slipped out somehow, but I regretted not having asked Rosemary for the exact number of Indian employees and hoped this disagreeable man wouldn't ask me to substantiate my exaggerated claims.

His thick eyebrows came together. "But don't most of the Indians in that area work for Microsoft and other high-tech companies?"

"No, sir. A number of them are in other fields. The pulp mills and the lumber industry do hire many Indians."

"Hmm." Rao's frown became deeper. He appeared to digest my information for a moment. Then he started to flip the pages in his folder rapidly, as if to refresh his memory about certain facts. He looked up at me and asked me to give him a couple of days to go over the information I'd given him.

Breathing a sigh of temporary relief, I nodded. We weren't out of the woods yet. His love of India and Indians should have endeared me to him, but that hadn't happened so far.

He probably viewed me as the quintessential Indian-American *coconut*—a traitor to my culture. "I sincerely hope this doesn't need to go to the next level, Mr. Rao," I said. "You'll see that my client's chemical levels are well under the EPA's safety guidelines."

Eventually, I left Rao's office on an uneasy note, unsure of the outcome. Had I done everything I could for my client? Was there anything I'd left out? I didn't think so. I had given it my very best.

I took a cab to my hotel. As I registered at the desk and rode the elevator to my room, I tried to put the Murzak case out of my mind. The accommodations were ordinary compared to the ones in Seattle, but they were comfortable.

Picking up the phone, I called Brenda. It was nice to hear her voice after so long, still so full of spirit and adventure. We decided to meet in the lobby at six o'clock, then figure out where to go from there.

Brenda Coleman had always been a lot of fun in college—

bright, vivacious, and brimming with mischievous energy. I looked forward to the evening. I was going to forget my diet for one night and even drink a glass of wine.

I needed something to chase the taste of Vasudev Rao out of my system.

The following week, Vasudev Rao called me to say he had made a strong recommendation to the judge to dismiss the Murzak case. I didn't ask him why. Whatever had made him soften up on my client, I was grateful.

"Thank you so much, Mr. Rao. I appreciate your efforts and your promptness," I said. "So what are your feelings about the judge's impending decision?"

"That's up to him, Ms. Giri. But usually our office's recommendations are taken seriously." He paused. "Chances of dismissal are generally about ninety-nine percent."

"My client and I really appreciate that, Mr. Rao. I'll be in touch."

After I hung up the phone I quietly pumped the air with my fist and grinned to myself. Ninety-nine percent was as good as one hundred. Yeah! Mac would be proud.

The framed picture of Lord Ganesh on my desk seemed to be staring at me expectantly, so I said a quick prayer to Him. He had taken care of a big obstacle. *Thank you, Lord!*

Sure enough, four days later, Mac walked into my office and offered me his congratulations in person. John Murzak was apparently pleased with my work. Mac beamed at me. "Good work, Soorya. I knew I could count on you."

Coming from Mac, that was high praise, so I merely smiled and thanked him.

That afternoon, a large floral arrangement arrived on my desk. The attached card read, *Soorya: A very special thank you from John Murzak and the folks at Murzak Pulp & Paper.*

Chapter 15

Just as I was packing my briefcase to go home and celebrate my little Murzak victory with my family, Sandy buzzed me. "Soorya, I know you're getting ready to leave, but you have a visitor."

"Did I forget a late appointment?"

Sandy cleared her throat. "The gentleman . . . has no appointment. He says it's personal."

Personal? I racked my brain for possible names. Nobody came to my office for personal visits. "Who is it?"

"Mr. Rajesh Vadepalli." Her pronunciation was nearly perfect.

Roger! A tingle raced through my bloodstream. What was *he* doing here? There was only one way to find out. "Send him in, Sandy," I instructed and laid down my briefcase.

What did he want? I wondered, despite the sense of elation at the prospect of seeing him again. Our accidental meeting at the Indian restaurant had been a while ago. All of a sudden he was here—with no appointment or even a phone call or e-mail.

The door opened and Sandy ushered Roger in. He looked like his usual casual self. He also made my pulse shoot skyward.

From what I could see, he'd charmed Sandy as well. Her eyes were twinkling in that special way when she genuinely took a liking to someone. Just before she left the room, she winked at me from behind his back, then mouthed, *"Cute."*

I gave her a bland look.

Looking as comfortable in these business surroundings as he did at my house several weeks ago, Roger threw me his killer smile. "Hi, Soorya. Hope you don't mind my coming over unannounced."

"No, not really," I said. Despite the blood rushing through my veins, I gestured to one of the guest chairs, inviting him to sit. "What brings you to my neck of the woods today, Roger?" I could tell he was irritated by my calling him Roger, but it gave me some satisfaction. It was fair retaliation for the havoc he was wreaking on my system at the moment.

He sauntered across the small room, sat down, and took in the surroundings at leisure. From his expression I could tell he liked what he saw. "I'm impressed, Soorya. This fits the image of a young and successful New York attorney's office." He pointed to the paintings on the wall. "Those landscapes are superb."

"Thanks." His approval made me feel like a kitten basking on a sunny windowsill on a warm spring day.

He moved closer to the wall to scrutinize the artwork. "This temple looks familiar. Are these all scenes from Andhra?"

"Yes—from the town of Arasavalli, where my father's eldest sister lives. Do you know the place?"

Roger shrugged. "Heard the name from my parents, but I've never been there."

I decided to give Roger a quick social studies lesson. "It has the only sun temple in the state. The Sooryanarayana temple is dedicated to the sun god. The shrine is in a unique location and constructed with such astronomical precision that the rays of the rising sun fall directly at the feet of the deity exactly twice a year, in February and June. And on those two days the temple attracts hundreds of thousands of pilgrims from all over the country."

"Amazing! Imagine the accuracy that goes into building an architectural and religious marvel like that." He turned back to the painting. "Who's the artist?"

"No one well-known. He's an old local guy from Arasavalli. His name is Reddy. He's brilliant, but other than a few people like my parents, mainly Indian-Americans and Indo-Europeans, I don't think he has too many customers."

"That's a shame. Maybe during my next trip I'll look him up and buy a painting or two myself." He looked speculatively at the landscape and then at me, with narrowed eyes. "Soorya-narayana? Does your name have something to do with it?"

I threw him an approving smile. "Apparently Mom and Dad visited the temple just before I was conceived. That particular deity is known to dispel infertility, so when Mom gave birth to me successfully after having suffered a couple of miscarriages previously, they felt compelled to name me Soorya. Some people believe the sun is a goddess and not a god."

"Your parents picked a great name. You're brilliant and bright as sunshine."

"Flattery isn't going to get you anywhere with me, Roger." Although immensely tickled at his comments, I wasn't naïve enough to believe all of it. I looked at him. "You still haven't told me what brought you here today."

Instead of answering me he threw a meaningful glance at my elaborate arrangement of flowers. "Must be from a rich ad-mirer, huh?" I smiled, allowing him to draw his own conclu-sions. His eyes moved to my briefcase. "I figured you must be getting ready to leave, so I came over to see if you'd like to have dinner with me."

Dinner with Roger sounded quaint and wonderful, but I wasn't sure I wanted to subject myself to the misery of drooling over his bedroom eyes and listening to him talk about his new fiancée or about-to-be fiancée. "Aren't you engaged to be married or something?" I asked, trying to keep my voice sufficiently aloof.

"Um . . . not yet." He had the decency to blush. "There's nothing wrong with a friendly dinner, is there? I mean, we both work in the city and all that. We could be friends."

I shrugged. "It's late and I have to get home. My folks worry if I'm too late."

"So tell them you're meeting a friend." He touched one of the flowers, then glanced at me. "Unless . . . it's not your parents but someone else who's waiting for you?"

It took me a second to realize what he meant. Could he be jealous? Nonetheless I decided to tell him the truth. "Those are from a grateful client, Roger. Don't read something into nothing."

"Then call your parents. I'm buying dinner this time, Soorya."

"Well, in that case I accept." I picked up the phone to inform my mother that I wouldn't be home for dinner. Mom asked me half a dozen questions, her voice taking on that mildly hopeful tone, but I assured her it was strictly business.

Roger, who'd been paying close attention to my conversation, widened his eyes in mock disbelief. "Business?" When I frowned at him, he grinned. "I thought you disliked lies and liars."

"For a good cause I don't mind a little fibbing. Once in a while."

His grin turned into a pleased chuckle. "I'm honored to be the good cause for some old-fashioned fibbing."

"Don't get carried away, Roger. If your ego swelled up any more it's likely to explode and I'd have to clean up the mess on the ceiling." I bit my twitching lip when his chuckle turned into roaring laughter.

We walked to Tandoor India, where we'd bumped into each other recently. Only one other table was occupied, so we had our choice of tables. Roger picked a quiet corner and we settled down to a drink before looking at the menu. He ordered Indian Kingfisher beer and I surprised myself and him by ordering a glass of white wine.

His eyebrows rose. "Off your special diet?"

I shook my head. "I'm celebrating something—a small victory of sorts."

"Oh yeah? Those flowers were meant for that?" He took a small sip of his beer and used a napkin to gently wipe the line of foam that settled over his upper lip. It served to draw my attention to his mouth, a sensuous mouth that had my head swimming with fantasies.

"They were," I replied. Without giving away confidential information and too many details, I found myself telling him all about Vasudev Rao. "He was the devil to deal with, but I think

I convinced him to see reason," I concluded and raised my glass in a salute to myself.

Roger raised his own glass and tapped it against mine. "Excellent job, Counselor. I'm proud of you." He took another sip. "In a sense we're both celebrating victories, aren't we?"

My puzzled look must have been obvious because he said, "I have an investor in my play and you won your legal battle. This is a joint celebration."

On my empty stomach the wine was beginning to go straight to my head, and the mellow feeling was marvelous. I nodded and raised my glass once again. "To a joint celebration."

What was I drinking to? Toasting Roger's upcoming engagement to a rich girl? His pending nuptials to some slim beauty while I fantasized over how he could heat my blood to smoking point? "So how's the play coming along?"

Roger offered me a pleased smile, turning my already weak legs to jelly. "It's coming along well. Auditions are over and my cast and crew are in place. Rehearsals have started. It's hard work and it's tougher than I'd imagined, but it's exciting. Being a writer, producer, director, and gopher-cum-janitor is difficult, sometimes frustrating, but I'm happy. It's what I've always wanted to do."

"So, who's the girl that's responsible for your good fortune?" I knew I was setting myself up for a major stab of jealousy and a painful wound—but I had to know.

His expression turned serious, his jaw tight and tense. It seemed like he'd neither anticipated nor appreciated my question. "What makes you think it's a girl?"

"You're looking for a rich woman to support your dream, aren't you?"

"I'm capable of finding a legitimate source of business capital, you know." He fixed me with a piercing look, the bedroom eyes not nearly as friendly as they usually were. Right now they seemed to be shooting twin arrows right into my irises. Ouch!

This was the first time I'd seen Roger actually looking angry. I'd apparently hit a nerve. "I'm sorry. I just assumed it was a girl since you'd told me that you were looking for a wealthy wife."

"Since that wasn't happening, I took an offer from a venture capitalist. I have a huge debt hanging over my head, but I'm confident I can repay it."

"I see." I felt like a first-class heel. "Does your father know about this?"

He gave me a measured look. "I don't keep secrets from my family."

I wondered if it was a mild dig at me for lying to my mother earlier. "I wish you lots of luck, then," I said.

"Thanks, Soorya. I appreciate that," he said, leaning forward, his voice once again reverting to that silk-and-sand, intimate quality that disturbed me so much.

With that we reached some sort of truce. I marveled at Roger's easy way of forgiving people. I was forced to admit he was very, very likeable. In about two minutes, despite his unconventional getup, he'd charmed Sandy no end. And it wasn't easy to hoodwink Sandy.

Roger and I could be friends, I concluded. And why not? He was charming, excellent company—and he was paying for the meal for a change. The tables around us slowly started to fill up. A multitude of voices chattering around us and the strong scent of Indian cuisine in the air were satisfying. The wine began to taste better and better.

Our food arrived—grilled *tandoori* chicken, lamb *roghan josh* curry, and saffron rice for Roger. And for me, *palak paneer*—a spinach and cubed cheese dish with white rice. It was a quiet and pleasant meal.

He told me about his play. It appeared that things were moving along briskly. He was talking about opening *Mumbai to Manhattan* within the next three or four months.

"That soon? I didn't realize a major production could be put on stage that quickly." I plunged my fork into the last of the delicious *palak paneer* and long grains of Basmati rice.

"It's not a musical and I don't have a large cast," he explained, fork held in midair. "Musicals can take years to produce with the choruses and the orchestras and the costumes.

Mine is a straightforward drama compared to those. Besides, I had started laying the groundwork before I actually started the project. Remember I'd told you about my trips to New York to meet with theater people?"

"Mm-hmm. So, am I going to get a peek at the preview?" I teased gently, watching him bite into a succulent grilled chicken drumstick and chew the meat slowly and thoroughly. It had been a while since I'd sunk my teeth into anything resembling poultry.

"Of course you'll get a preview. I don't have friends in the city yet. You're it at the moment."

I chuckled and sipped my wine. "With your personality I thought you'd have at least a dozen friends by now."

"Some of my cast members are certainly nice and friendly, and I am making some new friends."

"Mostly cute females, I gather?" The wine was giving me a buzz, and it felt good to sit there and rib Roger. Since we were both tall, our knees were touching under the small table and it felt right. God knows why, but it felt right. He was a fellow *desi,* that's why, I told myself.

"One or two cute ones," he replied. "Why don't you come to one of my rehearsals and find out for yourself?" His grin was wicked.

"You don't mind my watching a rehearsal?"

"Not at all. In fact, you may be able to look at it objectively and give me some constructive feedback."

"Okay." It pleased me no end that he wanted me to give him feedback—me, a woman who knew nothing about show business. "Tell me when."

He mentioned a day the following week when he'd scheduled an evening rehearsal and I promptly entered it into my planner. We lingered over Roger's dessert, almond *kulfi,* a rich frozen concoction, chock full of crushed almonds.

Since it was white and vegetarian, I ventured to try a spoonful. The sweet, icy creaminess was heaven on my tongue, but I refused a second spoonful despite Roger's efforts to entice me. It was with a sense of pride that I watched Roger pay for our meal with a shiny gold Visa card. The Broadway-bound Roger was making his way in the world.

In that moment I wished him success with all my heart.

He walked me to the train station and just before my train pulled in he surprised me with a hug. "Thanks for going to dinner with me, Soorya. I needed the company."

"My pleasure," I said, feeling breathless from the close contact. Despite the casual look, he smelled clean, with that vaguely familiar, citrusy cologne. I liked the feel of his hard chest against mine and the sandpaper coarseness of his stubble on my temple.

The train pulled in and I stepped out of his arms with great reluctance. "Thanks again for dinner, Roger. See you next week at the rehearsal . . . maybe."

A warm burst of something spread inside me. I'd never felt like that before, so I couldn't identify it. It had to be a result of the hug from Roger. That much I knew. And it was nicer, much more heart-wrenching than what I'd felt when Lou had touched me. That had been a purely physical reaction, whereas this was all-encompassing. Sweet.

As the train pulled out of the station, I turned around and saw Roger walking away, hands in his pockets.

I felt a baffling urge to break out of the train and catch up with him, ask him to hold me again.

Chapter 16

On the day I was scheduled to attend Roger's rehearsal, I was swamped with work. One of Mac's assistant attorneys was in the hospital with an emergency and Mac needed my help on a case that was coming up for a hearing soon. Since the Seattle case had gone so well, Mac had been requesting my assistance more and more.

It was a good feeling, but when one of the seniors put something in a junior's lap, it was meant to be done immediately. As the clock ticked away, I typed my notes into the computer and ended up making several mistakes and redoing them. Thank goodness for the undo and spell-check features in computers.

To make matters worse, Sandy had a dental appointment and I had to find files, folders, and miscellaneous pieces of information on my own. Although I knew our filing system well, it still took me time to locate things. I realized what a gem Sandy was. I always knew that, but then why did most of us recognize a person's worth only when they were absent?

I made a note in my planner to have yellow roses, Sandy's favorite flowers, delivered for her birthday coming up in a few months.

At precisely 6:09 P.M. I shut down my computer. Before I took a trip to the ladies' room to freshen up, I called Mom to tell her not to hold dinner for me. I wondered if Roger would mention going out to eat again. The last time we'd shared that meal at the Indian restaurant was so pleasant, I'd hoped to recapture it.

This time I meant to treat him—the poor guy was probably on a shoestring budget. How sadly ironic to have a rich father and yet have to watch one's pennies. Oh well, it was probably a valuable lesson in living for the carefree Roger—one he perhaps badly needed.

Once again, I used the business dinner excuse with Mom. Despite her naïveté Mom was smart and probably wondered if I had a boyfriend tucked away somewhere. It was only a matter of time before she started to question why I suddenly had these business dinners taking up my evenings. And if she didn't figure it out, Dad certainly would.

I was too tired to walk to the subway station, so I hailed a cab. Besides, my suede pumps and heavy briefcase were not made for walking. I asked the cabbie to take me uptown, to an area bordering Harlem. Roger and his crew were conducting rehearsals in some theater there. The traffic was heavy and the ride took over thirty minutes.

When I paid the cab driver and faced the building, I sucked my breath in. It looked decrepit, with the paint faded and the once-ornate cornice chipped in various places. I shivered in the cold wind that had picked up in the last hour. Although it was only mid-fall, it felt like approaching snow in the air. I was glad I'd chosen to wear a long wool coat.

I studied the surroundings. The small grocery store across the street was open. An Oriental man was unloading a crate of broccoli on the curbside display. He threw a cautious glance at me and returned to his task. A group of youths stood on the sidewalk half a block down and laughed about something, making my skin prickle.

Although there was a fair amount of pedestrian traffic as well as automobiles, it wasn't like the more upscale areas of Manhattan. A deli two doors down had a giant submarine sandwich displayed in neon lights in its window. A bar-restaurant at the end of the block was playing soft, soulful music.

The aroma of fried food met my nose, thrusting my diet-weary stomach into overdrive.

Although this block looked like a typical urban street scene, there was a seediness about it that made me uneasy. Why had Roger picked this place for rehearsals? Probably because the rent was cheap.

Once again I looked at the building before me. It didn't look like a theater. Wondering if I'd ended up at the wrong address, I checked my piece of paper. It was the right place. The young men laughing on the corner started walking toward me.

Panic flooded my brain. I didn't want to get mugged or gang-raped or something. I marched quickly and resolutely up to the front door. Thankfully it was unlocked, so I let myself in. My heart was thumping as I shut the door behind me.

I listened for approaching footsteps, wondering if those street punks had decided to follow me. When I heard nothing, I opened the door a crack and peered outside. They had saun-tered past the building. Their voices began to fade.

Taking a deep breath, I let my guard down and looked around. The foyer must have been lovely at one time. The build-ing had to be a hundred years old. An antique chandelier hung from the tall ceiling, but it looked dusty, and barely half the lightbulbs were lit.

I tried the single door in front of me and found it locked. Hearing muffled voices coming from below, I followed them down the narrow staircase toward the cold basement. A door to the right of the concrete landing had a sign that read AUDITO-RIUM.

Very carefully I opened the door. The voices grew louder and it felt warm inside. My eyes went straight to the raised and brightly lit stage at the far end and the people standing on it. The rest of the room was dark. It looked like I was in the right place after all.

Stepping inside, I stood for a moment, trying to discern things nearer to where I stood. This was probably some sort of amateur theater. There had to be a place to sit somewhere. As my eyes adjusted to the dark, the rows of chairs became visible. Gingerly placing my hand against the wall nearest me, I felt my way to about halfway down the auditorium and found an aisle seat for myself.

Throwing my briefcase in the adjoining chair, I sat down, suddenly feeling very weary. At least it was safe in here. The scene outside had been disquieting.

I noticed Roger on the stage, standing with his hands on his hips, giving orders to the cast. After some conferring and instructing he took the steps leading down to the seating area and parked himself in the front row. Then he yelled, "All right, once again, let's start from the beginning. I don't want any tomfoolery this time. Understand?"

They all nodded—two women, three young men, and an older man.

Roger hadn't noticed me sitting in the dark, several rows behind him. I wanted to keep it that way. It was fun to observe in secret the enigmatic writer, producer, and director at work. I was surprised at how forceful he was and how much in command. This was a new Roger, firmly in control of his cast and crew.

The actors took their places, ready for the scene. The lights dimmed, spooky background music reminiscent of the suspenseful scenes in *Jaws* and *Psycho* began to play, and suddenly the stage took on the atmosphere of a dark and menacing place. Shots rang out and a woman screamed—a bloodcurdling sound that echoed in the ancient theater.

I liked the mood created, the eerie quality of it that stirred fear inside me, like a good murder drama should.

The scene continued for a while, with a young Indian man running toward the fallen woman, pulling out his cell phone and calling 911. A dark, skulking figure watched them from some distance, then tiptoed away. The killer, I presumed. I knew the outline of the story since Roger had mentioned it the day we'd first met. But this wasn't just any ordinary thriller—there were some supernatural elements in it, a touch of voodoo and a mysterious clairvoyant who could communicate with dead people.

Roger's voice rang out. "Stop right there! Carrie, let's get a realistic fall. The scream sounded good, but your fall looked fake, like you were afraid of getting hurt. Shots from a gun slam into a person. I want you to portray that—the unexpectedness . . . the shock. The audience should feel it, okay?" Carrie nodded. "Now go."

The scene started all over again. Several times Roger cut the scene short and had them do it over and over again until he was satisfied. Eventually, after several attempts, I had to admit it came out looking and sounding good after Roger had his way. Gosh, what a lot of work for one little scene.

Sirens sounded in the background after that and one of the young men and the older man appeared on stage. Cops. Several other scenes were played out, but more often than not Roger seemed dissatisfied and had them reenact the sequence until they got it right.

However, he wasn't always the drill sergeant. He also applauded and praised the players when things went well, instructed when he thought he needed to intervene, yelled often at the person providing the background sounds, climbed onto the stage to get involved when they seemed confused.

More impressed by Roger's stance than by the scenes enacted, which by the way looked excellent to me, I smiled to myself. Who would have thought he'd be this no-nonsense, take-charge kind of guy?

No matter how much I resisted the notion, Roger was beginning to grow on me like a fungus. Except this one wasn't likely to be cured by antifungal medication.

At one point, when Roger was up on the stage, I noticed the young lady playing the murder victim giggle and put her hand around Roger's waist. "Wasn't that last run pretty damn good, Raj?"

In turn he placed his long arm on her shoulder and smiled at her, his eyes totally focused on hers. "Sure was. More of that kind of acting and we won't have to practice this late, eh? If you focus just a tad more, you'll make it straight to Broadway."

She nodded enthusiastically, her hair bouncing. Pretty woman, I decided, if one liked the sort. She wore hip-hugging jeans and a pale pink cropped shirt that exposed her midriff. A belly button ring glinted in the light every time she moved. Her shoulder-length hair looked coppery red under the stage lights. She was tall and slim and shapely. The smile she sent Roger was radiant.

The woman was flirting with Roger and he seemed to be enjoying it, returning that sweet look. I had the rare urge to march onto that stage and yank out that belly button ring and draw some blood. When I felt like I wanted to drive a fist into Roger's smug face, I skidded to a stop with my violent thoughts.

What was Roger doing to my brain? Why was I allowing him to do it? Closing my eyes, I told myself to get a grip on my emotions.

When I looked up, Roger still had his arm loosely hanging on the woman's shoulder. And to think he'd given me this song and dance about having no friends in this town. For a guy with no friends, he seemed to be doing well. If he had the redhead to play with, why had he invited *me* here?

I couldn't understand my irritation at some actress coming on to Roger. It was none of my business. He was only my friend. He meant nothing more to me. Hadn't I made that clear to him and to myself? Besides, he hadn't invited me here for a date. He'd asked me to observe the rehearsal and give him some constructive feedback. And constructive feedback was exactly what I'd give him.

Deeply immersed in my thoughts, I nearly jumped when all the lights came on, illuminating the auditorium. I blinked and looked up.

Roger noticed me then. His face broke into a surprised smile. "Soorya! I didn't see you come in. When did you get here?"

"A little while ago."

He hurried down the steps and toward me. "Did you get to see any of it?" he asked, gesturing to the stage behind him.

"The last half hour or so," I lied. It had been closer to an hour, but I felt a bit like a voyeur, sitting in the dark and observing him silently.

The familiar scent that clung to him reached me as he came closer, making me feel a bit woozy. "So, what did you think?"

"I'm impressed, Roger. In just a few weeks you've made tremendous progress."

He sank into the chair beside mine. "But I still have a long way to go." He clapped to get the attention of the chattering cast members on the stage.

A few other men and women had joined the ones in the two scenes and the noise level was up, so Roger had to whistle to get them to listen. "Let's call it a day. Tomorrow morning we start at eight sharp. No tardiness, please, and I don't want any excuses, either." After that curt order his tone relaxed and warmed. "So, who's still up for pizza?"

Four hands went up while the rest started to gather their coats and bags. I assumed the ones who weren't joining the pizza party were folks with families to go home to.

A bit disappointed that Roger hadn't mentioned going out to eat, I pondered if I should get out of the building with the departing cast members and go directly home. I'd feel safer with people around me than standing outside by myself, waiting for a taxi to show up.

Roger excused himself to talk to the people getting ready to leave. He gathered them around and talked in hushed tones and I noticed them nodding at whatever he said. I'd never thought of Roger as a managerial type, but these folks seemed to listen to him, respect him.

The four that had opted for pizza grabbed their coats and started walking toward me, with Roger bringing up the rear. He introduced them to me. "Soorya, I want you meet my coworkers. This is Carrie Blatt," he said, indicating the pretty redhead who was making me jealous.

I offered her my hand. "Hi, Carrie. Nice job. I was observing your performance."

"Thank you so much," she cooed, taking my hand.

I smiled back at her, wondering why she had to be so amiable. It was hard to dislike someone so full of friendly pep. With a pang I noticed Carrie was prettier up close than she was on stage. No wonder Roger looked like the king of the hill.

Then there was Satish Ayengar, the guy who happened to witness her murder in the alley; Ryan Smith, the guy who provided the background music and sound effects; and Theresa Collier, the older woman who was one of the spectators in the alley. I knew she was the clairvoyant who would eventually play a bigger role later in the drama.

I shook hands with each of them. "You guys are doing excellent work. I can't wait to see the finished product on stage." They looked pleased.

Roger touched my shoulder. "Guys, my friend Soorya is an attorney with a famous law firm in Manhattan." They looked sufficiently impressed. And the fact that he had referred to me as his friend wasn't lost on me, either.

Satish turned to me, his dark eyes taking on a curious gleam. "Have you defended any famous criminals?"

"I don't deal with criminals," I replied with a laugh. "I'm a boring environmental attorney and work with corporate types. Not at all glamorous."

Satish was a pleasant young man with deep-set ebony eyes and an Indian-American accent that suited his role. He looked awfully young and boyish, although I suspected he was in his mid to late twenties. The light in his eyes dulled a bit at my response. "Not even anyone mildly famous?"

I shook my head. Thanks to television, people believed attorneys led exciting lives. The O. J. Simpson case many years ago had even glamorized district attorneys to some extent, notwithstanding the meager salary, the deplorable working conditions, and the unkind glare of negative publicity at times.

Theresa was a woman in her forties with twinkling, mischievous eyes. I liked Theresa instantly. Ryan was a bit serious, with his severe crew cut and rimless glasses.

When I asked if they'd done stage work prior to this, Carrie and Theresa nodded, but Ryan shook his head. "This is my first time as sound artist."

"What about you, Satish?" I was interested in knowing how a *desi* had ended up in the world of theater. I wondered if he was like Roger, hoping to fulfill his Broadway dreams. Did he have a rich dad, too, someone who could keep supporting him while he tried his hand at show business?

"I was a drama major at NYU," he said. "My claim to fame

is bit parts in two Hollywood movies and some off-Broadway plays. Most people wouldn't remember the skinny Indian guy sitting at the bar or cheering at the ballpark."

"You never know what people notice or remember," I said in an effort to encourage him.

"Say, you didn't happen to notice the fellow carrying the water pitcher into the tent in the movie *Alexander,* did you?" he asked good-naturedly.

"Not really." I liked Satish's sense of humor.

After a few more polite words to the folks, I turned to Roger. "I think I'll be heading home. You guys must have a lot of things to talk about."

Roger put a restraining hand on my arm. "Soorya, come join us for pizza. We always order in when we do evening rehearsals."

I looked at my watch. "Well, I—"

"Will you stay? We're just going to eat in the adjoining room."

"My diet doesn't allow pizza."

"I'll order a salad for you." Roger grinned. "Lots of red and green veggies."

I hesitated for a moment, but the faces around me seemed friendly enough, so I nodded. Roger ushered us into a conference room, an ancient room that smelled mustier than the theater. The walls looked like they hadn't been painted in half a century. "Soorya, welcome to our executive lounge–cum–conference room. We plan, strategize, brainstorm, and argue here, but mostly we eat here."

"Thanks." I looked around. An oversized wooden table and a dozen chairs with faded upholstery were the only furniture in the room. Everybody found a chair to sit in and Roger ordered dinner on his cell phone. We talked while we waited for the food.

Carrie flirted outrageously with Roger as well as the other two men. I envied Carrie's lack of inhibition.

Satish and I talked. "So tell me about some of the roles you've played," I said to him.

He reeled off a few names of movies and plays. Unfortunately I hadn't seen any of them, so I couldn't comment. He tilted his head toward Roger. "*Mumbai to Manhattan* will be my first step into a major stage show."

"You think this will make it big?" I asked Theresa, who was sitting on my other side. She seemed to know the stage and the subject. I was curious on Roger's behalf.

"I think so. I'm really excited about the script. It's got potential, with its East-West mix and the current interest in multicultural themes—especially after *Slumdog Millionaire* became a hit movie. If it's done right, *M-to-M* could be a Broadway hit. Roger has the talent and the drive."

"You may be right," I said. "So you hope to see your name in lights soon?" I asked, turning to Satish once again.

"I've waited many years to see my name in lights." Satish's dark eyes gleamed with hope. "Sorry, I'm probably boring you to death."

"Not at all," I assured him. "What do you do besides acting?"

"I work as a programmer at an investment bank."

"Programming and acting? You're a man of diverse talents."

He rolled his eyes. "Programming is boring, but it pays the bills and allows me some flexibility to follow my passion."

Boring perhaps, but stable employment and a steady income, I concluded silently. Satish appeared to be a sensible man. He was also giving me the sort of attention that was flattering. I could tell he was interested. My ego was humming.

The pizza and salad arrived a few minutes later and we ate. When it was over and we'd cleaned up the table and got rid of the boxes and soda cans, I realized I'd had a good time, especially my conversation with Satish. I tried not to let Carrie's possessive attitude toward Roger bother me. I managed to keep smiling.

Ryan and Roger went into some deep discussion about sound effects and at one point moved to the far end of the table to talk about amps and acoustics in private.

I didn't mind one bit because Roger's actors were fun to talk to, even Carrie. They told me stories about bloopers in some of the roles they'd played over the years and the scandalous things that went on in some dressing rooms and behind the curtain.

It was vastly entertaining to learn how celebrities behaved behind the scenes versus how they were on stage. One or two stories were so outrageous I found myself laughing out loud, making Roger glance at me across the length of the large table and smile indulgently.

It was nearly nine-thirty when the party finally broke up.

Satish shook my hand and held it for a long time. "It was a pleasure meeting you, Soorya."

"Likewise." I withdrew my hand just as reluctantly. I wasn't mistaken about that look of interest in Satish's expression. My cheeks felt warm. Why hadn't I noticed earlier that there was something rather attractive about him? Was it the fact that he was more my type—plain vanilla?

"Maybe we'll meet again?" He handed me a business card.

"Maybe." I slipped the card in my bag. It gave me perverse pleasure that Roger noticed the exchange with great interest. A slight frown marred his handsome face—but it was gone in an instant.

The moment was interrupted when Carrie rose from the table and stretched. "See you guys tomorrow."

Roger looked at her. "You need someone to walk you to the bus stop, Carrie?"

She shook her head. "My boyfriend's picking me up. He's waiting outside."

Ah, Carrie had a boyfriend. That bit of information eased my mind like a good night's sleep.

Satish left on his own while Ryan offered to walk Theresa home, which she said was only a few blocks from there.

That left Roger and me. "Soorya, don't go out alone. I'll walk with you to the train station," he offered.

"That's okay. I can get a cab," I said.

He chuckled and nudged me out the conference room door. "Try hailing a cab in this neighborhood at this hour. You'll be standing there all night." Shutting off all the lights, he pulled out a set of keys from his jeans pocket and locked the door to the auditorium.

As we climbed the stairs toward the foyer, I turned to him. "That reminds me. Why did you pick this place for rehearsals? It's scary."

"Take a wild guess."

"Low rent?"

"Correct. And convenience." He opened the front door for me and followed behind, then used the keys once again and locked the massive door. "It's used mostly by community theater and off-Broadway productions for rehearsals. It's a popular place. I was lucky to get it on short notice."

We started walking toward the train station, which Roger said was only a couple of blocks. The stores were closed now, and the shutters drawn. The bar-restaurant was still open and the music still playing. The street looked nearly deserted. My disquiet returned.

Roger must have sensed my anxiety, because he patted my arm. "Don't worry. It's not as unsafe as it looks." He gave me one of those easy smiles of his. "I'm a brown belt in karate, if it helps any."

"Really?" One more thing that seemed so out of place with this odd man. But it was entirely possible he was telling the truth. I'd detected some steely strength in those long arms and chest when he'd hugged me the other day. I just hadn't made the connection then.

He shrugged. "When my sister took tap dancing and violin lessons, I was expected to find something appropriate for a boy. I picked karate."

"Not just picked but excelled at, apparently." It appeared that he did well in most whatever he *picked*.

"Turned out that I enjoyed it," he said.

"Just like you enjoyed theater arts," I prompted.

The subway station had a lot more people, making me feel much better. There were even a few business people and several student types on the platform, probably from my old alma mater, Columbia University, which wasn't too far from there.

We had a few minutes to kill before our train was scheduled to arrive. We talked, mostly about the play. Roger was deep into designing the playbill. He told me what it cost to get one printed.

I was aghast. "But it's an itsy-bitsy flyer. Why would that cost so much?"

"That itsy-bitsy booklet is a work of art, Soorya. It needs designing, professional photographs, color graphics, attractive front and back covers, and ads. It requires excellent writing and editing, too."

"All that for something people sit on, step on, fan themselves with, roll and toss at the end of the play?"

"Sad, isn't it? It means nothing to anyone else but those of us who are directly involved."

I agreed. Poor Roger wasn't likely to see any profits coming out of this venture. Maybe never. If, and it was a huge *if,* the play ever made it big, it would probably be months, or years, before he actually took home a paycheck.

Probably guessing my train of thought, Roger nodded. "Yeah, it'll be a long time before I go to the bank to make a deposit instead of a withdrawal."

All the more reason why I had to keep him at a safe distance, I reminded myself. And it was a good thing he'd moved on since our first meeting and the subject of marriage. Being married to a guy like Roger would mean dealing with the fact that I'd be the sole breadwinner in the family.

He'd be working long hours and putting a lot of effort and creativity into a job that could bomb in the end, and there would be no income. Only debts—and frustrations—and shattered dreams. It was an alarming thought.

And what would that do to a relationship, when roles were more or less reversed—the woman paying the bills and keeping the home fires burning while the man did more or less female things like dabbling in the arts? What would it do to the male ego and the woman's psyche?

Despite my negative thoughts I sent Roger an encouraging

smile. "You'll get there one of these days. You've got a dedicated crew and you've got the talent and determination."

"Thanks, Soorya. You're a good friend," he said and patted my arm again. "You're welcome to come and watch our rehearsals any time."

"I just might do that." I noticed his use of the word *friend* again.

"I'm sure Satish will be happy to see you, too," Roger said. "Looks like you've made a conquest with Satish."

I laughed. "Girls like me don't make conquests, Roger."

"You could have fooled me. Satish was definitely drooling." His eyes hardened a bit. Again, it was a mere flash.

"Nice to have a guy drooling, I suppose." Despite my lack of acting skills, I did my best to look nonchalant. Nevertheless I was flattered by Satish's interest. And I was dying to know if Roger was at least a little bit jealous. If he was, he wasn't showing it.

Instead he took me by surprise by asking, "What are you doing on Friday evening?"

"Nothing in particular." I gave him a wary look. "Why?"

"Want to go with me to the Ganesh Temple in Flushing?"

I hadn't thought of Roger as the religious type. When he had touched Pamma's feet I'd assumed it was more a cultural gesture rather than religious. But then he'd been throwing me one curve after another. "*You* are going to a temple?" I asked.

"Something wrong with that?"

"Nothing wrong. I just can't picture you as a temple-going, devotional kind of individual."

He smiled a slow, deliberately calculated smile that made my bones melt and shift a little. "You don't know a lot about me, Mizz Giri."

"So what are you going to do at the temple?"

"Pray for the Lord's blessings, of course. I could use a lot of those, as you know."

I clucked my tongue and slapped his hand. "The truth, Roger."

He pretended to soothe the imaginary wound I'd inflicted on the back of his hand. "Okay, Satish's uncle and aunt are performing a *puja* at the temple, and I'm invited to it and the *prasadam* dinner. I was asked to bring along a friend if I wanted to."

"So I'm the friend you thought of asking?" A *puja* was an elaborate ritualistic religious ceremony and *prasadam* was the feast offered first to God and then fed to the guests—consecrated food. So anyone who ate the meal reaped the peripheral blessings surrounding the occasion. It was a privilege to be invited to a *puja* and a *prasadam* meal.

"You're the one friend who's likely to know all about the temple and maybe even enjoy the visit," said Roger.

Going to the temple with Roger was tempting, but I wasn't sure I wanted to encourage him too much. Visiting a temple together was something typically done by engaged or married couples in our culture. And I didn't want to give Satish or his relatives the wrong impression. Did I want to risk that?

On the other hand, was this a deliberate move on Roger's part to send a subtle message to Satish that Roger and I were indeed a couple? But then he'd gone out of his way to call me his friend. I wished I knew what Roger was up to this time around. Beneath what appeared to be a forthright and uncomplicated personality I was beginning to discover some deep, complex layers.

So I made up an excuse. "I work rather late on most Fridays."

"I work late every evening. Besides, it shouldn't matter if we're delayed. You know how laid-back Indian gatherings are. People trail in at whatever time they feel like."

"Yeah, but still—"

"Why don't you call me on Friday when you're ready to leave the office? We'll take the train together into Flushing."

He was making it impossible to say no. And I so badly wanted to say yes. Besides, I hadn't been to the Ganesh Temple in ages. "All right, you twisted my arm."

"Excellent!" He looked genuinely pleased, making me speculate again about his real motive for inviting me.

When our train finally put in an appearance, I sighed in relief.

Although Roger had kindly carried my briefcase and was still holding it along with his own, my high-heels-clad feet were protesting. I gladly plopped into an empty seat with Roger beside me.

Despite his stop being elsewhere, Roger insisted on going with me to Penn Station, then waiting till my connecting train arrived and seeing me off. "It's late and I want to make sure you get home safely," he announced when I told him I was capable of taking care of myself.

I didn't complain. It was nice to know the unconventional Roger was so old-fashioned and chivalrous. In fact, no man other than Dad had ever shown me such consideration.

Roger never failed to surprise me. But it made him that much more enticing. That much more dangerous.

Chapter 17

Friday started out cloudy, and it got cloudier and colder as the day wore on. It was after seven when I hung up the phone and got up from my chair to stretch and look outside my office window. It was dark and raining.

I had informed Mom that morning that I was going to be very late returning home because I was going with a friend to the temple and eating a *prasadam* dinner.

Surprisingly Mom had neither expressed surprise nor pestered me for the friend's name, probably because she was on a long-distance call and too busy gossiping with my aunt in India to pay attention to me.

She and my aunt had been discussing some distant cousin's failed marriage—an anomaly in our community, and particularly in our family. And horror of horrors, the cousin's husband was cheating on her—overtly.

Mildly curious, I'd stood in the kitchen for a minute to eavesdrop.

Mom had looked distressed as she'd twirled the telephone cord around her finger. "She even *knows* about his dirty affairs?" Mom had groaned. "Poor thing must be so humiliated."

After another minute of listening to my aunt, Mom's eyes had opened wide. "He flaunts them in front of everyone? Is he suffering from some type of midlife crisis or what?"

From the look on Mom's face I'd figured the conversation was likely to continue for a while. Disgraceful affairs were not meant to happen in a decent family, and certainly not in rural Andhra. I had also noticed Pamma wasn't around. She was likely to be kept in the dark about this particular scandal. She was too old and delicate for such news.

Glad that I'd been saved the third degree, I had waved cheerily at Mom and headed out to work.

I studied the wet pavement now and the sea of umbrellas outside my window. Walking in the rain on a cold fall evening wasn't exactly inviting and I wondered if I should call Roger and cancel our appointment. But the idea of spending time with him was tempting.

Besides, the thought of a tasty temple dinner had become more and more appealing as the evening wore on and my belly began to rumble. I'd been on the phone most of the past hour and I needed a break from legal matters. So I called Roger.

"I'd nearly given up on hearing from you," he grumbled.

"Sorry, I was on a long conference call." I checked my watch. "Are we still on, or am I too late?"

"We're definitely on. Satish and I are on our way right now. It'll take us about fifteen minutes to get to the station near your office. Can you meet us there?"

"Okay." I fixed my hair and makeup with great care, then put on my coat, grabbed my umbrella, and started out.

I found Roger and Satish waiting for me at the entrance to the subway station. They were both dressed in jeans, pullover sweaters, and hooded parkas, making me feel overdressed in my wool skirt, turtleneck sweater, trench coat, and designer pumps.

Those two looked like college students while I could be mistaken for their staid and sensible older sister. On second thought, I decided that was a good thing. Maybe the crowd at the *puja* would think Roger and I were siblings—or cousins.

"Glad you made it despite the weather, Soorya." Satish gave me a long, admiring look. "My uncle and aunt are looking forward to meeting you and Rajesh."

Warm blood seeped into my face at his scrutiny. "Hope it's not an imposition."

Satish promptly dismissed my concern. "Not at all. They perform this *puja* once a year and they invite a huge crowd. It seems like every year the invitees list gets longer."

"What kind of *puja?*"

"*Satyanarayana puja.*"

"Then I'm glad I'm going." Satyanarayana was another name for the Hindu god Vishnu, the preserver of the universe. The *puja* was considered highly propitious, and no good Hindu would deliberately try to avoid attending one of those—or the sacred meal.

"I twisted her arm into going," Roger chimed in, placing a proprietary hand on my back, albeit for a minor second. This time I was almost sure he was making a subtle statement.

The short train ride was taken up with me listening to the two men talk about the day's rehearsal. It seemed like things hadn't gone all that well.

"Problems at work?" I asked Roger.

"Ryan is out sick with the flu—and it looks like Larry, another cast member, is coming down with it, too," Roger replied, looking worried.

"Did you notice Felicia sniffling? She may be next," said Satish. "I can't afford to get sick and take time off from rehearsal or my other job, man."

Roger nodded. "Neither can I. Looks like the flu epidemic is making its rounds early this year." But being an optimist, he added, "Maybe it's better that way if it means by the time the show opens it'll have come and gone."

The guys tried to include me in the conversation, but I preferred to let them talk. It was nice to see the two men getting along so well. Satish seemed like a decent guy. Roger could use some male friends for a change—stable and working friends. He had entirely too many females surrounding him.

The temple was mobbed as usual. Unlike churches, Hindu temples didn't have set timetables for services, so people went in and out at their leisure. Friday evening was a popular time for worshippers to congregate at the temple.

To add to that, it was *purnima,* a full moon. There it was again, a full moon, and Roger and I were together. For whatever reason, it seemed our fates were set to intersect during a full moon.

I stood on Bowne Street outside the shrine for a moment. Ignoring the raindrops falling on my face, I lifted my gaze to admire the soaring *gopuram,* the entry tower—the elaborately hand-carved pyramid, the equivalent of a church steeple, rising against the dark, sodden sky. Too bad that moon was completely concealed by clouds.

Builders and artisans from Andhra and other parts of southern India had been brought in over three decades ago to design and build the project as prescribed by the ancient Hindu principles of temple architecture.

The structure looked exactly like any South Indian house of worship. Inside, too, the atmosphere was authentic, with its smooth granite floors, towering ceilings and columns, and carved altars to seat the idols of the gods and goddesses. Every idol had been created by trained sculptors from India.

In the foyer, we left our shoes in the designated area. One did not enter a temple with shoes on, since footwear was traditionally made of animal hide. The Hindu principle of nonviolence toward animals was the basis for the practice.

Also, there was the matter of trailing in dirt from the outside and tainting the clean and sacred atmosphere of the temple. I left my dripping umbrella beside my shoes.

As we entered the sanctum, we were at once greeted by the combined odors of incense, sandalwood paste, roses, and chrysanthemums, and the sound of a priest reciting Sanskrit *shlokas* from the scriptures.

It was like stepping into another world, one far removed from the typical urban American street scene outside. Here the atmosphere was a riot of sounds, scents, flavors, and colors of India.

Women wearing colorful silk saris and the younger females in either the loose-fitting, two-piece *salwar-kameez* outfits or long skirts and tops like I was dressed in were scattered about. A few of the men wore a *sadra* and matching pants but most wore slacks or jeans and shirts.

The fact that everyone had to sit on the floor made it necessary for women to wear something loose and long in the interests of comfort and modesty. The kids, too, wore outfits that were a hodgepodge of East and West.

The temple's presiding deity was Ganesh, an impressive granite idol decked out in silk garments, fresh flower and fruit garlands, and gold jewelry. He was mounted on an elaborate throne in the inner chamber. Flanking the main deity were other Hindu gods and goddesses housed in their respective alcoves—a typical temple setup, spread out over a single, large room.

The three of us prayed to Ganesh first, and then paid our respects to the other deities. Most big gatherings were held in the community halls located in the basement, so we took the stairs to the *puja* hall.

Satish wasn't kidding when he'd mentioned the size of the gathering. What looked like over a hundred people were seated on the floor of one of the rooms. Half a dozen kids ranging in age from toddler to perhaps eight or ten were running around in the hallway, playing catch. We had to maneuver our way to avoid bumping into them.

The *puja* was taking place at the far end of the room. A picture of Lord Satyanarayana was mounted on a low table, surrounded by oil lamps, fresh flowers, and smoking incense sticks.

A few devout individuals sat with rapt attention in the front rows but most people were toward the back, huddled in small groups, carrying on whispered conversations, entirely oblivious to what was going on a few feet away.

I turned to Satish and Roger with an amused smile. "Typical Indian socio-religious scene, isn't it?"

"Is it any surprise that Hindu religious events become mainly social gatherings," Roger said, "when the ceremonies are in Sanskrit and they're so long?"

A Brahmin priest dressed in the traditional white cotton *dhoti* was officiating at the *puja*. Beside him sat a middle-aged couple, our hosts. Satish's uncle was a heavyset, dark-skinned man with a bald spot on the back of his head, wearing a cream silk *sadra*.

The aunt was an equally plump woman dressed in a yellow Kanjivaram silk sari with a maroon border. Her hair was pulled into a tight bun adorned with a string of fresh jasmine. She wore the traditional diamond cluster earrings and heavy gold jewelry around her neck and wrists.

Trays piled with cut flowers along with a variety of sweets, fruit, and nuts were placed before the deity. All of it was offered to the Lord to please Him so He would shower the worshippers with health, wealth, peace, and prosperity. The more people the hosts invited to the *puja,* the more blessed they were.

We found a spot in the back of the long room and sat on the floor. Despite our lateness, several minutes after our arrival, the rituals still continued, with no end in sight. The priest's chanting was so monotonous that I closed my eyes and let my mind drift.

With my eyes shut, I could pick out the herbal scent of the incense sticks that were an integral part of Hindu ritualistic worship, the sharp fragrance of the *tulsi* leaves, and the mingled odors of various perfumes and colognes worn by the people around me.

With the varied conversations buzzing in the background, the distant strains of wedding music coming from somewhere, the children's laughter, and the priest's monotone chanting, I felt very much at home in this South Indian temple buried in the heart of Flushing, New York. One's ethnic roots were probably too deep to disintegrate entirely, no matter where one planted them.

It brought back memories of my childhood, of visits to India, the ancestral home in Andhra, and the *pujas* I'd attended. Back then I'd sat amidst my parents, aunts, uncles, cousins, and grandparents, dressed in my latest long silk Indian skirt and blouse with the accompanying jewelry and the jasmine strings tucked in my braids.

I used to love the red *bindi* on my forehead, especially one of the fancy kinds that came in a variety of shapes and colors and encrusted with glitter and sequins. Less than halfway through the *puja* I'd start to fidget and whine and wonder when the service would be over. Eventually, bored out of my mind, I'd fall asleep in Mom or Dad's lap.

Tonight's nostalgic ambience, too, nearly had me dozing off. And my legs, not used to sitting on a hard floor, were beginning to go numb. I nudged Roger and whispered, "I think I'll go stretch my legs a little."

"Good idea. I'll go with you." He looked like he was about to nod off, too.

We both gestured to Satish and dodged our way out through the rambunctious kids still at play in the hallway.

I went in search of the ladies' room. When I returned, I found Roger standing outside another event room a couple of doors down. He seemed engrossed in observing something. When he saw me, he signaled to me to join him.

Curious, I went to stand beside him and realized there was a wedding ceremony taking place. So this was where the wedding music was coming from—poignantly sweet notes played on a *shehnai,* an instrument similar to an oboe. The bride and groom were poised to exchange flower garlands.

"They're about to become man and wife," Roger informed me.

"No shit, Sherlock," I teased him.

"Shh, watch your language! This is a temple," he reprimanded me.

I gave him a defiant grin. Not having attended a traditional Hindu wedding in a while, I observed the ceremony, fascinated. In ancient times, the bride and groom typically saw each other for the first time at this phase of the ceremony.

Then they would place the garlands around each other's necks and accept one another in marriage, for better or for worse. Family and friends would throw rice and flower petals at them to bless them with fertility and an abundance of good wishes.

It made me wonder about the perils of that kind of marriage, where one had no choice but to live with the luck of the draw. What if the groom turned out to be mean and abusive? What if he turned out to be like the guy my mom and aunt were discussing that morning—a philanderer?

My slight shudder must have been obvious because Roger looked at me strangely. "What?"

I whispered in his ear, "I was just imagining what it was like in the days when the bride and groom met for the first time while exchanging garlands."

"What about it?"

"What if the groom was an asshole?"

Roger's brow rose. "What if the bride was a bitch?"

"You have a point," I conceded, chuckling, and Roger shushed me again.

After that we observed the wedding in silence. The bride and groom took the seven steps with their accompanying vows, and walked the ceremonial circles around a small sandalwood fire burning in a metal grate. It represented Agni, the fire god, the ultimate witness to the bridal couple taking their sacred oath, thus making the union permanent.

As I studied the bride's traditional red silk sari with gold accents and the groom looking regal in his long, white, embroidered *shervani* and turban-style headdress, for a few brief moments I let myself indulge in a daydream. What if that were Roger and me in the marriage *mandap,* ready to exchange garlands and rings and promises of lifelong commitment?

Roger would no doubt look fabulous in one of those elegant groom outfits. I could look rather pretty, too, in all my bridal finery and makeup.

But that fantasy wasn't likely to become reality. Even though my views on his line of work had softened to a great extent, he hadn't bothered to bring up the subject of marriage—not since that first day. At the moment, it looked like we were merely friends.

Well then, I'd have to settle for friendship.

Roger glanced at me. "Shouldn't we go back? Seems rude to stay away so long."

I looked at my watch. "You're right."

We went back to the *puja*. The ceremony was coming to an end. We heard everyone singing and the brass bell clanging.

The *aarti* or the waving of lamps in a circular, clockwise motion before God had just begun. It signaled the last ritual when everyone rose to their feet and sang the prescribed hymns together. After that the guests stood in a line and took turns going up to the altar to pay their respects to the Lord.

Satish, Roger, and I went through the motions like everybody else in the crowd and received our blessings from the priest: a spoonful of *teertham*—holy water—placed in our palm and a Dixie cup with a sweet, rich dessert called *kesari*—made of cream of wheat, sugar, and clarified butter.

I ate every last morsel of the *kesari*, savoring its richness. So what if it didn't fit into my diet? I'd be riddled with bad luck if I didn't eat it.

When the rest of the guests proceeded to the dining hall for dinner and the room emptied out, Satish pulled Roger and me aside and introduced us to the hosts. "Soorya, Rajesh, meet my uncle and aunt, Nagraj and Saroja Varadan."

Both Roger and I greeted the Varadans with palms joined in an old-fashioned *namaste*. They seemed pleased that their nephew had brought his friends to the occasion. "Welcome," said his uncle, beaming, while his wife smiled in agreement. "We are honored that our Satish has brought you to our humble gathering." He patted Roger's shoulder. "A pleasure to meet my nephew's friends."

"Thank you for inviting us, sir," Roger said with genuine warmth, always the cordial guest.

Meanwhile Mrs. Varadan studied Roger and me, the dark eyes behind the glasses taking in every detail. I had a vague suspicion that she was jumping to certain conclusions—that Roger and I were a couple. My earlier fears were coming true. I quickly decided to put an end to that. "My parents and Rajesh's are good friends," I explained.

"I see." Saroja's head bobbed up and down.

I wasn't entirely sure she was convinced. In her mind young

couples didn't come to the temple together for nothing—but I had to leave it at that. She applied the customary vermillion dot and yellow turmeric on my forehead and offered me a flower—given to married and unmarried women, but not to widows.

Then the Varadans ushered us into a dining hall where tables and chairs had been set up around a buffet table with an array of chafing dishes. The aromas coming at me were pure heaven. They'd been driving me nuts since the moment I'd walked into the temple.

"Come, let us eat. You must be hungry," said Mr. Varadan.

He escorted Roger, Satish, and me to the buffet and pressed plates and forks into our hands. "Please help yourselves, and come back for seconds. The caterers here are famous—they were recently featured in *India Abroad* newspaper."

As Satish's friends we were being given special treatment. Thanking Mr. Varadan for his hospitality, we gleefully helped ourselves to the feast.

The temple cafeteria was indeed well-known for its fare, and it didn't disappoint me. The *sambar*—spicy split-pea soup—and the tamarind rice were seasoned just right. The *kosumbari* or salad and the mixed vegetable curry, which fortunately had plenty of green and red to satisfy my diet, were out of this world. The dessert, too, vermicelli *payasam*—angel-hair-thin noodles cooked in milk and sugar and flavored with cardamom—was excellent.

And as luck would have it, they were serving my favorite *jalebi*—deep-fried, pretzel shaped pastries dipped in syrup. Alas, they were saffron-colored and too rich, so I eyed them for a second, drooled privately, then decided to pass.

Some half an hour later, when the crowd had thinned out at the buffet table, Roger and Satish smiled at each other like co-conspirators. "Ready for seconds?" Even before the sentence was complete, they were on their feet. Roger glanced at me. "Coming, Soorya?"

I shook my head. "It gets slapped directly on my hips."

Roger pretended to study my body for a second. "Your hips look good to me. Very good."

"Get out of here, you big flatterer," I scolded him, trying not to giggle and blush like a teenager receiving her first compliment from a boy.

Satish tried to talk me into it. "It's *prasadam,* Soorya. You're supposed to eat till you're stuffed. The more you eat, the more blessed you are."

I shooed them away. "Any more edible blessings and I'll cry when I get on the scale next week." I'd been diligent with my diet and maintained my weight for nearly a year, and I knew I looked good these days. I was proud of myself and wanted to keep it that way, so I watched Roger and Satish make pigs of themselves.

Roger and I thanked our hosts for a lovely evening with more *namastes* before we left the dining hall.

Satish had planned to go to his uncle's house for the weekend, so Roger and I were going home on our own. I liked the idea of having some private time with Roger, even if it was just a subway ride.

Chapter 18

After retrieving our coats, shoes, and my umbrella, we stepped outside the temple. It was still raining. But it had turned to a fine drizzle, looking more like a dense fog.

Wet and droopy, the potted yellow and white chrysanthemums on the temple steps exuded their distinctive bitter-sweet scent. I buttoned up my coat and unfurled my umbrella.

Roger turned to me as we descended the steps. "Did you enjoy the evening, Soorya?"

"Yes, very much." I hadn't been here in nearly a year, so I needed to come and earn my blessings. Noticing he hadn't pulled his hood over his head, I moved closer to him so I could share my umbrella with him. "Thanks for inviting me."

He took the umbrella from me and held it up to protect us both. "Don't thank me; thank the Varadans and Satish. In fact, Satish was adamant that I invite you." Roger gave me a lingering look. "Like I said, Satish is drooling."

"But you're the one who asked me," I reminded Roger, and yet I was definitely tickled to have Satish's continued interest in me confirmed. Roger didn't look too happy about it, either. I indulged in a mental grin.

"Since you're being so utterly sweet and charitable tonight, Mizz Giri," he purred, throwing his arm around my shoulders, "may I invite you to a cup of coffee before we go back to the station?" He hesitated for a moment. "Or would that be too presumptuous on my part?"

"I'd love a cup of coffee," I said. "I know a little café right around the corner that serves good Indian coffee. Want to try it?"

"Sounds perfect," he said as we started in the direction of the café. A minute later, he let go of my shoulder, dug into his jeans pocket, then pulled out a red rose and presented it to me. "A pretty flower for a pretty lady."

I looked up at him and realized he meant it. "Why, thank you, Roger. I haven't received flowers in heaven knows how long." In fact, the last time I'd received flowers as a personal gift was when Dad and Mom had given me a bouquet of pink roses at my graduation from law school.

"That's not true," Roger said. "What about the extravagant arrangement you got from your client?"

"That's business. This is . . . personal, even if the flower came from the temple." I noticed the outer petals were a little bruised from sitting in his pocket, but I loved the sentiment, anyway. On an impulse I tucked it over my ear, Hawaiian style.

"It was the prettiest rose sitting on the *puja* tray," he said. "Since the service was over, I took it."

"Swiped it off the tray, you mean?"

"It had your name on it." He stopped for a moment to study my face. "It's very becoming, too."

"You stole a flower just for me? That's so darn thoughtful."

Roger's arm looped around me once again, giving me disturbingly pleasant goose bumps. But I tried not to dwell on it. I told myself to enjoy the moment, grab it and hold it in my hands for however long it lasted—just like the rose tucked over my ear. A spontaneous act of friendship—if that's what it was.

We ambled along the sidewalk, oblivious to the shuttered storefronts, the other pedestrians, and the cold rain falling around us. It might as well have been a leisurely stroll on a sunny afternoon.

The coffee shop was thankfully open despite the late hour. We ordered two old-fashioned Madras coffees at the counter, then sat at one of five small tables. The place was empty, so we had it all to ourselves. It was warm and cozy in here, and it smelled of rich coffee.

Within minutes the stocky young man at the counter brought our cups to our table. "Smells great," said Roger to the guy with an appreciative smile. "Thank you, Govinda."

Govinda beamed back at Roger, clearly thrilled at the compliment. "You are very welcome, sir. You tell me if you want extra sugar or anything, okay?"

When the guy returned to the counter, I whispered to Roger, "How do you know his name?"

"Didn't you see the picture on the wall?"

"What picture?"

"The one where he's serving coffee to some Indian diplomat. The caption clearly says, 'Golden Café employee, Govinda, serving the Honorable Mr. somebody or other.' "

"How do you do that?" I shook my head in amazement.

"Do what?"

"Notice such trivial details."

"When you're a writer like me, you tend to observe things—names, faces, places, objects. It's remarkable what one can learn from what you call trivial details." He stirred a heaping spoon of sugar into his coffee. "They're also a way to make people happy. And when people are happy, they give you outstanding service."

He was right. Mildred came to mind, the old lady he'd befriended that first day he and I had gone to the movies. Roger had an astounding capacity to make people feel important—and happy. It was a rare gift. Maybe I needed to learn some serious public relations strategies from this guy on how to be a more effective lawyer.

The coffee was piping hot, frothy, and loaded with thick milk. Pure heaven. Coffee was not on my diet, but it was the one thing I indulged in on special occasions—and today was one of those occasions. I took my first delicious sip and looked across at Roger. "Tastes wonderful on a cold, damp night, doesn't it?"

"Tastes wonderful on any night." He blew over the steaming

coffee, took a sip, and closed his eyes. "Mmm, reminds me of my last trip to India a couple of years ago. We were traveling through some obscure little town in Andhra, and Dad decided that he had to have a cup of coffee or he'd die of caffeine deprivation. So he had our cab driver take us to this place that was no more than a shack. We sat on wobbly chairs and had coffee similar to this. But there they served it in stainless steel *lotas*— those steel tumblers that get so damn hot, you can't even hold them."

"I know exactly what you mean. Done it a couple of times myself," I assured him.

"They called the brew *cah-pee*."

I cradled my cup in my cold hands to warm them. "So you forgave your dad for dragging you to the shack?"

"Sure. The coffee was worth it."

"Will you ever forgive him for the way he denigrates your choice of careers, Roger? He seems very harsh in his criticism of you."

Roger toyed with his spoon for a while, looking pensive. "I know, but he's not really a bad guy. He's a good father in other ways."

"I'm sure he is."

"Like most dads who belong to the old school, he wants me to have a decent career that'll pay my bills and then some." He lifted his cup and took a thoughtful sip. "You know what? I noticed something strange about Dad—he's been softening up on me lately. He's even sounding supportive to some degree."

"Why do you think that is?"

"I don't know what's come over him, but I suspect it might have something to do with his cousin in India dying of stomach cancer recently. He was about the same age as Dad. Maybe that's making Dad question his own mortality ... or something."

"Interesting." His father didn't seem like the kind to be influenced by some cousin dying in India.

"I also have a feeling my sister and mother might be lecturing

Dad on his attitude. He's even been calling and asking me how the play is coming along. And listen to this shocker—he sent me money to cover my living expenses for an entire year."

"Wow! What brought that on? He was livid about your career just a few weeks ago."

"I don't know. Whatever or whoever it is that's influencing him has my gratitude. My dad's approval means a lot to me. He's even talking about all of us taking a trip to India next year. I don't know if I can go, though. I'm going to be busy." He paused. "I'm hoping I'll be busy."

"Do you generally enjoy your trips to Andhra?"

"Oh yes." He licked the coffee off his lips, drawing my attention to his remarkable mouth. "I love visiting the extended family. Since we're considered special guests from America, they pamper us. They treat me like a prince over there."

"I bet you love playing the role, Roger. And I'm sure you eat all your relatives out of house and home."

His eyes danced with mischief. "All the old ladies pinch my cheeks and call me cute names like *puttu,* meaning little boy."

"I know what it means."

"They insist on feeding me by the truckload."

"And you have no problem eating all that and keeping your digestive system in order?"

"What's the point in going all the way to India if you can't eat and suffer a little Montezuma's Revenge? Or should it be called Gandhi's Revenge?"

I couldn't help chuckling. "You're incorrigible, Vadepalli."

"That's what they tell me," he said with a cocky grin. Swirling the coffee around in his cup, he sobered, then changed the subject. "So, what did you think of that wedding we observed?"

I felt a tiny stab in my side. Had he noticed my wistful expression earlier? "What about it?"

"Wasn't that nice, watching two young people tie the knot?"

Oh dear, he *had* read my mind. "My goodness, Vadepalli," I said, trying to make light of it, "don't tell me you're getting sentimental all of a sudden."

"I am a sentimental guy, Soorya. I may not look like it, but I am."

"This is *me* you're talking to, Roger," I reminded him.

"I mean it. I want to get married just like those two people someday and have a couple of kids that climb all over me and put their sticky fingers on my face and call me Daddy."

The stab in my side suddenly felt like an all-out assault on my body. I could clearly picture a couple of cherub-faced kids with their dad's captivating cinnamon eyes and silky hair. With his laid-back attitude and capacity for fun and laughter, Roger would probably make a marvelous dad, too. "I didn't realize you felt that way. I thought marriage was just a convenient arrangement to you—a way to have someone finance your project."

He downed the last of his coffee and sat back in his seat with his arms folded over his chest. "Nothing wrong in combining the practical with the sentimental, is there? That's exactly how Indian marriages work most of the time. Haven't you noticed? My parents have an excellent marriage and apparently so do yours. They were matched up for very pragmatic reasons and yet they've found love and long-term happiness."

"The romance is missing, though," I argued, although privately I agreed with his views.

"Believe me, they have their own kind of romance. They take good care of each other and stick together through the rough times. To me that's more romantic than flowers, champagne, and candlelight." He smiled. "Although I must confess I have a weakness for all those trappings myself. They can be fun."

"Speaking from experience?" How many women had he wined and dined and seduced by candlelight? I wondered.

"Yes," he replied, leaning forward to look in my eyes, making my nerves jump. "How many couples our parents' age can you find in that blissfully married state these days?"

"Not very many," I admitted.

"Our parents have it pretty good. I couldn't wish for better myself."

"Hmm." Good thing he wasn't a lawyer I'd have to go against at any point. He'd wear me down within minutes.

"If you ask me, it's the best kind of marriage there is," he continued, "where you go in with eyes wide open—there's not much chance of surprises and disillusionment later. It prevents unnecessary bickering and ending up in the divorce courts."

"You may have a point," I conceded.

He drew several dollar bills from his pocket and put them on the table, making Govinda's tip very generous. "I see a lot of couples building their marriages purely on sexual attraction, and a year or two later, boom, they're drifting apart. All the romance goes out the door."

My eyes went wide. "You, of all people, lecturing me on the practical aspects of life, Roger? You're the guy who gave up the chance for med school and every other sensible profession to become a playwright with a dubious future."

"I know I'm a dreamer in many ways, but I'll give it my best shot. If it doesn't work, I'll go join my dad's business." He shrugged. "I know my limits. By the same logic, I know a good marriage is based on both the sentimental as well as the humdrum."

I gave his words some thought. Damn, but he was right, and once again his ideas seemed to coincide with mine. "What about your sister, Roger? How did she meet her husband?"

"Semi-arranged," he replied. "Uday's parents and mine arranged for them to meet, just like you and I met—an old-fashioned Telugu bride viewing. Theirs turned into a success story. Uday and Renu went out a few times." His lips curved fondly as he recalled something from his sister's past. "Uday put the moves on my sister pretty quickly. Four or five dates and Renu was in love with the guy."

"No kidding?" I liked to hear sweetly romantic stories like that. It reaffirmed my faith in arranged love.

"Why would I kid you? They've been married for six years and they still hold hands and kiss when they think no one's looking. They don't have any babies yet, much to my mom's disappointment, but that's because Renu is too damn busy with her career. Mom's been on her case about the biological clock and all that female stuff."

"Are you and your sister close?"

"Sure. We sort of grew apart when we were teenagers. You know how it is—different interests, different universities. But as adults I think we've gotten closer than we ever were. You could even say we're friends."

I envied him for having a sibling who was also a friend. I'd always wanted a sister or brother. "How old is your sister?" I asked.

"Thirty-three. Two years older than I am."

I wondered if he'd thrown that last part in just so I'd know how old he was. But it was heartening to know that such arranged marriages still worked, in this day and age, and in this liberated American culture. "So, you think you'll find that kind of relationship for yourself someday?" I waited with my hands clasped under the table.

He nodded. "I do—if I go about it the right way and take things slowly, one step at a time." He gazed at me, his eyes turning darker. "I'm an optimist, Soorya. Haven't you noticed?"

I exhaled the breath I'd been holding in. The intense expression in his eyes made me look away. When we stood up, wished Govinda good night, and walked out of the café, I had this uneasy feeling in the pit of my stomach. It seemed like Roger was talking about *us* in some circuitous way.

I wanted to believe Roger, but then he hadn't mentioned the two of us specifically. Most likely he'd given up on me. I deserved it, of course, since I'd been prickly and self-righteous from the beginning. It was true that we now got along well, but that still didn't make him an ideal husband. Did one step at a time mean he was going to try and prove himself to me, or to some other woman?

As we started to walk toward the subway station, once again sharing the umbrella, but this time without Roger's arm around me, I wished I could accept things as they were. What did it matter that Roger wasn't going to make money for a long, long time? I earned a substantial income and my parents were wealthy. Besides, as their only child I stood to inherit their estate when they were gone. And Roger was the only son of even wealthier parents. He was rich in his own right.

Marriages of convenience happened in India all the time, where a well-to-do wife supported a husband oftentimes. As long as he was a good man, the marriage worked, and in many cases, worked well.

If I married Roger, I'd have a heck of a lot more than those women in India. He was good-looking, bright, generous, and I was attracted to him like a moth to flame. So why did I feel this slight reluctance? I wanted him—and yet some invisible force pulled me back.

Sometimes, the same analytical mind that made me a good attorney also proved to be my worst enemy. I frequently analyzed things to death. Maybe seeing him succeed as a playwright would make me see him differently. I'd have to give it some thought. And time.

Roger interrupted my musings when he said, "Tired?"

"I've had a long day." I realized we'd arrived at the station.

We found an empty bench to sit on while we waited for our train. At this time of the night, the trains were few and far between. The station was quiet, too. "I know what you mean. I'm looking forward to a hot shower and some sleep." He looked at me. "So, what plans do you have for the weekend?"

I shrugged. "I'm playing it by ear. Maybe I'll get together with some friends for drinks tomorrow. How about you? Are you working?"

He stifled a yawn. "I work seven days a week. Many of my cast members have other jobs, so they can spare more time for rehearsing on weekends." Then he did something that stole my breath. Reaching out, he pulled my head onto his shoulder. "The train's not due for another twenty minutes, so rest your head and relax, Soorya."

I let myself slump against him and closed my eyes. Roger's parka was still a bit damp and smelled of his signature after-shave mixed in with a hint of coffee absorbed from the café. His shoulder and arm were warm and firm.

The feeling was both sweetly satisfying and pleasant. It was right there, with other simple joys like the aroma of brownies baking, a bowl of Mom's *rasam,* a thick comforter on a cold night, and the sun rising above the red-gold trees in our back-yard on a fall morning.

I smiled to myself. After accusing Roger earlier, it was I who was now turning sentimental. But it had been that kind of evening. Roger had been a delightful companion.

To top it all, he'd displayed a hint of jealousy for Satish. That was the emotional equivalent of a dollop of whipped cream quivering atop a chocolate sundae.

Did I really want this for the rest of my life? And at the moment, was Roger experiencing the same feeling I was?

Chapter 19

After that hike-in-the-woods meeting, Lou and I met a few more times. Since his office was too cramped, most of the time he traveled to Manhattan. My client was adamant about increasing the number of homes, and the bureaucrats were fighting it. It kept both Lou and me sparring gently, but it also kept us both in business.

By then we had become friends, having learned to set aside our business differences and enjoy talking about a variety of things. We were both football fans, we liked Italian food, and we appreciated the same kind of music. Although when it came to movies and books, we differed, but then it was fun to compare notes.

However, I could sense something else developing between us. I couldn't say what. More and more, Lou's eyes had been taking on a different look.

I'd caught him staring at me a number of times, his expression hungry, filled with speculation. I'd never had a man look at me like that before. Satish's expression hadn't been this blatantly lascivious.

During my third trip to Pemberton, he took me canoeing on Oswego Lake. I stayed with a girlfriend in Cherry Hill on a Tuesday night so I could meet Lou at dawn on Wednesday—a day the forecast called for sunny skies and reasonably decent temperatures.

Getting out of bed when it was still pitch dark and freezing

cold outside was mild torture for me, but I didn't want to disappoint Lou. He had his heart set on showing me the magnificence
of Oswego Lake on a fall morning.

We started at daybreak to catch the sunrise shimmering over
the lake. As Lou had promised, it was breathtaking, with the
mist rising from the bogs, reminiscent of scenes from *Phantom
of the Opera*.

The canoeing was quite an adventure, with my nonexistent
rowing skills and fear of what lay in the murky depths of the
lake. But I had to admit the trip across the swampy water was
an education in itself. I'd never seen anything like this wild and
primitive beauty—much less experienced it.

It was almost spiritual—enough to restore one's faith in God.

The endless expanse of pine trees, the smell of the reed-filled
swamps, and the near silence were in direct contrast to the
sounds and sights of Manhattan. We went only a short distance
down the lake and returned, since we were both working that
day. The outing was part of educating me about the Pinelands,
as Lou chose to phrase it. And we'd accomplished it well before
the start of our workday.

After we returned to the shore, Lou loaded the rented canoe
on top of his Explorer and anchored it down. Then we had a
picnic breakfast of bagels and fresh fruit. It was freezing cold
beside the lake and I was bundled up in a down parka, wool
scarf, and insulated gloves.

The lakefront was deserted at this time of year. Early morning birds were out in large flocks, foraging for food. We threw
them bagel bits and then talked for a while. Looking at my
watch, I realized it was time to head back. Thank God! My
teeth were beginning to chatter.

I stood up and rubbed my hands together. "Let's head back,
Lou. It's too cold here and we've got work to do, remember?"

Lou smiled and rose to his feet. "There's a way to warm up
without going back."

"What way is that?" I asked in a hoarse murmur as he closed
the gap between us. I could sense the electricity in the air. It was
something live and palpable—pleasant yet frightening.

This was a conflict of interest, I told myself. We were working on opposite sides. We should have been arguing with each other, not getting closer. Besides, Lou was out of my league, slightly older than me, a man from a different world.

It was all wrong. And yet, out there in the woods, in a concealed spot amongst the majestic pines, overlooking Oswego Lake and the graceful aquatic birds, he put his beefy hands on my shoulders and kissed me, gently, softly, first on my forehead, then on my cheeks, and finally on my mouth.

I froze. This was my first kiss! A thirty-year-old woman who'd never experienced a real kiss was an aberration in America, but that's what I was. I stood there, scared stiff and speechless, my legs feeling like they'd give out any second.

Lou didn't do any more than press his lips to mine, but I started to tremble. Something stirred inside me, but I didn't know how to respond. Despite all the pretend kissing I'd done in my fantasies, I was a moron when it came to the real thing.

Was I supposed to open my mouth? That would mean his tongue would be touching mine. Oh boy! But then, that's how a kiss was supposed to be—a melding of tongues and teeth and lips and saliva—if the romance novels and movies were to be believed.

Gently pushing away from Lou, I thrust my unsteady hands in my pockets. I had no idea how to handle a situation like this. "I—I can't do this, Lou."

"I'm sorry, Soorya," he said. "I didn't realize you'd never been kissed before."

Oh hell, was my inexperience that obvious? I kept my eyes on the ground and hoped the heat suffusing my face didn't show. "I told you I've never dated anyone."

"I should've remembered. I'm sorry."

"It's not your fault. You're probably laughing at me, a grown woman and a professional who doesn't know how to handle a little physical contact."

"I think it's rather refreshing."

"What?" Surely he was kidding.

"I don't know any American woman who's even a virgin at your age, let alone remain untouched."

I stole a glance at him. He wasn't laughing. "So you don't think it's pathetic or laughable?"

"Not at all." He was frowning now. "You're not mad at me for coming on to you like that, are you?" He sounded uncertain, not at all like the bold, confident male who'd pressed his mouth to mine only moments ago.

"No, I'm not mad."

He sighed with obvious relief. "I thought I was setting myself up for a sexual harassment suit." This time his eyes glinted with humor. "It's a dangerous thing to do when it involves a powerful attorney from the city."

At the look on his face I burst into laughter. "You needn't worry on that score, Lou. I haven't had enough experience to distinguish between a plain old pass and sexual harassment. I'm a neophyte—literally an innocent babe in the woods."

He grabbed me by the arm and turned me around. "In that case, I'd like to teach you the difference." He was smiling.

"Oh yeah?" I grinned at him, although my insides were still a bit shaky. I wasn't good at flirting and didn't know how to play the game. Coyness had never come to me naturally.

"Yeah," he replied and let go of my arm. "But some other time, when you're a bit more comfortable being with me. Right now I feel like a lecher, trying to take advantage of a chaste and naïve young woman."

Chaste, innocent, naïve—they were all adjectives that had never been used to describe me. "Can I ask you something personal, Lou?"

"Sure." Lou was chewing on a mint and staring at something in the distance.

I wasn't sure if he appreciated my prying into his private life, but I was curious. It was my nature. "The first time we met and went to the Italian restaurant, you were so open about your marriage and the loss of your wife—basically your whole life. But when I looked at Lynne's photograph on your desk that time in your office, you clammed up. Did I do something wrong?"

Lou continued to stare at nothing for another moment, making me wonder if he'd tell me to go mind my own business. He had every right to do so.

But then he turned to me and lifted a hand to cup my face. "You did nothing wrong, Soorya. When you arrived that day in your jeans and college sweatshirt, you looked incredibly young and attractive, and I felt something I hadn't felt in a long time—not since Lynne passed away."

I frowned at him, puzzled.

"All of a sudden, the block of ice in me was thawing," he said. "It was nice to *feel* something positive after a year of pain followed by numbness. But I also felt guilty—like I was betraying Lynne in some way."

"I had no way of knowing that."

Lou removed his hand from my face and looked away. "Then when you started to stare at Lynne's picture, I felt worse, because I was tempted by the woman who was gazing at my dead wife's picture."

It all made sense now. Why hadn't I thought that perhaps Lou Draper was interested in me back then? I found the answer to that. I had never come across anyone who'd been attracted to me. I had no idea how to read the signs if they smacked me in the face, and no clue about how to behave around a man who was making a pass at me.

Perhaps I'd expected there'd be some sort of pheromones I'd sense, or signals that would make a man's attention as obvious as bells ringing or red flags flying. I was the poor little rich girl who didn't know the difference between a friend and an admirer. How pathetic was that?

So, why wasn't I feeling elated at Lou's explanation? I'd finally heard the words that most every woman in America had likely heard many times. Instead I felt somewhat deflated. The very first man who'd clearly expressed interest in me was a widower who still carried a torch for his dead wife, a man who knew very little about my private life.

Satish hadn't asked me out despite what Roger called his drooling. Roger himself was dancing around the issues of romance and marriage, and calling me his *friend*. So that left only Lou.

I smiled at Lou. "I don't know what to say. This is a first, so you'll have to forgive me."

We turned around to return to his vehicle. "Don't worry, kid. You're young and sweet and pretty. You'll figure it out soon enough."

"Thanks," I said with some relief. Sweet and pretty? I knew my looks had improved over the last year, but I hoped Lou wasn't suffering from vision problems or something. But then, I remembered Roger calling me pretty lady when we'd visited the temple. Two men saying the same thing?

I guess I was looking pretty good these days.

As we drove back, I thought about what Lou had just said. It was comforting to know that he was still a friend, that he wasn't offended by my lack of response.

After we returned to his office, we worked on the final details of the case. My client could build eighteen homes and would get most everything else they wanted.

Thanks to Lou's persistence and persuasive powers, my first major case was working out rather well. Coupled with my luck in the Seattle case, my career was definitely inching upward. During our latest Monday morning staff meeting, Mac and Al had made some glowing comments about me.

At noon, Lou and I ate lunch at the same deli we'd been to during my first trip. Back in Lou's office, as I started to pack my briefcase, my cell phone rang.

Pulling the phone out of my jacket pocket, I saw Mom's cell number flashing. She never called me unless it was an emergency. I hit the talk button. "Mom?"

Mom's voice sounded strained—so unlike her usual one. "Soorya, we have a problem."

"What is it?"

"It's Pamma. I had to call an ambulance."

"What happened to Pamma?" I asked, feeling my stomach muscles tightening.

"All of a sudden she couldn't breathe well."

My own breath quickened. "Where are you now?"

"I'm in the hospital emergency room." Mom paused. "I hope she's not going to die."

"Have you called Dad yet?"

"He's in surgery, so I left a message. He could be in it for hours. You know how it is with his work."

"I know." Poor Mom was alone and frightened. "How about Leela or Meera? You want me to call one of them?" Leela and Meera were her best friends and lived close enough to get to the hospital within minutes.

"Leela is in India. Meera is working. I can't disturb her at her office."

Mom was right. "Listen, I'm on my way. I'll get there as soon as possible." I groped for the right words to get her to calm down, but couldn't. "Which hospital?"

"North Jersey Medical Center."

I knew where it was. "I'll be there in about two hours. Have you called Aunt Pallavi yet?" When Mom said yes, I added, "Hang in there, Mom. I'll see you soon." I slipped the phone back in my pocket.

Lou, who'd been listening to the conversation, put a hand on my arm. "Your grandmother?"

I nodded, trembling with fear. Pamma had never suffered more than a cold or the flu since she'd come to live with us. She'd always displayed a tolerant attitude, excellent posture, and good health. And now she could be dying.

In spite of my efforts to keep my emotions under control, the sobs rose in my chest, squeezing it to the point of causing physical pain. "Oh, Lou, she could die."

It seemed only natural for Lou to put his arms around me. "Shh, I'm sure she'll be all right, Soorya."

"But she's never been this sick. When her cold wasn't going away, and her sniffling and coughing were getting worse in the last few days, I should have realized something was wrong."

"It's not your fault, honey. You're not a doctor."

"But my dad's a first-class doctor. Why didn't *he* notice something?" I was crying all over Lou's shirt and making wet stains. But he didn't seem to mind, and continued to hold me. I probably looked all swollen-eyed and unsightly. I wished I could cry like the women on the soap operas—look helplessly pretty and achingly feminine, all at the same time.

"These things happen sometimes . . . and your father's a busy man," said Lou in a clumsy effort to comfort me. All of a sudden, he said, "Give me your car keys."

"Why?"

"I'll drive you to the hospital."

Blowing my nose into a tissue, I shook my head at him. "You can't drive me all the way to Hackensack. How will you get back?"

"I can take a train."

His words dragged me back to my senses. "Lou, I can't impose on you. You'll have to change trains a couple of times to get back."

"I know that," Lou agreed.

"Even if you return by train, how will you get here from the train station to pick up your car?" I argued, zipping up my parka. "Don't worry about me. I'm capable of driving."

Lou shrugged into his jacket. "I have friends who can pick me up at the station." He grabbed my arm and nudged me out into the hallway. "Don't argue, Soorya. You're in no shape to drive. What if you got into an accident? Your parents already have one emergency to deal with."

Without further thought I handed over my car keys to Lou and followed him out.

Lou made a phone call to his office in Trenton and had a whispered conversation, probably with his boss, then had a word with someone about getting a ride from the train station to his office sometime that evening. We started out after that.

Several minutes later, as we merged onto the New Jersey Turnpike, I realized Lou was right. I was not fit to drive on the crowded highway. Guilt clawed at me as I thought about how I was flirting in the woods with Lou while my grandmother was gasping for breath.

I still couldn't wrap my head around the fact that Pamma was in a hospital emergency room. Could my hardy grandmother really be sick? Sick enough to die?

The traffic was annoyingly heavy, and it was more than two hours before I could call Mom for a status update and tell her we were getting close to the hospital. Unfortunately her voice mail came on. She had probably shut her phone off to comply with hospital policy.

I left her a message, hoping she'd be checking her voice mail regularly. With me navigating, Lou got us to the hospital. He dropped me off at the emergency entrance and drove off toward the visitors' parking area.

The blood pounding in my head, I ran all the way to the waiting room and found Mom sitting on one of the chairs, still as a rock. There were several other people scattered around, most of them looking somber and anxious. One little toddler sat on the floor amidst an assortment of wooden building blocks while his mother watched. Every one of these people looked like he or she was waiting for news of someone.

My heart crumpled at the sight of my perpetually cheerful mother with tearstains on her cheeks, her hair disheveled. She was staring at the opposite wall. The instant she noticed me, she shot up from the chair and gave me a hard hug. "I'm so glad you're here."

"How's Pamma?"

"They've put her on antibiotics and oxygen. They tell me she's breathing a little better."

Thank God she was still alive. "Have you seen her yet?"

Mom nodded. "Only for a minute. Dr. Shapiro says she'll be okay." Mom broke down into quiet tears. "I should have taken better care of her."

"What are you talking about, Mom? You take excellent care of her."

Mom shook her head. "But I should have insisted on taking her to Dr. Shapiro sooner."

Now that I knew Pamma was improving, a sudden surge of strength seemed to flow into me. I held my tiny mother in my arms and whispered, "She's going to be fine." I knew what was eating away at Mom. She felt guilty because Pamma now lived with us and she was Mom's responsibility.

In the old-fashioned Indian tradition, the daughter-in-law was expected to care for her in-laws, even more than her own parents. Anything less was considered dishonorable.

I led Mom to a brown vinyl couch and sat down with her. "Mom, don't blame yourself for this. Pamma's a stubborn old woman and refuses to see a doctor. She won't even take conventional medicines. She's been treating herself with *Amrutanjan* and sugar-coated homeopathic pills."

My temper stirred at Pamma for putting Mom through all this agony. But in the next instant I pictured my grandma with an intravenous tube attached to her arm and an oxygen tube in her nose and the anger drained away.

I loved that obstinate old woman and I wanted her to bounce back. Along with Mom and Dad, she formed my three-pronged anchor.

Lou appeared in the door and stood for a moment, perhaps feeling a little out of place. Never having had any real family, this was probably strange for him. But on the other hand, Lynne had been a cancer patient for years, so he had to know the waiting room scene well. I motioned to him to come forward. "Thanks, Lou. I'm grateful for everything."

"Glad to help," he said, handing me the car keys.

Mom eyed him curiously, then turned to me. I introduced them. "Mom, this is Lou Draper, the attorney I was meeting with today. Lou, this is my mom, Vijaya Giri."

They shook hands and I added, "Lou was very kind and drove me here."

"What about your car, Soorya?" Mom asked.

After I explained everything, Mom seemed satisfied and sank into quiet anguish. Lou asked if he could get us something to drink. Mom shook her head. She was too shy to accept anything from a stranger, so I nodded, once again grateful for Lou's thoughtfulness. "Diet Sprite for me and coffee with cream and one sugar for Mom. Only if it's not too much trouble, Lou."

Lou was striding out of the room before I could complete my sentence. To reflect privately for a moment, I rose and walked to the far window. When would I be able to see my grandmother?

At the moment, with my mother on the verge of a meltdown, I felt older than my age, felt I was responsible for her. Although tears were stinging my eyelids, I managed to keep them from spilling.

Until Dad arrived, I was in charge of both Mom and Pamma.

An ambulance, with its strobe lights flashing, came to a grinding stop at the emergency entrance. I watched as the rear doors of the vehicle flew open and a technician jumped out. Two others appeared from somewhere to help him lower a gurney from the vehicle and wheel it into the building. I couldn't see the patient's face—only a figure covered with a blanket.

The uniformed staff ran with the gurney through the glass doors and disappeared inside the building. All of it was accomplished in mere seconds. A sense of urgency encompassed the scene.

Was the person on the gurney dying? Pamma had been rushed here in the same fashion. While many came here to get healed, a great many also died. I said a quick prayer for Pamma. She was a great believer in the strength of prayer.

Hearing the glass doors sliding open behind me, I whirled around and saw Dad striding in. Seeing Mom rise and run straight into Dad's powerful arms and get completely enveloped in them released the tears I'd been holding back. I was free to let my guard down.

Dad released Mom and looked down at her face. "Viju, don't cry, dear. Amma is going to be fine. I just spoke to Shapiro a minute ago. It's a bad case of bronchitis. It happens in elderly people."

"Did you see her yet?" I heard Mom say.

"Oh yes. Shapiro was in and I could talk to him. Amma is coherent and comfortable."

I noted how Mom's shoulders sagged in relief. Her husband was here and she could relax and let him take control. It was clear in her expression and posture. With a tender arm around her shoulders, Dad led Mom back to the couch. I saw Mom nod and listen to Dad's whispered words. She offered him a watery smile.

I couldn't hear what he was saying to her. All I knew was that he was there for her. For me. For Pamma. It was the most profound sense of relief to have my father with us at the moment.

Pulling in a shuddering breath, I watched the two of them interact. It was so natural with them—so instinctive. I rarely saw Mom and Dad touch each other, and yet they were mutually devoted in every sense. Drying my tears with a tissue, I rolled it into a ball and tossed it in a nearby trash can.

This was what I wanted for my future—a husband who'd treat me like Dad treated Mom.

Dad hadn't noticed me standing at the window. He looked surprised at seeing me. "I didn't know you were here, dear." He stood up to give me a hug.

"I just arrived a few minutes ago. I was in south Jersey on business when Mom called."

"Good. Your mom needs you to be here." Without any reference to my swollen eyes he patted me on the back and gave up his seat so I could sit down. "I'm glad I was on my last surgery when I got the message."

Scooting over, I made room for him between Mom and me. "Dad, is Pamma *really* okay?"

"She'll be fine. Once mucus builds up in the lungs of an older person, it's hard to get rid of. It gets infected and turns into bronchitis, even pneumonia." He ran a tired hand over his wide forehead. "It was mostly my fault. Her wheezing and coughing should have made me more aware of her condition." He shrugged helplessly.

"But she's obstinate and won't listen to you or anyone," I supplied in Dad's defense, despite my questioning his perceived negligence earlier. Lou was right. Dad was a busy man and couldn't be expected to protect everyone, especially his stubborn mother who refused help.

I could see a lot of that same mulishness in myself and to some extent in Dad, too. Genes were strange things. "Maybe she'll learn a lesson from this?"

"Nothing like a ride in a speeding ambulance and a hospital bed to put the fear of sickness in an old woman." Dad laid his head back against the wall and shut his eyes for a few moments.

He looked beat. The poor man had been in surgery for hours and then received Mom's urgent message and rushed here directly, not knowing if his dear mother was dead or alive. He was still wearing surgical scrubs under his jacket. Well, at least his feet were clad in regular shoes and not paper booties.

The good thing about Dad's line of medicine was that he rarely had to deal with emergencies—the kind that had him on call at all hours of the day and night. Most of his surgeries were elective and on a planned schedule.

While I thought about Dad rushing here from work, I realized I'd done the same thing. It was late afternoon and I hadn't been in touch with my office. Telling Mom I'd be right back, I headed for the exit—and ran into Lou balancing two foam cups and a can of Sprite.

"I'll be right back. I have to call my office," I said and stepped outside. I explained to Sandy about Pamma and that I might not be able to report to work the next day. Sandy assured me that everything would be taken care of, and I went back inside.

Standing in the waiting room's doorway, I watched as Lou talked to my parents. Lou had forfeited his coffee to Dad. When I got near them, I heard Dad say, "That was very kind of you, Mr. Draper. I'll make sure you get a ride to the station."

"There's no rush, Dr. Giri. I can wait."

We chatted for several minutes, the coffee obviously making Mom feel better. Her tears had dried and she started to take an active interest in what Lou did for a living. "You work for the state government?" she asked, looking like she'd never heard of such a thing. "I didn't realize lawyers worked for any department other than the law-and-justice-related areas."

Lou smiled indulgently. "That's a common assumption, and quite understandable." For a man who'd never had a real mother, he showed remarkable deference toward Mom. "Every state agency has a few lawyers working in some capacity or other. But you're right—it is mostly the justice area that hires attorneys."

While Dad and Mom sipped their coffee, I offered to share my Sprite with Lou, who shook his head. "I'm fine."

Just then Dr. Shapiro appeared and informed us that Pamma had been moved from critical care to a regular room. We were free to visit her. "Family only," he emphasized, throwing a casual glance at Lou.

Mom, Dad, and I spent several minutes with Pamma. She was awake and in good spirits, considering the trauma she'd been through. She even smiled for our benefit.

Pamma needed her rest, so we headed out to the waiting room once again. Lou was sitting by the window, reading a newspaper. He put the paper aside and stood up when he saw us. "Everything okay?"

I nodded. He waited until my parents were seated and motioned to two empty chairs across the waiting room for the two of us to speak privately.

"I feel awful about bringing you all the way here," I said to Lou, "especially now that my grandmother's much better. All that fuss was unnecessary."

"Don't worry, Soorya." He patted my hand. "Just sit back and take it easy."

Taking his advice, I sank deeper into the chair and let my taut muscles relax. I sat in silence for a while, ignoring the people around us, the murmured conversations. It was the calm that came after dealing with an emergency. Exhaustion was catching up with me. A hot shower and bed sounded wonderful. I closed my eyes for one blissful minute.

Lou's next words forced me to open my eyes. "Looks like you guys have a visitor," he said, inclining his head.

Expecting one of Mom's friends, I turned my head in that direction. Every nerve in my body went on full alert, making me sit up. Roger!

Lou gave me a curious look. "Family?"

"No," I replied, my voice sounding hoarse.

Chapter 20

My heart rate shot up at the sight of Roger. So much for sitting back and taking it easy.

He wore his usual jeans, paired with a navy parka. Peeling off his gloves, he shoved them into his pocket and smoothed back his windblown hair with both hands.

After that temple visit, when he'd been all sweet and cute, offered me a flower, put his arm around me, and talked about sentimental things like marriage and love, he hadn't been in touch—not once. In fact, I'd been wondering if I had imagined that episode entirely, the walk to the coffee shop, the topics we'd discussed, the way we'd sat real close at the subway station.

He'd been teasing me.

After weeks of remaining invisible, here he was again, showing up at the worst possible moment. Every time I thought I'd successfully purged him from my system, he managed to sail in again and upset my balance.

I drew a deep breath. Lord help me.

Roger stood beside my parents and I noticed how my mother's mouth puckered into a shocked O when she laid eyes on him. She put a hand over her mouth and said something that appeared curiously like an apology.

Then Roger patted her hand, like he was forgiving her for whatever it was she'd done. What I wanted to know was why

Mom was apologizing, and what was her blunder that Roger had so magnanimously forgiven?

Dad gave Roger an enthusiastic handshake and slapped his back in that buddy-buddy gesture reserved for close friends. I didn't realize Dad even remembered him.

In general, after a suitor had come to our house and left, and then rejected me, Dad usually forgot the name, what the man looked like, or what he did for a living. Mom, on the other hand, remembered every little detail—the boy's height and weight, his vocation, his preferences, phone number, e-mail address, and God knows what other information she considered significant.

Mom belonged to the club that believed in passing along the details of such young men to other Telugu families with marriageable girls. Nothing was ever wasted or cast aside in our community, especially not a precious eligible boy in the marriage market. If he wasn't the right guy for Soorya he'd suit some other girl perfectly, just like trying on clothes at the store. If they didn't fit, one put them back on the rack. They could be perfect for someone else.

Lou must have sensed my prickly vibes. He smiled. "You don't care much for him?"

I shrugged. "He's all right. He . . . he's a friend of the family." What was Roger doing here? Who had notified him of Pamma's illness? Well, there was one way to find out. "Excuse me for a moment, Lou." I strode over to where Roger and my parents were discussing Pamma's condition and cut in, "What brings you here, Roger?"

He turned to me with that amazing smile and my traitorous heart leaped like a dolphin on steroids, then settled with a solid thump. "Soorya, nice to see you again."

His nonchalance was enviable. Roger had this habit of making me glad and angry, elated and irritated, pleased and exasperated, all at the same time. What was it about him that set my teeth and nerves on edge? "You didn't answer my question," I reminded him.

"Rajesh was supposed to have dinner with us this evening," Mom supplied before Roger could reply.

"What was the occasion?" I asked Mom in a bland voice. "I guess you were waiting to tell me after I got home from work?"

"No particular occasion, baby. When Pamma became ill, I forgot everything else." She sent Roger an apologetic look. "Poor Rajesh went to our house and was informed by Juan that we were at the hospital."

"What was the pool guy doing at our house in this weather?" And how convenient for Roger.

"Winterizing our pool." Mom threw me a "duh" look.

"Oh, of course." How could I have forgotten that our swimming pool needed winterizing at this time of year? In any case, why had Mom invited him to dinner and never mentioned it to me? Was she up to her matchmaking tricks again? If so, she was barking up the wrong tree. Roger wanted to be my friend, not my lover.

"Good thing your pool guy was there, or I'd never have known about Pamma and wouldn't have got a lift to the hospital," Roger added. Then he turned to my dad. "Uncle, I'm so relieved to hear that your mother is okay. I was worried when Juan told me that an ambulance had been summoned."

The Guatemalan man who maintained our pool wasn't exactly a friendly individual and spoke very little English, but Roger had managed to talk him into giving him a ride. Was there no end to Roger's charm and resourcefulness? I glanced at him. "How did you talk Juan into giving you a lift?"

"I didn't talk him into anything. Juan is a very nice man. He was just finishing up, so when I told him I'd taken a cab from the train station and had no way of getting to the hospital, he offered me a lift in his truck. We had a long and interesting talk on the way here."

"Juan speaks mostly Spanish." Despite my irritation I felt reluctant admiration for Roger's ability to get a private man like Juan to open up. "How did you manage that long talk?"

"I speak pretty decent Spanish."

"Impressive."

Roger shrugged. "Four years of Spanish in high school and one semester in Barcelona." He smiled. "Juan is an inspiring man."

I raised an eyebrow. "Juan is inspiring *because?*"

"Did you know he has four kids and the two oldest ones are in America's top universities?"

Mom nodded enthusiastically. "Carlos is at MIT and Maria is at Brown. The younger two are doing just as well in high school. Juan is so proud of his kids."

I should have known that despite her zero knowledge of Spanish, Mom would manage to break through Juan's reserve and get him to tell her his life story. No wonder he'd stuck with us for over a decade.

Talk of achievements reminded me that Lou was sitting there, entirely alienated from this cozy family scene. He was a talented and tenacious man, too. I turned around and gestured to him to join us. I noticed the reluctance with which he approached. "Lou, come meet Roger Vadepalli, a friend of the family. Roger, this is Louis Draper. He's an attorney with the Department of Environmental Protection."

"Pleased to meet you, Mr. Draper." Roger offered his hand to Lou. "And my name is Rajesh, by the way. Soorya insists on calling me Roger. As a joke, of course."

"Please call me Lou." Lou sounded grave, almost curt.

The underlying tension between the two men was palpable despite the handshake.

I remembered the first time Lou and I had met, when he'd told me "Mr. Draper" made him feel like an old man. Roger, with his long hair and lean, boyish physique, had to make him feel old. I had a feeling Lou's instincts told him there was more to my reaction to Roger's appearance than plain surprise.

He was sizing up Roger in that studious manner he had of evaluating something. I'd come to know that look well. He gave legal documents as well as individuals the same kind of penetrating gaze that meant his brain was computing facts.

There was something intense about Lou at the moment that made me uneasy, so I said, "Lou, it's getting late. I'd better drive you to the train station."

"Good idea." He looked at his wristwatch. "Just about rush hour—there should be plenty of trains available."

While I put on my coat and fished the car keys out of my purse, Lou said good-bye to Mom and Dad. They thanked him profusely for all his help.

Dad eyed Lou with the merest hint of suspicion—something so subtle that only I could sense it. A mild bolt of panic shot through me. Had he guessed that Lou had kissed me earlier? Dad was sharper than his Swiss-made scalpels. I could swear Dad was capable of reading minds and seeing through human brain tissue as if it were transparent glass.

Roger bid Lou good-bye with another handshake. But I noticed the smile was absent. There was a hardness in his expression that I'd never seen before—not even when Satish had shown interest in me. With some reluctance Lou took Roger's hand—in silence, dark eyes still watchful.

There was definitely hostility between the two men. I sensed that it had to do with me. How about that? I reflected. Two good-looking men having a mental duel over me. Nevertheless the negative energy was making me edgy.

"Okay, let's go." I rushed Lou out of there as quickly as I could. Lou had told me earlier that he'd parked my car in the multilevel parking garage.

As we rode the elevator up to the garage's third level, Lou folded his arms across his middle in that now-familiar gesture and raised his eyebrows at me. "So, what are we running from, Counselor? I don't recall hearing fire alarms or orders to evacuate the building."

The elevator doors opened and I spotted my car right away. "I didn't want you to miss the train," I said, marching toward my car. "Besides, your friend may not appreciate picking you up at the station at some ungodly hour."

"Okay." Lou's tone conveyed that he didn't believe one word

I'd said. Nonetheless he opened the passenger side door, settled back in his seat, and secured his seat belt. Pulling out a roll of mints from his pocket, he offered me one and moved on to a safer subject. "Any idea when your grandmother is going to be released?"

"No. They want to keep her for at least another day. Right now she's on oxygen and her fever's down, but at her age it could take a little longer for the antibiotics to take effect."

"I hope she goes home soon." Lou kept his eyes glued to the road.

The rest of the ride was quiet. In the station's parking lot I gave him the train schedule I always kept in my glove compartment and thanked him again. "Lou, I don't even know what to say other than thank you so much."

"You're welcome. Glad I could help."

"I'll make it up to you." I had no idea how I was going to do that or when, but the burden of obligation weighed heavily on my mind.

"Don't give it another thought." He leaned over and placed a light kiss on my temple. "Go home and get a good night's rest. I'll call you soon."

All the way back to the hospital I mulled over the way Lou had been studying Roger. I hadn't indicated by word or gesture that Roger meant anything to me. And yet Lou, a man who suddenly appeared more complicated than ever, had been overtly wary of Roger. Beyond wary. He seemed jealous.

Back at the hospital, there was no sign of my parents or Roger in the waiting area, so I made my way to Pamma's room. I discovered all three of them standing around her bed, talking. Pamma looked more comfortable than she had earlier. She was smiling at something Roger was saying to her.

The devil was trying to charm a sick old woman. And I wasn't surprised one bit. That man could charm the shell off a tortoise.

I went in and joined the three of them. A nurse appeared sometime later and informed us that visiting hours were over. So we reluctantly wished Pamma good night. Dad laid a hand on her forehead and asked her to take it easy, while Mom straightened her covers.

Then we walked out of there. My heart felt like a lead ball. Leaving Pamma behind with those tubes stuck into her was awful. She'd never been alone since she'd come to live with us.

Stopping at the door, I turned around for one last look and waved at her. She gave me an encouraging half smile.

Tears welled up in my eyes yet again. She was going to spend the night in a strange bed. Alone.

A warm, reassuring hand descended on my shoulder. "I'll be okay, Dad," I whispered. But it wasn't Dad. It was Roger. It felt good to have him there. And that in itself irritated me.

He put his arm around me as I left the room. Together we walked down the long, fluorescent-lit corridor with waxed linoleum floors, stark white walls, and the smell of disinfectant.

At Dad's suggestion we went to a Mexican restaurant to eat. Dad and Roger traveled in Dad's car and Mom rode with me. Roger and Dad ate with gusto, while Mom and I ate very little.

Pamma weighed heavily on our minds. I could tell Mom was consumed by guilt, although God knows why. We were in a booth and Mom was next to me, so I placed a hand on hers on the red vinyl seat. It felt small and cold.

After the meal, Mom and I drove home. Dad took Roger to the train station. I turned to Mom when we stopped at a red light. "How come you invited Roger to dinner? I didn't realize you knew he lived in the city these days."

Mom hesitated. "Venki and Sharda gave us his address and phone number, so I contacted him."

"Hmm." It made sense. Roger's parents and my family had gotten along well right from the beginning. It was only logical that they should inform my parents about Roger's move to the city. Although, and this brought on a grudging smile, he was capable of taking care of himself. I didn't bother to ask Mom where Roger lived. I didn't want to let on that I was curious.

As soon as we reached home, I went directly to my room. It had been a long and exhausting day, both physically and emotionally. But once I got into bed I lay awake, staring at the ceiling.

Lou's kiss had been disturbing. I kept analyzing it in my mind, and still couldn't decide whether I liked it. The sensation had been pleasant—very pleasant—and yet something was missing. Was I expecting fireworks? I didn't have anything to compare the experience with, so I couldn't say how good or bad it was.

I couldn't discuss it with Amy, either. She had been sexually active for years, and at present she and David were having wild and wonderful sex at every opportunity, so discussing my first kiss at this age was like talking to a teenager about potty training.

Then there was my grandmother, lying in a hospital bed and looking entirely helpless for the first time in my life. What if something went wrong in the middle of the night? What if she was too weak to call for help? Would the nurses get to her in time? But then Dad had assured Mom and me that Pamma was going to be all right, and I trusted his medical judgment.

A little later, I heard the garage door opening and closing, then Dad coming inside the house. I wondered what he and Roger had talked about while they drove to the train station. Was Dad trying to set me up with Roger once again? Was that why he and Mom were so eager to invite him to dinner and treat him like a son?

Chapter 21

Pamma came home three days later. It was a relief to have her back with us. She looked a bit thinner. For the first couple of days she confined herself to her room and Mom carried her meals to her and helped her bathe and dress, but Pamma soon got back into her routine.

However, her unexpected illness had served me a jolt. A woman who'd seemed invincible was very human—and the fear of losing her was real now. I could clearly see it was the same for Mom. She treated Pamma with kid gloves. Dad, being a macho male and a doctor, didn't show it all that much, but I could see he was more solicitous of Pamma now, although very subtly.

The Saturday after Pamma's return was Amy's bachelorette party. Amy and the girls, seven of them in all, arrived at our house that afternoon, since it was centrally located and large enough for everyone. We all went out to a beauty salon and got ourselves manicures and pedicures. We also treated Amy to a full body massage and facial.

That evening, we donned our party dresses. As a luxurious special touch, we had arranged for a limousine to pick us up and transport us to the city and later bring us back.

I was keyed up. It had been a while since all of us had gone to a nightclub together. In our younger days we used to go bar hopping and partying, but now we were all grown women with jobs and responsibilities. Three of the women were now married, and two of them were mothers, but it was still exciting to plan a girls' night out.

Mom seemed out of touch, too, since I hadn't hosted a sleep-over in several years. She looked a bit overwhelmed by eight young women scampering around the house, putting on makeup, fixing their hair, and leaving behind a mess in her sparkling bathrooms.

Being the perfect Indian hostess, Mom kept asking everyone if they wanted something to eat or drink. She looked disap-pointed when they shook their heads and went back to their mascara and hair spray.

At the moment, she was sitting on my bed, watching me put on my makeup. I could tell something was bothering her. I could see her in the mirror, biting her lower lip.

"Don't worry, Mom, we'll get something to eat and drink at the restaurant," I told her.

"It's not right to send away guests on an empty stomach," she grumbled.

"Mom, you did your part by asking them, so stop obsessing about it," I admonished her.

Of course, there were other minor issues that disturbed her. She wouldn't be Mom if there weren't. "Is it safe for decent girls to go to a place where men dance naked?"

I should have known she'd zero in on that. "The men wear shorts; they're not naked." I tried to keep my voice casual. I'd been to strip clubs before, but Mom didn't know about that part of my life. Although I had to admit, the thought of looking at scantily clad men had me slightly breathless and excited.

How many seminude men did I ever get to see, let alone touch?

"But still, they wear thongs or something like that, so they're mostly naked, right?" Mom argued. "Even the name of the club, Monk's Hunks, sounds a bit suspicious."

"The owner's last name is Monk, Mom. It has nothing to do with a monastery. It's a popular place and lots of women go there. It's very safe."

"Why couldn't you choose a nice Indian restaurant where

they play elegant music and serve a nutritious buffet? Leela told me about that new restaurant on Fiftieth Street. She says it is really nice and trendy. It has disco dancing and fusion cuisine. Even your non-Indian friends would enjoy that."

I tried hard not to smile. "Mom, nobody has a bachelorette party with *parathas,* fusion curry, and disco dancing to Indian classical music. We have reservations for dinner at a French restaurant and we'll go to the club later at night."

"Okay, but is that naked fellows' club in a safe area at least?" Mom's frown deepened. "All you young and pretty girls out there in some rowdy club with drunkards and predatory men worries me."

Just then Sue walked into the room to borrow my flatiron. A curiously amused look came over her face. She had caught Mom's last remark.

I glanced at Mom in the mirror. "Mom, relax. We're not kids anymore."

"But Manhattan at night can be dangerous, dear. Just the other day I heard Kate's granddaughter got mugged outside a bar in Manhattan. Her shoulder was dislocated and her purse was gone—eighty-three dollars and all credit cards stolen."

"Sorry to hear that," I said. Kate was a senior citizen who volunteered at the local library, which Mom frequented.

"We'll be careful. I promise." I met Sue's amused glance in the mirror. "We're not going to walk anywhere. The limo will drop us off at the front door and pick us up at the same place when we're ready to come home."

Mom's frown eased a little, but she continued to chew on her lower lip for a little while longer before sliding off the bed and walking away. As soon as Sue and I heard Mom's footsteps going down the stairs we started chuckling.

"Your mom has an active imagination," said Sue.

"My mom leads a very sheltered life and thinks Manhattan at night is a jungle filled with murderers and pimps," I explained.

Thank God Dad had stayed away from what he called "girly things" and was watching television downstairs. He was worse than Mom when it came to protectiveness.

Meanwhile Pamma had wisely removed her hearing aid to take a snooze on the family room couch, completely oblivious to the noise on the second floor.

My friends thought Dad was cool, Mom was a doll, and my grandma was adorable. I was glad to hear that. However, I had warned Amy and others who were planning to wear cocktail dresses to put on their long winter coats before going downstairs. An obscene amount of exposed cleavage and thigh would not sit well with my family—mainly Dad.

I wouldn't be surprised if Dad ordered me to stay home and quietly told the other girls to go out by themselves. As things stood right now, everything was going smoothly. The family was pleased that I had offered to open up our home for everyone to gather and get ready for the big night. My parents had known all my close friends for many years and generally approved of them.

As I brushed my hair, I recalled my teenage days when things weren't so harmonious in our house. I was going through my rebellious adolescent years, when I'd thought parents weren't meant to be heard or seen. I had wanted them to disappear into the woodwork whenever my friends were around.

I was ashamed of Mom's department store clothes, her accent, and the strong smell of Indian spices in our home. I was mortified at the gaudy furnishings in our living room and the Hindu gods and goddesses in the small alcove off the kitchen that served as Mom's altar room.

Whenever Dad had insisted on carrying on a conversation with my friends or brought out his movie camera to *create happy memories,* as he called it, I'd wanted to hide in some dark corner. Pamma's saris and her Telugu ways were always a topic for curious questions from my friends—questions I didn't want to answer.

Mom and Pamma's concerns over my spending time outdoors and getting sunburn and consequently making my dark skin even darker had always turned into a major argument in those days.

I recalled one particular Saturday afternoon during summer. Amy and Sue had come by to swim in our pool. I was sixteen years old. Amy and Sue had worn tiny bikinis that left little to the imagination. I was a roly-poly teenager and wore a one-piece outfit that covered as much of me as possible, all the while wishing I could look like the skinny, brown-eyed and brown-haired Amy with the sunny smile, or like the blond, green-eyed Sue—not so skinny, but still cute and vivacious.

One look at the girls' bikinis and Pamma's jaw had dropped. "Oh Lord Venkatesha! Why are your friends not wearing any clothes?"

Dad's mouth had flattened into a grim line. He'd taken me aside for a brief talking-to. "Soorya, is that any kind of attire for your girlfriends? Do their parents know what kind of trashy outfits they're wearing?"

"Dad, it's a bathing suit. And their parents don't mind."

"It's two tiny strips of cloth. They're not exactly five years old."

"It's what all the girls wear, Dad." I had to defend my friends.

"You don't."

I'd glared at my father with my lips quivering, eyelids burning with tears. "I'm too damn chunky to wear a little bikini. If I had the figure, don't you think I'd wear one, too?"

"Over my dead body, Soorya! Even if you lose weight I will not allow you to wear such ridiculous outfits. In our culture, women don't go around exposing their bodies."

"But we don't live in your culture, do we? We live in America." It had given me immense satisfaction to note my father's eyes turn wide with shock. "If you wanted me to wear those stupid saris and *salwar-kameez* outfits, you should have lived in India, not in New Jersey."

Before my stunned dad could say another word, I'd turned on my chubby heel and dashed out of there, only to bump into Mom.

She'd obviously heard everything. She'd held me by the shoulders and looked at me with such visible pain in her eyes that I'd let my eyes drop. The basset hound look used to get to me even in those days, when mutiny stirred in my veins. "How could you say such hateful things to your father, Soorya?"

"He started it," I'd pouted defensively.

"He loves you, dear. He wants what's best for you."

"No, he doesn't. If he did, he wouldn't be so mean. He wants everyone to dress like little Telugu girls. And he hates my friends. I'll never ask them to come here again. Ever!" With the dreaded tears streaming down my cheeks, I'd run to the bathroom, allowed my emotions to settle over the next several minutes, and then gone out and joined my friends in the pool like nothing unusual had transpired between my parents and me.

I'd have died before I'd let them see what was going on. It was bad enough that I looked different from them—the last thing I needed was to make it obvious that our language and dress and culture were different, too.

When Amy had asked me why my eyes and nose looked red and swollen, I'd told her my allergies were acting up.

Later that afternoon, Mom had insisted on making mango *lassi* for my friends—a yogurt shake made with mango juice. Amy had wrinkled up her small, tip-tilted nose. "What's this? It smells funny." Sue had bravely ventured to take a sip but grimaced. "It's got a weird taste." That was the end of the *lassi*-drinking session.

Mortified yet again, I'd marched up to Mom. "Why didn't you just give them soda or punch or something American?"

Mom had cringed and picked up the glasses, then brought out cans of soda along with chocolate chip cookies and potato chips. She had quietly put away the chicken *samosas* she'd made as a special treat for my friends.

There had been other instances like that one, where I'd shot my mouth off and insulted my parents and grandmother. I had seen Mom shedding tears over my hurtful words and Dad consoling her. "She's only going through a phase, Viju. She'll come around soon."

I had heard Pamma complain that this American culture was ruining me. "Who will marry a girl who is behaving like this?

Why she is making her skin look more black when she is already having dark color? Everyone will say she is not suitable for a Telugu boy."

Once again, Dad, the peacemaker, had tried to put Pamma's troubled mind at ease. "She's a typical teenager, Amma. They all do that in this country before they settle down. Just wait and see."

I hadn't experienced much guilt at what had occurred during those tempestuous arguments, not until I was nearly twenty years old. It was a shameful way to treat a warm and caring family. Appreciation for what I had with my parents and grandma had begun to sink in much later, after a year or two of college, after I'd had a chance to see some of the real world, the dysfunction that plagued so many families, the poverty that forced some students to work two jobs to put themselves through college, the bleakness that existed outside my comfortable home.

Furthermore, some of my closest friends had been hit hard. Amy's parents had gone through a bitter divorce during our sophomore year, leaving Amy to envy me. Jen's mother had been diagnosed with multiple sclerosis and eventually ended up in a wheelchair. My roommate's father had died, leaving the family with a failing business and such staggering debts that she had to quit college and work as a clerk at the age of nineteen.

Every one of those incidents had served as a tough lesson to me. I had it good.

Eventually, realizing how blessed I was, I had come to love and appreciate my parents. Pamma was an added blessing. She, too, in many ways, had been a pain in the rear in my teenage days, when she'd made me say Sanskrit prayers each evening before dinner, or wash my feet when I came in barefoot through the door after playing outdoors, or apologize to Mom for insulting her cooking or her clothes.

My worst nightmare was when Pamma forced me to apply all kinds of homemade potions on my face and body to make me fairer. She was obsessed with making my skin lighter. Lately it was those fairness creams that were all the rage in India that she insisted on giving me, but at least they came in plastic tubes and smelled pleasant. I even made an effort to use the Fair and Fabulous cream.

I still argued with my parents and Pamma over various things, but essentially I'd come to see their point of view to a large extent. I had come to a phase in my life when I was proud of my Indian-ness, my sweet little mom, my big and smart and somewhat famous dad, and even my deaf grandmother. Where would I be without them?

Forcing my mind back to the present, I looked at the bedside clock. Time to go. I shrugged into my coat, picked up my purse, and announced to the girls that the limo would arrive in fifteen minutes.

Slowly they all emerged from the various rooms, and one by one we went downstairs, like a parade of beauty pageant contestants, with me in the lead, and Amy, the lady of the hour, bringing up the rear.

We all had our coats buttoned up, so nobody could see above our knees, although most of us were clad in decent enough dresses. But I was glad Amy was wearing a calf-length coat. It covered her black minidress with sequined spaghetti straps, practically no back to speak of, and a front that left half her breasts spilling over like ripe mangoes.

Mom stood at the foot of the staircase and clapped her hands, eyes aglow behind her glasses. "Oh my, how lovely you girls look!"

Perhaps hearing her excited words, Dad ventured out of the family room and stood with his arms crossed. "Well now, isn't this a sight for sore eyes! You girls better be careful, or someone might kidnap you or something."

I gave Dad a friendly punch in the arm. "Get the ransom ready."

Dad took the joke with a chuckle, went back to the family room, and promptly came out with his camcorder, dragging Pamma out at the same time to watch the procession of beauties.

Pamma ground her dentures and announced, "All of you are

looking very beautiful." She turned serious after that. "The bride might get the evil eye, no?" Then she instructed Mom to do something about that evil eye in whispered Telugu.

"Amy, stay where you are, I'll be right back," said Mom and hurried to the kitchen.

Amy looked at me, one perfectly tweezed eyebrow raised, so I explained, "Some old-fashioned ritual. She'll wave a pinch of salt and a chili pepper in front of your face, then throw it in the flames on the stove. It's supposed to ward off the evil eye." Dad grinned at Amy and I winked at her. "Just stand there and look pretty until she's done."

Mom came out with the salt and chili and waved it before Amy three times in clockwise circles and then returned to the kitchen to dispose of it.

Dad had his camcorder recording that and the rest of us. He made us go back upstairs and come down the steps once again, very slowly, then smile and gather in the living room—smile and stand by the front door—and smile again so he could add to his *happy memories.*

For the next three decades I'd probably be subjected to viewing a DVD of myself descending the stairs in high heels and a black coat and a happy smile on my face.

While we posed for the last group shot, Pamma cautioned us, "All of you come home before it gets too much dark outside, okay?"

We all nodded obediently. There was no point in reminding her that it had turned dark hours ago. We'd be returning home closer to sunrise.

The doorbell rang. Our limo had arrived.

Chapter 22

The French restaurant was a small and pleasant but modestly priced eatery only a block from the strip club. Since we were splurging on Amy's shower gift and the luxury of a limousine, we'd decided to keep the dinner relatively affordable.

A small bearded man opened the restaurant's door and welcomed us in with a gracious bow, making it look as authentic French as it could be in the middle of Manhattan.

Since the manager had been warned that ours would be a chattering, noisy group of young women celebrating a special occasion, she'd reserved for us a table in a remote corner with muted lighting.

There would be plenty of drinking later at the club, so we decided to skip alcohol and go straight to the food. I drooled over much of the rich fare listed on the menu before I settled on a dish made of zucchini, cauliflower, and mushrooms cooked in white wine. It was their only vegetarian entrée.

Everyone else ordered seafood, meat, or poultry laden with butter, cream, wine, and cheese—heavenly dishes that I could only dream of.

We were having a fantastic time until halfway through the dinner. Just as I was popping a piece of zucchini into my mouth I noticed a couple being shown to a table across the room.

Oh no! Roger and a young blond woman were just getting seated. Was he following me, or what? Wherever I went lately, there was Roger—even in this little French restaurant where I'd least expected him. Was there some kind of conspiracy going on here, with fate bringing him and me together constantly? Why else would he be everywhere I was?

"Of all the damned places!" I didn't realize I'd said that aloud until my friends looked at me curiously and then turned their heads to look at what had me swearing. Then one by one they all turned back to stare at me.

Amy was the first to speak. "Soorya, what's the matter?"

I blinked and took several sips of water. The zucchini was nearly choking me since I'd swallowed the chunk without chewing it. Once I felt it sliding down my throat I coughed and shook my head. "Nothing."

Gretchen threw me a knowing look. "Is it that couple that just walked in?"

I pretended to be inordinately interested in the medley of vegetables on my plate. "I sort of know that guy . . . a little."

Megana glanced at me and quietly went back to eating. Being a fellow Indian-American, she'd probably guessed something out of the ordinary was going on.

She was the same age as I and her parents had been harassing her about getting married, too. Megana and I often traded stories about the guys we met through our respective parents' matchmaking efforts. Sometimes we laughed. At other times we groaned or sighed.

"An old boyfriend?" Sue asked, then turned around and studied Roger again. "It seems he's moved on."

Once the curious looks were over, we went back to eating and chatting, but my cheerful evening was spoiled, and I couldn't even pinpoint the exact reason. So Roger was having French food with a pretty blonde. So what was it to me? Nothing, I told myself. Absolutely nothing. But no matter how many times I repeated that in my mind, the urge to march across the room and tear into the blond woman was clawing at me.

The thoughts swirling in my brain were vaguely familiar. Then it came to me—it was the same emotion I'd experienced when Roger was flirting with Carrie on the day I'd attended the rehearsals for *Mumbai to Manhattan.*

Good Lord, I was jealous! But I couldn't be. I'd never thought of myself as the jealous kind, but here I was, thinking violent thoughts against a woman I'd never seen before. I'd always prided myself on not having a single sadistic bone in my body, and now Roger was making me a crazed, evil person. I hated myself for feeling this way.

Jen, who'd been watching me thoughtfully, nudged me with her elbow. "You feeling all right?"

"I'm fine," I assured her. "A piece of zucchini went down the wrong way." With a forced smile I tried to concentrate on the topic of conversation at our table—Amy's wedding and honeymoon. I plunged into the discussion wholeheartedly. The heck with Roger. I was here to enjoy the party.

Despite my resolve not to let Roger's presence bother me, my eyes went to his table frequently. He was wearing a maroon dress shirt and khakis today, a change from his trademark jeans and sweatshirt. His hair was neatly brushed and his jaw looked smooth, like he'd shaved recently.

So he'd tried to look nice for this woman he was taking out to dinner tonight, and despite his lack of money he was trying to impress her. She must mean a lot to him if he had gone to that much trouble. I wondered where and when he'd met her. Only a few weeks ago he'd claimed he had no friends in this city. From the way he was getting along with that woman, it seemed like he was acquiring new friends rapidly.

He sat at an angle with mostly his back visible to me, but the woman sat facing me and I noticed her smiling at Roger often, laughing a few times, a throaty sound that carried across the room. She seemed to have a habit of flipping her hair back from her face every now and then. It was probably a gesture men considered sexy and adorable. To me it was an attention-seeking mechanism.

Although I couldn't see much of Roger's face, I could tell he was talking a lot. I could see his expressive hands moving, his head thrown back in laughter. It was a good thing he hadn't noticed me. I wasn't in a mood to talk to Roger tonight, not after I'd seen him having a pleasant time with an attractive woman.

A thought struck me then. She could very well be the woman who had financed his play.

The restaurant was crowded and the service was slow, so even after our plates were cleared away, our check hadn't arrived. While we waited, Roger rose to his feet and turned around, started to walk across the room.

I hadn't realized the restrooms weren't too far from where we sat. Hoping the lighting was too dim for him to notice me, I turned to the group and pretended to listen to something someone was saying.

My luck ran out soon enough. A shadow fell across our table and there stood Roger, beaming at me. "Soorya, what a pleasant surprise to see you."

My cheeks warmed instantly. I looked up at him and quirked an eyebrow. "Oh, hello, Roger!" I wasn't sure if my attempt at looking startled had fooled him, but he looked like . . . well, he looked like Roger—friendly, relaxed, happy. "Fancy running into you here."

"Colette suggested this place," he said, inclining his head toward his table. "I must say it's nice. The food's very good."

With all eyes at our table focused on him, I couldn't avoid introducing him. After I'd mentioned all my friends' names, I said, "This is Roger Vadepalli."

He nodded at each of the women in turn before saying, "Ladies, my name is Rajesh, but Soorya prefers to call me Roger." He grinned in a charmingly self-deprecating way. "But it's entirely my fault, because I lied to her about my name the first time we met." With a good-natured shrug he added, "Now she won't let me forget it."

When he put on an expression of mock distress, they all went, "Aww!" He'd done it again. Seven faces were smiling back at him in sympathy.

"So, is this a special occasion? You ladies look very lovely." Roger gazed at them in frank admiration.

And boy, did it work. In roughly one minute my friends finished telling him about the bachelorette party and Amy's approaching wedding. Roger wished Amy good luck and all of us an enjoyable evening. Then he ambled away.

All eyes turned to me. They all started to speak at once. *What a great guy. Isn't he cute? So friendly. How come you don't like him?*

I held up my hand. "All right."

Jen turned her wide baby blues on me. "What's your problem? He seems like a nice guy."

"So why don't you like him?" Sue demanded.

I sighed. "I like him just fine, but he's . . . different, and if I were you, I wouldn't fall for that laid-back charm." The check arrived and one of the girls calculated how much each of us owed. We put our money down, and with a sense of relief I got up and pushed my chair in. "Time to go to the club."

Amy got in the last word. "You've got the hots for him and he's here with another woman. It bothers you, doesn't it?"

"Of course not! What Roger does is none of my business." My face felt hotter than ever. I marched to the coat stand and yanked my coat off the hanger, nearly ripping off the fur collar in the process.

The rest got to their feet and started putting on their coats. I heard at least two voices say, "But his name is Rajesh."

Amy came up to me and whispered in my ear, "It's the guy you met recently, isn't it?"

I nodded and put my coat on. One look at my face and she'd guessed my secret. I was tempted to tell Amy to mind her own business, but managed to keep my mouth shut. It wasn't worth spoiling her evening just because mine wasn't going well.

We walked the single block to the club, a bevy of laughing young women wearing fancy high heels clicking on the sidewalk. It was a cold night but not cold enough to keep the crowds indoors, so there were enough people looking at us curiously.

The chilly air served to cool my temper and warm my feelings toward Amy once again. None of this was her fault.

Being a Saturday night, the strip club was already packed to capacity. Women of all ages, colors, sizes, and ethnicities were there, drinking, laughing, talking. A variety of perfumes mingling with the bitter odor of beer hung in the air.

Although the entertainment was exuberant and exciting, with a bunch of hunks gyrating to keep the women screaming, stomping, and whistling, my thoughts kept wandering to Roger and Colette. Had he gone to her place after dinner, or had he taken her to his apartment? Were his long hands all over her creamy white body?

I knew my mind was traveling to disturbing places, but I couldn't help it. I wanted Roger next to me. I wanted his hands all over me. Did he have a sprinkling of dark hair over his chest just like he did on his arms? Was he a good kisser?

Where were all these erotic thoughts coming from? All those twisting and undulating men on stage were driving my libido just a little bit nuts. Nuts? I was even beginning to dream up silly puns. What was happening to my mind?

Amy was so right. I had the hots for Roger and I couldn't stand to see him with someone else, and yet, I didn't want him for myself, either. He was still bad husband material. So what did that make me? The proverbial dog in the manger.

After a drink or two, we all went slightly crazy over the hunks. I had to admit they had beautiful, sculpted bodies that made my mouth water. I even tucked several dollar bills into one or two sweaty crotches.

I watched Amy living it up—her last wild party before she turned into a staid and sensible wife. Of course, the Amy I knew could never turn into a staid and sensible anything. But seeing her laugh so much was the only good thing about the evening. Tonight she looked like a Barbie doll in a cocktail dress, her sequined straps barely holding the tiny outfit in place.

This celebration was all for Amy, so I was glad she was having so much fun.

Recalling Mom's earlier concerns about seminaked men, I smiled to myself. I wondered how Mom and Pamma would've reacted if I'd brought them to a place like this. There were a few older women in the crowd and some of them were having a rip-roaring good time.

Mom would have been agape, her enormous eyes unblinking, while Pamma would probably have labeled all this "bad-bad, dirty things" and yanked off her hearing aid and eyeglasses.

I stuck to two glasses of white wine and watched my friends savor a variety of high-calorie cocktails. Fortunately nobody was an irresponsible drinker, so everyone remained relatively sober.

Once it was past the midnight hour, I couldn't wait for the party to end. A headache was beginning to bloom like a tight band around my head, and all I wanted to do was go home to bed.

Some two hours later, when it was all over and the limo dropped us back home, I was relieved to note that all my friends looked alert enough to drive. I was in no mood to have a sleep-over. I stood on the stoop and waved as one by one they climbed into their respective cars and drove away.

"Drive carefully," I reminded them.

Letting myself inside the house, I disarmed the security system, then reset it after locking the door behind me. My head was throbbing. I dragged myself upstairs for aspirin and my bed.

Finding it hard to unwind, I booted up my computer instead of going to bed, and checked my e-mail messages. There was one from Lou: *If you're not doing anything on the Saturday after Thanksgiving, would you like to meet me somewhere? Lou.*

Was it nearly Thanksgiving already? I glanced at the calendar by my desk. Thanksgiving was less than two weeks away. Did I want a rendezvous with Lou? Was he asking me out on a date?

I hesitated, not sure if I wanted a rerun of what had happened in the woods the last time I'd seen Lou, when he'd made it clear that he found me desirable. But then the image of Roger and the pretty Colette popped into my mind. I quickly typed a reply: *Sounds good. What time and where?*

I wasn't sure if I was setting myself up for a load of grief. If I thought Roger wouldn't fit into my life, Lou was even more of a misfit. Having an affair with Lou was like playing with fire. However, I'd always been a goody two-shoes, mostly because fate had dictated it, while I'd observed my friends and acquaintances living on the edge. I hadn't been offered the chance to do it.

Finally I had a man who was attractive and sexy. But was I ready to start seeing a man seriously and perhaps get my first taste of sex? Ready to start a torrid affair? Willing to lie naked beside Lou, with his big shoulders and hard body? Could I picture giving up my virginity to a man still half in love with his dead wife? A man who could be using me to satisfy no more than a physical need?

Moreover, was I willing to face my parents' shocked outrage and the possibility of hurting their sensibilities? Someday in the future I'd *have* to separate myself from them and be my own person, but that was always with the understanding that it would happen after I acquired a husband and home of my own, or at least a career that required me to move out of state.

Nevertheless, could I honestly go against my conservative culture to chase after what I considered superficial fun and entertainment, just because everyone else was doing it?

And deep down, the real reason was my need to lash out at Roger. He hadn't exactly led me on, but his behavior after the temple visit had sparked something in me, a certain something I couldn't put my finger on. Was it hope? Infatuation? Love?

Was it a brief, tantalizing glimpse of the future, including two brown-eyed kids, or was it simply my imagination inspired by witnessing a sentimental wedding followed by the talk at the coffee shop and the tender way Roger had touched me at the subway station?

In all honesty, Roger had done or said nothing to hurt me. If anything, he'd been kind and attentive and warm, so I had no right to feel hurt or betrayed. And yet I was.

So was I ready for an all-out affair with Lou? I didn't know. I really and truly didn't know.

What I knew for certain was that it was daunting.

Chapter 23

Almost every year, since I was a toddler, we'd had a Thanksgiving feast at our house. Having lived in America for more than half their lives, my parents had blended comfortably into American culture, slowly absorbing Thanksgiving, Christmas, Easter, and other holidays into their own customs.

Most of the non-Hindu holidays in our home were a combination of East and West—a little *masala* or spice mixture added to good old-fashioned American food—like *tandoori* paste rubbed over the Thanksgiving turkey and chopped green chili peppers generously mixed in with the potatoes. Our Christmas tree topper, instead of the traditional angel or star, was an image of the goddess Lakshmi, dressed in a red sari.

A week before Thanksgiving, at the dinner table, Mom suddenly announced, "You know what? This year we should invite Rajesh over for the holiday dinner." Dad thought it was a brilliant idea. When I showed little enthusiasm, Mom frowned at me. "Where is your holiday spirit, dear? Poor Rajesh is all alone in a big city. Can't you be a little kind?"

After she'd succeeded in making me feel rotten, she called him right away. Being Roger, he promptly accepted the invitation, and must have said something ridiculously gracious, because Mom looked delighted as she hung up the phone. "Such a nice boy."

A cousin named Krishna, a recent immigrant to the U.S., was

also going to be one of the invitees. He lived and worked in Maryland and he'd been coming over for Thanksgiving and Christmas every year for the past five years, ever since he'd come to America as a contract worker with some IT company. His mother was Dad's cousin. Now Krishna was waiting to acquire a green card with his employer's help, so he could make this country his permanent home.

I tolerated Krishna because he was family, but I didn't particularly like him. He was pompous, full of himself, and somewhat greedy. He was always looking for freebies.

Mom and Pamma assured me it was Krishna's Indian-ness and that it would wear off eventually, that it was natural for him to want what he hadn't had while growing up in Andhra.

Whenever he visited us, he took home leftovers, pots, pans, dishes, and flatware that Mom donated to him, and all the gifts my parents and Pamma insisted on giving him. And yet, he never once bothered to thank my family. He took everything like it was his birthright, and that's the thing that bothered me.

Apparently expressing gratitude was not part of old-fashioned Hindu culture. And I didn't like that part one bit.

Cousin Krishna must have asked Mom if he could bring a guest this year, because Dad and I heard her say, "You're welcome to bring him, Krishna." A second later, after some hesitation, she added, "Girlfriend? Sure . . . please bring her."

Intrigued, Dad and I looked at each other. His heavy eyebrows climbed up. When a frowning Mom hung up the phone, Dad was the first to ask, "Krishna has a girlfriend?"

"Looks that way." Mom was still frowning. "When he asked if he could bring her, I couldn't say no."

"Of course not," agreed Dad, always the gracious host, just like Mom. Nobody had brought a girlfriend or boyfriend to our home before, so it was only natural for my parents to dissect the subject. "What's her name?"

Mom chewed on her lower lip. "He didn't say, and I didn't want to ask. A girlfriend is . . . well . . . kind of awkward." From the way Mom was hemming and hawing, it sounded like

Krishna was suffering from a serious sexually transmitted disease instead of merely being involved with a woman.

"Is there something wrong with a guy having a girlfriend?" I asked. This was an ideal opportunity to bring up the delicate subject since I'd made that date with Lou.

"Nothing, if she is a nice Indian girl," replied Mom.

"What if she's not?"

Dad clucked his tongue. "Then Krishna's in a shitload of trouble." That earned Dad a fierce look from Mom, but he seemed too worried about the imminent *trouble* to pay attention to Mom.

"Why, Dad?" I asked, more curious than ever.

"Ah, princess, you don't know Krishna's mother, Shantha. She's looking for a good Telugu girl with a big dowry for her only son. And Shantha's husband, Raju, is even worse. He's been dreaming about dowry since the day Krishna was born."

"That's disgusting." I'd always found the dowry system revolting, but my own family indulging in it was doubly so. Thank God, my dad had not accepted any dowry from my mom's family.

Dad had apparently been working as a medical resident in the U.S. for two years by the time he'd been ready for marriage, and his ideas had changed. He didn't want a dowry. All he'd wanted was a nice, educated woman who could speak English and would fit into his life and American culture.

I respected my father for going against tradition and doing what was right.

Dad chuckled at my response. "Disgusting, yes, but it's all part and parcel of being a Telugu, my dear."

"But you're Telugu, and you didn't demand a dowry from Mom's parents."

Mom rolled her eyes, an uncharacteristic gesture for her. "And thank the Lord for that, or I wouldn't be sitting here today. My parents were lower middle class. They would never be able to afford the kind of dowry the Giris would have commanded. Your dad's father was a landowner and well-known doctor with a big practice and a huge house. My father was only a clerk in a government agency."

"So how come Krishna's parents are so different?" How could cousins, practically raised in the same household, be so diverse in their philosophies?

"Different personalities, princess," Dad replied patiently. "Besides, you don't even know the half of it. Do you remember when Krishna first came to the U.S., and spent a month with us?"

"I most certainly remember," I said with a groan. At the time, Krishna was a typical FOB, as in fresh off the boat, with his tight pants, shiny silk shirts, hair puffed up with some kind of glossy gel, and his cloying cologne that made my allergies go berserk. He was covered in that scent, so much so that it announced his presence seconds before he entered a room.

He used to strut around our house like the lord of the manor and expected my mom to wait on him hand and foot. Most of the time he'd treated Pamma like a batty old woman unworthy of his attention. But what had bothered me most was Krishna's habit of staring at me with those dark, deep-set eyes, all the while fingering his mustache. His silent, contemplative gaze and sly vigilance had given me the creeps.

"Shantha and Raju were hoping Krishna would marry you," said Dad.

"What!" I squeaked.

"It's true, dear. That way he would not only get a hefty dowry, but also have a guaranteed green card and future inheritance."

"I can't believe it." I felt like someone had dealt a blow to my gut. Marry my cousin? No wonder Krishna had walked around like he owned our house, and everyone in it. And that look in his eyes—all the while he'd been mulling over being my husband, having control over my inheritance, maybe visualizing me in his bed.

It was sickening. Did he still think of me that way? "What

did *you* guys have to say to that?" I demanded of Mom and Dad, the revulsion still scorching my insides.

Mom patted the air with her hands. "Shh, calm down, dear. Your dad and I don't believe in that sort of thing. That was in the old days, when family money stayed within the family and inbreeding was considered normal. Of course we said no to Shantha and Raju's idea."

"Thank goodness for that," I murmured. But the disbelief remained. I'd never be able to look at Krishna the same way again. "Can you imagine Krishna for a husband? It's even yuckier than Uncle Srinath marrying a eunuch to keep the money within the family."

Dad roared with laughter. "I agree."

Mom looked horrified. "Stop it, you two! She is *not* a eunuch. The poor woman had some hormone problems. After the facial hair was removed, she looked very nice, quite feminine."

"Okay, she's a hermaphrodite, then." Dad snickered.

Mom turned a ferocious frown on him, although her version of ferocious couldn't scare a newborn babe.

Recalling the tail end of Krishna's month-long stay with us, I grinned. "Is that why he left in a such a huff, because you turned him down? I'd wondered about that."

"Yes," Dad confirmed. "He and his parents were furious with us. They didn't speak to us for months afterward."

Mom looked sad. "That boy was so angry, he didn't return our calls for a long time."

"Are they still mad, or are they talking to you now?" I inquired.

Dad nodded. "The temper tantrum dissolved eventually when they realized we were still of some use to them. They're after your mom to find a good, wealthy girl for Krishna, preferably an American citizen with a high-paying job."

I couldn't help laughing. "So, Mom, have you found a rich Telugu girl for our Krishna yet?"

Mom gave a rueful sigh. "I'm trying, believe me. But no girl is good enough for Shantha and Raju's boy. So far they have turned down every girl I have suggested. Some of them are really good and smart girls, too. What a shame." She got to her feet and started clearing the table. "And now Krishna has a girl-friend."

I chuckled some more at Mom's expression. It looked like Krishna's affliction had been upgraded from sexually trans-mitted disease to bubonic plague.

Chapter 24

On Thanksgiving Day, I woke up early to help Mom with the preparations. She could whip up an Indian meal in a jiffy and with no help, but she seemed a little unsure of herself when it came to non-Indian food. I generally pitched in, especially because Pamma stayed away from the kitchen. As a strict vegetarian, the sight and smell of a turkey seemed to nauseate her.

By noon Mom and I had everything under control. The turkey was turning to a nice shade of russet with the added red tint of the *tandoori* spices. The two vegetable dishes were well on their way, and the salad and Jell-O mold were ready and chilling in the refrigerator. Mom had made a mango cheesecake and pumpkin pie for dessert the previous day.

While I put the finishing touches to the gravy, Mom cleaned the kitchen. In less than twenty minutes she had the place back to its gleaming neatness. Fresh flowers sat in a lovely antique silver vase on the dining table. The pumpkin colored tablecloth and plump cinnamon-scented candles in silver holders gave the place a nice, old-fashioned Thanksgiving aura.

I tasted the spicy vegetable dip that I'd made earlier. "Mmm, pretty good, even if I say so myself," I said, and tasted a little more.

Mom sprinkled fried onions over the green bean casserole and slid it back into the oven before giving me a dubious look.

"Good job with the dip, but it's about time you learned some Indian cooking."

"Why, sure." I arranged the baby carrots and celery sticks around the bowl of dip. "If I put my mind to it, I bet I could easily cook up a gourmet Telugu meal."

"Learn how to make some simple lemon rice and *sambar* first. Then maybe you can dream big," Mom quipped.

The doorbell rang. Our first guest had arrived. I heard Dad opening the door. Mom and I both went out to greet the guest—or guests.

It was Krishna and . . . oh my . . . a Caucasian woman. Mom and I briefly exchanged baffled looks. Despite all our speculation about her the other day, for some reason we'd assumed Krishna's girlfriend would be Indian, or at least Asian—perhaps because Krishna was so Indian in his ways.

My lips twitched at the look on Dad's face. I'd never seen one like that before, like he was suddenly suffering from hemorrhoids. After the moment of astonishment passed, he broke into a polite smile and welcomed them.

What a contrast they were, Krishna and his girlfriend. He was tall, broad-shouldered, with skin that looked like polished ebony. She was short, white as whole milk, with golden brown eyes and blond hair teased into a halo. She was pretty as a doll and looked older than Krishna.

Krishna cracked a smile, his brilliant white teeth gleaming against his dark lips. His hairstyle looked different this year—the stiff, gelled look was gone. Instead he had longish hair that rivaled Roger's careless tresses. The heavy mustache was still there, the macho symbol that gave him the look of a Telugu movie villain.

He made the introductions. "This is Carol Stanton, my girlfriend. Carol, meet my uncle and aunt, Dr. and Mrs. Giri." He gestured toward me. "Soorya, their daughter."

Carol shook hands with each of us. "Welcome to our home, Carol," said Dad, and took their coats. I noticed Carol was chubby, which made me warm up to her instantly. She wore black pants and a black pullover sweater with an embroidered pumpkin on it.

"Thanks for having me over," Carol said in a shy voice. "I've heard so much about all of you." She handed a white cardboard bakery box to Mom. "This is from Kris and me. I hope you like chocolate cake."

"Thank you so much. We love chocolate cake," Mom lied with a sweet smile. "It is very kind of you and . . . Kris."

Truthfully, I'd give up my law degree for a slice of rich chocolate cake, but my diet got in the way. Dad didn't like chocolate. Pamma didn't eat anything with eggs in it. And Mom, with her dislike for sweets, barely tolerated it. And yet she held the box like it housed the family jewels.

But then that was Mom—she'd never hurt anyone's feelings.

Ushering the guests into the living room, Mom requested them to take a seat while she put the cake away and informed Pamma that it was time to emerge from her room. Meanwhile I asked Krishna and Carol what they'd like to drink. Krishna asked for scotch and soda and Carol asked for red wine. Dad offered to take care of the drinks, so I went into the kitchen to bring out the appetizers.

Mom pounced on me the second I walked in. "She's American. Did you see that?" she whispered to me.

"Yes, Mom. It's hard to miss." I grinned. "By the way, we're American citizens, too."

"But not in the same way." She bit her lip. "Oh my goodness, what will I tell Shantha and Raju?'

"Tell them the truth."

"How? They will curse me out. They will think your dad and I didn't do our duty in looking out for their son."

I couldn't help snorting. "Mom, Krishna's an adult. He's not your responsibility. If he has a girlfriend, it's his business. Besides, Carol seems very nice."

"Nice yes, but rather old for him, right? She must be at least in her late thirties?" Mom placed the cake in the fridge. "I better inform Pamma that her great-nephew is here. I don't know how to tell her about this scandal. She's going to have a seizure when she meets Carol."

"Scandal, eh?" I picked up the appetizer trays and headed toward the living room. "Then you better prepare her thoroughly before you bring her out," I advised with a wink.

I could sympathize with Mom and Dad, but this was turning out to be quite amusing.

At least Krishna wouldn't stare at me in that creepy, lascivious way anymore. He had Carol. And wasn't it ironic that he'd found someone who was the complete opposite of me—short, fair-skinned, gentle, and sweet. Oh well, like Pamma always said, the Lord's ways were strange and one's karma dictated everything.

Just as I laid down the trays on the coffee table, I heard the doorbell ring again. A wild thrill of anticipation raced through my veins. Roger! I told myself I had to stop behaving in this giddy fashion around Roger. The guy was playing the field with beautiful girls bearing cute names like Carrie and Colette, besides which, he was busy producing a play and trying to live on a shoestring budget.

I might have the hots for him, but he wasn't being anything but friendly toward me. I had to keep that fact in mind. *Friend.*

Dad was still busy getting the drinks, so I hastened to answer the door.

Roger stood on the stoop, looking taller than ever, his hair getting tossed about in the cold wind. He wore a black leather jacket, jeans, and sneakers. Even before he could take off the jacket I knew there would be a sweatshirt underneath. I had to resist the mad urge to throw my arms around him.

"Hi, Soorya," he greeted me, stepping inside. Then he handed me a bouquet of mixed flowers—carnations, lilies, and mums. "Happy Thanksgiving. These are for the three charming Giri ladies."

He wants you for a friend, I reminded myself once again, trying not to think of the rose he'd given me outside the temple not too long ago. I wondered if he remembered it.

"Thank you, Roger. It's very sweet of you," I said, making sure not to sniff the flowers or I'd start sneezing despite my antihistamine. "Just hang your jacket in the closet," I instructed him.

"Something smells delicious," he remarked, sliding his jacket over a hanger.

"That's Mom's *tandoori* turkey," I said. I could bet Roger would do full justice to the food, too. "My cousin Krishna and his girlfriend Carol are in the living room with Dad. Please join them."

"Soorya."

"Yeah?"

"You look very nice today, more casual but festive," remarked Roger, with a heart-stopping smile.

I looked down at myself. Festive? All I had on was a pair of black slacks and a coral-colored pullover sweater with a black and coral scarf around my neck. I wasn't sure how to take his compliment. "Uh...thanks." A bit flustered, I turned around and went back to the kitchen to find a vase.

By the time I finished arranging the flowers, I heard Pamma being introduced to Carol. I hoped the old lady's heart could withstand the shock. She was just now recovering from the bronchitis attack.

When I returned to the living room, I found Pamma sitting on the couch, staring at Krishna and Carol, a slightly purplish tint to her face, her mouth clamped shut. The dentures were positively not clicking.

Krishna was sitting glued to Carol, a possessive arm around her shoulders. Any closer and Carol would be in his lap. I could see why Pamma's face looked flushed. To pry her gaze away from those two, I announced cheerfully, "Look, you guys, Roger brought us flowers."

It was a smooth move on my part. Both Mom and Pamma switched their attention to the bouquet. "Such beautiful fall colors. Thank you, Rajesh," Mom said. Pamma's dentures clicked.

Roger, God bless him, immediately put Carol at ease by asking her about her job. In the few minutes that I'd been out of the room, how had he managed to draw her out? His ability to make people feel comfortable was always a delight.

"So, Carol, what is it like working as an executive assistant at a high-tech corporation?" he said, popping a baby carrot smothered with dip into his mouth. His left hand curled around a frosty glass of beer. He looked very much at home. If he accidentally found himself in a snake pit, he'd probably find a way to make himself comfortable.

Carol, looking thrilled at being asked about her career, replied with a modest smile, "It can be overwhelming sometimes. It's not easy being an assistant to two executives with such diverse personalities and management styles. One of the guys is especially difficult."

"I'm sure it's a tough job, but something tells me you're very good at it. Am I right?" Roger shot her a killer smile, making Carol blush with pleasure.

Krishna ruffled Carol's hair. "You should see how efficient she is. She can juggle six things at once." So it appeared that Krishna and Carol worked for the same employer and that's where they'd met. And for a change, Krishna was saying something nice about someone.

Good for Carol. She was making a better man out of Krishna. I was beginning to like her more and more.

"Thank you, Kris!" Carol cooed and kissed Krishna's cheek, making him send the rest of us a smug, self-important grin. He was basking in the adoration this sweet woman was laying at his feet.

Pamma's face went back to the earlier purple tint. Even my cool, confident dad looked like he'd just grown another pesky hemorrhoid. So I quickly jumped in. "Anybody need their drinks refreshed? I know I could use a soda."

Mom sprang to her feet and headed for the kitchen with a murmured, "I better see about getting dinner on the table."

It was pretty much smooth sailing after that. Dinner was lovely, with the turkey coming out looking delectable and the vegetables cooked to perfection. The candles, besides adding a warm glow, lent a homey aroma to the dining room. Pamma looked every inch the Giri family matriarch as she looked around the table with a smile.

When Dad asked Roger how his play was coming along, he said it was only a few weeks to opening night and that he was working the crew and himself to the point of exhaustion. "Today's the first day my cast and I have taken time off in weeks," he said with a sigh. "Of course, they'd have slaughtered me if I hadn't given them Thanksgiving off," he added with a hand at his throat, imitating a swift cutting motion.

I had to admit Roger was working extremely hard toward fulfilling his ambition, something I hadn't expected when I'd first met him. If there was one thing I admired, it was dogged determination to realize one's dream.

Krishna, with his superior computer software job, tried his best to belittle Roger's unusual career. Several times he made snide remarks about show business and Roger's assumed American name. I was itching to defend Roger, who appeared unconcerned about Krishna's jibes. Mom looked a little distressed, too. Dad continued to eat his turkey like he hadn't eaten in a year.

Why the heck wasn't Roger giving Krishna back in equal measure? I knew he was an easygoing individual and let very little upset him, but this was the limit.

Eventually, just when my temper was about to reach boiling point, Roger unexpectedly and cleverly threw a knockout punch at Krishna. It wasn't just me that he took by surprise. Everyone at the table looked at him in awe.

"Let me tell you something, Krishna," explained Roger in a calm tone. "I could have chosen the trite path to medicine or computer science or engineering. I had the grades, the brains, and the resources for any of those fields, but I decided to be different. It takes guts and creativity to try what I'm trying. I'm following my vision. And Roger's a rather nice name." He took a sip of water and smiled, deftly removing the sting from his words. "I might fail miserably, but at least I will have tried. It's better than being bored to death."

I was proud of Roger. He'd proved he could handle the worst kind of pompous asses, and they couldn't get any worse than my pretentious cousin.

Carol looked impressed. "Roger, that's so admirable. Very few people have the vision and courage to do what you're doing." When she beamed at Roger, Krishna decided to shut up once and for all.

As I studied Krishna and Carol across the table, I sincerely hoped that Krishna had enough decency to treat her well. Carol seemed to be genuinely in love with him. My primary concern was for her. Precisely what were Krishna's intentions toward her? Was he serious about Carol, or was he merely toying with her while he waited for the ideal Telugu virgin to materialize?

It made me angry to visualize such a scenario. He had no right to play with a girl's heart, use her for sex, and then trash her. It wasn't all that uncommon for young men coming from conservative cultures to seek out a good time before settling down with a suitable wife.

After dinner Mom and I cleared the dishes and loaded the dishwasher. Then I shooed Mom out of the kitchen, telling her to relax with the guests and give herself a break while I put the coffee on and got the desserts out.

Mom had been working since dawn, and she seemed tired. I had a feeling this whole Krishna-Carol affair and Krishna's parents' potential reaction to it were placing Mom under a great deal of stress.

While I got the dessert plates, Carol unexpectedly came into the kitchen. "Soorya, can I help you with anything?" she asked hesitantly.

"Sure," I replied with a smile. "You can get the cups and teaspoons, if you don't mind."

"No problem." She went to the cabinet I pointed to.

I glanced at her back as she stood on her toes to reach the cups on the top shelf. She was a pleasant person, open and friendly. There was something very innocent and likeable about her. After a second of debating whether I should get nosy or not, I said to her, "Carol, can I ask you something personal?"

She put the cups on the counter and turned around to face me, looking uneasy. "Yeah . . . sure."

"How long have you and Krishna been seeing each other?"

Carol opened one of the drawers, looking for flatware, conveniently avoiding my gaze. "Almost a year."

"Wrong drawer," I said, opening the right one for her.

"He's really a great guy," she assured me, picking up several teaspoons. "He's quite thoughtful."

Thoughtful? Were we talking about the same man here? "That's nice." I kept my uncharitable thoughts to myself.

"I never thought I'd fall for someone from a completely different culture."

"How did you guys meet? At work?"

She finally looked up at me. "At an office party. He and I started talking, and we hit it off right away." She waited a moment for my reaction before adding, "He asked me out the following week."

"He sure didn't waste any time," I remarked. Krishna knew a good thing when he saw it.

"He was so different from anyone I'd met," said Carol. "So down-to-earth and kind of shy."

Down-to-earth . . . maybe. But shy? Either Krishna had made a 180 degree turn since the last time I'd seen him or Carol was so totally in love that she was seeing things. But the next thing that came out of her mouth stumped me. "I'm really sorry, Soorya. I know you must hate me."

I stopped what I was doing and faced her. "Why would I hate you, Carol?"

"Maybe I shouldn't have said anything. Kris is going to be mad at me."

"Mad about what? What are you talking about?" I had my hands parked on my hips. Carol backed up a step or two. I was easily half a foot taller and a whole lot heavier than she. I probably looked like a raging bull ready to charge at her.

"Kris told me about how the family expected the two of you to marry and . . . that you're in love with him . . . but he didn't return your feelings."

I narrowed my eyes at her. "Is *that* what he told you?" The nerve of that lying, egotistical weasel! I was tempted to march out into the living room right that second and confront my smug, self-serving cousin. But I took a deep breath instead.

"He broke your heart when he"—Carol said with a remorseful pause—"when he said he didn't want to marry you, right?" All of a sudden she rushed forward, threw her arms around my waist and gave me a hug. "I'm sorry, Soorya."

"Sorry for what?" Taken by surprise, I awkwardly patted Carol's head resting against my chest. Her hair smelled like peaches.

"I know this hurts, but it's not a good idea for cousins to marry. It's not healthy."

"I know that, Carol. It's definitely not healthy."

She pulled away. "So you do understand?"

"Perfectly. And don't worry, I never had any feelings for Krishna." I gave Carol a casual shrug. "I don't know where he got the insane idea that I was interested, but I never was and never will be. To me he's just another cousin from India. I have several of them."

Carol's shoulders sagged with relief. "I'm so glad you see it that way. I was worried and nervous about coming here today." She gave a tremulous laugh. "God, am I relieved!"

Poor Carol. She was taking this way too seriously. And how hilarious was that, now that I'd gotten over my initial fit of rage at Krishna and could actually see the humor in all this? The man had an ego as big as California, and since it had suffered a blow he'd come up with some ridiculous explanation to soothe it.

I wondered if bringing Carol here was his way of throwing it back in our faces. Was that why he'd looked so smug when she'd made a public display of kissing him?

I went about readying the forks and plates. "So, are you and Krishna serious?"

Carol's golden eyes lit up like light bulbs. "He's talking marriage. I don't know when, but I know he's serious. Of course, I have to think about Adam's future and then—"

"Adam?" My radar beeped.

"He's my son."

My hand stilled for a second before uncovering the pie. "Oh."

"My ex has him every other weekend and part of the summer. Kris and Adam get along okay, but Adam's a little shy around him right now."

"How old is Adam?"

"Eight."

"I guess he'll adjust in time," I offered. What did I know about how an eight-year-old boy's mind worked? But I had to say something supportive.

"He's only a little boy," Carol said, defending her son. "And unfortunately he's never been around anyone other than white people. That's my fault, of course."

I smiled. "I understand." Actually I didn't. What was Krishna getting into? Had he even thought this thing through clearly? Marrying a divorced woman with a son was a lot to take on, especially for a spoiled brat raised in India. Clearly Carol was older than him, and a young son and ex-husband made the situation more complicated. What about the rest of her family? How did they fit in?

And then again, was Krishna really serious about Carol or was he merely leading her on? The thought made me start fuming again.

I could only imagine the fireworks this *scandal,* as Mom called it, would set off in my aunt and uncle's home. My only hope was that Carol and her little boy didn't get hurt in the crush. Carol seemed very trusting, from what I'd learned so far. And very much in love.

The ruckus would erupt the moment Mom called Shantha. I

had the uncomfortable feeling that Shantha and Raju would soon be arriving in the U.S., ready to do battle and rescue their precious son from what they'd consider a life sentence.

Well, I actually began to feel a wee bit sorry for Krishna, but mostly I reserved my sympathy for Carol.

Later, after everyone had dessert and coffee, I once again sent Mom out of the kitchen. I wanted to give her a real break. Another surprise awaited me as I turned on the dishwasher and started hand-washing the crystal. Roger came in with an offer to help. I thrust a towel in his hands. "I'll wash and you can dry. Be careful. Those pieces are delicate and my mom loves them."

"Aye, aye, Captain. I'll do my best." Roger happily dried every last glass with all the delicacy he could put into those lean fingers while he whistled some cheerful tune.

"So, when is your opening night?" I asked him.

"In ten weeks." He inclined his head at the glasses he'd lined up on the counter. "Tell me where these go and I'll put them away."

I pointed to the cabinet and he neatly arranged them on the shelf by height. The boy was handy in the kitchen. He was full of surprises lately, and good ones, too. I was beginning to see the eccentric Roger in an entirely different light, especially since our visit to the temple.

"Are you nervous yet, Roger?" To me he looked cool as an ice cube.

"Absolutely. The tension is killing me," he answered, pressing a hand to his belly.

I laughed and wiped the wet countertop. "*You* experiencing tension, Vadepalli? You don't know the meaning of the word."

He picked up the salad bowl from the draining board and dried it with great care. "I may not show it, Soorya, but I do get nervous. Lately I've been having nightmares that things are going to go terribly wrong at the last minute."

I could see he was serious, and I believed him. It was a huge production and he probably had no one to confide in. I'd have been a basket case if I were in his shoes. "I'm sure it'll be all right," I soothed. "Just have faith in yourself." It came as a shock when I realized I genuinely wanted to reach out to comfort him, to cheer him up.

Setting the last bowl down, he draped the damp dish towel on the handle of the oven and sprang another surprise on me. "Soorya, if you're not busy on Saturday, will you have dinner with me?"

"Why?"

"My flagging spirits could use a boost."

"I can't. I have plans for Saturday."

He looked at me for a long, speculative moment. "You have a date?"

"Why are you looking at me like that?" Irritation sparked. "You think someone like me can't have one?"

"I didn't say that."

"I'm too plain to have a date? Is that what you're trying to imply, Roger?"

"Damn it, Soorya, why do you get so defensive? Why can't you accept the fact that you're not plain? I've told you that, more than once. Why can't you just let go of all those teenage hang-ups of yours and enjoy life for a change? You're an attractive woman with a brilliant, spirited personality—when you're not angry and prickly, that is."

"You don't really mean that—the part about me being attractive." He'd told me that before, but he was so full of bullshit sometimes.

"Don't tell me what I do and don't mean. You just finished telling me to have faith in myself, so why don't *you* have a little faith in yourself for a change?"

"It's not easy for me. It's never easy. I was always the tallest and the biggest girl in school. The boys always gravitated toward the cute, petite girls. My parents talked my cousin into coming all the way from Arizona to take me to the senior prom because no boy had asked me. But then you'd never understand that kind of humiliation, Mr. Cute and Captivating."

On the pretext of putting away the bowls, I turned my back

to him. Tears were gathering in my eyes and I didn't want him to see them.

I heard him breathe out a deep sigh. "But I do understand, Soorya. I was always the gawky kid with his head buried in Shakespeare and Molière when boys my age were into sports and computers and robotics. In my twenties I went around looking like a homeless bum when my classmates wore business suits. I worked in a musty community theater while they performed surgeries or sat in plush offices and had their own executive assistants.

"My father reminded me what a loser I was no less than five times a week. I've been rejected by a dozen girls so far—well, thirteen, counting you. If that's not living the life of an outcast, then you tell me what is?"

I turned around to face him. "I'm sorry. I didn't realize that." Hearing Roger's words quickly put an end to my tears of self-pity. Not for a moment had I stopped to think that he might have serious issues of his own. He always displayed such relaxed confidence. Well, now that I thought about it, he was the ultimate misfit in the Indian-American culture, with its doctors and engineers and scientists and computer geeks—especially the young Indian males.

Why hadn't I seen it as something that perhaps hurt him, alienated him from the other kids? He'd mentioned it the first time we'd met, during our walk in the park—the rejections, the awkwardness, everything. I'd also seen his father's denigration of Roger firsthand. And yet, because of his looks and careless attitude, I'd dismissed it as nothing. It looked like Roger and I had more in common than I'd realized.

He ran his fingers along the edge of the counter. "Well, now you know that Rajesh Vadepalli, or Roger, as you insist on calling me, has a few issues that he constantly battles with, just like you."

"I'm sorry. And for your information, Saturday's appointment is a friendly business thing—sort of killing two birds with one stone—a little business and a little socializing with a fellow lawyer."

"Ah, one of those. I understand perfectly. Maybe Sunday for lunch, then?"

"Sunday's fine, but don't you have a date with Charlotte or ... the actress, Cassie?" I wasn't quite finished grilling him. Just because he had some emotional issues, didn't mean he wasn't the world's biggest flirt.

A dark eyebrow inched up. "Are you by any chance jealous, Soorya?"

"Of course not! Who you choose to spend your time with is your business." The nerve, trying to put me on the spot when he saw two, maybe more, women in his spare time. All my sympathy for him melted like ice cream zapped in a microwave oven.

"Well, for *your* information, the actress's name is Carrie, and she has a steady boyfriend, a big guy with tattoos that I wouldn't want to mess with. As for Colette, not Charlotte," he said with a mysterious smile, "she's my stage manager. We were discussing business the other day at the French restaurant. Just like you said—killing two birds with one stone."

"Ah, is that what they call a date these days—discussing business? I'll make a note of it. It just might come in handy someday, when presenting one of my cases before a jury."

"Very funny. If you have to know the truth, Colette suggested dinner because we were meeting after her working hours. She works on weekends, and since I don't exactly have an office, we had to meet somewhere." He shrugged. "And she came up with that restaurant because she works half a block from it."

"Isn't that handy? Admit it, Roger, it was a date."

"Fine, if you insist on calling it that."

"What else would you call it?" I knew I was belaboring the issue, but I couldn't stop needling him a bit more.

"A business dinner. Of course, I could have invited her to my little loft apartment for a glass of wine and my home-cooked chicken curry. Now *that* would've been an interesting discussion," he added with a sly grin.

I picked up the damp towel and threw it at him. "You are insufferable, Roger Vadepalli."

Catching the towel in midair, he put it back in its place and stood with his hands on his waist. "So will you go to lunch with me on Sunday, or not?"

"Give me one good reason why I should."

He stood in silence for several seconds. "Because I'm interested in you. Is that good enough?" He paused. "I want to get to know you better, Soorya. I want to prove to you that I'm a nice guy. I want to show you that you're an attractive woman who's capable of capturing any man's interest."

Stunned, I stared at him. For the first time he'd come out and admitted he was interested in me. And for the first time I actually believed he meant it when he said I was attractive. I was tempted to take a few steps forward and ask him to put his arms around me, prove to me that I could ignite a fire in him like he did in me.

But I couldn't bring myself to do it. A few barriers stood in the way—not the least of which was that my family was in the next room. I couldn't throw myself at a man, no matter how much I wanted to. Besides, self-respecting girls just didn't do things like that.

Like a fool I stood rooted to my spot and bit my lip. I was very rarely left speechless. Roger was one of the few people who managed to leave me in that state.

Probably tired of waiting for my reply, he tilted his head and looked at me. "What'll it be?"

"Yes," I murmured at last.

"Excellent. I'll pick you up at noon. I have a car now," he said. Then he threw me a curve. "By the way, Satish wanted to know if you and I are an item."

"Why?" I sort of knew the answer, but wanted to hear it from Roger.

"He's interested in you, Soorya. Didn't he make that abundantly clear?"

"We've only had a couple of brief conversations, that's all."

"He said he wanted to ask you out but didn't know whether you and I were seeing each other."

"So what did you tell Satish?" I asked, hiding my grin. I was feeling like a pampered cat. It was wonderful to have three men interested in me—three very different personalities.

"I told him I had the first claim, so he didn't stand a chance."

"You didn't!" I was flattered by all this attention, but Roger had some nerve to assume I'd fall in line.

His response was to smile and saunter out of the kitchen, the picture of male confidence, hands in his pockets. But my heart was doing a tap dance.

I'd done it again. I'd fallen under Roger's spell.

Chapter 25

On Saturday morning, I woke up with a headache and stuffy nose. I wasn't sure if it was my allergies or a genuine cold, but along with my antihistamine I swallowed a couple of aspirin to play it safe.

The weather was cold and the sky a drab gray. The forecast called for snow flurries later in the day and I dreaded driving in bad weather to meet Lou. But I was going only up to Edison and not all the way to Pemberton like the last couple of visits, so I'd be driving forty-five minutes at the most. Despite the miserable feeling, I told myself I could do it.

Lou had suggested Edison because he was interested in visiting the quaint icon known as Little India, a neighborhood filled with Indian restaurants, sari shops, jewelry and grocery stores, music shops, and novelty boutiques crammed with arts, artifacts, and souvenirs. The area even smelled of India.

In his e-mail Lou had mentioned his interest in sampling Indian food and perhaps an Indian movie with subtitles. Lou was in for a shock to his system—spicy food, colorful clothes, accented English, and a movie with lots of dancing and singing and outlandish costumes.

I hoped he wouldn't get turned off by a heavy dose of ethnicity. I had a suspicion he was doing all this to learn more about my culture, in essence to please me. It was thoughtful of him.

When the headache and stuffiness refused to go away, I called

Lou on my cell from my room. "Lou, I don't feel all that good and I hate driving in bad weather. I'm not sure what to do."

"I'm sorry to hear that, Soorya." He became quiet for a minute. "Look, why don't you take the train to Edison and I'll pick you up there. That way the only driving you'll have to do is from your home to your local train station and back."

"I suppose I could do that." I looked up the train schedule on the computer while I had him on the phone. "There's one that'll put me at the Metro Park station around noon." Lou agreed to that.

Mom and Dad gave me concerned looks when they noticed my red eyes and sneezing fits. "You feeling okay, princess?" asked Dad, who was sipping coffee while Mom made brunch.

"It's just a mild cold, Dad." I poured myself a glass of milk. "I've already taken something for it, so don't worry."

Seeing me dressed in outdoor clothes, Mom remarked, "Should you be going out? You'll end up getting sick, dear."

Pamma looked up from her newspaper. "Too much cold outside. You stay home and rest. Good Indian movie on TV today. We all see it together."

I got up and put my empty glass in the sink. "Don't worry so much, you guys. I'm just going out to lunch with some friends in Edison and then we're going to see a Hindi movie inside a nice, warm theater. We won't be hanging outdoors all that much."

"But they're forecasting snow tonight," Mom added.

I shot the three of them my most cheerful smile. "I'll be home before the snow arrives. I won't stay out late—promise." I patted Pamma's shoulder. "Don't look so grim, Pamma. I'll be home in a few hours."

A half hour later, as I sat in the train, I felt guilty about having lied to my family. I tried to tell myself that theoretically I hadn't lied. I was indeed meeting a friend for lunch and a movie. But my folks thought I was going out with a bunch of girls and boys as usual, not a single man, and definitely not someone like Lou.

And then there was Roger flitting around in my mind. He had

indicated interest in me. At last. But I still didn't know how deep my emotions went. Lusting after a handsome face and sexy body didn't mean permanence. I'd have to explore that a bit more tomorrow. Maybe if Roger and I saw each other a few times I'd know what my true feelings for him were. There was also the chance that he'd tire of me.

In the meantime, I had Lou to deal with.

Was it only three months ago that I was a woman with no men in my life? Now I was juggling two—with Satish a possible third. My new diet, despite the hunger pangs, was worth it. I wanted to howl aloud. The feeling was so damn heady, so powerful. Soorya Giri with three men claiming her attention—and all of them good-looking in their own way.

Was this how my popular friends felt when they had to deal with more than one man chasing after them? How did they decide which one to go steady with? How did they weigh one against the others? Looks, speech, manners, education, job security, sense of humor?

I blew my nose and pocketed the tissue, then resolved to stop analyzing the situation and enjoy the day. I hadn't had anything beyond a glass of skim milk, so my stomach was already growling, looking forward to lunch in Edison.

When I emerged from the train station at Metro Park, I found Lou waiting at the curb in his Explorer. He honked to catch my attention. When I climbed in he leaned over to place a warm kiss on my cold cheek. "It's great to see you again."

He was wearing khakis, a brown leather jacket, and a matching golf cap. He smelled of some kind of spicy men's cologne. My sense of smell was still somewhat alive despite the stuffed-up sinuses.

"Likewise, Lou," I said and fastened my seat belt.

He touched my arm with a gloved hand. "Feeling any better, babe?"

"A little." He'd called me babe. Pleased with the endearment, I smiled and told him which way to turn after exiting the parking lot.

Little India was crowded despite the unseasonable cold and

the cloudy skies. I suggested eating at a North Indian restaurant that served a buffet. A buffet was always the safest choice. There was bound to be something that appealed to a first-timer.

The restaurant's ambience was typical—some Rajasthani prints on the walls, Indian lantern-type light fixtures, green vinyl upholstered chairs, and a buffet set up against a wall with the food served in wide copper *handis*.

Hindi songs played in the background. Just as I'd anticipated, the first thing Lou asked me was why the falsetto voice sounded like high-pitched shrieking. I gave him my stock answer: "That's Indian music for you. And this singer is considered one of the top voices in the world."

Poor Lou looked like his eardrums were ready to split. I asked our waiter to turn down the volume so we could eat in peace.

Lou tried eating a variety of things from the buffet. He didn't seem particularly pleased with anything other than the grilled chicken. For dessert we had cashew-raisin ice cream and co-conut *burfi* accompanied by spiced tea.

As I sipped the scalding tea and savored its aroma, I glanced at Lou. "So, what did you think of your first Indian meal?"

"Interesting."

"That's a polite way of saying you hated it."

"No, honestly, a couple more times and I could get into it se-riously," he replied with a grin. "I think dessert was the best part, though."

I made a face at him. "Can't take the spices, eh? Where's your sense of adventure, Lou?"

"I ate the grilled chicken and rice." He didn't seem to like the tea much, either. I noticed he'd pushed his cup away with most of the tea still in it.

"I recall a certain individual encouraging me to walk amidst the Pinelands' snake nests, calling it an adventure, and now the same individual is afraid of a few harmless spices." I made a tsk-tsk sound and finished my tea.

Lou laughed and caught my hand across the table in both of his, sending a mild flutter up my arm. Since we were surrounded by Indians and we were already attracting curious stares, I quickly pulled my hand back. An Indian girl eating an intimate lunch with a black man was a rare sight in this milieu.

And what if my parents' friends were lurking around? Many of them visited Edison on weekends. I was afraid Lou might pick up my hand and place a kiss on it or something. Then I'd be in real trouble.

An elderly woman sitting at the next table had been eyeing us nonstop since the moment we'd been seated, making me squirm in my seat. She reminded me of Pamma.

Minutes later, it was a relief to walk out of the restaurant and those gawking, censorious eyes. I could only imagine the comments behind our backs: *Did you see that Indian girl with the black man? What is the matter with our girls these days? They cannot find an Indian man, or what? Such nonsense this is. I hope she is not married to that fellow.*

The movie wasn't until much later, so we wandered down the sidewalk on Oak Tree Road, looking at window displays in the long line of stores. Again, we seemed to attract some curious looks. By now the Indian community had grudgingly come to accept their children marrying Caucasians, but they had yet to accept African-Americans.

Lou seemed intrigued by the clothes, the colors, and the elaborate gold and silver embroidery, even on men's clothes.

"The men really wear such girly clothes in India?" he asked me.

"Not all the time, Lou," I replied. "What you're looking at is special-occasion attire—weddings, fancy parties and such. Those long, close-necked embroidered tops are called *shervanis*. Would you like to try one on?"

Lou scowled at me. "I'd look like an idiot in all that fancy gold stuff."

"Come on, Lou, be brave and try something different. You asked to come here so you could have a taste of India." I pointed to a male mannequin wearing a dashing gray and silver outfit, looking very proud and regal. "Doesn't that look elegant?"

He shook his head. "I'd look like an Arab sheikh's harem guard in that."

"Harem guards are usually eunuchs," I whispered.

"Oh, please!" The look of pure disgust on Lou's face was enough to make me laugh.

"I think you'd look nice, like a maharaja. All you'd need is a headdress and a pair of those pointy hand-embroidered shoes called *mojdis,* and you'll look very posh."

He chuckled, then took my arm and marched me down the street.

We looked at a few more displays as we made our way back to the car. The wind was brisk and chilly, and my hair was blowing over my face. I shivered inside my thick coat. My nose felt runnier than ever. I fished out a wad of tissues from my purse and blew my nose.

The movie was typical Bollywood, as India's film industry was referred to, with lots of interesting garments and dances. The hero and heroine burst into song every few minutes, irrespective of where they were or what their mood. They sang in the middle of a busy street, a lonely park (with over one billion Indians, I didn't think there were any deserted parks in India), a field of yellow flowers, on a rooftop, and even a window ledge.

Every time they broke into spontaneous song, they also danced, and dozens of chorus girls and boys appeared out of nowhere, all dressed in identical clothes. And they all danced in perfect coordination.

Lou was fascinated for the first half hour, but then started to squirm and chew on more mints than ever. And this time they were no ordinary mints—they were antacids. His stomach was clearly revolting against the spicy Indian food he'd eaten. Meanwhile, the warm air inside the theater was making my eyes and nose run more freely than ever.

Things weren't going all that well on my first real date.

"Bored to tears yet?" I asked Lou.

He shrugged. "Maybe another fifteen minutes and I'll be there," he said, stretching his legs and throwing his head back on the headrest.

We were in one of the back rows of the theater and there was no one nearby or behind us. Lou reached for my hand and massaged it with his thumb. It felt hard and warm and soothing, and it sent a pleasant shiver through my system. Lou certainly had an electric effect on me.

During the intermission, which was customary in a three-hour-long Hindi movie, we decided to get out. Lou wanted a cup of coffee, so we found a Starbucks nearby and went in.

We lingered for nearly an hour over Lou's coffee and my bottled water, mostly talking about my client, Solstice.

While we talked, it got dark outside. It was always a pleasure to talk to Lou. Since we both talked legalese, I never had to explain myself. He was an intelligent man and therefore stimulating company. But I'd had enough. Along with my head, my throat was also beginning to feel achy. "We better head back to the station," I said. "I can catch the 6:05 train."

"Do you have to go so soon?" He took my hand again, but this time we were surrounded by non-Indians and nobody bothered to throw us a second glance.

"The forecast is for snow this evening, Lou, and my cold seems to be getting worse."

"All right then, let's go." Lou looked thoroughly disappointed as he shoved his chair in. And annoyed.

What had he expected? That we'd go spend the night somewhere together? The thought made me uncomfortable. I'd never given him any cause to think that. I had presumed this was a simple first date—get to know each other, talk, eat, and maybe take in a movie, all of which we had already done.

Wasn't that enough?

Outside the train station, once again Lou stopped by the curbside directly in front of the building. The train wasn't due for another fifteen minutes, so I requested him to park in one of the empty twenty-minutes-only slots where we could talk. "Thanks for a really nice day, Lou," I said to him.

"I should be the one to thank you for coming out when you have a bad cold and for showing me Little India."

"But you didn't much care for it, did you?"

"Why do you say that? I liked it. The food was pretty good, the stores were a lot of fun, and—"

"But you don't want to do it again," I interrupted. At the look on his face, I chuckled. "That's okay; I'm not offended. I can't expect everyone to fall in love with my culture. I still like you, so don't worry."

Feigning relief, Lou clutched at his chest. "Thank God! I was worried there for a moment."

"You're a terrible actor."

"So you're saying it's a good thing I went into legal work and not the stage?"

"That's what I'm saying."

Lou's eyes went from amused to intense as he continued to gaze at me. With an abrupt movement he grabbed me by the shoulders and pulled me toward him. His lips descended on mine, warm, solid, challenging. "I've been dying to do that all afternoon," he murmured against my lips. He tasted of coffee and mints. "Put your arms around my neck, Soorya," he whispered.

"You'll catch my germs, Lou. I don't want you getting sick." Our bodies were awkwardly twisted over the armrest between the seats.

"Just do it, Soorya."

Despite my reservations, I closed my eyes and did what he asked. For the first time in my life a man had said he couldn't wait to hold me in his arms, to press his mouth against mine, to feel my body straining against his.

Although Roger had told me he was interested in me, he hadn't touched me in the real sense. So I wanted to savor this feeling of being wanted, desired, and fantasized about.

Throwing caution to the winds, I let Lou's tongue slide into my mouth and explore. It was a wonderful feeling that went clear through my system all the way down to my toes. I could see why my friends talked endlessly about something as primitive as kissing. It was the most intimately erotic way a man and woman could connect—short of making love.

Lou's hand gradually slid to my neck, down my shoulder,

then shifted to cup my breast. I shivered some more, but figured it was from the cold. The sensation of being touched intimately was alien to me.

The hot kiss lasted awhile, and I poured every bit of my emotional energy into it. His fingers kneaded and caressed my breast, and the heat of his large hand burned through the fabric. A strangely tight and tingly feeling settled in my groin. So this is what it felt like to be touched by a man. It wasn't quite what I'd expected. It was better, and yet—

He withdrew abruptly. "Sorry."

The disappointment was like a lead balloon: heavy, dark, and cold. I'd failed completely in the seduction department. I looked up at him. "Was it . . . *that* bad?"

He shook his head. "It was *that* good."

"Couldn't have been if you were repelled."

"Repelled?" He raked his fingers through his cropped hair. "Believe me, Soorya, I was far from repelled. It was great. I wanted more. A lot more."

"But Lynne got in the way, I suppose," I said, unable to keep the bitterness out of my voice. My very first real kiss—and a dead woman had to get in the way. Talk about rotten luck.

Without a word he leaned back, his silence confirming my words. I wanted to tell him not to look so guilty, because I had my own issues with the close encounter. For some inexplicable reason I'd been seeing Roger's face as Lou's tongue had touched mine, as his mouth had hungrily devoured my mouth.

I'd had an insane desire to know what it would feel like to be held by Roger, kissed by Roger, whispered to by Roger, fondled by Roger.

Oh God! That's when it dawned on me. Besides the common cold, I was also suffering from a bad case of Rogeritis. Was I falling in love with that rogue? Was I sliding down that tricky hill? If I didn't watch out, I was likely to fall hard and get hurt.

Lou turned to me with a rueful look. "I'm sorry, babe. It's me, not you. I promise to make it better the next time."

"I'm sorry, too," I said, sniffling. "My cold seems to be getting worse. I couldn't kiss and breathe at the same time."

"Then let's make sure you get home to a warm bed and a hot cup of tea."

"You're right." I gave a great sigh of relief at how we'd both managed to escape embarrassment.

After a moment of what appeared to be introspection, Lou turned to me, one arm resting on the steering wheel. "Tell me the truth, Soorya. Does it bother you that I'm a black man?"

I shook my head. "No, Lou. I think you're a great guy. I'm not a racist."

"Good. I'd like to see you again. When you're feeling better, of course."

"Sure." I blew my nose hard, further stuffing up my sinuses. Bed and a hot drink were beginning to sound better and better.

The dashboard clock read 6:00 P.M. I unfastened my seat belt. "Time for me to go."

This time Lou picked up my hand and kissed the palm softly. "Take care of yourself, okay? Call me tomorrow if you can. Tell me how you're feeling."

"Thanks, Lou." I shut the door and stood on the sidewalk, watching him drive away, then trudged up the stairs to the platform and found a bench to sit down and wait for my train. My headache was getting worse. I felt feverish, too.

It looked like Mom was right. I was coming down with something.

I'd waited many long years to be asked out on a date, and when I'd finally bagged one, it had ended up being with the wrong man—wrong color, wrong race, wrong religion, wrong everything.

The only good thing about today's strange date was that it had made the differences between Lou and me as clear as night and day. He was never likely to be comfortable in my environment and I'd probably never fit into his. My Indian-ness was manifesting itself despite my efforts to suppress it. And Lou had turned out to be considerably more set in his ways than I'd anticipated.

Was I doomed to be a virgin all my life? I was ready to throw my hands up in frustration and scream. If Pamma's philosophy had any basis, my bad-bad karma was not only in full play but it had arrived with a generous dash of cynicism and dark humor. I had to have a serious talk with my grandmother about this karma business.

Speaking of twisted karma, I had a date scheduled for tomorrow with the man who occupied my mind, but it looked like I was going to be too ill to go. Damn it, I had been looking so forward to it, too. Roger had said he wanted to prove to me that I was attractive, that he wanted to get to know me better.

Was he planning on kissing me like Lou had, or was he going to give me that nonsense about us being good friends? Despite my chills and achy head, I could well imagine what kissing Roger would be like. I knew it would be wonderful. I just knew it in my bones.

The arriving train's squealing brakes sent a sharp stab through my head. A miserable fit of shivers forced me to pull my coat closer. This was so like Amy's mother often said, "You know why some of us miss the boat? Because when our boat comes in, we're at the train station."

Such wise words. And in my case true—literally.

Chapter 26

I cursed that snowy Sunday the moment I woke up in the morning. I had a high temperature, and the so-called dusting of snow that had been predicted for Saturday night had ended up being nearly two inches. Imagine that in November.

Despite my calling Roger and warning him that I was ill, he still stopped by at noon. Brave man, considering his worries about getting sick when he could least afford it.

As soon as he saw me huddled under a blanket with a red nose and a feverish glaze in my eyes, he knew our date had gone down the toilet.

But he gave me a box of sugar-free white chocolates. How thoughtful! I felt guilty for standing him up. When I apologized, he dismissed it. "Don't be silly. We can do it as soon as you're feeling better."

But all was not lost. Mom, God bless her generous heart, invited Roger to join us for lunch. And Roger, being the adaptable sort, accepted. So the five of us ate at the kitchen table. Although mine was a bowl of vegetable soup while the rest of them feasted on *pesarattu*—thin, crisp crepes made from a batter of ground mung beans and served with a pungent chutney, the meal was still pleasant.

Roger spent the afternoon with us, watching a movie on DVD with Dad and Mom and chatting for a while. Despite my lying on the couch and dozing on and off, I liked having him there, listening to his deep voice. It made the afternoon go fast. Too fast.

Later, after Roger left, I called Lou to give him an update on my condition. He sounded contrite. "I shouldn't have forced you to come out and meet me. This is all my fault." I told him it was a virus and it would have made me ill no matter how much I'd coddled myself.

After that Sunday lunch, Roger sent me a few brief e-mails and managed to keep me informed of his progress with the play. He again extended an invitation to attend the rehearsals if I wanted to. I kept away from them because I didn't want to spoil my viewing the finished product on a real stage.

There was no mention of another date, though. That troubled me. By the time the winter holidays arrived, he still hadn't bothered to reschedule the date we'd missed because of my unfortunate bout of flu.

Mom invited Roger, Krishna, and Carol to Christmas dinner. In recent years, although we still put up the Christmas tree, we'd given up the gift exchange thing. I had lost interest in that part of the holiday after my teenage years were gone. Now it was just a pleasant and festive meal with family.

Roger appeared thrilled at being included in a family gathering once again. Krishna and Carol were still acting like hormone-bitten adolescents and Pamma continued to eye them with mild repugnance. I was happy to hear from Carol that Krishna was still talking about the two of them getting married.

Roger surprised me when he took me aside after dinner to have a quick word. "Soorya, I'm sorry I haven't been in touch since Thanksgiving," he whispered. "I haven't forgotten our date. It's just that everything's been very hectic."

"Don't worry about it, Roger," I assured him, relieved that he remembered it after all. "Your premiere is right around the corner and things are bound to be chaotic."

He threw me an appreciative look. "Thanks for understanding. Between rehearsals and stage sets and musical scores and lighting equipment, and three of our cast members getting sick, I'm happy to grab about four hours of sleep each night. But after the opening, I promise I'll call you."

"No problem." He was working impossibly long hours, poor man. I'd be a total bitch if I didn't comprehend something as simple as deadlines and dedication to one's work.

Between Christmas and the middle of January, Roger called me twice, once to wish me happy new year and another time to chat, but he seemed to be in a rush. Opening night was coming up soon and I could sense the tension in his voice. I wished I could help him in some way, but I didn't know how.

It didn't come as a surprise when all of us received an invitation to preview night. Even Krishna and Carol were invited. Mom still hadn't mentioned Carol to Krishna's parents. By this time Dad had decreed that Mom should not get involved. It was Krishna's affair and it was his responsibility to tell his parents.

On a freezing Friday night, at the end of January, we all got dressed to attend the preview. Thank goodness there was no snowstorm in the forecast to ruin the occasion.

My excitement mounted as I put on my silvery gray pantsuit and coordinating oxidized silver jewelry I'd bought in Rajasthan two years ago.

I hoped the theater looked perfect. This was the night the media would be present, looking at everything with razor-sharp eyes and ears, mentally writing their reviews even as they sat silently in the hushed darkness of the theater.

When I'd first met Roger, I hadn't given two hoots about his venture, but now I felt differently. Slowly it had become very personal. Now I was both thrilled and afraid for him.

Roger had called the previous night to make sure we were all attending. His parents, sister, and brother-in-law were flying in from Kansas City. Several of his friends from out of town were expected to attend, too. I hoped his father would give him a break for a change, even if the show flopped.

I prayed hard that it wouldn't flop. It couldn't.

Dad looked important in a charcoal Armani suit. Mom looked elegant in a pink Dharmavaram sari accessorized with pearls at her throat and ears. And Pamma was dressed in a soft, white tussore silk and matching shawl for the occasion. We bundled ourselves in our most fashionable winter coats. Dad drove us into Manhattan in Mom's Honda.

Outside the theater, I read the billboard—*Mumbai to Manhattan* in lights, along with Roger's name. The sign was almost exactly as I'd imagined it, except, to my surprise, the name said Rajesh Vadepalli and not Roger. He had decided to use his real name.

Inside the theater, tense anticipation was in the air, or perhaps I felt that way because my nerves were taut. There had been much pre-opening hype generated by the marketing and public relations firm Roger had hired. The public's expectations were probably high.

At the champagne reception for attendees in the lobby, I took only one small sip to wish Roger good luck. I caught scraps of conversation in passing, and all of them centered on Roger—they made him sound like some mysterious character. To keep the mystery element alive, Roger was curiously absent—probably another ploy recommended by the publicity folks.

The playbill was a glossy work of art with colorful graphics and Roger's and each cast member's photograph airbrushed to perfection. I could see what Roger had meant when he'd described the effort that went into designing it.

We located the Vadepallis. Roger's dad looked distinguished in a dark suit. He greeted Dad like a long-lost friend. "Pramod, good to see you."

Dad slapped him on the shoulder. "Likewise, Venki." Dad looked around the crowded room. "Quite an impressive gathering."

Mr. Vadepalli nodded and took a sip of his champagne, looking like the father of the groom on the wedding day—edgy and impatient. I was glad he had come to attend Roger's opening and that he'd been reasonably supportive of Roger's project in recent weeks. It meant so much to Roger.

Mrs. Vadepalli was dressed in a turquoise chiffon sari and lots of gold jewelry. She reminded me of the doll that sat atop the fireplace mantel in our family room. The red lipstick was brighter than ever and her diamond earrings sparkled under the chandelier's lights.

She hugged Mom, Pamma, and me by turns. "I am so happy that you could come. This is so exciting." She looked more nervous than her husband.

It was Roger's sister, Renuka, who filled me with both admiration and envy. She shook my hand warmly when we were introduced. "Pleasure to meet you, Soorya. I've heard so much about you from Rajesh."

"You have?" I asked with a quizzical smile. "Good things, I hope?"

"Everything he's said about you is fabulous."

Insanely pleased to hear that, I grinned back at her. She was an attractive, willowy woman. The resemblance between her and Roger was strong—the arched brows, the narrow nose, the long and lean body.

She had on a burgundy silk jacket layered over a black turtleneck sweater. A narrow, calf-length black skirt and black jewel-embellished shoes made her look cool and stylish. Small diamond earrings and a diamond pin completed the ensemble. Her dark, glossy hair fell well below her shoulders.

Renuka could have been a fashion model, but I doubted that her parents would've let her, especially with their attitude to Roger's career.

Roger had mentioned that Renuka was a systems analyst and worked in the IT industry—a sensible and practical career lauded by their father. The Vadepallis had lucked out with their children—they'd produced two good-looking and bright kids. Renuka's husband, Uday, on the other hand, was rather plain, but he was a friendly sort with a sparkling sense of humor. And I, of all people, had no right to call anyone plain.

We chatted for a while, the conversation mostly about their eventful trip from Kansas City, plagued by snowstorms in the Midwest and delayed flights.

Krishna and Carol showed up a while later. Carol greeted us with warm hugs—like family.

I noticed Pamma's expression. It looked like she'd come to terms with the fact that her great-nephew would most likely marry a non-Indian woman. I wasn't sure if Pamma had been told that Carol was a divorcée and had a young son.

Inside the auditorium, we found the best seats in the house reserved for us. The butterflies in my tummy were fluttering with ferocious intensity. I couldn't wait for curtain time.

The show started with an orchestra playing before Roger appeared on stage to a drum roll to introduce himself and his play. I drew a surprised breath. He was wearing a tuxedo! The creases in his trousers were knife-edge sharp, his black tie looked perfectly centered, and his shoes were glossy.

The image was so un-Roger-like that I had to quash the laughter bubbling up inside me. His hair was trimmed and combed back neatly. He looked great on stage, with the bright lights showcasing the planes and angles of his face. He was a born showman, and articulate, if nothing else. He welcomed the invitees warmly, with a touch of humor, and ended with a charming smile—slightly crooked and seductive.

After the applause died down I heard one woman in the row behind me say, "I'd like to take him home. He's adorable." I silently agreed.

The lights dimmed and the heavy curtain lifted. I held my breath. The opening scene was the one I'd witnessed during rehearsal, but now, with the professionally designed set, it had a frighteningly real quality. If I'd experienced a few goose bumps that day, today the hair on my arms stood on end.

The dramatic elements were marvelous, with the dark alley, the dog howling in the distance, the homeless man huddled in a corner, the killer stalking his quarry, and the eerie background music causing me to nearly chew on my manicured fingernails. I was beginning to recognize what Roger had said about the high cost of sets and everything else.

I stole a glance at my family and the Vadepallis. Everyone seemed mesmerized by the drama unfolding before our eyes. I was breathing hard when the stalker appeared and the killing occurred. Carrie's scream was spine-chilling, and when she fell, she did it with just the right touch.

Satish was great as the passionate but naïve diamond merchant who comes to Manhattan to start a jewelry store but instead gets caught up in a web of crime. Theresa, as the madcap clairvoyant, was amazingly credible.

Roger had to be proud. I found myself fighting back tears during the emotional scenes and laughing at the funnier ones.

The play was highly entertaining. Toward the end, I ventured a peek at the others in the audience. Most of them were critics from the media, advertisers, and publishers. They seemed as enthralled as I was, but perhaps I was reading in their expressions what I wanted to read.

What were they going to do to Roger's masterpiece? How was it going to play out in the weekend reviews?

Would the Indian guy coming to America to strike it rich and ending up running for his life be a story that the critics would love or hate? Had Roger put too much Indian-ness in his play, or not enough to make it interestingly exotic? It was a tough call. The play *Bombay Dreams,* despite its popular appeal, had sadly folded after a brief run.

When the curtain fell on the final scene and then lifted once again to showcase Roger and his cast and crew taking a bow, the audience gave them a standing ovation, bringing tears to my eyes all over again.

Then Roger came forward and took his final bow.

He had worked hard for tonight and deserved every round of applause and every whistle. I suspected the whistlers were mostly his friends who'd flown in from out of town.

Mom and Mrs. Vadepalli were sniffling. Roger's sister and her husband couldn't stop applauding. Dad was slapping Mr. Vadepalli on the back, but Mr. Vadepalli still looked a bit constipated. I hoped it wasn't because he'd hated the play. Krishna and Carol were whispering to each other. Pamma's dentures were getting a good workout.

That night we celebrated—all of us and the Vadepallis. We

went out to an Indian restaurant in midtown and had a lovely dinner. Roger joined us halfway through the meal and stayed only for a little while, glowing with excitement.

When I got up to go to the ladies' room he must have followed me, because he called my name and I stopped in the corridor outside the restrooms.

"Soorya, wait." He jogged up to me. His hair was now in its usual disarray and his black tie was askew. But what else did I expect? It was all I could do to stop myself from reaching up to straighten that tie. "What did you think?" he gasped, perspiration glistening on his forehead. "I want a brutally honest opinion."

"It was outstanding, Roger. It was everything I'd expected and more."

"You're not just saying that?" he asked on an uncharacteristically insecure note.

I shook my head. "I think all of you did a great job. Even Ryan, despite this being his debut play, did well with the sound and light effects."

"Thank you, Soorya. It meant a lot to have you and your family in the audience."

"Our pleasure, Roger. Thanks for offering us the best seats."

He flushed at that remark and glanced down at the floor. Roger was clearly suffering from opening night nerves.

When I joined the group once again, Dad ordered champagne and proposed a toast. "To Rajesh, Broadway's new star, and *Mumbai to Manhattan*'s magnificent opening night. May they both enjoy continued success and many awards," he pronounced proudly and raised his glass.

We all joined Dad in toasting Roger and his play.

Roger thanked Dad profusely and then the rest of us. "I couldn't have done it without you, Uncle, and all of you, and certainly not without my fantastic cast and crew."

Dad grinned at him. "Looks like I made a wise investment, Rajesh. Congratulations!"

"Thank you, Uncle," replied Roger. "You made the whole thing possible, sir. We'll talk some more tomorrow?"

Dad nodded. "Anytime you have a spare minute, call me. You're going to be an extremely busy man now." He raised his glass again. "May every one of your shows be SROs."

What the heck were my dad and Roger talking about? Had Dad just said *investment?* Suddenly my stomach dropped. I looked at Dad, my hands under the tablecloth shaking. "Dad, what's all that about?"

"I'll tell you in a moment, dear." His spirit remained buoyant.

The churning in my gut was a sign that I wasn't going to like his answer.

Chapter 27

Dad casually sipped his champagne and inclined his head at Roger. "That boy is going places, Soorya, if my hunch is right."

"You mean you're the investor who financed Roger's project?" I hoped I was wrong. It had to be a mistake. My dad couldn't have tried to buy me a husband. Or could he? Why else would a shrewd guy like my father invest in a risky venture like an unknown playwright?

Was that why Roger had been so nice to me, asked me out, invited me to his rehearsals, and even gone as far as telling me I was attractive?

He'd been trying to kiss up to his financier's daughter.

"Yes, princess," replied Dad. "I even talked Venki into accepting Rajesh's ideas. Venki's a hard man to convince, I can tell you that," he said with a wink at Roger's father. "Took me several long-distance calls to get this guy to see my point of view."

Mr. Vadepalli shook his head. "You're more stubborn than I am, Pramod. But I have to say this: Because of your persistence, at least my son and I are talking now—without coming to blows, anyway." He turned to Roger and said something to him. They fell into a conversation.

The elders as well as Renuka and her husband seemed unaffected by the news. Mom and Mrs. Vadepalli were still busy chatting. Pamma looked a little overwhelmed and tired. Krishna and Carol had left early because they had a long drive back to Maryland.

Surprisingly, I noticed Roger staring at his father with a dismayed frown. Who knew what *that* was all about. Were they arguing again, despite what his father had said just moments ago?

No one else seemed to be bothered by what was happening around us. Was I the only one disturbed by the bombshell?

Bitter resentment against my dad rose in my throat like bile. How could he have humiliated me like this? What exactly had he said to Roger? *If you promise to take my plain daughter off my hands, I'll give you money for your play?* Or was it more like, *Let's make a deal, boy: You get all the money you want if you marry my daughter.*

Damn it! How could Dad do this to me?

Roger came to stand beside me a minute later, his coat on, and a scowl on his face. "Soorya, we need to talk."

"There's nothing to talk about, Roger."

He touched my arm. "I'd appreciate a few minutes of your time."

"We've said everything there is to be said, Roger. I'm in no mood to talk to anyone right now." My eyes were trained on my glass of water. I wanted to fling something at someone. The half-full water glass looked tempting.

I couldn't and didn't want to face the man who'd been bought by my father. This whole episode was even more despicable than the dowry system. At least that was open and upfront deal making, with no lies and deceit involved.

"Stop acting like a brat and come with me, Soorya," said Roger in a tight voice. "Unless you want to cause a scene here." I'd never heard that steely tone before. I'd heard him sound serious, businesslike, angry, frustrated, excited, warm, and cajoling, but never like this.

"Fine, I'll go outside with you, but only for a minute." I stood up, put on my coat, and followed Roger toward the front door, but not before I sent my parents a blistering look.

By God, I was going to make them pay for this.

I could feel all eyes on Roger and me. The tension between us was so thick that our respective families had finally stopped conversing and lapsed into silence. Even the handful of patrons left in the restaurant and the two waiters hovering over them were gazing at us wide-eyed.

There was plenty of traffic outside even this late at night, mostly because it was a Friday and this place was close to the theater district. A few pedestrians hurried along the sidewalks. Frost had gathered on the windshields of the vehicles parked on the street and shimmered like crushed glass.

A blast of frigid air blew in my face the moment I stepped outside. Shivering, I thrust my hands deep inside my pockets. "Now say what you have to say, Roger, and then leave me alone," I ground out.

"I don't intend to," he replied, sounding equally peeved.

"What does that mean?"

"It means I plan to ask you out, break down your defenses, make you like me a little—maybe even accept my marriage proposal."

It was like a fist connecting with my chest. Marriage! Good God, he was actually going to stoop to that level—let my dad buy him like a side of beef hanging in a butcher shop. Was that what he and Mr. Vadepalli were discussing earlier, when Roger's face had taken on an odd expression? Was his dad forcing him to marry me as a payback for my father's generosity?

Being mildly attracted to me was one thing, but marriage was entirely another. No wonder Roger had looked enraged and then come to drag me out here with a vicious glower on his face. Like a good Hindu boy he was going to perform his duty, do his father's bidding, even if it killed him. But that didn't mean he had to like it.

I threw Roger my most disgusted look. "Accept your proposal? When hell freezes over." At the moment my nose was freezing over and my teeth were chattering.

He leaned against the brick wall of the building with a loud sigh. "Why, Soorya? Why are you behaving like this?"

"You lied to me—again. You took money from my father and never told me. I abhor liars, remember?"

"I didn't lie to you, Soorya. I only kept certain information from you. I wanted to tell you about the loan. Your parents didn't want me to, but—"

"But what? Lying comes so easily to you that you couldn't help yourself?"

His jaw tightened. "I wanted to tell you tonight, after the opening, when you were likely to be in a good mood, more willing to listen."

"Well, ha-ha, I'm in a fantastic mood. Can't you see?"

"Sarcasm is your middle name, Soorya. Practically every sentence coming out of your mouth has an edge to it. But I know you have the capacity for understanding and forgiveness. You have a heart underneath all that scorn, even if you prefer to keep it under wraps. I've caught glimpses of it on occasion."

"And flattery is *your* middle name," I reminded him.

He ignored my remark. "I wanted to tell you about your father's offer to fund my project a long time ago, but your mom and dad swore me to secrecy."

"Of course they did." It was a conspiracy right from the start.

"And by the way, you're not the only one to be shocked by all this. I just had the biggest jolt of my life."

"What is that, Roger? That not everyone falls in love with you? That there are a handful of us who are capable of resisting your considerable charms?"

"I just found out that your father put up fifty percent of my funding while the other half came from guess who? My father. How do you think I feel?"

I was speechless. His father had shelled out money for the play? Was that what was going on between father and son a few minutes ago?

Roger pressed his fingers to his temples, like he was fighting a headache. "Go figure that. Remember I'd mentioned to you that he'd changed his tune recently? All those concerned phone calls and offers to foot my living expenses? It was your father who convinced the stingy old bat to ease up on me and even invest his money in my venture."

"Sure, that's my dad—philanthropist, mediator, and diplomat. He's so good at it that he even managed to talk you into proposing to his daughter."

"That's where you're totally wrong. I'm grateful to your father for all he's done for me, Soorya, but you and I are a separate issue. My interest in you has nothing to do with your dad's money."

"You could have fooled me."

"Initially, when I first met you, it started out with the idea of marrying a wealthy woman and possibly borrowing money from her or her family. But things changed. I got to know you better. Even on that first day, when we took a walk in the park and then went to a movie, I found you very intriguing."

I laughed. "Sure, and my name is Cinderella."

"Don't be snide, Soorya. When will you accept the fact that everything about a person does not hinge on physical appearance? There's so much more to a person besides—"

"I don't need a lecture on philosophy, Roger," I cut in, looking at my wristwatch. "Now that you've said your piece, I'm out of here." I turned and started going back inside the building.

I wished I had my own car, so I could have driven around a bit, maybe given myself some time to absorb all this. I badly needed some privacy, but I had arrived with my parents and Pamma, and I was stuck going home with them.

Roger came up behind me and grabbed my arm. "Soorya, wait, hear me out."

"Unhand me, Roger." When he didn't let go, I eyed the passersby. "I said let me go, or I'm going to have the cops here in a minute." Indeed, a couple walking past us, hearing my raised voice, stared in speculation for a second before continuing on their way.

Roger dropped my arm but held my gaze, his eyes turning cold with fury. "Go ahead, call the cops. What are you going to say to them? That I'm asking you to forgive me for something that wasn't really my mistake? That I'm asking you to consider me as a suitor?"

"I don't have anything to say to you, Roger. I have nothing to say to my parents, either. You lied to me, all of you. You guys went behind my back and planned this thing—money in exchange for proposing to poor Soorya."

"That is not true and you know it."

I made a dismissive gesture with my hand. "All I know is I'm disgusted with you. Every one of you."

"If you're trying to deceive me or yourself, you're failing miserably." His eyes narrowed on me, like he was looking into my soul. "Deep down, I know you care about me, Soorya, at least as a friend, if not more. I've seen it in your eyes. That wall of self-defense you've built around yourself doesn't fool me for one second. I know *I've* come to care for you a great deal."

He paused for a moment, as if to gather his thoughts. "Our families get along so well. On their part, they're keeping the communication lines open so you and I have every opportunity to get to know each other better. God knows I've tried to get you to go out with me."

"Is that why there were long, unexplained silences between the times you got in touch with me?" I recalled the times he'd remain invisible for weeks, and then just sort of sail into my life, upset my equilibrium, and then disappear once again.

"You're a fine one to complain about silences. By asking you to come to the rehearsals, I tried to leave an open door at all times, hoping you'd use that as an excuse to see me. Being who you are, an Indian woman, I knew you'd hesitate to initiate a date, so I thought of that idea. And yet you wouldn't budge. It was always I who contacted you. Your parents had my phone number and you had my e-mail address, and yet you never bothered to use either. You never tried to call or write to me. Not one damn time!"

I frowned and stared at the ground. He was right, but I didn't want to accept it, much less admit it.

Getting no response from me, he continued, "Our parents are

hoping the two of us will get married someday. I'd sincerely hoped that would happen, but it takes two to build a relationship and a marriage. We could come to love each other, Soorya. We're already there to some degree, aren't we? When it comes to Indian culture and marriage, one couldn't ask for a better foundation than that."

"That's a hunk of baloney," I said, impatiently pushing my windblown hair away from my face. Oh God, he was talking about love. Finally, he was talking about love—caring. And he was right, at least about me. I was half in love with him. But about him being in love with me, I didn't know. He could be mistaking gratitude to my father for love.

"No matter what I do or say, you'll find a way to turn it into something ugly and dishonest. I don't know why the hell I even try." He groaned and looked at his watch. "Never mind, I don't have the time or the desire to argue with you anymore. I'm already late for the cast party."

He turned to go but seemed to change his mind. "Damn it, Soorya!" In the next instant I was hauled against his chest, and his mouth clamped over mine, hard, demanding, ruthless. His arms around me felt like iron bands. The breath swept out of my lungs as his teeth scraped my lips and his tongue plunged in and plundered my mouth. It was a punishing, bruising kiss, meant to inflict pain.

I didn't want to feel anything other than anger and contempt. But despite my efforts at keeping a tight rein on my weaker emotions, something uncoiled inside me. Need slammed into me with the force of a gale. With my limbs turning weak, I instinctively leaned into him. He felt warm and hard, and he smelled wonderful, like fresh herbs in a country garden.

Grabbing the lapels on his coat with both hands, I held on for dear life. I'd never felt so needy in all my life, so helpless, so desperate for a man's touch. I needed *this* man so damn much, it was painful. A knife thrust into my heart and twisted again and again would have been less agonizing.

In spite of the havoc he was creating in my brain and heart, I never wanted the kiss to end.

Nevertheless, before I could respond appropriately his mouth abandoned mine. I staggered when his arms unclamped me. For a second he held my shoulders to steady me, and then let go.

His voice was a whisper. "I've had it with your attitude, Soorya. Go ahead, get on your high horse and stay there. I refuse to beg anymore. Good-bye."

With that he turned on his heel and left me standing there, stunned, my sense of balance still uncertain, my heartbeat thundering, and my ego in shreds. I watched him stride down the street and enter the parking garage on the corner, the tails of his coat flapping in the wind.

He didn't hesitate or look back. There was a certain finality to his gait.

I stood rooted to the spot, shivering uncontrollably. Oh my God! Roger was gone from my life.

Chapter 28

Icontinued to tremble, the panic rising. Was Roger gone for good? I put my fingers to my lips. There wasn't any blood there but they felt tender and swollen—like he'd put a branding iron on them.

To go to the extent of bruising my lips Roger had to have been pushed to the extreme. He wasn't a violent man by nature. That much I knew. Had I turned him into a brute?

But then, how dare he talk to me like that? And how dare he use me as a punching bag with that cruel kiss? And damn it all, why was I obsessing over *his* feelings in all of this? Several minutes later, I still stood on the sidewalk, huddled against the chill, still fuming.

And yet, the rage was minor when compared with the fear of losing Roger forever.

Once I recovered somewhat from the shock of that kiss and his parting words, I slowly went back inside the restaurant to face my parents—and Roger's family.

The second they saw me approaching they stopped talking. Then they all stared at me in silence. The women looked wide-eyed and anxious, the men curious.

Too mortified to meet the Vadepallis' gazes, I stood in front of the group with my hands in my pockets and turned to my parents. "Can we go home now, please?"

Renuka gave me a suspicious look. "Where's Rajesh, Soorya?"

"He went to the cast party." I could tell they were all dying to know what had occurred between Roger and me. Perhaps my swollen lips had given away some of what had happened? If they had guessed, they wouldn't say anything, anyway. Folks like ours didn't openly talk about such matters.

Dad recovered quickly and said, "Sure, princess. I'll be right back." He pushed his chair in and walked over to the front desk to settle the bill. Mr. Vadepalli sprang to his feet and followed him. The others at the table turned their gazes on the men, shifting their attention away from me. *Thank you, God.*

The restaurant was small enough and quiet enough at the moment for us to hear the men arguing. Mr. Vadepalli pulled out his wallet and grabbed my dad's wrist. "Pramod, this is my treat—my son's debut. Please let me pay. It's the least I can do."

Dad slapped his shoulder with a grin. "Next time, Venki, when we come to visit you, I'll make sure we go to the most expensive place in Kansas and make you pay, my friend."

"You promise?" Mr. Vadepalli put his wallet back in his pocket.

"Of course. You're a rich man, Venki, and I plan to take advantage of it," said Dad with a good-natured chuckle. After Dad signed the credit card bill, I saw the two men put their heads close together and have a whispered conversation, none of which I could hear. But it didn't take a genius to figure out they were talking about Roger and me.

What other kind of upheaval were the two old men cooking up now? Hadn't they created enough chaos?

I stood with my face to the window, rocking on my heels and pretending to be absorbed by the street scene visible through the tinted glass. That way I could avoid looking at everyone at the table. But I could feel their eyes on me, like laser beams fixed on my back.

Finally, after some more whispering, Dad and Roger's father returned to the table. Everyone shuffled to their feet and put on their coats. I was dying to get out of there. With all those silent, speculative looks aimed in my direction, the room felt stifling, like the walls were closing in on me. Even the two waiters were still eyeing me.

We said our good-byes standing on the sidewalk. While the rest of the folks hugged and shook hands and promised to call each other, and my family wished theirs a safe flight back to Kansas, I limited my farewell to two words: "Good night."

But Renuka took my hand and held it between both of hers. "It was lovely meeting you, Soorya. I hope you'll stay in touch." She fished out a card from her purse and pressed it in my hand. "E-mail me when you get a chance." She whispered in my ear, "Call me if you need to talk. Anytime."

Despite the sincerity in her eyes, I merely put the card in my purse and gave her a polite smile. I didn't trust my voice to say anything civil at the moment.

Dad walked to the parking garage with the Vadepallis while Mom and I waited outside the restaurant with Pamma. Several minutes later, I noticed Renuka's husband at the wheel of their rental car as they drove away, waving at us. Dad brought our vehicle around to pick us up.

I settled in the backseat beside Pamma and closed my eyes for a blessed second. How had a pleasant day morphed into a total disaster in an instant? Earlier that evening, when I was getting dressed, I'd been excited, looking forward to having a good time.

It had turned out to be delightful at first, but had plummeted and crashed sometime during dinner. Finally, it had turned into the worst day of my life.

I sat in silence as Dad drove us home. Mom, in the passenger seat next to him, tried to start a conversation. "That was such an exciting play, wasn't it?"

Dad nodded, trying to help her along. "Even Amma seemed to enjoy it."

"The rice *pulao* at the restaurant was a bit undercooked, but the rest of the food was pretty good. What did you think, Soorya?" asked Mom, obviously babbling to draw me out of my surly mood.

But I had nothing to say. I kept my gaze focused outside the window.

Pamma took my hand and stroked it. I reclaimed my hand

and thrust it inside my coat pocket. I wanted nothing to do with any of them. Although I wasn't sure why I was mad at Pamma. Her only offense was that she liked the Vadepallis, especially Roger. And that fact more or less made her my enemy, too—at the moment.

After a few more failed attempts at getting me to thaw out, Mom gave up. We drove the rest of the way like silent ghosts riding in a phantom automobile.

When we got home, Pamma announced that she was going straight to bed. But before heading for her room she cupped my cheek in her wizened hand. "Baby, too much anger is not good. You think about everything very careful like, okay? You are a big girl now. You must have little more understanding."

Ignoring her counsel, I peeled off my coat and headed for the staircase. I needed to be alone and wanted to reach the sanctuary of my room as quickly as I could.

I couldn't stand to spend another moment with my parents. They were schemers of the worst kind. How could they treat me like a sack of potatoes to be given away? Was I that much of a burden to them?

As I undressed and brushed my teeth with enough vigor to make my gums bleed, I felt something rising within me. All the teenage rebellion that had leached out of my system sometime ago was seeping back with a kick.

Looking at myself in the mirror while I removed my makeup, I made the decision to call Lou. The heck with convention and the unwritten code of behavior for young women.

No one was going to arrange my life for me. No one. I was born and raised in a free country and I had a right to live like other Americans. I could make my own decisions—mistakes included—and carve out my own life.

I'd invite Lou to go to dinner with me tomorrow. And then I'd seduce him. I could at least try, couldn't I? He was certainly attracted to me. He'd admitted it the day we went to Little India. He'd found me kissable enough despite my stuffed-up nose and puffy eyes. He'd surely find me doubly enticing when I was healthy and looking my best.

In spite of my earlier misgivings about Lou never being able to fit in with my family, it was that very fact that made him the ideal man for my plans. My parents would never accept him—at least never wholeheartedly. Perfect.

Now wouldn't it be a great big surprise for Lou if *I* took the initiative in the matter? I'd make him forget his precious Lynne while I was at it. It was time he got over his dead wife and moved on. It was time I forgot about Roger and moved on as well.

It would be a real date this time. I'd make sure I enjoyed every second of my time with Lou.

And later, I'd tell my parents about it in excruciating detail.

Chapter 29

I dressed very carefully on Saturday afternoon for my dinner date with Lou. Wearing a black wool skirt, turquoise top that showed a bit of cleavage, and subtle makeup, I looked my very best. With a dose of antihistamine, I could even indulge in a squirt of perfume. My calf-length suede boots were the perfect finishing touch.

Lou and I were going to meet near his home in Hamilton. He'd been a little surprised at my suggestion but was delighted that he wouldn't have to drive much and neither would I. He was going to pick me up at the Princeton Junction train station and we'd have dinner at a cozy restaurant on Witherspoon Street, close to the Princeton University campus.

As I descended the stairs and went to the hall closet to grab my coat, Mom came out of the kitchen, wiping her hands on a towel. "Going to a party?" Her expression said she approved of my outfit—despite the risqué neckline.

"I have a date."

"That's nice," she said. "I'm glad you're not angry at Rajesh anymore."

"I'm not meeting Rajesh." I pretended to rummage in the closet for the right coat. It was hard to make eye contact with my mother.

"Is it someone Dad and I know?" The disappointment in her voice was unmistakable.

Just then Dad emerged from the powder room off the foyer,

making me groan inwardly. Now I'd have to face the two of them.

"Did I hear something about a date, princess?" Dad queried. I had a feeling he'd hurried out of the bathroom as soon as he'd heard me mention it. His hearing was keen.

"Yes." I drew a quick breath and looked squarely at both of them. "I'm meeting Lou Draper for dinner."

"Oh." Mom's mouth stayed puckered for a moment before the puzzled look set in. "The man who brought you to the hospital?"

"Correct." I buttoned up my coat.

Dad's eyebrows plunged. "I didn't realize you had a personal relationship with that man."

"I do. That's why we're having dinner together." I wanted to tell them about my previous date with him in Edison, but I refrained.

"Where?" demanded Dad.

"In Princeton." I pulled on my gloves.

"You're driving all the way to Princeton? There's still some black ice on the back roads."

As if I hadn't been driving on icy roads for years now? I sighed long and hard. "No, Dad. I'm only driving up to the station and then taking the train. Lou's picking me up at the Princeton Junction station."

Dad threw me a pointed look. "You're sure you know what you're doing, Soorya?"

"Positive. I'm thirty years old and getting older and wiser by the minute," I quipped.

That didn't stop Dad. "But have you given any thought to the consequences of seeing a man like that?"

"You mean because he's black?"

"That and a few other things, like his family background. You don't know anything about his personal life, do you?" Dad had to be bristling underneath the controlled façade.

"Welcome to the twenty-first century, Dad." I smirked. "How many of your rich and famous patients are black?"

"Quite a few," he replied with enviable calm. "That doesn't mean they're part of my family."

"Well, who knows, you just might end up with a black son-in-law someday." I slung my purse over my shoulder and started toward the door leading into the garage, feeling a perverse sense of satisfaction at seeing my mother wince. "By the way, Lou's a widower." I threw my parents a beatific smile. "A mature and experienced family man."

"If this is your idea of getting even with your mom and me and Rajesh, I pray that you come to your senses before you do something you'll regret, Soorya." There it was again. He'd called me Soorya. His quiet voice told me he was trying hard to keep a lid on his temper. If I were much younger, he'd have lashed out at me.

Nevertheless it was my temper that erupted right then. I turned on them, my eyes burning. "It's *my* life to mess up, isn't it? I'm sick and tired of being a good Telugu girl whose Mommy and Daddy have to pay some guy a huge dowry to take her off their hands."

For once Dad became quiet, probably because he'd never heard anything this crushing coming out of my mouth since I'd reached adulthood. His expression slowly changed from controlled annoyance to dismay.

He stared at me in silence, his hands clenched into tight fists. Mom looked like she'd received a blow to her stomach.

But I'd come this far, and I wasn't about to back down. "I'll be late coming back. Don't bother waiting up for me."

As I opened the automatic garage door and got behind the wheel of my car, the wicked gratification I'd felt a moment ago began to recede.

By the time I parked at the station and ran to catch the train, which was just pulling in, a strange sense of numbness settled over me. I'd hurt my parents like never before.

Their wounded faces were all I could picture in my mind, all the way to Princeton Junction.

After I got off the train, seeing a smiling Lou waiting for me on the platform thawed my brain a little. He looked and smelled good, like a man eager for a date. He gathered me in his large arms, gave a me tight hug, and kissed me on the cheek. "I'm so glad you called. I'd been resigned to spending a lonely weekend."

"I'm glad, too." I told myself I was very glad indeed.

As we got into his Explorer and drove toward Princeton, I managed to tuck away most of my misgivings beneath a cheerful veneer. This was my date, my evening, my chance to enjoy them as I saw fit.

We chatted easily during the drive along Washington and Nassau Streets, about Pamma's improving health, about my work, Lou's work—everything but the reason why I'd called him out of the blue.

He didn't ask. I didn't tell. He seemed pleased that I had called. And that was enough.

The restaurant was small but packed. I let my eyes roam around the place after we were seated at a table. "Popular place."

"It's always crowded, especially on weekends. They get reservations weeks in advance."

"How'd you manage to get reservations on short notice?" I asked.

"Clout," he bragged. "A friend of mine is a chef here."

"So that's your secret," I said, looking at the wine list the waiter had left us with. After some deliberation I decided to stick with my Diet Sprite while Lou ordered a glass of Merlot.

The food was delicious, charmingly served in old china. My Greek salad and leek soup were seasoned to perfection. Lou pronounced his prime rib excellent. I was quiet through dinner, listening to Lou talk about some of the more interesting things he'd been doing lately.

As I smiled and deliberated and commented appropriately on his anecdotes, Dad's words began to come back to me. *You don't know anything about his personal life, do you?* I knew about his life, all the way from childhood, and yet, I didn't

really know a whole lot about the man's personality or character beyond what I'd seen so far.

A couple of times Lou looked at me curiously. "Are you
okay? You've been very quiet," he remarked.

"I'm fine, Lou," I assured him. "It's nice to hear another attorney talk about his work for a change."

That and a second glass of wine had spurred Lou into talking
some more, which was fine with me. I was getting more and
more introspective instead of participating actively in my much-
anticipated date.

By the time Lou had his coffee and insisted on picking up the
tab despite my offer to split the hefty bill, my spirit was all but
gone. I kept seeing my parents' pained faces. Thank goodness
Pamma's face was missing from that mix. That would have
made it worse.

It will get better later, I advised myself. Lou was likely to kiss
me, if nothing else, and then things would heat up—get really
interesting. My feminine instincts would kick in, just like the
last time he'd kissed me.

I would have a great time yet.

"Is everything okay, Soorya?" Lou asked again as we walked
back to his car, careful to skirt around the icy spots on the sidewalk.

"Yeah, sure," I said, looking up at a small patch of sky visible
beyond the cluster of tall roofs and treetops. It was a clear night.
"Just wondering what time it is."

Lou looked at his watch and turned to me. "It's not even
seven o'clock yet. You're not thinking of leaving already, are
you?" He pulled out a roll of mints from his pocket and offered
me one, then tossed one into his mouth.

"Not yet. I have plenty of time." I was surprised it was still
that early, in spite of our leisurely dinner.

He took my arm and started walking briskly toward his car.
"Good, because I have plans for us."

"What kind of plans?" I asked with a coy smile. Flirting wasn't
part of my personality, so I had to put some effort into it. But in

the next second I wondered why I was trying so hard to flirt. Something in Lou's words and expression told me his plans could be of the intimate kind.

For the first time since I'd made this date I began to feel a smidgen of alarm.

"I'm taking you back to my house." He smiled down at me, teeth gleaming in the lights shining from nearby businesses, confirming my suspicion.

My pulse skittered. "You are?"

"It's just a little rancher. Nothing compared to what you're used to, I'm sure. But it's my home. I'd like you to see it."

"Is it far?"

"No, only about fifteen minutes from here."

"I'm sure you have a lovely house, Lou." The word *home* made me swallow hard. His home and Lynne's. I wasn't sure if I wanted to set foot in the place where his wife and he had made a happy life for themselves, made love, made plans for the future—the future that wasn't meant to be.

It was also the house where she might have died.

Lou came to a stop beside his vehicle, then leaned toward me and engaged me in a hard kiss, filled with promise—probably a taste of what was yet to come.

He tasted of mint and . . . desire. The kiss didn't last long since there were too many pedestrians milling around to allow privacy. But the message was clear. The man fairly reeked of lust. Even I could sense it.

The alarm bells in my head went up by a few decibels.

I started to get the feeling that Lou's plans included an evening of sex—in the bed he'd likely shared with Lynne. And what did he mean when he said he'd like for me to see his house? Was I giving him ideas about a possible future together? Was seeing a woman a couple of times enough to have a man thinking about a permanent relationship? I wished I knew the answers.

What was I thinking when I'd called him to suggest this rendezvous?

I was still a virgin, an embarrassment at my age. And then there was the fact that I wasn't prepared for intimacy with this man. Any man. Was I ready to give up my virginity to a widower I barely knew, just to prove a point?

Why the heck had I imagined I could enjoy a normal date like my friends? I wasn't like them. I could never be exactly like them.

Dad's words started pounding in my head again. *If this is your idea of getting even with your mom and me and Rajesh, I pray that you come to your senses before you do something you'll regret, Soorya.*

I couldn't do this, I realized, the panic rising as Lou turned on the ignition and slowly maneuvered the car out of its spot and merged into the traffic. I couldn't sleep with Lou. Not now. Not ever.

Besides, I couldn't lead him on and then break up with him later. He was still hurting from losing his wife. I couldn't add to that pain.

Setting up this date with him was a mistake. But it wasn't too late to correct it.

"Lou, I think we better skip any further plans for the evening," I murmured as we came to a stoplight.

He chewed vigorously on his mint and angled a confused glance at me. "Didn't you say you were in no hurry to get back?"

"Yes, but I'm beginning to realize it's a long train ride and then another drive back to my house."

He went quiet for a minute. "Are you mad at me? Did I say something wrong?"

"No, Lou." I fidgeted with my gloves. Perhaps the truth would be best. "It's just that . . . I'm not prepared to go to your house yet. It's too soon for that."

"Humph," he grunted and accelerated again as the light turned green.

I noticed we were already on Washington Road. His house was probably not too far. I had to make him take me back to the train station before we ended up in his driveway, before it became too late to turn back. I put a hand on his arm. "Lou, no offense, but I think I should take the next train back home."

"Why?" He looked tense and irritated, and I couldn't blame him.

"I don't want my parents worrying about my safety."

His jaw tightened. "They think I'll take advantage of you? What kind of a man do they think I am?"

"It's nothing like that," I replied. "They think you're a great guy, especially after the way you came through for me when my grandmother was ill."

"Then what is it?" he demanded as he drove through yet another busy intersection—this time a bit too fast for my comfort. "Is it because I'm black?"

"It's not that, either." I didn't have an answer, even for myself. I liked Lou immensely and enjoyed his company. His ethnicity didn't matter to me one bit. And yet there were too many things that seemed wrong with the two of us coming together as more than friends—like a puzzle where no matter which way you tried, the pieces didn't fit. So all I said was, "It's difficult to explain."

He drew an audible breath and slowed the vehicle, clearly trying to calm himself. Maybe he was trying to understand my capriciousness, or trying to summon patience to deal with an unpredictable woman like me. "Tell me honestly, why did you ask me to meet you today?" he demanded.

I shook my head. "I don't know, Lou. It seemed like a good idea at the time."

"But now you're regretting it."

My silence was enough of an answer.

"Fine, I'll take you back to the train station." We drove the rest of the way in silence at a reasonable speed. The dashboard clock read 7:12 P.M. when we reached our destination and found a temporary parking spot. The next train wasn't due for several minutes.

"I'm really sorry, Lou," I mumbled, feeling more foolish and rueful than ever. "I guess I'm not used to this sort of thing."

He sat staring out the windshield for a long time, his face frozen, his thick fingers drumming a tattoo on the steering wheel, making me wonder if this was the calm before he exploded in a fit of rage. I didn't know him well enough to gauge his every mood.

Then slowly he turned toward me. "That's okay, Soorya."

"No, it's not okay. It's all my fault." I was on the verge of tears and my voice wobbled. "I—I don't know how to make it up to you, Lou. I've treated you very badly. I've been selfish and stupid."

He patted my hand. "Don't punish yourself. It wouldn't have worked between us, anyway."

"Why do you say that?"

"We'd probably end up having an affair, but it wouldn't have gone anywhere. We're from different worlds. You've had a lavish life and I grew up in a ghetto."

"Our lifestyles have nothing to do with this," I countered, trying not to sniffle. The tears were close to spilling. "I'm proud of who you are and what you've done with your life."

"But you just can't accept me as a guy you could go out with."

I chewed on that for a bit. "I can't explain it, Lou. I know something doesn't feel right about us in the romantic sense. I've come to respect and like you very much. I want us to be friends, if you're willing to accept that."

He took his time responding. "I'll accept that."

"Thank you. That means a lot to me."

He let out a resigned sigh. "To tell you the truth, I still miss Lynne. I think I was only trying to prove to myself that I'm still alive, and still able to feel something."

"I can understand that." I really did, to some extent. He was desperately trying to put the past behind him and get on with his life, and I happened to be there at the right time. It was generous of him to confess his sentiments instead of letting me wallow in guilt.

"My mistake was in trying to do it with someone like you,

inexperienced and unprepared for an affair." He put a hand on mine and squeezed gently. "I'm sorry I came on strong."

"You didn't," I assured him, vastly relieved at the mature way he was handling all this. "You're not mad at me, then?" When he shook his head, I started to cry in earnest. How could he forgive me so easily?

"I'm not mad at you, honey. Please don't cry." He wiped away my tears with his thumbs. It was an unexpected and tender gesture. Instead of consoling me, it only brought on more tears. "I'm mad at myself for being foolish enough to think a woman like you could have a relationship with a man like me."

"You're not foolish, Lou." I sniffled. "Some things are meant to happen, while some are not. I'm sure you'll meet the right woman one of these days."

"You're a kind young lady, but I believe your mind is on that young man who came to visit your grandma in the hospital." He looked at me closely. "Am I right?"

I frowned at him and blew my nose with a tissue. "Roger? He's just a family friend." Was I that transparent?

Lou chuckled, allowing me to breathe easier and regain my composure. "I saw you staring at him, my dear. I got the distinct impression he's more than a friend. Your parents seem to like him a lot, too."

"They certainly like him," I said.

"I admit I was a little jealous of him. I still am."

I wasn't surprised to hear that. Lou's reaction to Roger that day in the hospital had been a clear case of jealousy. "You've no reason to be," I said. "But I'm flattered."

Lou looked at the clock and unhooked his seat belt. "Your train should be here in about five minutes. I'll wait inside the station with you."

"You don't have to do that. I'm a big girl and there are plenty of people on the platform."

"You're sure?"

"Absolutely. Thanks for a lovely dinner." Gingerly I kissed his cheek. "Again, I'm sorry for ruining your evening."

"You did not ruin my evening," he assured me. "Let me know you got home safely, Soorya."

"I will." I hurried toward the platform with my head down. What I'd done was pretty disgusting—using a vulnerable man for my petty, selfish purposes.

I couldn't let it happen again.

He'd wait in the car until I boarded the train. I was certain of that. Lou was a gentleman.

Chapter 30

As I approached the house, I noticed the lights on in the family room and foyer. Mom and Dad were probably watching TV or reading. There was no way to avoid them. They'd wonder why I was returning home hours earlier than their estimate.

It was likely to raise a lot of questions. Thank goodness, I'd had enough time on the train to compose myself after my fit of tears.

Since I'd promised Lou I'd call him when I reached home, I stopped on the street outside for a minute and used my cell phone to let him know before pulling into the garage. I got out of the car and shut the door reluctantly.

I entered the house, bracing myself for the third degree.

As expected, Mom was the first to appear in the foyer. She was in her usual nightgown, face glistening with moisturizer. "You're early."

"Yes." I unbuttoned my coat.

She bit her lower lip and studied me. "Is everything okay?"

"Sure."

"I thought you would be very late."

Hanging up the coat, I shut the closet door. "I was a little tired and decided to come home early."

"Is that the only reason?" It was Dad who asked that, emerging from the family room. He was dressed for bed as well, a robe covering his pajamas.

"Yes." I wasn't about to confess that I'd had cold feet, that his earlier words of warning had hounded me all evening. I wouldn't give him the satisfaction. Instead I walked toward the staircase. "I'm off to bed."

I saw Dad and Mom exchange a private look—a familiar look. It generally preceded a lecture.

"Stop right there, Soorya," commanded Dad. "Your mother and I want to talk to you." His tone, too, had a familiar ring—it meant I had no choice but to concede. He was in *Indian Dad* mode.

"I have nothing to say, Dad," I informed him wearily.

"But *we* have something to say to you. Stop behaving like a petulant child and sit down," he said, shepherding me into the family room. "This nonsense has gone on long enough."

From habit I sat on the edge of the recliner, keeping my eyes trained on the carpet. Dad and Mom sat side by side on the couch. Again, this was a familiar scene from my childhood, when I was about to be reprimanded for some wild or stupid thing I'd done. Even the tightening in my tummy was reminiscent of those days.

"Soorya, why are you behaving like this?" Dad asked.

His words echoed what Roger had said to me the previous night. "Behaving like what, Dad?" My defenses were already up and Dad's question only served to reinforce them.

"I know exactly why you're giving us the silent treatment since last night—and why you're having an affair with that Draper fellow."

"I'm not having an affair with Lou."

"Didn't you say you had a date with him? Isn't that your way of punishing me and your mother?"

"That's not true!" My voice sounded whiny and defensive even to my own ears.

He held up one index finger. "Remember one thing, though. That kind of retribution will end up hurting *you* more than anyone else. It's self-destructive."

I suppressed my urge to tell him that I'd already recognized that. All through the evening I'd been obsessing over my impulsiveness. My mistake. My stupidity.

"What happened to you last evening?" asked Dad. "You were fine until I mentioned my involvement in Rajesh's venture. After that you immediately put on a face and clammed up. Why?"

I sat there for a long time, my thoughts spinning in my head, my lips trembling. I felt like I was thirteen again. I finally looked up. "You want to know why? Because you bought Roger with your millions. Isn't that what this so-called investment is all about? An attempt to purchase a husband for your loser daughter? And how different is that from the dowry system that you allegedly condemn? What you did is worse. It's underhanded. It's bribery, Dad, plain and simple."

"No, it is not. When I offered to fund Rajesh's project, it had nothing to do with you. Do you remember the day the Vadepallis visited us, when Rajesh talked about his play and how Venki maligned him? Well, that night the boy convinced me that there was something to this Broadway idea. I admit it sounded like a vague, unreachable dream, but he had a vision, the willingness to work hard, and all he needed was the money to reach it. He got me thinking."

"That's bullshit, Dad. It had everything to do with me. You wouldn't have just gone out and found a penniless Broadway dreamer and given him half a million dollars. This was all about me."

"Oh, shut up, Soorya! The universe doesn't revolve around you. Your mom and I do have other things to occupy us. I believed in the boy's dream and wanted to offer him support. I did it partly for my own pleasure, too—my contribution to the world of theater, which I love so much. Besides, the story was intriguing—all about a young Indian man coming to America with big dreams, and despite the many hurdles, succeeding in realizing those dreams. It was a tale I could relate to, so I not only decided to help out Rajesh but I also called his father and shamed him into putting up half the capital."

"And I bet Roger just grabbed it with both hands!"

"Not at all. Contrary to what you think, Rajesh is a decent young man with scruples."

"Really? He didn't have a problem looking for a rich wife to fund his play."

"Looking for business backing is not unscrupulous. It's practical thinking. Besides, Rajesh was reluctant to accept money from me. You know why? Because he felt you would jump to precisely the conclusion you have. But when I convinced him that it was strictly a loan, he agreed."

"Of course he did." Roger was a talented actor.

"Thirty years ago, I had a dream of becoming a famous cosmetic surgeon," continued Dad, ignoring my sarcasm. "I had to beg and borrow money to set up my practice in a dreadfully expensive place like Manhattan, so I knew how the boy felt."

"Then why didn't you tell me all this earlier? Why did I have to wait until tonight to find out?"

"You never gave us a chance to explain last night. You ran off to hide in your room." His eyes narrowed on me. "I don't know what made you come home early this evening, but you seem kind of . . . down." His expression turned more suspicious as he leaned closer to study my face. "Did something happen in Princeton? Did that man—"

"No! Lou's a decent guy." Damn, but my eyes were probably still red and puffy. "We had a very pleasant dinner together, that's all."

"Okay," Dad murmured. He didn't pursue the subject.

"Told you I was merely tired," I reminded him, breathing a sigh of relief.

"In that case it's time to have this out, Soorya, once and for all."

"Let's hear it, then." I compressed my mouth into a tight line.

Mom, who'd been quiet all this time, spoke up. "Baby, we want you to know that Venki had asked us to keep it quiet. He said you were likely to react badly—exactly like you're doing now. Besides, he wanted his son to think all the money came from your dad, so he'd work hard to make it a success. He was afraid Rajesh would take it easy if it was his own father's money. Last evening's revelation was a shock to poor Rajesh. Did you see the expression on his face?"

"Hmm." That explained Roger's discomfort outside the restrooms, when I'd thanked him for inviting us. He owed it to us. It was Dad who'd made the whole thing possible. "Why didn't Roger tell me about your offer? He made it sound like he'd found some capitalist to finance his project, but he never as much as hinted it was you."

Dad's stiff shoulders relaxed a bit, probably because the secret was finally out in the open. "He wanted to tell you long ago, princess, but I prevented him from doing it. I knew you'd explode. You have a mean temper, you know."

"What difference would it have made if I exploded then or exploded now?"

"Big difference. Now you've had a chance to get to know Rajesh better. If you had known this months ago, you would have dismissed him as a greedy, devious opportunist. You'd never have agreed to see him, let alone talk to him or spend time with him."

I didn't want to admit it, but Dad was probably right. "Well, now that you've generously funded Roger's play, I suppose he can go on his merry way. Venki and Sharda can find him a pretty little wife somewhere and we can all get on with our lives." I stood up. "I'm going to bed."

Dad glared at me. "I'm not done yet. Sit down!"

I wondered how long this grilling was likely to last. "I'm exhausted, Dad," I said and remained standing.

"So am I, Soorya, with your juvenile attitude. Now sit down and hear me out." After I sank back onto the chair, he leaned forward, his arms resting loosely on his knees. "You were the one who turned him down. Rajesh told me that he'd mentioned marriage the day you guys met, and that you'd more or less made it clear you weren't interested in a man with no money and no career prospects."

"I didn't say that."

"Not in so many words, but that was the impression you gave Rajesh, isn't that right?"

"If you were in my shoes, would you have considered someone as unconventional as him? He even lied about his name. And you should have seen his picture. I've seen homeless men who look more respectable than that." I looked at Mom. "If Dad had been like Roger, would you have thought of him as a potential husband for yourself?"

Mom took a moment to respond. "Probably not. But I saw the look on your face when you met Rajesh. You nearly dropped the coffee tray. After that day I could see the disappointment in your face when there was no call from the Vadepallis. You were interested in Rajesh the man, but not Rajesh the dramatist. Am I right?"

I shrugged, reluctant to acknowledge it and yet marveling at how accurately Mom had read my mind. I hadn't realized she was that perceptive. "I guess."

"So when we realized you and Rajesh could make such a good match, and the only thing stopping that from happening was his career, Dad and I decided we might be able to help."

"So you guys set out to rescue Rog . . . Rajesh?"

Dad shrugged. "I suppose you could call it that. And rescue *you* from your silly hang-ups to some extent."

Mom's basset hound eyes focused on mine like soft moonbeams. "Was that so wrong, dear? We want to see you happy, and Rajesh could make you happy. He told us he liked you since the day he met you."

"You're making that up." Something stirred in my chest—despite my doubts.

"I'm not. He said you were different from the other girls he had met. He liked your candid nature and your feistiness. He called the other young women he had met insipid—demure little Telugu girls that bored him to tears."

"That's just sour grapes because all those women turned him down."

"So did you, and yet he liked you a lot more than he did those girls, enough to want to stick around and stay in touch with you. He has been trying very hard to win you over."

I rolled my eyes. "Exactly how is he doing that, Mom?"

Mom groaned. "Are you blind? He invited you to dinner and then to lunch, which you couldn't go to because you got sick. But he still brought you chocolates and stayed with you all afternoon in an effort to cheer you up. He even asked you to attend his rehearsals."

"How do *you* know all that?" I asked with a scowl. I thought I'd successfully kept my dealings with Roger a secret.

"Recently he told us about all the times you two had met, including how much he enjoyed your trip to the temple."

That Roger needed to have his big mouth sewn shut.

"He said quite frankly that he admires you. He thinks you're a brilliant young lady," Mom said. "He wants to propose to you. What more do you want from that poor boy, Soorya?"

"He really said all that?" I wished my parents had told me this a long time ago.

Dad gave a dry laugh. "He said that and more. I just wish you'd give the man a chance. He's a good kid. And you know what? He's promised his father that if he fails in this venture he'll join Venki's consulting business. So there you go. Rajesh can still be a rich businessman and a suitable husband for a successful and bright lawyer. Either way you have nothing to lose."

I shot Dad a wary look. "Does this mean you guys are going to force me to marry Roger?"

Mom rose wearily to her feet and turned toward the door. "No, dear. We don't believe in forcing you into doing anything you don't want to do. It's up to you. And I wish you would start calling him Rajesh. Even his professional name is Rajesh Vadepalli now."

"What about his parents? How do they feel about me?"

Dad got up to follow Mom. "They think you're a strong and practical young lady, a good complement to their creative and idealistic Rajesh."

"Strong and practical is just another way to describe bossy and boring, Dad."

"Nothing wrong with that. I'm bossy and boring myself, and proud of it. Rajesh could stand to learn some of your discipline and business sense." Since I opened my mouth to retort, he promptly held up a hand to shut me up. "Now go to bed and think about this before you start shooting your mouth off."

Mom gave me one of her stern looks. "And remember, nice Telugu boys don't grow on trees. Rajesh is not going to hang around forever. If you keep pushing him away, he will be gone from your life before you know it."

He was already gone from my life, but I wasn't about to reveal that to Mom and Dad. Let them think what they wanted.

"Other girls find him very attractive," Mom added. Her face broke into a fond smile. "I must say he looked very handsome and sexy in that tuxedo last night."

As if I didn't know that. Wait a minute! Had Mom actually used the word *sexy*? Had Dad looked pleased with her using such language? What was happening to my old-fashioned family? It was all Roger's fault.

I turned off the lights after my parents retired upstairs, reset the alarm, and went to my room. But I was too wound up to sleep. My mind was in turmoil. Too much had happened in one day for my tired brain to absorb.

Lying on my bed in the dark, I rehashed the scene in Lou's car. I was lucky that he'd let me off the hook that easily. He could have lost his temper at me for leading him on, or worse, he could have taken me to his house and forced himself on me. But he'd been a gentleman and would hopefully remain a friend. On a professional level, too, having a friend at the DEP was definitely an asset.

I couldn't stop obsessing over what my parents had just told me, either—and what Roger had said about his feelings for me. Could it be true that he was genuinely fond of me? I knew he liked and respected me in a certain fashion, but could he really be interested in me as a woman and not merely a cash cow?

And that kiss outside the restaurant. I'd never realized Roger was capable of that kind of raw, savage emotion. On some level it was exciting to know that the easygoing Roger had some interesting and complicated facets to his character, fiery passion and keen temper, and that I was able to bring them to the fore.

But then, half in love was not really head over heels in love. Roger had not confessed to being in love with me. On the other hand, we'd met only a few times, mostly surrounded by others, and none of them were dates, so love was not likely to happen.

And if Mom and Dad, all the other couples in my family, the Vadepallis, and more importantly, Renuka and her husband, who were closer to our age, could start with basic liking and let it mature and grow into something beautiful and lasting, why couldn't Roger and I?

As Roger had pointed out, Mom and Dad and the Vadepallis had given me every opportunity to get to know him better, and for his part he was trying, too. Also, like he'd said, in our culture, there couldn't be a more solid foundation than what the two of us had—complete support from both families combined with mutual affection.

There were so many pluses when I thought about marrying Roger. I made a mental list. According to Mom, our horoscopes were a good match. His parents and mine had bonded in an instant, something that hadn't happened with the other guys who'd come bride-viewing to our house over the last few years. Roger and I got along well. And last but not least, I found him very attractive—another thing I hadn't felt with any of the others. Not even close.

Okay, so if I'd really let him court me, if things had gone well for us, and we'd ended up getting married, I'd have had to start a whole new life—give up everything that was safe and secure and so easy to take for granted. Living in this big, comfortable house with my parents and Pamma had lulled me into a sense of security, and it was difficult to imagine a future without it.

Roger had served me a tremendous jolt by leaving me standing on the sidewalk the previous night. Perhaps I needed a wake-up call like that—to take a hard look at where my life was going. I had no other interested suitors. There had never been any.

This had been my last chance at grabbing a life with a certain amount of promise. If I'd wanted any kind of marital happiness, I was in no position to throw away an opportunity like this.

There were no guarantees in life, and this proposal hadn't come with a warranty either, perhaps not even a limited one, but it was the only offer I'd had. And yet I had chosen to cast it away.

Unable to sleep, I wandered over to the window and opened the blinds. I was bathed in moonlight. Not quite a full moon, since that had occurred last night—but still ethereal and lovely. I'd completely forgotten that Roger's debut had occurred on full-moon night. I recalled it as a pristine and beautiful night, crisp and clear, making the stars appear to be almost within one's reach.

Roger had probably planned his debut to coincide with *purnima,* an auspicious time. Perhaps his parents had advised him to do it—after consulting an astrologer about lucky dates, astral projections, best chance for success, and all those old-fashioned beliefs. A December full moon, coming at the beginning of the winter solstice, was believed to be full of promise for new ventures. How appropriate that Roger had his opening on just such a night.

And . . . oh God! He had more or less proposed to me last night, too, albeit in an angry and most unconventional fashion. We had met on a full moon day, had our first evening together outside the Ganesh temple on a full moon, and he'd proposed to me on a full moon.

Three times? Was that some weird coincidence? Was it a sign from the Gods?

With my eyes fixed on the moon, and my mind in overdrive, I

was finally willing to admit that I was ready for a commitment—willing to set aside my ego and make a concession.

Yes, I was a spoiled brat. I had a mean temper, as Dad had
pointed out. And yes, I had a chip on my shoulder. Perhaps if I'd
had a sibling or two I'd have been less self-centered?

And with that understanding came another, more significant
realization: I didn't want to lose Roger. I couldn't afford to lose
him.

Alas, it was too late to win him back.

Chapter 31

The next morning, gritty-eyed and exhausted from analyzing and lamenting over my mistakes all night, I trudged downstairs to the kitchen for a glass of skim milk. I hadn't bothered to change out of my pajamas and robe.

Dad, Mom, and Pamma were sitting around the kitchen table, drowning in newspapers. Pages were scattered on the table, the counter, even the floor.

"What are you guys doing?" The paper mess was so contrary to Mom's habitual neatness. "This place looks like a newsstand caught in a tornado."

Mom clapped her hands and beamed. "Come here, dear. Look at all the reviews for Rajesh's play."

The reviews! I shut the refrigerator door with a thud before I could reach for the milk. Oh no, amidst my self-centered pondering, I'd forgotten all about Roger's big night. Again. "So, what are they saying?" I fervently hoped it was good. "And exactly how many newspapers did you buy?"

Dad waved a page at me. "Every paper I could find at seven o'clock on a Sunday morning. Take a look. Didn't I tell you that boy was smart?"

"Yeah, Dad, you did." Short of twirling his nonexistent mustache, Dad was doing everything a proud father would do. He and Mom looked like the parents of a newborn baby boy, bursting with satisfaction. Pamma's dentures clicked briskly as she read a review through the reading glasses perched on her nose.

"They're calling him a fresh and brilliant new voice on Broadway," Dad informed me.

I gathered up some of the newspapers and settled myself in the family room. With a sense of rising euphoria, I read the reviews in the major papers: *Vadepalli's* Mumbai to Manhattan *is a promising debut. . . . A cleverly crafted tale of the macabre, the morbid, and the malicious. . . . Refreshing and vibrant. . . . Vadepalli's debut is stellar. . . . Vadepalli is a master storyteller. . . . An intriguing mix of urban crime and the paranormal with a side order of spicy Indian chutney. . . .*

There were a few negative reviews and some ho-hum ones, too. It wouldn't be realistic if there weren't. But those were from the lesser-known critics. And anyway, nobody was *that* perfect. But Roger had come close, that charming devil. He was probably walking on air right this minute, crooked grin and all.

Oh God, I missed him. I'd been with him only a day and a half ago, and it already seemed like ages since I'd seen him. Why hadn't I done something to stop him from leaving the other night? Apologized to him, at the very least? He had described me aptly: I was sitting atop a very high horse, a bitter woman so full of scorn that I couldn't see anyone or anything on the ground.

He was right. So damn right.

By rejecting Roger, I had thrown away the best thing that had ever happened in my life. Was it too late to make amends? If nothing else, Roger had a tremendous capacity for goodwill and forgiveness. But would he be big enough to forgive me and my arrogant ways? I had whittled away at his patience and kindness time and again. Would he be willing to help me dismount that imaginary horse?

I'd never know if I didn't try, and I'd never forgive myself, either. As much as I hated it, it was my turn to pick up the phone and call Roger. Even if he wanted nothing to do with me, at least I could apologize and get that load of guilt off my chest. I didn't want to feel like a first-class bitch for the rest of my life.

Picking up the address book resting by the phone on the end table, I leafed through it. Sure enough, Mom had listed the senior Vadepallis' and Roger's numbers. She even had his cell phone penciled in. That was probably the best way to catch him.

Upstairs in my room, I shut the door and retrieved my cell phone from my purse. With shaky fingers I dialed Roger's number.

On the fifth ring, he answered the phone. "Hello."

"Hi, Roger. This is Soorya."

"Oh . . . hi." His voice was subdued, distant, but more seductive than ever, and it felt like a shot of electricity rocketing up my spine.

I swallowed to moisten my dry throat. "I hope I didn't wake you up."

"No, I'm on the road."

"You're traveling?" I tried to keep the dismay out of my voice, but failed.

"Just going out for breakfast . . . and running an errand."

"Oh." Of course he had to eat. I felt tongue-tied, but managed to say, "Congratulations, Roger. I've been reading the reviews."

"I couldn't have done it without your parents."

"I know."

His tone was cool. "I've had a long couple of days, Soorya. I have to—"

"Roger, wait," I interrupted him. "I'd like to apologize for my behavior the other night."

I could hear him take a deep breath. "What brought that on? Did your mom and dad ask you to apologize?"

"No. I'm doing this entirely on my own. I was out of line."

"Okay. Apology accepted."

"I'm sorry about all the times I've been rude and nasty and . . . difficult." Now that I'd broken the ice, I wanted to finish what I'd started.

"That's all right, Soorya."

"Do you mean that, Roger, or are you just saying it to get rid of me?"

"I always mean what I say." He was silent for a minute, making me wonder if he'd hung up or his phone battery had died. But he spoke again. "I suppose I've given you sufficient cause in the past for some of that resentment."

"Can you blame me? When we met, you came across as a cold, calculating guy who wanted a rich wife and nothing more. Later, you went and told my parents about your feelings for me, yet not once did you have the decency to tell me to my face."

"I wasn't sure how you'd handle it, Soorya. You'd made it very plain that I was a drifter, not exactly your type. You know what I mean."

"Hmm." I knew what he meant. And I was glad we were talking, really talking like mature adults—instead of squabbling.

"Besides, if I told you that I liked your personality, you wouldn't have believed me anyway," added Roger. "You'd think I was lying to you just to get my hands on your money. You have a very suspicious mind, Soorya. Maybe that's an asset. It's probably what makes you an effective lawyer."

"It has served me very well in my profession, thank you," I informed him. "I don't need to defend myself on that count."

"You don't, but it's a deterrent in your personal life. It won't let you live life to the fullest—you always assume everything in this world comes with a catch—the fine print that'll bite you on the ass. And that chip on your shoulder about your appearance is so damn big, you can't see past it."

"That's not a fair shot," I retorted, despite knowing he'd hit the nail on the head. Put in so many words, it was hard not to admit I had some serious self-esteem issues, which he had pointed out so eloquently on Thanksgiving Day, and again two nights ago. "But I guess I deserve it."

"I didn't mean to insult or hurt you, Soorya. I'm just trying to get you to face the truth." Roger sounded genuinely apologetic.

I took a deep breath and counted to ten, reminded myself that he was right and I was wrong. Also, I was the one who'd called to apologize to him. I was the one who needed forgiveness. He was quite a shrewd psychoanalyst, besides being a few other things.

"I realize I have a bit of a problem, Roger. The minute I met you I was convinced that you were going to reject me." Just like all the other men before him had done, and consequently I'd wanted to be the one to decline Roger first and not the other way around.

"So you decided to behave like you didn't give a damn. You were trying to protect your ego."

"I suppose." I still couldn't admit it. It was too painful.

His voice turned wary again. "So, despite the apology you're still holding a grudge."

"No, I'm not. . . . Really." What I considered deception on his part as well as my parents' still rankled, but I wasn't raving mad any longer. Two nights of brooding and the fear of having lost him had taken the edge off my temper. He had only done what my parents had asked him to. I thought I heard Roger yawn. He sounded exhausted. "You must be dead on your feet, Roger. Go get some rest."

"Later. Right now, I think we need to talk some more."

"Not a good idea at this time." I looked at the clock on my nightstand. We'd already been talking for several minutes.

"Soorya, I've worked my tail off to succeed in a tough business." He was beginning to sound extremely tired. "When we first met, you thought I was a good-for-nothing rolling stone. After Friday night, do you still think I'm a loser?"

"No, Roger. Whatever you are, you're not a loser. Never that." Oh God, he sounded so . . . hopeless, dejected. Had I done that to him—completely crushed his spirit? I knew what rejection and disdain felt like, and yet I was inflicting it on a perfectly nice guy—and for what reasons other than pure spite and the obsessive need to protect myself from possible pain? I was being unreasonably selfish. "I'm happy for you, Roger. I'm glad you're realizing your dream."

"You mean that?"

"Absolutely," I said with all the enthusiasm I could muster.

"Look, I'm just about to enter the tunnel and the traffic is bad. I'll call you back in a few minutes," he said abruptly and hung up.

I stared at the phone for a second and ended the call. Was the tunnel a legitimate excuse or had he just dismissed me? I sat on the edge of my bed and decided to wait for a few minutes. If he didn't call back within half an hour, I'd know he didn't want anything more to do with me.

With every minute of silence that followed, my heart sank a little lower. He wasn't calling back. Well, at least I'd apologized. I'd offered him some moral support. He probably didn't believe a word of it, but I'd tried my best to patch things up between us. Only it didn't make me feel any better. Too much was left unsaid for any comfort between us in the future.

Startled by the phone ringing some twenty minutes later, I nearly let it slip out of my hand before hitting the Talk button. He was calling me back.

He started to talk instantly, like there'd been no break in our conversation. "Soorya, I need to know what you want to do about us."

"You're exhausted, Roger. We can talk another time." Although I enjoyed going head-to-head in a professional setting, I wasn't good with confrontations in personal matters, especially of the intimate variety.

"I admit I'm tired, but I won't be able to rest much until I have your answer to my question."

"Fine then, we'll talk. Where do you want to meet?"

"At your front door, in thirty seconds."

"What?"

"Open your front door, Soorya."

"Right now? You mean you've been in our driveway all this time?"

"I was in my car when you called me, driving toward your house to meet with your parents."

I frowned. "But my parents didn't tell me you were coming."

"They don't know that I'm coming. I wanted to surprise them."

My heartbeat took a giant leap. "You crazy man!"

"I'm standing on your front porch. Are you going let me in or not?"

I ended the call and tossed the phone on my bed. Then I ran down the stairs and through the foyer. I probably looked like a mess, but I didn't care.

Chapter 32

I opened the door and let Roger in. There was no cheery greeting on his lips today, only a bleak nod. He wore that well-worn leather jacket. As he walked past me I got a whiff of soap and aftershave. He had found time to shave and shower. But it didn't look like he'd slept at all. Still living on the euphoria of two nights ago? I wondered.

Hearing voices in the foyer, Mom came out of the kitchen. "Rajesh! What a pleasant surprise."

"Good morning, Auntie." He smiled at Mom, the usual boyish charm bubbling to the surface. "I hope I'm not interrupting your Sunday morning schedule."

"Not at all." Probably sensing the tension between us, Mom's gaze bounced from Roger to me a couple of times. "I'll let the two of you talk. Would you like some coffee, Rajesh?"

"No, thanks, Auntie. I'm here to see if I can talk Soorya into going out to brunch with me."

"Okay." Mom gave me a long look that was almost pleading in its intensity. She was silently telling me not to make the biggest mistake of my life. I saw it all in her expressive eyes. She gave Roger an encouraging nod and walked away.

Hushed voices in the kitchen indicated that she was probably explaining to Dad and Pamma what was going on in the foyer. I also knew the three of them were going to give Roger and me all the privacy we needed.

Roger shrugged out of his jacket, folded it over his arm, and followed me into the family room. I motioned to him to sit, but he waited to do so until I sat in the recliner. Always the gentleman—even when he was tense and exhausted.

Pulling my powder blue chenille robe tighter around myself, I glanced at him. "Well, here we are."

He returned my glance, but there was caution in his. "Were you sincere in your apology?"

I nodded. "I meant every word."

"Good." He came straight to the point. "In that case, will you consider marrying me, Soorya? I know this isn't the conventional way to do it—no diamond, no candlelight or flowers. But then ours isn't a conventional American courtship."

"You got that right." Heck, the most romantic thing we'd done was walk arm in arm outside a temple on a cold, wet night, have coffee, and then sit close together on a grimy subway station bench. So much for romance and courtship.

"We're both Indian-Americans who met at an old-fashioned bride viewing," he admitted. "I realize things didn't start out smoothly between us, but I still feel we're right for each other."

"Why is that?"

"Instinct—destiny—karma, if you wish to use a popular and clichéd Indian term. I can be as romantic as the next guy, but only if you tell me you're serious about us, about me. Then you'll see what I'm capable of."

I was sure he was capable of romance. This was the charmer who'd had lots of relationships. Nonetheless I stared at the design on the area rug. "Things haven't changed all that much since we first met, Roger. They have in some ways. Your play is up and running, and it's a success so far. But you still don't have a stable income and that means I'll be supporting you, maybe for a long time."

"Possibly," he conceded.

"Wouldn't you, as an Indian male, have a problem with that—the reversal of roles? It could become a bone of contention between us in the future."

He shook his head. "I've given it serious thought, Soorya. By this time next year, if *Mumbai to Manhattan* is not bringing in some profits, I'm planning to fold up and start working with my father. I know my limits."

I'd heard that from him once before and also from Dad, but now that Roger had reconfirmed it, I felt a lot better. And yet, I wanted his play to succeed, have his dream come true. Viewed realistically, the show could go either way, in spite of the great reviews. Broadway plays were notorious for their high failure rate. "If it comes to that worst-case scenario, and I'm hoping it doesn't, aren't there other restrictions to consider, Roger? My career will be here while you'll be forced to work out of Kansas City."

"Not necessarily. My father has several large clients on the East Coast and I could very well stay here and work out of an office in the city or even in New Jersey. Dad and I had discussed this some years ago, when I was still an undergrad—when we had both assumed I'd join his business, most likely in the sales and marketing areas."

"I'm sure you'd be great at sales and marketing." I could easily see him in that role.

"With today's technology one can work basically anywhere, even in one's home." He arched his eyebrows at me. "Have I answered all your questions?"

"Not quite." Since we were laying all our cards on the table, I had to know just one more thing. "Did you mean it when you said you find me attractive and that Dad's money plays no part in it? I have to have the absolute truth, Roger. I won't settle for anything less."

His gaze was steady. "I swear to it. If it weren't the truth, I wouldn't have asked you, Soorya. I'm too damn selfish to settle for someone I don't find attractive and don't care about. Marriage is too intimate and permanent a relationship to end up with a woman I don't like and don't want in my bed." He gave me a second or two to digest that. "So, what'll it be?"

Last night I'd realized that my life would be very empty without the unpredictable Roger in it. He had a way of making me laugh and delight in simple things like a movie, a crushed red rose, a stroll in the rain, and a quiet cup of coffee.

He had taught me how important it was to observe and appreciate people—genuinely look into their souls and see them as individuals. He had so easily forgiven his father, too, despite the bitterness. Heck, he'd forgiven me in an instant just now, although I didn't deserve it. Roger even made me feel pretty and attractive and important. Moreover, he treated me like a refined lady, something very few Indian men knew how to do, and that mattered to me very much.

Yes, I wanted him in my life. Needed him. It was no use denying it. "I've given your proposal a lot of thought." I stood and went to stand beside the window.

"And?"

"And I think you're right. If our parents could make a go of it, with just about one percent of the pre-marriage channels of communication we've been blessed with, maybe we could, too."

For the first time since the other night a gleam of warmth crept into his eyes. "You really believe that?"

"I do. If we try hard, I think we could make it."

He actually smiled. "I agree. Why don't we start trying right now by going out to brunch? I'm starving."

I chuckled. "Aren't you always?"

He got to his feet and joined me at the window. Very slowly, with some hesitation, he put his hands on my shoulders and drew me closer, giving me plenty of time to back away if I wanted to. The heat from his hands reached my skin through the layers of my pajama top and robe.

I didn't step back. He stood still, allowing me the opportunity to splay my hands on his chest and feel his hard, muscular warmth beneath the well-washed softness of the sweatshirt, inhale his scent, and study the texture of the freshly shaved skin on his face. It was like letting a new puppy get used to its master's presence, his bouquet, his voice, his personality.

"I'm sorry I hurt you the other night with that kiss," he murmured. "It was an emotional evening and I was—"

"I deserved it. In fact, I deserved a good spanking." I was surprised at my own willingness to admit my culpability.

"I promise I can do a hell of a lot better than that." He traced my lips with a gentle thumb. "Would you like me to show you?"

I nodded, feeling the first stirrings of nervous but heady anticipation. I'd never really done this. Not like this, anyway.

Then his mouth touched mine, light as a butterfly, tender, excruciatingly sweet. It was nothing like the other time and definitely nothing like Lou's aggressive kisses. I closed my eyes and surrendered to the experience. Instinctively I responded to his tongue seeking out mine, relishing the taste of him and the feel of him, despite my lack of skill.

I never knew a kiss could be so touching and yet so enchantingly sexy. And Roger was obviously a master at it. Good thing at least one of us knew the technique.

The kiss didn't last all that long, but it was enough to convince me that he was telling the truth. If I could turn the rascal on with no makeup, my hair in tangles, and dressed in a shapeless robe, I was doing just fine.

"There, does that convince you?" He kept his hands on my shoulders. His gorgeous eyes were clouded with desire. My own were probably just as hazy with need.

I narrowed my gaze on him. "Only if you can tell me you don't do that with other women."

"I haven't kissed anyone since I broke up with my last girlfriend ... over two years ago," he said on an amused laugh. "Don't tell me you're jealous, my spirited Soorya."

"Dream on, Vadepalli." I gave him a look of mock indignation, but he'd called me his spirited Soorya. I could kiss him silly just for that.

Feeling reckless, and also since he'd accused me of never taking the initiative, I slipped my arms around his neck and put my lips to the hollow of his throat, where his skin felt like warm, fragrant satin. His long arms tightened around me, telling me he liked my bold gesture. I was learning a lot about him in this short interlude. And about myself.

I had no idea being held flush against a man's hard body and feeling it pulsing next to mine could be so exciting, so empowering. I could stand like this for the next ten years and not be tired or bored. Why the hell hadn't I given this a chance earlier? His heart was thumping wildly in keeping with mine. Wow, I could do that to him?

"Well?" he said after a while. "Yes or no to my proposal?"

"Yes. But we'll still have to talk about some things."

"I should have known that legal mind of yours would find a way to ruin a perfect moment," he said, but his tone was blithe, and his fingers sifted playfully through my hair.

"Just so you know, I'm a neatness freak like my mother, and I use only unscented soap because of my allergies. I like white towels, too."

"Not a problem," he replied.

"We'll have to decide where to live," I added. "Then there's my special diet versus your unlimited capacity to eat junk." I took a step back but stayed within the circle of his arms. "We need to discuss all those small, everyday things before you run out and shop for a ring."

"I agree," he said, his trademark grin returning. "Maybe we can do the ring in a month or so?"

"Fair enough. But I want the candles and flowers. Even if it's arranged, I won't settle for a haphazard proposal. I'm a perfectionist and I have my standards," I informed him firmly.

"Yes, dear," he said in a meek voice. "Anything else?"

"That's it for the moment," I said, trying not to laugh at his submissive act. Reluctantly disengaging myself from his arms, I turned toward the door. My legs were still trembling from that kiss. I wanted more of that with him, lots more. "I'll get changed and we'll go have brunch," I told him. "Then we'll talk about all those things, Roger."

"Now that you've decided to accept my proposal, although it comes with a couple dozen legal clauses, do you think you could make an effort to call me Rajesh? At least Raj?"

I pretended to think about it for a second. "Guess I could handle Raj." Then turning around, I started upstairs to get changed and swallow my daily dose of antihistamine.

"I'll go chat with your parents and Pamma while you're getting ready," he said.

While I dressed and put on my makeup, I heard Roger conversing and laughing with my family in the kitchen. They clearly loved him. And so did I.

There, I'd finally acknowledged it. I loved him.

Despite acknowledging my feelings for him, I had to face the fact that ours was not the usual Indian match: two well-placed nerds marrying, buying the house in the suburbs, a BMW and an SUV, and giving birth to two kids who won every math and spelling bee in the universe. A Hindu-American's ultimate dream.

I was about to get engaged to the most unconventional, modern-day hippie this side of the Atlantic. God help me.

And honestly, Roger was going to be a handful when it came to women—of all ages. He seemed to like them and they seemed to reciprocate. I had no idea how I was going to keep the predatory females away from my private pot of honey. It was sure to be a challenge.

"Nothing like a good challenge to make life interesting, right?" I whispered to the flushed, starry-eyed woman staring back at me in the mirror.

Then I picked up my purse and went downstairs. My destiny was calling.

Author's Note

Dear Reader,

After writing about some serious social issues like India's dowry system, female-fetus abortions, the repressive lives of some women, and political violence in India, I decided to introduce my readers to a slightly different kind of story in this latest book—the Indian-American immigrant experience.

Many young second-generation Indians are constantly trying to maintain a fine balance between meeting the expectations of their conservative families and those of their emancipated American peers. This novel portrays the life of a young Indian-American woman, Soorya Giri. She has most everything a young lady could dream of: wealth, intelligence, a successful legal career, and a family who dotes on her. And yet there is something lacking in her personal life.

She faces a number of challenges: plain looks and lack of self-esteem. When all her friends are actively dating and seemingly enjoying their lives, Soorya is the perpetual wallflower, always afraid to take that first step toward meeting a man and cultivating a relationship. As a result she has developed a caustic sense of humor to cover up her inadequacies. And yet she dearly wants to experience the enchantment of romance, and the comfort of marriage and children. Nevertheless, before she can attain all that, she has to find a way to accept and love herself.

It is going to take a very special kind of man to break down her defenses. And my hero tries very hard to do just that. But will he succeed in winning her over?

I sincerely hope you will join Soorya Giri on her bumpy journey to find that nebulous, elusive thing called "love."

Happy reading!

Shobhan Bantwal

THE FULL MOON BRIDE

Shobhan Bantwal

ABOUT THIS GUIDE

The suggested questions are included
to enhance your group's
reading of this book.

DISCUSSION QUESTIONS

1. Despite having a supportive family and a healthy childhood, why is Soorya Giri an unhappy woman?

2. After multiple rejections, Soorya finally meets a dream of a man, and yet she can't trust him. What are her reasons for such distrust?

3. What role does Soorya's father play in her life? Discuss the positives and negatives of having a parent who is neither good-looking nor charismatic but is highly successful.

4. Are Roger's casual, laid-back ways merely a façade to cover up deeper personality issues?

5. Discuss Soorya's relationship with Lou Draper. What does Lou bring to her life and to the story? Discuss the pros and cons of a potential relationship between them.

6. Soorya's mother is a submissive and old-fashioned Indian woman. Is there a hidden core of steel within her? If so, how does it affect Soorya?

7. Discuss the conflicting effects of Indian and American cultures on Soorya's personal and professional lives.

8. After admitting to herself that she's falling in love with Roger, Soorya continues to resist him and her own instincts. Why is she determined to keep him at arm's length?

9. Do any of the characters in the book remind you of someone you know? If yes, which character and in what way?

10. Discuss the role of Roger's family in the story. How does each member enhance the plot?

11. Originally I had titled this story *A Twist of Karma*. Do you believe in fate, and that everything happens for a reason? That Soorya and Roger were meant to be together?

12. As the family matriarch, what kind of impact does Pamma, the grandmother, have on Soorya's values?